Jackie Collins is one of the world's top-selling writers, with five hundred million copies of her books sold in more than forty countries. Her twenty-seven bestselling novels have never been out of print, and have all been *New York Times* bestsellers. She lives in Beverly Hills, California. Visit her website at www.jackiecollins.com

PRAISE FOR JACKIE COLLINS

'Jackie Collins is the queen of the bonkbuster – I'm simply the scullery maid' Jilly Cooper, *Telegraph*

'Sex, glamour and big hair and more sex, Jackie Collins's dissection of Tinseltown is as razor sharp as ever' *Daily Mail*

'Her style is pure escapism, her heroine's strong and ambitious and her men, well, like the book, they'll keep you up all night!' *Company Magazine*

'A generation of women have learnt more about how to handle their men from Jackie's books than from any kind of manual . . . Jackie is very much her own person: a total one off' *Daily Mail*

'Bartender, pour us a dirty martini and keep them coming. This is vintage Jackie Collins and we'll be here 'til closin'' *Heat*

'Jackie is still the queen of sexy stories. Perfect' *OK!*

'Cancel all engagements, take the phone off the hook and indulge yourself' *Mirror*

'The Proust of nips and tucks' *Daily Telegraph*

Jackie Collins

LETHAL SEDUCTION

SIMON &
SCHUSTER

London · New York · Sydney · Toronto

A CBS COMPANY

First published in Great Britain by Simon & Schuster UK Ltd, 2000
First published by Pocket Books UK, 2001
This edition published by Simon & Schuster, 2011
An imprint of Simon & Schuster UK Ltd
A CBS COMPANY

3 5 7 9 10 8 6 4 2

Simon & Schuster UK Ltd
1st Floor
222 Gray's Inn Road
London WC1X 8HB

www.simonandschuster.co.uk

Simon & Schuster Australia
Sydney

A CIP catalogue record for this book is available from the British Library

ISBN 978-1-41651-188-5

Printed in the UK by CPI Group (UK) Ltd, Croydon, CR0 4YY

In memory of my darling Frank,
who will live in my heart forever

BOOK ONE
MANHATTAN

Chapter One

'What's the best sex you've ever had?' Jamie Nova asked her best friend, Madison Castelli. At twenty-nine Jamie was heartbreakingly lovely. A cool, willowy blonde with classic style and an impeccable pedigree, she was a cross between a young Grace Kelly and a contemporary Gwyneth Paltrow.

'Huh?' Madison said, glancing quickly at the adjoining table in the packed Manhattan restaurant. The couple sitting there were deep in their own conversation and had failed to hear Jamie's provocative question.

'You know what I mean,' Jamie said, brushing a lock of fine blonde hair from her forehead. 'Mind-blowing, earth shaking down and dirty sex. The kind where you never want to see the guy again, but at the exact moment you're doing it – anything goes.' A long, wistful sigh. 'And I *do* mean anything.'

'Well . . .' Madison said, wondering where Jamie, her former college roommate, was going with this.

'Come *on*,' Jamie said impatiently. 'Answer me.'

'Hmm.' Madison thought for a moment, realizing

3

this was not a question Jamie was about to drop. 'Miami,' she said at last. 'Vacation with my father. I was sixteen and the guy was a forty-five-year-old major playboy with all the toys. Penthouse, Porsche, porno videos.'

'Porno videos!' Jamie said, rolling her aquamarine eyes in exaggerated horror. 'Doesn't sound too sexy to me.'

'I can assure you it was,' Madison retorted crisply. 'He had the oversized water-bed covered in rose petals. A pitcher of champagne with sliced peaches. Sexy European body oil. And,' she paused for full effect, 'an extraordinarily talented tongue!'

'Ah . . . the old talented tongue trick,' Jamie retorted a touch bitterly. 'Gets 'em every time.'

Madison raised an eyebrow. 'What's *with* you today? Why all this sex talk? You're a married woman – and, if what I hear is true, once you're married, sex is supposed to be nothing but a distant memory.'

'Very funny,' Jamie said glumly.

'I was joking,' Madison said, sensing trouble in the paradise that Jamie inhabited. It was a fact that everyone who knew Jamie and her Wall Street hot-shot husband, Peter, considered them the golden couple. They seemed to have everything, yet today Madison sensed a lurking storm. 'So, what's up?' she asked, leaning across the table. 'Tell me everything.'

'Well,' Jamie said, biting her lower lip, 'last night we were at a dinner party and the question arose.'

'*What* question?'

'The best-sex-you've-ever-had question,' Jamie said, toying with her salad. 'And here's the thing – everyone was coming up with *really* good answers.'

'Yes?' Madison said curiously.

4

'Naturally, when it came to me, I carried on about it being the first time Peter and I made love. Told a cute little story about it, and everyone oohed and aahed. Then it was Peter's turn, and he suddenly went very quiet, muttered that he couldn't remember and abruptly changed the subject.'

'Maybe he was embarrassed.'

'Peter?' Jamie shook her head vigorously. 'Not him.'

'Had he been drinking?'

'Not at all.'

'Then . . . *what?*' Madison asked, perplexed.

'I think he's having an affair,' Jamie blurted.

'Come *on!*' Madison exclaimed. 'You've only been married three years. Give the guy a *chance* to get bored.'

'Thanks a lot,' Jamie said huffily. 'What makes you think he'd *ever* get bored?'

True, Madison thought. How could any man be bored with a woman like Jamie by his side? She was perfect. Everyone knew that. Besides, in a proper world, no man would cheat on Jamie.

But the world wasn't proper, and most men were dogs, so maybe Jamie was right, maybe Peter *was* exercising his precious manhood in another neighbourhood.

'What makes you suspect Peter might be screwing around?' she asked.

'Intuition,' Jamie answered. 'That and the fact that we haven't made love in two weeks.'

'Two weeks!' Madison exclaimed teasingly. 'Jesus! Send in the Marines!'

'You don't understand,' Jamie muttered, twisting her diamond wedding band on an elegant French-manicured finger. 'Peter is a *very* sexual man. He likes sex every day.' A meaningful pause. 'Sometimes more than once.'

'Hmm . . .' Madison murmured, thinking that *she* hadn't had sex in almost a year. Her choice, because who needed to sleep with assholes? And unfortunately that's all she'd come across in the last year – major assholes. The truth was that ever since her live-in love of two years, David the TV producer rat, had run out on her, she'd been off men. Although there *was* that very attractive photographer she'd met in L.A. earlier in the year while on assignment for *Manhattan Style*, the upscale magazine she worked for. His name was Jake Sica and they'd had chemistry. Unfortunately he'd been involved elsewhere.

Too bad.

Then there was the one-night stand in Miami where she'd been interviewing The Donald. She'd met a male model at one of the happening clubs in South Beach. He was not very smart, but quite beautiful, with a muscular body and an untamed mane of sun-streaked hair.

One long passionate night of unbridled lust, accompanied by a condom, and later a feeling of 'Why the hell did I do *that*?'

No. One-night stands were not for her.

'What do *you* think I should do?' Jamie wailed. 'I can't *stand* not knowing. It's driving me insane.'

'Well . . . uh . . . find out, I guess,' Madison offered.

'Very helpful,' Jamie snapped. 'You're supposed to be the smart one with an answer for everything.'

Madison sighed. What a label to be stuck with. Unfortunately it was true. In college she and Jamie were known as 'The Beauty' (Jamie) and 'The Brain' (Madison). And a third friend, Natalie De Barge, a pretty black girl, was nicknamed 'The Sexpot'. The three of them had been inseparable.

College had ended seven years ago, and in those seven years they'd all made their mark. Apart from marrying Peter and leading a hectic social life, Jamie had her own successful interior design firm in Manhattan. It helped that her rich daddy had put up the money *and* partnered her with Anton Couch – a gay genius with connections up the kazoo.

Natalie, with nobody to back her, had carved out a career on television. She was currently living in L.A. and co-hosting *Celebrity News*, a successful entertainment show.

And Madison had an interesting, challenging job and quite a reputation. Her profiles of the rich, powerful and infamous were an important part of *Manhattan Style*'s outstanding success as *the* magazine of the moment – regularly outselling *Vanity Fair* and *Esquire*. In fact, the piece she'd written on Hollywood call-girls earlier in the year had caused quite a stir – she'd even sold the film rights, although she doubted if the movie would get made.

'Okay, here's the plan,' she said, deciding that Jamie needed help.

'Yes?' Jamie said, placing her elbows on the table, wide aqua eyes eager for an answer to her problem.

'Have him followed.'

'Followed!' Jamie exclaimed, causing the couple at the next table finally to take notice. 'I can't do that, it's so . . . so . . . *cheap*.'

'Expensive actually,' Madison corrected. 'But worth it, I'm sure.'

'How can *that* be?'

'Peace of mind. If he's cheating you'll find out. And

if he's not . . . hey, it'll have cost you a few bucks and normal life resumes.'

'Maybe . . .' Jamie murmured hesitantly, followed by a much firmer, 'Okay, I'll do it!'

'Let me check into our options,' Madison said briskly, 'find out who's the best.'

'*And* the most discreet,' Jamie added quickly. 'There's no way this can get out.'

'I understand,' Madison said, sure that her editor, Victor Simons, would be able to come up with exactly who they should hire. Victor knew everything and everybody. Maybe he even knew if Peter was hound-dogging after some sexy nymphet.

Then again, maybe not. Victor and Peter did not travel in the same social circles.

'I'm certain you're wrong,' Madison said reassuringly, 'but at least this way you'll know.'

'Right,' Jamie agreed, and felt sick at the thought of catching Peter with another woman.

* * *

After saying goodbye outside the restaurant, Madison strode along Park Avenue, heading for the offices of *Manhattan Style*. Heads turned, but she didn't notice; she was too busy thinking about Jamie and her suspicions.

Madison was a striking-looking woman, tall and slender, with full breasts, dancer's legs and a cloud of long black curly hair that she usually wore pulled back. She tried to play down her good looks, but nothing could disguise her green almond-shaped eyes, sharply defined cheekbones and full, seductive lips. She was a beauty, although she did not consider herself one – her idea of beauty was her mother, Stella, a statuesque honey blonde whose quivering lips and dreamy eyes reminded most people of Marilyn Monroe.

Looks-wise, Madison took after her father, Michael. Dark and handsome, Michael Castelli was the best looking fifty-eight-year-old in Connecticut. He also possessed a beguiling charm and steely determination – two qualities Madison had definitely inherited, which had not hindered her rise to success as a well-respected writer of revealing and insightful profiles of the notorious and powerful.

Madison loved what she did – going for the right angle, discovering the secrets of people in the public eye. Politicians and super-rich business tycoons were her favourites. Movie stars, sports personalities and Hollywood moguls were low on her list. She didn't regard herself as a killer, although she wrote with searing honesty, sometimes upsetting her subjects who were usually sheltered in an all-enveloping cocoon of protective PR.

Too bad if they didn't like it, she was merely reporting the truth.

She'd worked under the watchful eye of Victor Simons for five years. They had an excellent relation-ship, although sometimes Victor could be a total pain, especially when he wanted her to interview a subject she had absolutely zero interest in. Usually they com-promised, and she'd reluctantly agree to interview some ding-bat movie-star sex symbol in exchange for a crack at a nuclear scientist or a computer genius.

Victor had discovered her fresh out of college when she'd written a provocative piece on the still rampant double standard between men and women, and it had been published in *Esquire*. He'd taken her to lunch, told her to get more experience, then two years later hired her to write short question and answer pieces for his magazine. A year later she'd graduated to brief interviews, then suddenly she'd come up with her signature work – Madison Castelli, Profiles in Power.

Her first subject was Henry Kissinger. She'd captured the essence of the ageing politician with a sharp, wry wit. After that it was easy. One interview a month, which gave her plenty of free time to work on her novel – a book about relationships, which was making slow progress while she got over her anger at David for walking out. It wasn't easy writing about relationships while she was still so hurt.

Why had David left? That was the question. Was it something she'd done to turn him off?

No. Deep down she knew the answer. David hadn't been able to accept that she made as much money as he did. It was as simple as that. He was searching for a woman who stayed home and did what *he* wanted, not an independent free spirit with ambitions. Two years of great sex did not make a lasting relationship, because after the passion settled down, what was left?

In their case, apparently nothing.

A few weeks after David's abrupt departure, she'd heard that he'd married his childhood sweetheart, a vapid blonde with fake boobs and an annoying overbite. So much for good taste.

* * *

Victor was crouched on the floor in his spacious office playing with his precious model train set, which wound its way across the room and back again. He was a big, cuddly man in his late forties, with a mop of frizzy brown hair that appeared to stand on end, matching eyebrows, several chins and puppy-dog eyes.

'Maddy!' he exclaimed, in a loud, booming voice. 'I wasn't expecting to see you today. Come in.'

'Hi, Victor,' she said, stepping carefully over a chugging red engine. 'Working hard as usual, I see.'

'Of course,' he said, with a hearty chuckle. 'Keeps the old heart pumping. Besides, Evelyn won't let me do this at home.'

'I wonder why,' Madison murmured, thinking of his skinny-as-a-stick pristine wife, with her permanently uptight expression and designer wardrobe.

'Wouldn't do to mess up her living room,' Victor responded, hauling himself up.

Madison perched on the edge of his desk. 'I need a favour,' she announced, picking up a heavy glass paperweight and examining it.

'Good,' Victor boomed, sitting down in his leather chair. 'There's nothing I like better than people owing me favours.'

'I'm not *people*,' Madison pointed out, irritated that he should regard her as such. 'And it's not exactly a favour, more a request for information.'

'What kind of information?' Victor asked suspiciously.

'Nothing earth-shattering,' she said, putting down the paperweight. 'I simply require the name of the best private investigator in New York.'

Victor tapped his index finger on the desk. 'And what makes you think I'd have that?'

'Because you know everything. And besides,' she added quickly, 'didn't you use someone to follow your first wife before you divorced her?'

His bushy eyebrows shot up. 'Who told you that?'

'Office folklore.'

'I hate gossip,' he snapped.

'You thrive on it,' she responded.

'Why do you need this?'

'For a friend.'

'What friend?'

'None of your business.'

'Bitch!'

'Slave driver!'

They exchanged smiles.

Madison was extremely fond of Victor, even though he sometimes drove her crazy with his loud voice and often overbearing attitude. And Victor adored Madison, whom he considered his own personal discovery.

Placing the train remote on his desk, Victor buzzed Lynda, his personal assistant, who had worked for him for twelve years and closely resembled a cross-eyed basset hound, with her lank brown hair and lacklustre smile.

Lynda materialized immediately, unrequited love oozing from her every pore. 'Yes, Mr S?' she asked anxiously.

'It's confidential,' Victor said.

Lynda threw Madison a dirty look as if to say, 'Then what's *she* doing here?'

'Get me the name and number of the, uh . . . person who trailed Rebecca,' Victor said. 'Do it now.'

Lynda snapped to attention. 'Yes, Mr S.'

And she was gone.

'So . . .' Victor said, turning to Madison. 'You don't care to tell me what this is about?'

'Hey,' she answered, purposely keeping it vague, 'it's not about *me*, that should be enough.'

'Well, it isn't,' he grumbled.

'Don't sweat it, Victor,' she said casually. 'You wouldn't be interested anyway.'

'You need a man,' Victor said, his favourite comment whenever she pissed him off. 'How long is it since David walked?'

'Stay out of my private life,' she warned.

'You're twenty-nine and you *have* no private life,' he reminded her.

God! How she hated it when Victor tried to get into her business. 'Fuck you!' she said vehemently.

'Any time you're ready.'

She burst out laughing. There was no way she could stay mad at Victor. After all, he meant well, even though he was forever trying to fix her up with any single man who came his way. He didn't care how old they were or what they looked like: as long as they had a reasonable bank account and a working cock he was determined she should give them a try.

She'd given up accepting dinner invitations to his home. The last one she'd attended she'd found herself seated between an ancient astronaut and a twenty-one-year-old computer nerd. Both interesting men – but dating material? No way.

I don't mind being alone, she told herself.

Yes, you do, an annoying little voice that lived in the back of her head replied.

NO! I don't!

Ten minutes later, armed with the name K. Florian and a phone number, she left the office, cutting down Sixty-seventh Street towards her apartment on Lexington. Now that she had the number she decided she'd better check with Jamie before using it. That evening they were both attending a dinner party at

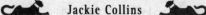

Anton Couch's penthouse apartment, so she'd be able to find out *exactly* what Jamie wanted her to do.

Yes, and she'd also be able to check out Peter, see what he was up to.

Her people skills were excellent. If Peter was screwing around on Jamie, she'd know it. No doubt of *that*.

Chapter Two

'I want him dead!' Rosarita Vincent Falcon screeched, red in the face. 'Dead! Dead! Dead!'

'Lower your voice,' her father growled, his heavy-lidded eyes filled with disapproval at his daughter's petulant outburst. 'Ya want the whole fuckin' neighbourhood t' hear?'

'Who cares?' Rosarita yelled. 'You *own* the fucking neighbourhood!'

'Nice language,' sniffed Chas Vincent, a large bear of a man with ruddy cheeks and a rough-edged voice. 'Is that what I sent ya t' college t' learn?'

'Fuck college! Fuck the neighbourhood! I want Dex fucking Falcon *dead!*'

'A little louder,' Chas growled, sweat beading his forehead. 'The maid next door didn't hear ya.'

Rosarita stamped her foot on the thick pile rug. What was *wrong* with her stupid father? *Why* wasn't he getting it?

At five feet four, Rosarita was bordering on anorexic, helped along by bulimic tendencies. She was twenty-six, with red hair worn in a shoulder-length bob, a thin pointed face, over-full lips (thanks to her busy plastic surgeon, who'd also helped out with a new nose, cheekbone and chin implants – not to mention the best boobs in Manhattan) and plenty of attitude. Especially when it came to her husband of eighteen months, struggling actor and sometime model Dexter Falcon. She'd married him because he was unbelievably handsome, had an enormous underwear billboard hovering above Times Square and was absolutely crazy about her.

She'd thought he was destined to be a movie star. But no, the only acting job Dexter Falcon had managed to land was on an about-to-be cancelled daytime soap that paid shit and nobody watched. Damn him!

Now Rosarita wanted out because she'd met someone else, someone of substance with an attitude to match her own and an even bigger dick than Dexter's – who was no slouch in the size department. Someone she planned to go places with.

But how could she go anywhere with a loser husband trailing along behind her?

When she'd brought up the subject of divorce, Dexter had freaked. 'Over my dead body,' he'd said.

Well . . . if that's the way he wanted it . . .

'I thought you was so in love,' Chas said, swigging from a large glass of Scotch. 'I gave ya the big fuckin' weddin' with all the trimmin's – exactly like ya wanted. I bought you a fuckin' house an' a fuckin' Nazi car. I thought you was all set.'

'Sorry, I'm not,' Rosarita said, gritting her teeth. 'Dex is a deadbeat actor with no prospects and I want you to get rid of him for me.'

'Just like that,' Chas said, wondering how he'd

managed to get himself such a difficult daughter. Her year-younger sister, Venice, was a sweetheart with two kids and a down-to-earth husband who sold insurance for a living. Why couldn't Rosarita be more like her? 'I warned ya about marryin' a fuckin' actor,' he said dourly. 'They got birdcrap for brains, not ta mention fagola tendencies.'

'He's not *gay*,' Rosarita sniffed, insulted that Chas would think that any man who was with her might be gay, 'merely *dumb*.'

'I coulda told ya that,' Chas grumbled. 'Only *you* wouldn't listen.' He put on an exaggerated voice. 'Miss I-gotta-have-everythin'-the-moment-I-want-it.'

'Daddy!' Rosarita wailed, changing tactics because she knew how to play him like a violin. 'Please help your little girl. I *need* you.'

Chas could barely resist Rosarita when she was sweet – during those rare times she reminded him of her dear departed mother who'd died giving birth to Venice, leaving him alone with a newborn baby and an infant to raise. In his opinion he'd done a good job – with the help of an army of girlfriends, none of whom had lasted more than a few months. Chas Vincent was not a one-woman man. He liked big tits and a closed mouth. Two or three months into the game and they got on his nerves with their whiny demands and money-spending ways.

Maybe Rosarita took after him when it came to living with someone. He couldn't blame her. Dexter Falcon was a white-bread putz with only a pretty face to get him through life. He had no balls – Chas could've told his daughter *that* the first time he met the dumb shit. Rosarita should've *fucked* him out of her system. But no, she'd had to *marry* the asshole.

Her wedding had cost a fuckin' fortune. Rosarita demanded – and got – only the best. Now Chas had a powerful urge to say, 'I told you so.' But his strong-willed kid didn't take kindly to criticism, so he choked back the words and patted Rosarita's bony shoulder as she tried to perch on his knee, tears streaming down her cheeks.

They were actually tears of frustration and anger because she was having to fight to get her own way, but Chas didn't know that. 'What shall we do, Daddy?' She sniffled. 'I'm . . . so . . . miserable. Dex is so *mean* to me.'

'Get a divorce,' Chas suggested, sure that if Dexter was mean to her, he had good reason.

'Don't you understand? He won't give me one,' she moaned. 'And that means I'll have to wait and go through lawyers and depositions and all that horrible, degrading stuff. He's threatening to go after half of everything I own. I don't *want* to wait, Daddy. It's not fair.' A pause for a few deep sobs. 'Besides, I've met someone else, and I can't have Dex getting in my way and ruining everything.'

'Not another dumb actor, I hope,' Chas said, taking a second hearty swig of Scotch.

'No, Daddy. This one's got money. He's a *someone*, not a nobody like Dex.' She narrowed her eyes. 'I *hate* Dex.'

'I'm gettin' the picture,' Chas said, scratching his chin.

Rosarita wriggled off his knee, which was good because he wasn't as young as he used to be, and last night he'd gone three rounds with a pneumatic blonde whose knockers alone must've weighed five pounds apiece.

'Lemme speak t' him,' Chas said. 'He'll listen t' me.'

'Talking won't do any good,' Rosarita wailed. '*Killing* him *will*.'

'Enough of that crap,' Chas snapped, suddenly angry. 'I ain't in the killin' business. I'm in construction, an' don't you forget it.'

'Ha!' Rosarita said.

'Ha, what?' Chas responded.

Rosarita stared at her father, a malevolent expression on her sharp, pointed face. 'Whatever happened to that foreman you didn't like?' she said, knowingly. 'You remember, the one who stole from you. And then there was Adam Rubicon, your ex-partner, who mysteriously disappeared. And –'

'Shut your fuckin' mouth,' Chas yelled, jumping up, red in the face. 'I *never* wanna hear ya talk like that again. Ya hear me?'

'Then do it,' Rosarita said, all cool and collected and sure of herself. 'And do it soon.'

* * *

Unaware of the ominous conversation taking place at his father-in-law's house, Dexter Falcon left the mid-town TV studio, where they shot the daily soap *Dark Days*, with a smile on his handsome face. His name wasn't really Dexter Falcon, it was actually Dick Cockranger – a name too ridiculous even to contemplate keeping, unless he planned on being a porno star, and when he'd first come to New York from a small town in the Midwest four years previously, that had *not* been his plan at all. Oh, no, Dexter Falcon had far grander aspirations.

The name change was first on his agenda – Dexter,

in honour of a good-looking character on his mother's all-time favourite night-time soap, and Falcon – because it was powerful and strong, and sounded very masculine.

So Dexter Falcon was born. Again. It was a memorable day. He was twenty and ready for anything, and a few weeks after arriving in the big city he found 'anything' in the person of Mortimer Marcel, a French-born designer whom he bumped into while jogging in Central Park.

'You a model?' Mortimer had asked.

'Actor,' Dexter replied. He'd never acted, never even thought of it. But acting sounded like a far more exciting profession than washing dishes in a deli on Lexington – which was what he was currently doing.

'You could be right for my new underwear line,' Mortimer said brusquely. 'I'll audition you tonight. My house. Seven o'clock.' And he'd fished in the pocket of his fashionable running shorts and handed Dexter an engraved card.

Dexter had stood considering the possibilities while watching Mortimer jog out of sight. He was not naïve. He knew what went on – especially in a big city like New York. Mortimer Marcel was obviously gay. And Dexter was not.

Mortimer Marcel was also obviously successful. And Dexter was not.

Was there a choice about what he should do?

Yes. He should *not* pursue it. But he'd been handed an opportunity, and it was clearly his destiny to follow it through.

Within six months he was the Mortimer Marcel boy – on television, the Internet, in print ads. Marcel even took him to Paris and had him strut the runway wearing the latest line of Mortimer Marcel men's leisurewear.

And he didn't have to do anything sexual. Mortimer had a live-in lover – Jefferson, a handsome black ex-model, who was as jealous as a wildcat guarding its young, so Mortimer never laid a hand on Dexter, leaving him free to sleep with whoever he liked. And he did. Every night was supermodel night, each girl more gorgeous than the next.

For two years Dexter fulfilled every sexual fantasy he'd ever had, but deep in his heart he wanted more than transient sex. He desperately craved a real relationship with a woman who cared about him. His main desire was to get married, have babies and be forever happy like his parents, who were still together after forty-five blissful years.

One night he met Rosarita at a party. She wasn't supermodel pretty, but she was attractive and seemed to be caring and sweet and, best of all, she hung on his every word. Since he never had much to say, this was flattering. He liked it. He liked her. They started to date.

Over several dinners she talked about family values and how she loathed the whole New York social scene. He couldn't agree more.

She chatted about her sister's children, and how one day she hoped to have children of her own. Several. She was full of all the old-fashioned virtues he'd been searching for. What a girl!

A month later he asked her to marry him and she said yes. Six weeks later they did the deed. And on their wedding night they had sex for the first time and it was quite something. Dexter was sure that marrying Rosarita was the best thing he'd ever done.

After they'd been married a few weeks, Rosarita informed him he was far too smart to continue being a model, and she arranged for him to see an agent at William Morris. He did so, and the agent assured him they could make him a star and immediately began sending him out on auditions.

Dexter was elated. So was Rosarita.

Over the next two months he almost landed a Clint Eastwood movie. Very nearly got cast in a Martin Scorsese masterpiece. Just missed being Gwyneth Paltrow's lover in a Miramax film. And then, on his agent's advice, after several months of no auditions at all, he signed for a one-year stint on *Dark Days*.

'Do it,' his agent insisted. 'Once you get the experience behind you, they'll all be chasing after you.'

From the moment he signed on for the soap, Rosarita's attitude changed. From sweet she turned to sour, complaining about everything, including the fact that they were unable to go out most nights because he had a five a.m. call every day. She nagged him continually. Nothing he ever did was good enough. Until finally, six weeks ago, she'd started muttering about divorce.

Dexter could not believe it. Divorce! They'd only been married eighteen months. Divorce was unthinkable. Not in *his* family. For a start it would kill his parents. Besides, he was quite happy with the way things were.

So after much thought he'd devised a plan to calm her down. When they were first going out he'd taken her home to meet his mom and dad – Martha and Matt. She'd loved them and they her. The only other time she'd seen them since was at their wedding, which had turned out to be an enormous affair. Fortunately,

22

Rosarita's father had paid for the lavish event, *and* bought them a large apartment in Manhattan, plus a sleek Mercedes as a wedding present – which they hardly ever got to drive because it was difficult to find a parking spot in the city.

Martha and Matt Cockranger were Dexter's secret weapon. He was flying them into New York for a surprise visit. He'd already instructed the maid to prepare the guest bedroom, and he'd booked a limo to meet them at the airport. They were arriving tonight, hence the smile on his face.

If Martha and Matt Cockranger couldn't talk some sense into Rosarita, *nobody* could.

Chapter Three

Anton Couch gave great party. A stickler for detail, he hosted dinners that were always the best. Two tables of twelve – twenty-four people who were either glamorous, talented, witty or extraordinarily rich. A New York mix with flavour.

As Madison entered Anton's fire-red living room she immediately checked out the group. Once she'd seen John Gotti there – before his incarceration. And there were often movie stars, politicians and rock stars in attendance.

Tonight she spotted the legendary Kris Phoenix – rock icon supreme, with his trademark spiked hair and intense blue eyes. Although past fifty, he still had a magnetic quality. Like Mick Jagger, Rod Stewart and Eric Clapton, he never seemed to change. Kris was deep in conversation with music mogul Clive Davis. Since she knew Clive, she began heading in their direction, only to be stopped by Jamie's husband, Peter, who stepped in front of her, martini glass in one hand and a silly grin on his somewhat bland face. Peter had that 'just-came-back-from-a-weekend-in-the-Hamptons' look. Like his wife, he was tall, with a light year-round tan, aquamarine eyes and tousled blond hair. He and Jamie made a spectacular couple.

'How's my wife's best friend?' he asked, favouring her with a lascivious leer.

'Fine, thank you,' she said, thinking, *Uh-oh, one more martini and he's over the edge.*

'I hear you and my gorgeous wife had lunch today,' he remarked.

'We certainly did.'

'Talk about me, did you?' he asked, flirting.

'We *always* talk about you,' she answered lightly. 'Surely you know you're the most interesting subject in our universe?'

'Wish I was,' he said ruefully, sipping his martini. 'Truth is, I think my wife's going off me.'

'Why would you say that?'

'I don't know . . . I sort of sense it.'

Madison shrugged. 'What can I say?'

'Nothing. If she *does* go off me and throws me out, I'll simply have to come live with you.'

'That'll be fun,' Madison said drily. 'You can sleep with the dog.'

'You *know* I've always had my eye on you,' he said, edging closer.

Oh, God, she hated it when Peter drank. He invariably came out with the same tired old lines, and nobody ever complained to Jamie because they all knew he didn't mean it.

'How's the stock market?' she asked, hurriedly changing the subject.

'You wanna talk stocks with me?' he said, licking his lips. 'You want me to *investigate* your portfolio?'

25

'Excuse me, Peter,' she said, backing away. 'I must find Anton.'

'Y'know, Maddy, I don't get it,' he said, coming after her. 'What's a beautiful woman like you doing all by herself?'

'My choice, Peter,' she said coolly.

'David was a fool.'

'We simply had different agendas.'

'Yeah.' He laughed scornfully. 'Have you *seen* David's agenda? Big tits and no brains.'

'When did *you* see her?' Madison asked, frowning, unaware that Peter and her ex-boyfriend were still in touch.

'We had dinner one night when Jamie was out of town. He'd been calling, bugging me to get together with him and his new bride.'

'*Bugging* you?' Madison said, remembering David's less than flattering opinion of Peter. He'd once invested in the market with him and lost a bundle. This did not sit well with David, who expected to win at everything he did.

'I said yes. Had nothing else to do.'

'What was she like?' Madison couldn't help asking, furious with herself for doing so.

'Bimbo, you know the type.'

'No, actually, I don't,' she said coldly.

'He was crazy to give you up,' Peter said, getting so close she could smell his boozy breath.

'Where's Jamie?' she asked abruptly, once more backing away.

'Met Kris Phoenix and had a total melt-down. What *is* it with you women and these rock stars?'

'We grew up watching him, Peter. In college he was our idol, the best of the older rock stars.'

'Really? First sexual stirrings and all that?'

'Wouldn't *you* like to know.'

'As a matter of fact I would.'

'Well, you're not going to.'

'Hmm . . .' he said, rocking on his heels. 'Since you lunched with my wife today, isn't it only fair that you lunch with me tomorrow?' Another deeply horny look. 'I could examine your portfolio in detail.'

She knew he wasn't serious, it was only the booze talking – or was it, in view of Jamie's suspicions? 'How about *not* ordering another martini tonight, Peter,' she said gently. 'You know Jamie hates it when you drink.'

'How about . . . minding your own business?'

She looked around for someone she knew. This conversation was going nowhere and it was time to escape. 'I really do have to go find Anton,' she said. 'See you later.'

'I hope we're sitting together,' he called after her.

Yeah. Right. She was just about to make sure that they weren't.

Anton was pleased to see her. He was a diminutive man with inquisitive eyes, a spontaneous smile and expansive gestures – he had a warmth about him that was most appealing. Somehow he and Jamie had turned out to be a great business mix, much in demand to decorate the homes of the rich and frivolous – homes that eventually appeared between the covers of *Architectural Digest* and *In Style*. Anton usually came up with an innovative concept for their clients, and Jamie followed through. Since putting them in business together, Jamie's father had more than recouped his original investment.

'Amazing turn-out, as usual,' Madison said, survey-ing the room and spotting the powerful agent, Mort

Janklow, talking to publishers Sonny Mehta and Michael Korda in one corner, while across the room, Betsy Bloomingdale, visiting from California, dominated the conversation with a group of New York wives – including a striking Georgette Moschbacher.

'I always try to mix it up,' Anton said modestly.

'And you *always* succeed,' Madison said. 'I wish you'd let me write about *you*.'

'No personal publicity – that's why all my ladies trust me. You'd be amazed what they tell me when I'm suggesting a new fabric for their dining-room walls.'

'Knowing you, I wouldn't be surprised if you stashed a little microphone in the wall,' Madison said, grinning. 'You *love* hearing all the gossip.'

'I certainly do, my dear,' Anton replied. 'However, my strength is that I don't repeat it – not even to you.'

They both laughed.

'If I were looking for Jamie, where would I find her?' Madison asked.

'In the guest bathroom,' Anton replied. Lowering his voice, he added, 'I think Kris Phoenix propositioned her. She's run off to recover.'

'And what was Peter doing while all this was going on?'

'Getting drunk,' Anton said. 'Haven't you noticed?'

'I'll try to keep an eye on him for you.'

'Do,' Anton replied. 'If there's one thing I crave, it's peace and harmony.'

'Sure,' Madison said, disbelievingly. 'If you liked peace and harmony, you wouldn't throw such incredible dinner parties every month.'

'One's got to have a social life,' Anton said, with a sly smile. 'By the way, your mother called me.'

'*My* mother?' she said, surprised.

'You do have a mother, don't you?' Anton said crisply. 'You didn't just spring from the streets of New York with a pen in your hand.'

'Of course I have a mother, but why would she call *you?*'

'Stella, isn't it?'

'Yes, the beautiful Stella.'

'If she's anything like you, she must certainly be *very* beautiful.'

'Oh, c'mon,' Madison said, embarrassed by his compliment. 'My mother is a *real* beauty. Marilyn Monroe in her heyday.'

'How exciting,' Anton said. 'I would've *loved* a mother who resembled the divine Marilyn.'

'What did Stella want?'

'To inquire about a design concept for their new apartment.'

'*What* new apartment?' Madison said, puzzled. 'My parents live in Connecticut. They haven't lived in New York for ten years.'

'Apparently they're moving back.'

'I don't get it,' she said, completely bewildered. 'First of all, why would Stella call you and not Jamie? And secondly, how come I don't know about this so-called apartment?'

'Maybe they're planning to surprise you.'

'Yeah, sure – that'll be the day. The only surprise my mother ever gave me was when she once complimented a piece I wrote on Eddie Murphy.'

'Eddie Murphy?'

'Yeah. Can you believe it? I write about politicians and all these other fascinating people, and the *only* one she has anything to say about is Eddie Murphy.'

29

'Maybe she likes them black and bold,' Anton said with a chuckle.

'Have you *seen* my father? He's the best-looking man walking.'

'*Really?*' Anton said, perking up. 'How old is he?'

'Fifty-eight. Too old for you. Rumour is you don't like 'em over twenty-five.'

'Oh dear,' Anton said, feigning dismay. 'My reputation's out.'

Madison laughed. 'I'm finding Jamie. I need to talk to someone sane.'

Jamie wasn't in the guest powder room.

'Miss Jamie is in Mr Anton's bedroom,' Anton's Filipino housekeeper informed her.

'Thanks,' she said, still wondering about Stella calling Anton. What was *that* all about? Her parents *loved* Connecticut, why would they consider moving back to New York? *Especially* without telling her.

Oh, well . . . she'd find out tomorrow.

Jamie was sitting in front of Anton's Art Deco mirrored vanity, applying lipstick with a trembling hand and a long, thin brush.

'What's up with you?' Madison asked, perching on the edge of the tub.

'Kris Phoenix wants me to meet him at his hotel,' Jamie said, her voice husky.

'*What?*'

'You heard. He asked me to meet him.'

'When?'

'Later.'

'Are you kidding?'

'No.'

'What about Peter?'

'What about him?' Jamie answered defiantly.

'He thinks you're going off him.'

'Ha!'

'This is crazy,' Madison said.

'Why?' Jamie said stubbornly. 'I *know* he's screwing around on me.'

'You don't *know*, you merely suspect. You can't go running off in the middle of the night to meet with some ageing rock star.'

'I can if I want to.'

'Did you and Peter have a fight?'

'No.'

'Then why are you acting like this?'

'To see if he cares.'

'Of *course* he cares,' Madison said, quite exasperated. 'He wouldn't be with you if he didn't.'

'People stay together for many different reasons,' Jamie said mysteriously, applying a touch of blush to her already glowing complexion.

'Anyway,' Madison said, 'I have the number of a private investigator, and I think you should meet with him.'

'Me? What about *you?*' Jamie wailed.

'Correct me if I'm wrong, but isn't it *you* with the might-be-straying husband?'

'Yes, but you're going to help me, aren't you?' Jamie said pleadingly.

Madison sighed. 'If you insist,' she said. Jamie always *had* been the champion at getting her own way.

'I can't do it alone, Maddy. Will you make the appointment and come with me?'

'Okay, okay,' Madison said impatiently, wishing she could learn to say no. 'But only if you stop all this Kris Phoenix crap. He's a horny old rock star, for Crissakes. *Definitely* not for you.'

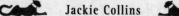

'I promise,' Jamie said, an angelic expression on her lovely face. 'However, I swear to you, if I find out that Peter is screwing around, I'll track Kris Phoenix down and fuck him in the middle of Times Square!'

Chapter Four

I n bed with Joel Blaine, Rosarita realized he was
everything Dex was not. Joel was a down-and-dirty
lover, servicing her in ways she had only ever
dreamt about. He pushed her around, making her do
things Dex wouldn't dare try. When he was inside her
he wanted her all the way – forcing her legs around the
back of his neck, popping amyl nitrate vials under her
nose whether she liked it or not – biting her nipples
until she screamed with a mixture of pain and pleasure.
He was all man. Eight and a half solid inches that he
made her deep-throat until she gagged.

When she finally came – spreadeagled on top of him
– she let out a scream so loud and out of control that
he clamped his big hairy hand over her mouth and told
her to shut the fuck up.

She liked a man who was in charge.

Personality-wise he reminded her of her father. In
the looks department he was no Dex. He was not very
tall, dark and stocky, with plenty of thick body hair,
brooding close-set eyes and fleshy lips. The
combination made him attractive in a sexy, flashy way.

33

This was their second assignation – their first one in a bed. The time before, right after they'd met at the opening of an art-gallery show, he'd parked in a dark SoHo side street, shared a vial of coke with her and made rough love to her in the back of his gleaming grey Bentley while a couple of transients looked on through the open window. It was one big turn-on.

Tonight was even better. More coke. More sex. Her two favourite things.

'Jesus!' she exclaimed, reaching for a cigarette and lighting up. 'That was sensational!'

Joel was already on his way into the bathroom. She took another drag on her cigarette and peeked at her watch. It was past six, time for her to go home and spend another boring evening with Dex. Was it any wonder that she wanted him dead?

If Dex was out of her life she would be free to pursue a proper relationship with Joel. Right now he was playing it poker-faced because he knew she was unavailable.

She'd give anything to spend the night with him. Dinner at a nice restaurant. Drinks at a happening club. Then back to his place for more of the same. Idly she wondered what it would be like to be married to a man like Joel. He was a goer, a doer. At thirty-two – according to what he'd told her – he practically ran his father's enormous real estate business. What a match they would make. They both had powerful rich fathers – men from whom they'd learned plenty. Together they could rule New York.

Only Dex stood in her way.

Damn him! He was a dumb nobody. Why had she married him?

Oh, yeah, yeah, she'd thought he was destined to be a movie star . . .

34

End of *that* story.

She could hear the sound of the shower coming from the bathroom. Surreptitiously she slid open Joel's bedside drawer and checked out the contents. A gun. Excellent, it showed he had balls. Six boxes of peppermint Tic Tacs. A porno video entitled *Hot Spurts*. An unopened package of extra large condoms. And a pale blue envelope with *Sweetie* written across the front. Quick as a flash she extracted the note inside. *Babykins. I love you. Always will. See you next week. Keep my place warm.* It was signed – *Honeystuff*.

Honeystuff! Who in *hell* was *Honeystuff*?

Rosarita was outraged. Did Joel have a girlfriend he hadn't told her about?

She was about to rummage further when she heard the shower stop. Quickly she slid the note back into the envelope and closed the drawer.

Joel strode back into the room, a towel knotted loosely around his waist. If she wasn't mistaken he still had a hard-on – the jut of his cock beneath the thick towel was unmistakable.

It was about time she put her mark on him – something Rosarita knew how to do better than anyone.

'Come over here, hot stuff,' she crooned, beckoning him to the bed. 'I've got something for you.'

Joel didn't need asking twice.

* * *

Dexter paced around the living room, glancing at his watch every five minutes. Where was Rosarita? He had hoped she'd be home before his parents arrived, making it the perfect surprise. But at six thirty she was still not there.

Reluctantly he picked up the phone and called his father-in-law, breaking out in a sweat as he did so. Chas Vincent scared the heck out of him – he looked like a refugee from *The Sopranos*, and acted like one too.

Early on in their relationship Rosarita had proudly informed him that Chas was king of construction in New Jersey. He didn't know or care *what* Chas was king of, he simply preferred to keep as much distance as possible between them.

'Hi, Chas,' he said, making sure his voice sounded strong. 'Is Rosarita there?'

'Why'd she be here?' Chas growled suspiciously. 'She left two hours ago.'

'Did she say where she was going?'

Probably to buy a gun and blow you away, Chas thought. 'Naw,' he said. 'Most likely she's hittin' the stores. You know women – spend till their titties drop.'

Dexter faked a laugh. Even though he'd been involved in the world of modelling, he still couldn't stand vulgarity.

'Call me if she's not home by midnight,' Chas said jovially. 'I'll send out the cops.'

A concerned father. How nice.

Dexter roamed around the apartment, stopping at the guest room to make sure it was all ready for his parents' imminent arrival. He'd personally gone to the flower shop and chosen twelve perfect red roses – his mother's favourites. Conchita, the maid, had placed them in an exquisite amber vase on the dresser next to the television. He'd also bought roses for Rosarita, white ones, which he planned to present to her later when they were alone.

Tonight was going to be special. He was absolutely sure of it.

* * *

'Shit!' Rosarita screeched, snagging her expensive tights as she entered a cab outside Joel's building.

'Where to, lady?' asked the cabbie, not even bothering to turn around.

'There's a sharp edge on the bottom of your door,' she complained. 'You'd better do something about it.'

'Where to?' he repeated, cracking his knuckles. She leaned forward to get a look at his ID. Moussaf Kiridarian. Another foreigner not worth arguing with. Chas said they should all be lined up and shot. Sometimes he could be a bit of an extremist. After all, if that ever happened who would be around to drive the cabs and trains? Get rid of the garbage? Run all the electronic and camera shops?

'Sixty-first and Park,' she said brusquely. 'And make it fast. I'm in a hurry.'

The cab set off with a jerk, almost throwing her off her seat. She muttered an insult under her breath and groped in her purse for a cigarette. She was about to light up when Moussaf caught her eye in the rear-view mirror and announced sternly, 'No smoking. See sign.'

'Shit,' she muttered, putting the cigarette away. What kind of stupid rule was *that*? And how come a lowly cab driver was allowed to tell her what to do?

If she was very nice to Chas maybe he'd spring for her own car and driver, especially if she suggested it as a Christmas or birthday present. He was rich enough to afford it, and there was no reason for her to ride around town in a filthy cab with some crazy foreigner who wouldn't allow her to smoke. Of course, Chas would ask why she didn't drive the Mercedes he'd bought her. But who could park in Manhattan? It was a fucking nightmare.

For a moment her thoughts drifted to Joel. What a guy! Although he'd been really pissed when she'd sunk her teeth into his neck so deep that any little cupcake trying to put her claim on him would notice immediately that he'd been playing elsewhere. He'd jumped back a foot. 'What the *fuck* have you done to me?' he'd yelled, rubbing his neck.

'Sorry,' she'd murmured innocently. 'You shouldn't be such a turn-on. I couldn't help myself.'

'Fuck!' he'd complained. 'This is gonna swell up.'

'I know something else that's gonna swell up,' she'd giggled, reaching for his ever-ready dick. It was solid and thick, just the way she liked them.

Now, sitting in the cab, she wondered what little Honeystuff would have to say when she got a load of her boyfriend's neck. Well . . . ex-boyfriend, because Rosarita had big plans for Joel.

He wasn't going to be easy, she could already tell that. He was stubborn, didn't care to be pushed. And, like most men, he was probably shit-scared of commitment.

However, Rosarita was confident enough to think that she was quite capable of changing all that.

'When can we get together again?' she'd asked, before leaving his apartment.

'You're married, aren't you?' he'd said gruffly.

'Since when did that make a difference?'

Joel had laughed, more a throaty growl. 'I get off on an office matinée occasionally,' he'd said. 'Y'know, close the door, raise the shades. There's plenty of tall buildings around – you never know who's watching. You into that?'

'When?' she'd asked eagerly.

'Call me in a coupla days. We'll make a plan.'

She knew that she couldn't ask *him* to call *her*. It wouldn't do for Dex to pick up any message Joel might leave. 'You *do* know I'm planning a divorce?' she'd said.

'You told that pretty-boy husband of yours?'

'Not yet, but I will. My father's getting involved.'

'How come?'

''Cause he'll make damn sure Dex doesn't give me any trouble.'

Joel had looked at her admiringly. 'You're a piece of work, you know that?'

'Never said I wasn't,' she'd answered, with a knowing smirk. Then she'd given him a long French kiss he wouldn't forget in a hurry, and left his apartment.

Now she was groaning inside because she had to go home and face that big lox of a husband. And she knew exactly what he'd say. 'Guess what happened on the set today?'

Who gave a flying fuck what happened on the set today? *She* certainly didn't.

Dex simply didn't get it. She wanted a divorce, and tonight she would hammer the point home. Because, if he didn't get it soon, he would be one *dead* pretty boy – with or without her father's co-operation.

Chapter Five

'I gotta tell you . . .'

'Yes?' Madison said, completely uninterested in what the man sitting next to her had to say.

'You have *the* sexiest lips.'

'Really,' she responded, hardly taking a beat. 'How interesting. I was about to say the same thing to you.'

Her dinner companion looked at her, perplexed. 'That's what I like about you, always got a smart answer.'

That's what I don't like about you, she wanted to say, but she didn't. It wasn't worth the trouble.

She was seated to the left of Joel Blaine, playboy son of real-estate billionaire Leon Blaine. Leon was an interesting man. Joel was not. Joel was the typical rich man's son who thought the world should kiss his ass because of his father. What a crock *that* was. As far as Madison was concerned, Joel Blaine was a bad joke. The last of the useless playboys.

'What's the matter?' Joel said, wondering how he could get her to put out. 'Can't take a compliment?'

'What happened to your neck?' she asked, pointedly

staring at an offending red and swollen hickey.
'Girlfriend get a little too . . . frisky?'

Joel glowered. That bitch Rosarita. Two rounds
with her and he felt like Mike Tyson. Why couldn't a
woman like Madison go for him? Smart, stylish and
beautiful, she was the kind of woman he *should* be
with. Not some coked-out married whore like Rosarita
Falcon. Although he had to admit that Rosarita *was*
something in bed, horny as a wildcat, with claws to
prove it.

'If you like my lips, how 'bout us going out some
time?' he said, with an encouraging wink. 'You an' me,
Maddy, we could make things happen.'

'Make things happen?' she said, laughing derisively.
'What century are *you* living in?'

He didn't like that. Women were all the same, a
bunch of bitches, his father had taught him that. And
that's about the only thing Leon had taught him. 'Has
anyone ever told you you're a balls breaker?' he said
with a sharp scowl.

'Has anybody ever told *you* you're barking up the
wrong woman?' she replied coolly.

'Jesus!' he muttered, turning away.

Madison reminded herself to have a little talk with
Anton about his seating. Surely he knew better than to
stick her next to Joel Blaine?

Why was Joel there anyway? He was a most unlikely
guest, hardly on Anton's A list.

She turned to the man on her other side, Mortimer
Marcel, the designer. Mortimer was gay, and always
entertaining. A tall, slim man in his early fifties, he was
elegance personified. 'You must come visit our
showroom some time,' he said, chic as ever in a pin-
stripe suit with crisp white shirt, pearl-grey tie and

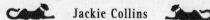

diamond cufflinks. 'I'm presenting some divine outfits this year. You'll love everything.'

'Do I get free clothes?' she asked jokingly.

'For you, yes,' Mortimer said, taking her seriously. 'You're an excellent advertisement.'

'I am?' she said, surprised. Hmm . . . first of all she had gorgeous lips, now she was an excellent advertisement. *Hey, girl*, she thought wryly, *you're certainly scoring tonight!*

She glanced across at the other table, where Jamie was glowing as Kris Phoenix plied her with compliments. Peter was slumped in a chair a few seats away from his wife. He did not look too happy. Next to him was a stick-thin, heroin-addicted supermodel – a girl who was failing to hold his interest.

Tonight is not Anton's greatest seating triumph, Madison thought. She feigned a yawn. 'I have to leave early,' she whispered to Mortimer.

'So do I,' he whispered back, indicating his live-in love at the next table. 'Perhaps Jefferson and I can offer you a ride?'

'Great,' she said, and was relieved to find that Joel had turned his full attention to the woman on his other side – a gorgeous black opera singer.

Poor soul. There was no greater punishment than being hit on by Joel Blaine.

As soon as they finished dessert she was out of there, sitting in the back of a town car with Mortimer and the black, bald and sexy Jefferson. *What a waste*, she thought. *Why are all the good ones either taken or gay?*

David hadn't liked gay men: they'd threatened his masculinity or some such garbage. She remembered how they'd often argued about his homophobic tendencies. Of course, gay women were fine with him. There were many times he'd tried to persuade her to do it with another girl. To his annoyance she'd always refused. Threesomes were definitely not her scene.

On reflection, there were quite a few things about David she hadn't liked.

So why the wasted two years?

Great sex, she was forced to admit. Great, uncomplicated, satisfying sex.

'How important do you think sex is?' she asked Mortimer.

'What?' he said, not quite sure he'd heard her correctly.

'I'm conducting a survey. How important is sex between two people?'

Mortimer glanced quickly at Jefferson. 'What's *your* answer?'

Jefferson grinned. 'Sex, man – it's the most important thing in the world.'

'I disagree,' Mortimer said, adjusting one of his diamond cufflinks. 'Getting along with somebody is more important, *especially* when you live together.'

'How long have *you* two been a couple?' Madison asked.

'I discovered Jefferson when he was a mere child,' Mortimer said, patting his boyfriend on the knee. 'Eighteen or nineteen . . . he'd just arrived in America from Trinidad. I was living with an older man at the time, so Jefferson and I became friends first.'

'That's nice,' Madison said.

'He was my favourite model,' Mortimer said, turning to his significant other. 'Isn't that right, dear?'

Jefferson grinned again. 'No way, man. You came on to me in the dressing room the first show I did. It

43

was like, "Oh, here we go!" Everybody was laughing about it.'

'Who's everybody?' Mortimer said huffily.

'The people who work for you – they know what you're like.'

'They know what I *used* to be like,' Mortimer corrected. 'Then *you* came along, and now I'm a changed man.'

'Yeah, you'd better believe it!' Jefferson said, with another huge grin. ''Cause I don't take kindly to nobody messin' around on *me*.'

'I'm duly warned,' Mortimer said.

'So be it,' Jefferson said, and they exchanged a long, intimate look.

Madison began to feel as if she was in the way. Maybe a cab would've been a better idea.

'Are you interviewing us for the magazine?' Mortimer asked curiously.

'No,' she said, shaking her head. 'I was merely thinking about relationships. Y'see, I was in one where I hardly had anything in common with the guy. I mean, we didn't even like the same music.'

'*Not* good,' Jefferson interjected. 'You gotta get off on the sounds.'

'Right,' she agreed. 'I'm into soul and jazz, and he was a classical freak. We never read the same books, or watched the same TV programmes. He loved sports. I'm bored by them. I guess we were totally different.'

'Then what was the big attraction?' Jefferson asked.

'Sex, of course. And now that he's gone I realize that maybe I simply got too comfortable. Y'know what I mean?'

'Were you planning on getting married before you

broke up with him?' Mortimer asked, ever the practical one.

'*He* broke up with *me*,' Madison explained. 'That's why I feel so kind of . . . like it's unfinished business.' She paused for a moment before continuing. 'Then he ran off and married someone else to make me feel really good.'

'What an asshole!' Jefferson said.

'Agreed!' Madison said.

'How'd you like to see him again?' Jefferson ventured. 'Y'know, fun times on the side. Do to *her* what *she* did to you.'

'She didn't do anything to me,' Madison said calmly. 'She was merely around when he was ready for something different.'

'But you're still pretty pissed, huh?' Jefferson said, nodding his bald head like he understood perfectly.

She laughed, slightly embarrassed because it was true, and she didn't want to be pissed, she wanted to forget all about David once and for all. 'Oh God, I feel like I'm sitting in a shrink's office,' she groaned.

'Maybe that's what you *should* do,' Mortimer suggested. 'It certainly helped me.'

'No way. I hate shrinks – all they do is sit there on their smug asses, nodding, telling you what you want to hear. Either that or they don't say anything at all. Screw that!'

'Get yourself to a shrink, girl,' Jefferson said succinctly. 'You need help.'

Before she could summon up a suitable reply, the car stopped outside her building. She invited them up for a drink, but they declined, which was okay with her because she was tired and edgy and ready to crawl into bed.

Her dog, Slammer, a large black Labrador, greeted her at the door. Well, he wasn't really her dog, she'd reluctantly agreed to look after him for a friend who'd gone to Australia for a week. The friend had got engaged, and the week had turned into three months.

In spite of herself, Madison had grown quite fond of the big dog.

Slammer didn't need walking because she'd given the doorman a key to her apartment and he'd already taken him out, which was good news because she wasn't into late-night strolls with a pooper-scooper for company.

Wandering into her small kitchen she checked her answering-machine. No messages, so she picked up the phone and called her father.

Michael sounded half-asleep, but she didn't care. 'Why you calling so late, sweetheart?' he mumbled. 'Everything okay?'

'Are you sleeping?'

A very audible yawn. 'I was.'

'Sorry,' she said, not sorry at all.

'What's goin' on? You sound down.'

'No, no . . . It's simply that I do not appreciate hearing from Anton Couch that you guys are getting an apartment in New York.'

'Hey, sweetie, I really *am* asleep.' A pause. 'Can we talk about this tomorrow?'

'Sure,' she said, slamming down the phone.

She couldn't stand it when her father didn't give her his full attention. Michael had always been there for her – unlike her mother, who was a more distant figure in her life. It had always been that way. As far back as she could remember, her mother, Stella, had been this exotic-smelling, glamorous creature she hardly ever

46

saw. As a child she'd been raised by a nanny, then sent to boarding school at eleven; vacations at summer camp; and finally college.

The day she graduated, Michael had handed her the keys to her own small apartment. It was quite obvious there was to be no going home, and that was fine with her. She loved her parents, although there were times she felt she hardly knew her mother, but that was okay too. Michael more than compensated. He was a dynamic, interesting man, and she was glad he was her father.

She undressed, got into bed and attempted to read. After a few minutes she found her mind wandering; it was impossible to concentrate.

Slammer jumped on the bed, snuggling up beside her. She didn't push him off. It was comforting that *somebody* cared – even if that somebody was only a dog.

She thought about Anton's dinner and how she'd hated every minute of it. It hadn't been up to his usual standard. Joel Blaine hitting on her. Ugh! And Peter Nova, drunk. Double ugh!

Tomorrow she'd fix an appointment with Victor's private eye to sort out Jamie's problems. *Oh well, that's what friends are for.*

She switched off the light, but after ten minutes realized there was no way she was falling asleep. It was destined to be one of those nights. Maybe Jefferson was right, maybe she *did* need to see a shrink. Of course, Victor would know the best one in town, but how could she ask *him*?

She tossed restlessly, finally gave up and clicked on the television, flicking past several porno stations, marvelling at a soft-core movie where the girls' breasts jutted to attention without a sign of gravity. What a

bunch of freaks. You didn't see guys running out buying themselves perky silicone balls.

Silicone balls. What a hilarious thought!

She began to giggle. Slammer started to pant, a sure sign that he, too, was not ready for sleep.

Finally she got up and padded into the kitchen where she fixed herself a cheese and ham sandwich with plenty of lettuce and pickles.

Slammer got the crusts. He was one happy dog.

Finally satisfied, they both returned to bed.

Chapter Six

'*What?*' Rosarita shrieked bad-temperedly, staring at Dex, who stood in the front hall blocking her way. It occurred to her that maybe he'd found out about her and Joel, and she was all set with a thousand excuses. Not that she needed excuses – but until this was over she had to keep up *some* kind of show.

'Got a surprise,' Dexter said.

'Good or bad?' she snapped, cagey as ever.

'Good.'

'Then perhaps I can come in the fucking apartment,' she said, attempting to push past him.

'Don't swear,' he admonished her, in a fierce whisper.

Maybe, just maybe he'd landed the lead role in a major movie and was about to tell her. Wouldn't *that* be something?

She could dream, couldn't she?

Suddenly Dexter jumped to one side, making an extravagant gesture with his left arm. And, to Rosarita's horror, there stood Martha and Matt

Cockranger, his goddamn parents.

'Shit!' The word slid out of her mouth before she could stop it. 'What in hell are *they* doing here?' nearly followed, but she was able to refrain from actually saying it aloud.

'Hello, dear,' said Martha, a plump, faded blonde in a lime-green polyester pant-suit, with jangly rhinestone earrings and white plastic open-toed sandals. 'How lovely to see you.'

Rosarita was still in shock as Matt stepped forward, giving her an all-encompassing hug. Dex's dad was a florid-faced man in his mid-fifties, with close-cropped grey hair and faded blue eyes. Once handsome like his son, he'd been beaten into submission by the passing years. Plus he had a huge protruding gut – solid as a football.

'How's our Dick's –' he began.

'Dexter,' Dexter interrupted, frowning at his father.

'How's our *Dexter's* little girl?' Matt corrected himself quickly, wary of his famous son's wrath.

For once in her life, Rosarita was speechless. This was a nightmare. What had she done to deserve a visit from the Cockrangers?

'Mom, Dad, I didn't tell Rosarita you were coming,' Dexter said, beaming. 'She's kind of overcome. You know how much she loves you.'

Oh, yes, Dex, pour it on. How could he do this to her? How *could* he?

'They're staying with us, honey,' he continued. 'I had Conchita fix up the guest room.'

'You did?' she croaked, wishing nothing more than an immediate shower and a long night of uninterrupted sleep.

'Isn't it a neat surprise?' Dexter said, squeezing her

arm. 'I knew you'd be pleased.'

'I'm . . . I'm . . . shocked,' she stammered. Then turning to his big, blustery dad, she added, 'How'd you get away from your job, Matt?'

'Took a three-week leave of absence,' Matt replied proudly. 'Everyone at work watches our boy on *Dark Days*. Makes me something of a celebrity back home.'

Three weeks! This was getting worse every minute. Goddamnit! She asked for a divorce and the motherfucker flew in his parents! Unreal!

'We wanted to be sure to spend plenty of time with you,' Martha said. 'Remember when you came to see us before you were married? The family is *still* talking about your visit.'

'Yes,' Matt agreed, rubbing his hands together. 'And *I*'m looking forward to getting together with that dad of yours. He promised to show us the town.'

Oh, that was rich. How about a tour of all the strip clubs and a few drop-ins at Mob-connected restaurants? Matt and Martha would fit right in.

'I wish I'd known you were coming,' Rosarita said, struggling for something to say. 'I would've planned dinner.'

'That's all right,' Dexter said – *Mr I've-got-it-all-under-control*. 'I made a reservation at Twenty-one.'

Valiantly she tried to keep her scowl down to a minimum. 'You did?'

'Eight o'clock.'

'Eight o'clock,' she repeated.

'So let's all get cleaned up and meet in the living room at seven thirty,' Dexter said.

'Should I wear a tie?' Matt worried.

'Can I wear a pant-suit?' Martha asked anxiously.

51

Rosarita couldn't stand it. Her life was turning to shit right before her very eyes.

* * *

Somehow Rosarita got through dinner, seething all the while. They were not given a good table at the restaurant, and she could understand why. Matt and Martha Cockranger had suburbia written all over them, and apparently the name Dexter Falcon meant nothing.

She didn't mind that they were shown to a lousy table, because the truth was she didn't wish to be seen with them. Christ! Going out with Chas to one of his gangster hang-outs would be better than this. In fact, *anything* would be an improvement.

So far she had not had Dex alone. When she did, she planned on giving him an earful. How dare he invite his parents to stay without consulting her? Especially when he *knew* she'd been talking divorce.

The way he acted it was as if they were the happiest couple in the world. Was he *losing* it?

She spent the better part of the dinner worrying that Joel might come in and spot her, although everyone else appeared to be having a wonderful time. Martha downed two vodka martinis in a row and promptly got tipsy. Matt ordered several beers and kept jumping up to visit the men's room, while Dex had a big stupid grin on his big handsome face all night. Boy, was he living in Dreamland.

On their way out, a female customer stopped Dex and asked him for his autograph. It made Matt and Martha's night. It put Rosarita in an even worse mood than before. Didn't the stupid fan standing there with a pen and a dopey look on her moon face realize that he was nothing but a stupid nobody well on his way to nowhere?

Rosarita squelched a strong desire to scream. Why did she have to stand for this crap? Why couldn't her father co-operate and arrange to have Dex whacked, thereby putting an end to this charade?

'It was *such* a lovely evening, dear,' Martha enthused, when they got back to the apartment. 'You make my little boy so happy. It truly warms my heart.'

Oh, God, was she going to have to face Martha at the funeral? Would she be forced to play the bereaved widow and pretend to be desolate?

The moment she and Dex were alone she started a litany of complaints. 'What *do* you think you're *doing?!*' she shrieked. 'Inviting your goddamn parents without checking with me first. This is unfucking-acceptable.'

'Why are you so upset?' Dexter asked blankly. 'You've always told me you love my parents.'

'When did I ever say *that?*'

'When we first visited them. Remember? Before we were married.'

'Ha! Before we were married I said a lot of things I wouldn't say now.'

'You did?'

Was he obtuse or what? God had given him exceptional looks, but He sure as shit hadn't given him any brains.

'Listen to me,' she said, spitting her words out very slowly, making sure he heard every single one. 'You don't seem to get it. I . . . want . . . a . . . divorce. That means I do *not* intend to sit around playing nice with your parents.'

53

'You're a bitch, you know that?'

'Yes,' she said spitefully. 'I know that.'

'You're certainly not the girl I married.'

'Hey, when I married *you*, I thought you were on your way to being a movie star for Crissakes, not a TV hack.'

'I suppose that's *why* you married me, huh?'

'Yes, as a matter of fact, that's *exactly* why I married you. I expected we'd move into a big Beverly Hills mansion and mix with all the other movie stars.' She threw him a stony glare. 'You haven't lived up to your side of the bargain, Dex.'

'I didn't know we *had* a bargain,' he countered. 'However, we *are* married, Rosarita, and I refuse to give you a divorce.'

'You do, huh?' she said, her tone getting shriller by the minute. 'Well, let me tell you this – if you *don't* agree to a divorce, you'll be very sorry indeed.'

'Is that a threat?'

'Sounds suspiciously like one, doesn't it?'

He stared at the woman he'd given his name to. How could she be so cold? Surely this wasn't the same sweet girl he'd walked down the aisle with? Where had that darling girl gone?

'I thought we were planning a family,' he ventured sadly.

'For the number of times *you* get it up a week, we're lucky to have a fucking *cat!*' she responded.

'My call is five a.m. every day,' he said evenly. 'I need my sleep.'

'Weekends too?' she sneered.

'Are you saying we don't make love enough?'

'I'm saying we *never* do it, and when we do, it's always in the missionary position.' She placed her hands on her hips, glaring at him accusingly. 'Do I *look* like a fucking missionary to you?' He shook his head. 'I thought you were such a swinger,' she continued, her voice one long, monotonous whine. 'Didn't you fuck your way through a bunch of horny models before we were married?'

'I wish you wouldn't use language like that,' he objected.

'When did *you* turn so holier than thou?' she said tartly. 'I married this hunk with his *dick* on show all over Times Square, *now* look at you.'

'It wasn't on show,' he objected. 'I was wearing underwear.'

'Give me a fucking break,' she jeered. '*Everyone* saw your package. And I must say it looked pretty damn good up on that billboard. It got *me*, didn't it?'

'I've never done nudity.'

'No?' she snapped back. 'How about privately for dear old Mortimer?'

'Absolutely not,' Dexter said, his face reddening.

'He's gay, isn't he?' she taunted. 'He discovered you, didn't he? So don't tell *me* you didn't have to suck his dick to get where you are today. Not that it's very far, but I suppose you *were* a successful model. You should've stayed one.'

'It was *you* who wanted me to start acting.'

'It was me, was it? *C'mon*. You were forever watching those movies with Kevin Costner and Harrison Ford. You *always* wanted to be exactly like them. So tell me, Dex, why aren't you?'

'I will be, one of these days,' he said, truly believing.

'In a pig's ear.' She snorted derisively.

'Look,' he sighed, 'all I'm asking is for you to be nice to my parents while they're here. If you can do that, then, when they leave – if it's what you still want – we'll talk about divorce.'

She didn't believe him, but what else could she do?

'Okay,' she said. 'Deal. But it's not a twenty-four-hour thing, I've got to get out and breathe.'

'Be nice to them,' he repeated. 'Especially my mother. She thinks the world of you.'

'Yeah, yeah,' she said. 'I'll take Martha to Saks and let her loose with my credit card – is that nice enough?'

He didn't believe her, but what else could he do?

Chapter Seven

'Hello?' Madison said, reaching for the phone. Slammer immediately began licking her bare arm with his wet, floppy tongue. 'Hello,' she repeated, attempting to push the overly affectionate dog away.

'Hi, sweetheart, it's Michael.'

How come he never said 'Dad'? It was weird, but ever since she could remember she'd called her parents by their first names. Stella and Michael. Sometimes she kind of wished for the Dad thing.

'I'm asleep,' she mumbled.

'Now you know what it's like,' he said, good-naturedly. 'Call me back when you wake up.'

'No, no, don't go away,' she said quickly. 'What time is it?'

'Eight.'

'On Saturday?' she said, struggling to sit up.

'I was thinking that if you were available I'd drive into the city and we'd go for brunch.'

'That'd be great,' she said, stifling a yawn. 'You *and* Stella?'

'No,' he said shortly. 'Stella can't make it.'

'Why?'

'It doesn't matter. Where would you like to go?'

'How about the Plaza?' she suggested. 'It's all kind of, like, you know, grown-up.'

He laughed softly. 'My intelligent big girl is such a kid sometimes.'

She smiled. Why not? He was her father, and it was fun to feel like a kid again. 'Will you pick me up at my apartment?' she said, stifling another yawn.

'I'll do that.'

She put down the phone and hauled herself out of bed. Slammer followed, panting and watching her with his big, soulful brown eyes as she headed for the bathroom.

'I suppose you want to go out,' she said. He barked once. Sometimes she could swear he understood every word. 'Okay, okay, let me clean my teeth and put some clothes on, then you and I will hit the streets.'

She wriggled into a pair of faded jeans and a sweatshirt, tied her hair back and left the apartment, an eager Slammer trotting obediently beside her.

In the elevator she remembered she'd left the pooper-scooper behind and had to go back to get it. It was humiliating walking the streets and picking up dog crap. Whoever came up with *that* rule?

Outside, the crisp morning air woke her up. She began thinking about her conversation with her father. If Michael was coming into town without Stella on a weekend, it definitely meant he had something to tell her. It must be about why they'd decided to move to Manhattan, why they'd called her best friend's partner to tell *him*, and not bothered mentioning it to her. It was all too bizarre. What could his excuse possibly be?

As she walked briskly along the street she wondered how Peter and Jamie had managed the previous night. Had they gotten into a mammoth fight? Or maybe they'd indulged in one of the long lovemaking sessions that Jamie said Peter desired every day.

Hmm . . . David had been like that. She remembered the time they'd gone to the theatre to see *Joseph and the Amazing Technicolor Dream Coat*. After that she'd nicknamed him *David and the Amazing Insatiable Cock*.

Now the insatiable cock was performing elsewhere. Too bad.

A familiar face jogged by. A tall, rugged soap actor, whom she spotted every weekend. They exchanged nods of recognition. Around the corner she bumped into BoBo, the area's famous Scottish dog walker. Short and squat, with a mop of carrot-coloured hair and numerous freckles, he was quite a character. Somehow or other he managed six dogs while wearing a kilt and carrying a Saks shopping bag in which to deposit his charges' offerings. Slammer was in love with one of BoBo's charges, Candy, a sexy miniature poodle who refused to have anything to do with him.

'Morning, Miss,' BoBo said, cheerful as ever.

'Morning, BoBo. How's it going?'

'It's a wee touch chilly up the Khyber Pass,' he said, with a saucy wink. 'But I'll live.'

'Glad to hear it,' she said, idly wondering if he wore anything under his kilt.

'If you ever need me t' look after Slammer, just say the word,' BoBo offered, fishing in his pocket for a treat with which he proceeded to tempt the big dog.

'I'll keep that in mind,' Madison said, thinking of

how much she was looking forward to getting together with her father. The last time she'd seen him was a few months ago when she'd spent a weekend in Connecticut at their house. She'd rented a car and driven there on Friday night, returning to the city twenty-four hours later. Sometimes the anticipation of spending time with her parents was better than the actual event. When she had Michael to herself she was much happier than hanging out with both of them. Stella was hardly the warm and loving motherly type.

While she was there, Stella had languished in the garden lying on a *chaise-longue* under a striped umbrella, sipping iced tea, while Michael had walked her around the grounds, showing off his roses.

'Isn't it awfully quiet here after New York?' she'd asked, surprised that he was so settled.

'I like it here,' he'd said. 'No pressure.'

'No action either,' she'd replied. 'When I was a kid you and Stella *loved* getting all dressed up and hitting the restaurants and clubs. Action was your middle name.'

Michael had nodded thoughtfully. 'Sometimes Stella misses the action. Although most of the time she's perfectly happy, like me.'

Sometimes Madison couldn't help wondering if he'd ever screwed around on the beautiful Stella.

No. Her father wasn't that kind of guy. Michael had integrity.

Madison often wished that *she* could find a guy with integrity. It was more important than a great butt any day.

Back at her apartment, she took a shower and tried to decide what to wear, finally settling on tight black pants, boots and a man's white shirt knotted at the waist. For a change she wore her hair down, then added tinted shades. David had always liked her in tinted shades. 'Makes you look like a movie star,' he used to joke. Ha! Only David would call her a movie star. She added a couple of crosses strung around her neck on black leather thongs, and some Indian silver hoop earrings. Then, with nothing else to do while she waited for Michael, she picked up the phone and called the private detective Victor had recommended.

A woman answered the phone, terse and unfriendly. 'Yeah?'

'Oh, um . . . hi. I'm looking for K. Florian.'

'You want to set up an appointment?'

'That's right.'

'Can you make it at four o'clock today?'

'The weekend isn't good. How about Monday or Tuesday?'

'Monday, ten o'clock.'

'Where?'

'You want to come here? Or shall I come to you?'

'Are *you* K. Florian?'

An aggressive 'What's the matter? You shocked I'm a woman?'

'No,' Madison said quickly. 'I guess I was expecting a man, but a woman's fine with me.'

'I'll come to you then. What's the address?'

'Uh . . . you do realize that this is confidential. Y' see, it's not *me* hiring you, it's my friend. So uh . . . I'll make sure she's here at ten on Monday.'

'What's this about? A cheating husband?'

'How did you know?'

'It's always the same story.' A beat. 'Listen, if he's cheating, I can get the goods within twenty-four hours.'

'Sounds very efficient. I'll give you my address.'

She did so, then decided she'd better contact Jamie to let her know.

Peter answered the phone. 'Bad news!' he groaned. 'Me have major hangover.'

'I'm not surprised.'

'You're *not*? Why? Were you drinking with me last night? What did I do?'

'No, I wasn't your drinking partner, but for a moment you were knocking it back pretty good in front of me.'

'Did I say something I shouldn't've?'

'You were fine, Peter – really.'

'Remind me never to drink again.'

'I always remind you of that.'

'Even my eyelashes hurt!'

'Is your wife around?'

'Jamie!' he yelled. 'It's Maddy.'

'Coming,' Jamie called out in the background.

'What are you up to today?' he asked. 'Anything exciting?'

'Meeting Michael for brunch. And you two are –'

'Shopping,' he complained. 'My punishment for being bad.'

'Maybe I'll catch up with you guys later.'

'You'll find us at Barney's, followed by Bergdorf's and Saks. Doesn't that sound like a fun afternoon for a reformed drunk?'

Jamie picked up the extension. 'Hi!' she said happily. 'How are *you* today?'

'Great,' Madison said. 'And you?'

'Last night was something, wasn't it?' Jamie giggled.

'*I* had a lousy time. Can you imagine getting stuck next to Joel Blaine? I mean really!'

'Don't be so down on him,' Jamie said. 'Joel's not so bad. In fact, I find him sort of attractive in an odd kind of earthy way.'

'*What?*' Peter said, still listening in on the extension. 'The guy's a moron. His dad's the one with the smarts.'

'You only say that because Leon's a multi-billionaire,' Jamie said. 'You and money, Petey, you revel in it.'

'So do you, sweet thing, so do you.'

'Put down the extension, Peter. I'd prefer to speak to Madison *without* you joining in.'

'Don't mind me,' he said. 'I'm taking a cold shower and swallowing a bottle of aspirin. I'm still trying to understand why you didn't give them to me last night. You could've saved me a monster hangover.'

'What am I – your nurse?' Jamie said crisply.

'Oh, I forgot,' Peter said. 'You were too busy flirting with Kris Phoenix.'

'Hey, listen, guys,' Madison interrupted, 'much as I love listening to you two bicker, can you please do it on your own time?'

'Sure,' Peter said. 'See ya,' and he clicked off.

'Has he gone?' Madison asked.

'Yes,' Jamie said. 'I can always tell if he's still listening in.'

'*You* were having fun last night.'

'As a matter of fact I was,' Jamie said, giggling softly. 'Kris Phoenix was saying some *very* flattering things.'

'No big one, Jamie, you've been hearing very flattering things since you were ten. Guys have *always* been on your case.'

'But, Maddy, this was Kris Phoenix! We used to buy his records, follow his romances in the magazines. It's a huge kick being hit on by a guy like that. It'd be like Mick Jagger coming on to me.'

'I'm sure that can be arranged any time you want,' Madison said drily. 'Apparently Mick Jagger comes on to anything that breathes!'

Jamie laughed.

'Anyway,' Madison continued, 'enough about your love-life. Remember that thing we discussed?'

'What thing?' Jamie said vaguely.

'You know what I'm talking about. It's set for Monday, ten o'clock, my apartment.'

'Oh . . . you mean the detective thing.'

'What's the matter?'

'Well . . .' Jamie said, hesitating for a moment. 'Do you honestly think I should go through with it?'

'If you're suspicious, yes.'

'I'm not so sure any more. We had such a fantastic time last night when we got home. I know Peter was drunk and everything, and I was kind of, like . . . well, I guess I was on a high. Getting hit on by a rock star certainly revs the old adrenaline!'

'Are you saying you want me to call it off?'

'No . . . I guess I *should* do it. No harm done, right? Only I'm not that suspicious any more.'

'Then *don't* do it,' Madison said, exasperated. 'Nobody's forcing you. I'll call back and cancel.'

'What would *you* do?'

'It's not *my* situation,' Madison said. 'I know how you hate making decisions, but this one is all yours.'

'Okay, okay,' Jamie said. 'I'll do it. Just so I can say to myself, silly suspicious me.'

'That's a fair decision.'

'Nothing lost, right?'

'Right. Peter tells me you're going shopping at Barney's.'

'Yes, my darling husband has promised to buy me whatever I want.' A soft chuckle. 'And after last night, believe me, I deserve it.'

* * *

Madison was right, Michael Castelli *was* the best-looking fifty-eight-year-old in Connecticut. Six feet tall, he was slim and well built, with black curly hair, smooth olive skin, and the same sharply defined cheek-bones and seductive lips as his daughter. They looked alike. This pleased Madison.

Maybe she was prejudiced, but it seemed to her that age suited him – Michael got better looking each year. He wasn't handsome in the traditional way, not like that soap actor she saw jogging every weekend. No, he had an Al Pacino/Robert de Niro edge – a look of danger – which apparently turned women on, because for as long as she could remember women had always had eyes for her father.

'Hi, Michael,' she said.

'Hey, sweetheart,' he said, hugging her. 'It's good to see ya.'

'You too,' she responded.

'Still living by yourself?' he inquired, strolling into her apartment.

'Why? Would you sooner I had a resident man?' she teased, wishing she'd had more of a chance to tidy up.

'I'd sooner you were *married* to a guy.'

'As opposed to *married* to a girl?'

'Cut the comedy. I'm not joking.'

'I'm only twenty-nine,' she protested. 'Why this sudden desire to see me married off?'

''Cause we live in a tough world, sweetheart,' he said. 'And I'd prefer to see you protected.'

She found herself giggling. 'Protected? You sound like a scene out of *The Godfather*.'

He threw her a look.

'I'm making another joke,' she said.

Slammer padded over and drooled on Michael's black Armani pants. He didn't appreciate the dog's attention. He took a quick step back. 'Keep that animal away from me,' he said, brushing off his pants. 'I hate dogs.'

'You sound like Stella.'

'Not me.'

Since it was such a clear and crisp morning, they decided to walk to the Plaza. Madison felt pretty good strolling along Lexington with her father. She wished she could see more of him, but a few times a year was better than nothing.

'So,' she said, as they headed towards the hotel, 'when am I going to hear what's going on?'

'Can't you wait until I get a cup of coffee?' he said.

'No,' she replied, unable to hold back any longer. 'I'm really pissed, Michael. How could you not tell me you're moving back to the city?'

He looked at her blankly. 'What are you talking about?'

'Anton told me.'

'Who's Anton, and what did he tell you?'

'Anton is Jamie's partner. They have an interior design business. He told me that Stella called him about decorating your New York apartment.'

'Did Stella tell him where she could be reached?'

66

'I guess so. I didn't ask. What's going on?'

'You're just like me. Impatient. Have to know everything immediately.'

'This isn't exactly immediately,' she pointed out. 'I doubt you'd be telling me anything at all if I hadn't busted you on it.'

'You know if I didn't tell you there had to be a reason, right?'

'Right. So when am I going to hear?'

'Jesus!' he said irritably. 'Take it easy.'

'Okay, I'll be patient. How *is* Stella anyway? And why didn't she come with you today?'

Michael stared straight ahead. 'No idea. Haven't seen her in a while.'

Uh-oh, this is not good. 'What do you mean? How could you not see her when you live together?'

'You couldn't wait until we're sitting down eating brunch like two civilized people,' he said harshly. 'No, you have to find out now.' He took a long ominous beat. 'The reason I haven't seen Stella is because she left me.'

'She did *what?*' Madison said breathlessly.

'You heard.'

'Stella left you?'

'You got it. Ran off with some twenty-six-year-old kid.'

'I don't believe it!'

'Believe it,' he said flatly. 'It happened.'

'But you and Mom, you've always been so close.'

'That's what *I* thought.'

'How did it happen?'

'Who knows?' he said evenly. 'I'm merely the guy who got left. Came home one day and she was gone. I haven't spoken to her since.'

'Oh, my God!' Madison exclaimed, trying to digest this shocking news.

'That's the story, Princess,' Michael said calmly. 'I guess it's *her* who's moving to New York, not me.'

They walked in silence for a few minutes, until Madison suddenly stopped and faced him. 'How . . . how can you let her do this to me?'

Michael laughed drily. 'Nobody's doing anything to you,' he said.

'You're my parents,' she said accusingly, knowing she sounded unreasonable but unable to stop herself. 'I don't *want* divorced parents.'

'You don't want divorced parents, huh?' he repeated. 'What are you – eight?'

'No,' she said heatedly. 'But I've always looked up to you both as an example. Your marriage was . . . well, anyway, *I* thought it was so idyllic. The two of you . . . for ever together.'

'Everything isn't always what it seems,' he said grimly. 'Stella wanted a younger body in her bed. Harder abs. Harder everything.' A cold laugh. 'Hey, guys do it all the time. Thing is – I don't happen to be that kind of guy.'

Madison clung on to his arm. 'Are you okay?' she asked, realizing that he was taking this far too calmly.

'Me? I'm fine,' he said. 'I was planning on telling you when I was ready. Didn't want to spring it on you out of nowhere.' Another dry laugh. 'Guess we blew that.'

'How long ago did this happen?'

'A few weeks.'

'Why hasn't she called *me?*'

'You were never exactly close, were you?'

'She *is* my mother. Don't you think I should have heard it from her?'

'Madison,' he sighed, 'you're all grown up. You've got a great job interviewing lots of interesting people, and you do it well. You've achieved plenty, which I know wasn't easy.' A long, slow beat. 'Truth is, you didn't always get the attention from either of us that you deserved, and somehow that bothers me.'

'I guess . . .' she mumbled, feeling totally mixed up and sad. 'It was you and Stella, I was the outsider.'

'Don't get carried away.'

'No, Michael, I was. That's why I'm so shocked at this news.'

'Listen, sweetheart,' he said, speaking fast, 'there's something else I have to tell you – something that might help you understand things better.'

'What?' she asked, holding his arm tighter.

'It'll have to wait until we're sitting down.' She nodded blankly. Today was definitely going to be a day to remember.

Chapter Eight

'I hope you're thinking about babies,' Martha Cockranger said, her round cheeks flushed.

'What?' Rosarita said, as Martha trailed her around the ground floor of Saks.

'Babies,' Martha repeated with a coy chuckle. 'Little ones.' A confidential whisper. 'Dick wants three, you know.'

'How many times do I have to tell you? He's not called Dick any more,' Rosarita said irritably. 'And while we're *on* the subject, how could you stick him with a name like Dick when your surname is Cockranger?'

'Dick was his grandfather's name,' Martha said, managing to look hurt. 'He never should've changed it. His daddy is *still* upset.'

Oh, Christ! Rosarita thought. *What am I doing here? This unsophisticated dolt simply doesn't get it.*

'I'm not planning on becoming pregnant any time soon,' she said, putting what she hoped was an end to *that* discussion.

'You're not?' Martha said, disappointed.

'Definitely *not*,' Rosarita said, dragging her mother-in-law over to the accessory section, and quickly pulling a long chiffon Armani scarf off the stand. 'What do you think of *this?*' she asked.

'It's lovely!' Martha exclaimed.

'I'll buy it for you,' Rosarita said, waving her Saks charge card at a salesperson.

'I can't let you do that,' Martha objected.

'Why not?' Rosarita said airily. 'Dex'll pay.'

'Please, no,' Martha said, getting all flustered. 'I can't have him spending his hard-earned money on me. He works so hard, and this scarf is . . .' her voice rose in horror as she took a peek at the price tag '. . . three hundred and fifty dollars!'

Ha! Rosarita thought. *Works hard? He goes in early, has makeup slapped on his face, sits around with a bunch of mediocre actors, then comes home. What's so hard about that?*

Instead she nodded understandingly. 'I know, it must be tough for him.'

'Yes,' Martha agreed. 'But at least he has *you* to come home to.' Another confidential whisper. 'He adores you, dear, you should *see* the letters he writes us.'

'He writes you letters?' Rosarita said, surprised.

'Once a week we get a handwritten letter from him telling us all about your exciting life together.'

'What does he say?'

'He tells us about the places you go to dinner, what you wear, the meals you eat. I love to hear all the details, and he knows it.' A happy sigh. 'He's *such* a good son.'

'I'm sure,' Rosarita muttered. *Good and boring and he won't give me a divorce. It'll be the death of him.*

71

'The morning he appeared on *Regis & Kathie Lee* was the most exciting day of my life,' Martha confided dreamily. 'Kathie Lee's my favourite, you know, such a delightful woman. I don't believe a word about those nasty sweat shops, it's all lies.'

'He wasn't on the show by himself,' Rosarita pointed out. 'He was there with the rest of the cast, and he only appeared at the end of the programme. It was actually an interview with the witch who plays the lead.'

'Ah . . . Silver Anderson,' Martha said admiringly. 'Such a lady! I'm hoping Dick . . . I mean Dex, will take us to the studio one day to meet her.'

'I'm sure he will,' Rosarita said, bored with this conversation.

'What night are we seeing that lovely daddy of yours?' Martha inquired, flinging the chiffon scarf around her neck and parading in front of a mirror.

'I'll call him later,' Rosarita said, spotting a girlfriend in the distance.

Quick as a flash she pulled Martha round to the other side of the counter.

She couldn't be seen with her. It was far too humiliating.

*   *   *

'When are you starting a family, son?' Matt Cockranger said, as he lifted weights in Dexter's makeshift gym.

'Dunno,' Dexter mumbled, busy on the rowing machine.

Clearing his throat, Matt lowered his voice. 'I shouldn't be telling you this, but when I married your mother she was already pregnant with your older sister.'

'She was?' Dexter said, quite shocked at this intimate revelation.

'She'd kill me if she thought I'd told you,' Matt said, looking around to make sure that Martha was not about to appear suddenly. 'The secret is to start early.'

'Thanks, Dad,' Dexter said, hoping to shut him up.

Matt had no intention of shutting up. 'No point in waiting,' he said. 'Knock her up, boy, that's what you've got to do.'

'Dad,' Dexter said, frowning, 'where did *you* learn phrases like "knock her up"?'

'I was quite a ladies' man in my time,' Matt said, with a boastful chuckle. 'Handsome, like you. Captain of the football team. And my Martha was the prettiest girl in school. All the fellows were after her.'

'They were?' Dexter said, eyebrows rising at the thought that his dear old mom might once have been a sex magnet.

'Yes, indeed,' Matt said, moving over to the Life Cycle. 'But I knew she was the one for me as soon as I met her.'

'Really?' Dexter said.

'Oh, yes,' Matt said, nodding to himself. 'She wouldn't let anyone else near her except me. Had to wait weeks before she'd give me so much as a good-night kiss. What a girl! To this day I'm the only man she's ever had.'

'You're telling me too many details, Dad,' Dexter said nervously.

'I know what I'm talking about, son. You've got to knock your wife up, keeps 'em in their place.'

'Right,' Dexter said, thinking that nothing would keep Rosarita in her place.

'Has she been getting uppity with you lately?' Matt asked.

'Why would you say that?'

'I was in the kitchen last night when I heard shouting coming from your bedroom. Not that I'd ever interfere.'

'You didn't tell Mom, did you?'

'No,' Matt said. 'Wouldn't do to upset her.'

'Don't!' Dexter said. 'She'd hate to think we were fighting.'

'What were you fighting about?'

'I want to start a family,' Dexter mumbled. 'Rosarita doesn't.'

'Is she on the pill, son?' Matt asked, slowing down.

Dexter shook his head, sweat beading his brow.

'What does she use?' Matt asked. 'One of those rubber diaphragm things?'

Dexter nodded, embarrassed to be discussing such a personal subject with his dad.

'I'll tell you what to do,' Matt said, stopping his machine. 'And you'd better listen to me, 'cause I'm wiser than you – not more famous, but older and wiser.'

'Yes, Dad,' Dexter said, resigned to the fact that there was no stopping him.

'You take a pin, find her diaphragm and prick a few little holes in it. She'll never know you've done it, and before long she'll be pregnant. After that things will be fine. Take it from me, son, once they've had a baby they calm down.'

'You think so?'

'I *know* so,' Matt said. 'Heed the voice of

74

experience, son. Matt Cockranger *knows* what he's talking about.'

* * *

Back at the apartment Rosarita escaped to the bedroom, locked the door and sat staring at the phone. Should she call him? Shouldn't she? She was ready for action with a vengeance, and Joel was certainly the man to give it to her. But there was no way she could see him over the weekend, not with the Cockrangers on her case every single minute.

Damn! She wanted him more than she'd ever wanted anyone, and Rosarita *always* got what she wanted.

On impulse, she picked up the phone and got through to Chas. 'You know that little favour I asked you to do?' she said, picking at her nail polish – a nervous habit she couldn't shake.

'Ha!' Chas said. 'Some *little* goddamn favour. I wanna talk to you 'bout that.'

'Anyway,' she said casually, 'put it on hold. His parents are in town.'

'Dexter's mom and dad?'

'Yes, they're here in New York, staying with us. Which brings me to favour number two.'

'And what's that?' Chas said sourly. 'Ya want I should arrange t' whack the whole family?'

'Funny,' Rosarita said.

'What *do* ya want?' Chas said, thoroughly steamed at his unpredictable daughter.

'Daddy,' she said, reverting to little girl tactics, 'don't be so mean. Dex's stupid parents are here and I've got to entertain them. They're *dying* to see you. Can we all have dinner tonight?'

'No way,' Chas growled. 'I gotta hot date.'

'You can *bring* your date,' Rosarita said persuasively. 'It doesn't make any difference to me.'

'The last time you was in the company of one of my dates, ya ended up callin' her a cheap whore to her face.'

'I did?' Rosarita said innocently, remembering the incident well.

'Yeah, an' that kinda behaviour I don't appreciate, considerin' me an' the broad was in the middle of a very cosy relationship.'

'You were?'

'Don't go playin' innocent tootsie with me,' Chas said. 'Ya know what ya did. My ladyfriend ran out on me so fast she forgot her panties.'

'Lucky you,' Rosarita said, with a wicked laugh. 'You can parade around wearing them.'

'You're gettin' a real smart mouth,' Chas said angrily.

Rosarita changed tactics again. 'Anyway,' she said, as sweetly as she could, 'how about if we all come to dinner at your house? You've got a cook who sits around doing nothing all day. Please, Daddy, *please*.'

'Jeez!' Chas grumbled. 'This is *all* I freakin' need. What's their name? Shipranger?'

'No, Daddy,' she said patiently. 'Cockranger.'

'What kinda name is *that?*'

'At least Dex was smart enough to change it,' Rosarita said, with a wild giggle. 'Can you imagine if I was Mrs *Cockranger?*'

Yeah, Chas thought. *You would've gotten the name you deserve.*

* * *

76

The moment Chas got off the phone with Rosarita he phoned his other daughter.

'Hello, Daddy,' Venice said. 'How are you?'

Venice always had a happy face and a kind word – not to mention these two adorable small kids and the pleasant, low-key husband whom she was *not* nagging Chas to dispose of.

'How ya doin', baby doll?' he said, happy to speak to her.

'We're all fine, thank you, Daddy.'

'Glad t' hear it.'

'I was thinking of bringing the children over tomorrow. Would that be okay with you?'

'Sure, I wanna see 'em. But I also wanna see you an' . . .' He hesitated, never quite certain of Venice's husband's name.

'Eddie,' she reminded.

'Yeah, yeah – I know, Eddie, for Crissakes. I want you an' Eddie t' come for dinner tonight at the house. Rosarita's in-laws are in town.'

'Martha and Matt,' Venice said. 'I remember them from the wedding, they're nice people.'

'I'm glad *somebody* remembers 'em.'

'What time shall we be there, Daddy?'

'Around seven thirty.'

'Should Eddie wear a tie?'

'Yeah, good idea.' He hesitated again – Venice was his sensitive daughter, he didn't want to shock or surprise her. 'Uh . . . hon – is it okay with you if I got a date? It won't upset you or nothin'?'

'Why on earth would it upset me? I know how much you loved Mommy, which is why you never remarried. I'm *happy* you have a date. I'm sure if she's with you, she must be someone special.'

'Yeah, honey, she is, she is.'

'What does she do?'

Chas fumbled for a moment. 'She's, uh . . . she's a nurse,' he said finally, trying to decide how he was going to tell his current stripper girlfriend that she had to pretend to be a nurse for the night.

And *how* was he going to get her to hide those huge silicone jugs?

Jesus! Problems, problems. Nothing he couldn't deal with.

'See you later, kiddo,' he said, and hung up.

* * *

Dexter felt like a criminal, he'd done as his father had advised him, located Rosarita's diaphragm – which he'd found conveniently stashed in her bathroom cabinet – and poked a few minuscule holes in it. Doing such a thing had made him feel bad about himself. Was it right to trick her? On the other hand, was it right that she wanted a divorce after only eighteen months of what *he* considered a pretty good marriage?

Since their argument last night Rosarita was behaving. She'd taken his mother shopping and bought her a beautiful scarf. She'd actually sat down and had a conversation with his father about a Clint Eastwood movie they'd both seen and liked. Then she'd informed him that she'd organized dinner at Chas's house.

The Cockrangers were duly pleased. 'What shall I wear?' Martha kept on fussing.

'Don't worry about it,' Matt said, winking at his son. 'I suggest we all take an afternoon nap and let the two lovebirds alone.'

Dexter knew exactly what his dad had in mind.

After his parents retired to the guest room, he followed Rosarita into the bedroom, shutting the door behind them. 'Good idea,' he said.

'What's a good idea?' she said.

'Taking a nap before we go to Chas' tonight. You've had a tough day. I know it's not easy taking my mom shopping. She doesn't make quick decisions like you.'

'Is that a dig?' Rosarita asked suspiciously.

'No, what I mean is you're an excellent shopper. I remember when we went to Bloomingdale's and you bought me some shirts. It was like wham-bam. You chose right, and they looked great. I still wear them.'

'Why are you being so nice to me?' she asked, regarding him with narrowed eyes.

'Because . . . I love you.'

Rosarita sat down on the edge of the bed. 'Love's not what makes the world go around, Dex,' she said. 'Sorry about that.'

'You look beautiful today,' he said.

'I do?' she replied, enjoying the compliment. She'd never told him about her various plastic surgeries and he was under the impression she was a natural beauty. God! She'd better tear up all her old photos, it wouldn't do to get busted; her previous face had been a horror.

Dex walked over and stood in front of her. Her eye-level was at his belt buckle, and she couldn't help noticing that he had the beginnings of a hard-on.

You're just a raving sex magnet, she thought. *As soon as anyone gets near you, it's let's go, Mama!*

Idly she wondered if she should teach Dex a thing or two before bowing out of this marriage. He certainly had *the* most gorgeous body. And his cock wasn't bad either. Of course, he wasn't Joel, but maybe while she was waiting for Matt and Martha to leave town, she could teach him some new tricks.

Brilliant red nails sprang into action as her hands snaked forward, preparing to pull down his zipper.

His dick popped out immediately – one of the advantages of wearing no underwear.

'Ooooh, Little Dexie is lookin' good today!' she crooned, putting on her I'm-ready-for-sex voice.

He picked up the remote and activated the drapes, closing them.

Not exactly Joel's style, Rosarita thought. Joel was more interested in people watching his sexual antics, which was a major turn-on.

She gave Dex a little lick to encourage him, then jumped up. 'I'll be right back,' she said, hurrying into the bathroom.

He walked over, locked the bedroom door, removed his clothes and lay back on the bed, waiting.

He wondered if she'd notice the damage he'd done to her diaphragm and emerge from the bathroom screaming with fury.

How could she possibly notice it? The holes he'd made were tiny – just big enough for those pesky little sperms to fight their way through.

It was a sneaky thing to do, but she hadn't given him any choice. And when they had their first child, a healthy bouncing baby boy, she'd thank him.

Oh, yes, she certainly would. Dexter was sure of it.

Chapter Nine

'Here's the deal,' Michael said, his worldly green eyes fixed firmly on his daughter's face.

Deal? Madison had no idea what he was talking about. She was already upset enough, she didn't need to hear anything else.

They were sitting in the restaurant of the palatial Plaza Hotel. She'd ordered a mimosa to drink, and eggs over easy with bacon and sausage to eat. Now the food sat on a plate in front of her, abandoned – because she couldn't touch a thing. And the mimosa was almost finished.

'Yes, Michael,' she said, staring back at him, her green eyes alert.

He was on his second cup of coffee. For the first time she noticed he had dark shadows under his eyes, and tiny flecks of grey in his jet black hair. Was her handsome father finally getting old?

No. Not Michael. It was impossible.

'I never thought I'd tell you this,' he said, his voice serious enough to match his expression. 'Somehow it didn't seem necessary. But now that Stella has taken this step, you *should* know the truth.'

'The truth about what?' Madison asked, wishing that this wasn't happening.

'About you and me,' he said steadily. 'About our family.'

She felt queasy. Something bad was going to come out of his mouth, something she didn't want to hear.

'You know, sweetheart, I've always loved you and I always will,' he said. 'You're very, very precious to me.'

In a rush it came to her. Oh, God! HE WAS ABOUT TO TELL HER SHE WAS ADOPTED.

So *that*'s why she'd had to call them Stella and Michael all these years. *That*'s why they'd never wanted to be called Mommy and Daddy like normal parents. Of course. It all made sense.

Her stomach lurched. Her hands were clammy. She felt sick and faint all at the same time. This was so bad, the last thing she'd expected.

Pull yourself together, she told herself sternly. *Get a grip and listen to what he has to say.*

'Yes?' she said blankly. *Spit it out fast, Michael, because I cannot stand the suspense.*

He gave a long drawn-out sigh. 'This isn't easy,' he said, tapping his index finger on the table.

You think it's easy for me? she wanted to yell. *You're about to tell me I'm adopted, and you're sitting there telling me it's not easy. Screw you! Screw you, Michael! I hate this.*

'Here's the thing,' he said, his eyes still fixed firmly on hers. 'Stella . . . she's, uh . . . she's not your mother.'

No big surprise. She waited patiently for him to add, *And I'm not your father, but rest assured that we desperately wanted you. In fact, we chose you. Picked you out*. Isn't that the kind of crap adoptive parents usually came out with?

'So, you adopted me,' she said, barely able to get the words out.

'No,' he said, vigorously shaking his head. '*I'm* your father. Your *real* father.'

This was all too weird. 'You are?' she murmured faintly.

'You bet I am. I *never* would have abandoned you. Never.'

'I – I – don't understand.'

'Let me try explaining,' he said, taking a gulp of coffee to fortify himself. 'I . . . I was a single guy. I had a girlfriend, Gloria. Well, Gloria and me, we were cosmic twins. Inseparable. We grew up together, did everything together. Eventually we made a baby together.'

Now her world was really spinning. He was telling her that *STELLA WASN'T HER MOTHER.* How could that be?

A long pause before he continued. 'That baby was you, sweetheart.'

'Me?' she said blankly.

'I was involved in something at the time that wasn't exactly legitimate. It was a mess, and when you were six months old, the people I was dealing with decided they had to punish me.'

'Punish you?' Madison said, frowning. 'For *what?*'

Ignoring her question he continued with his story. 'The deal was that, uh, either I gave them what they wanted, or they'd take away my family. I didn't believe them – besides, I had both of you well protected. Anyway, one day Gloria managed to get out of the house without anyone knowing. She wanted to buy me a birthday present. That's when they shot her.'

'*Who* shot her?'

'It's too complicated to get into now. It was a long time ago – twenty-nine years. They killed her. The bastards killed her.'

'Oh, God!' Madison cried.

'Truth is,' Michael said, 'I've never gotten over her. And Stella knew it.'

Madison felt like she was in the middle of some insane soap opera as she listened to his story. Everything she knew was crumbling around her. Stella – the beautiful Marilyn Monroe-like Stella – was not her mother. And who was Gloria? She wanted to see a picture, find out everything about her. What happened when she was shot? Did she die immediately or was she injured?

Oh, God, so many questions, and who was going to give her the answers? Her mind was racing in a million different directions, and at the same time she was sick to her stomach and totally lost.

'A year later I met Stella, who was everything Gloria wasn't,' Michael continued. 'When we started talking about marriage I gave her the conditions. If I married her, she had to become your mother in every way. And no more kids. You were it. She agreed, but I know she was never there for you the way Gloria would've been.' He shrugged hopelessly. 'What could I do? And now . . .' his voice hardened '. . . the bitch has betrayed me. And believe me, as far as I'm concerned, she's dead.'

All of a sudden Madison had a blinding headache. Maybe it was the mixture of champagne and orange juice. Maybe it was simply staring at this man whom she now realized she didn't know at all. For God's sake, was this her life? All these years had she been living a lie?

'I – I have to go home and – digest this,' she managed, standing up.

'Don't run away from me,' Michael implored, grabbing her hand. 'I need you, sweetheart. I've always needed you.'

'Maybe you do,' she said, feeling a sharp pain burning within her. 'But this is too much of a shock, and I have to deal with it on my own.' Pulling her hand away from his, she stood up and hurried from the restaurant.

Outside on the street everything seemed different. She didn't know what to do or where to turn. All she really wanted to do was burst out crying.

Why do you want to cry? a little voice within her asked.

BECAUSE I DON'T KNOW WHO I AM ANY MORE.

* * *

Jamie and Peter spent almost the entire day cruising around Barney's. After one of Peter's drinking bouts, he got a strong attack of the guilts, and to assuage them he spent freely.

Jamie took advantage of every moment. She charged boots, jewellery, shoes, sweaters and a long blue cashmere coat – which when she snuggled into it made her look like a blonde Russian princess.

'You *do* know you're the most gorgeous girl in New York?' Peter told her admiringly. 'And *I'm* the luckiest man alive to be married to you.'

Jamie smiled. Why had she ever suspected him? He was the best, and they had the greatest marriage. Just because he'd gone off sex for a few weeks didn't mean there was another woman. Plus last night he'd made up for it. And how!

No. There was absolutely no reason for her to meet with Madison's detective. Peter was one hundred per cent a loyal and loving husband – he'd proved it to her today.

They left Barney's at last, both loaded down with packages.

'Madison said something about meeting us later,' Peter said as they stood kerbside searching for a cab.

'Is your phone on?' Jamie asked.

'Of course it is,' he said, patting his pocket.

'Then she must've got tied up.'

'About time!' Peter said with a dirty chuckle. 'Hasn't it been rather a long dry spell?'

'You know Madison,' Jamie said airily. 'She's *very* particular about the guys she gets involved with. *Especially* after David.'

'I liked David,' Peter remarked.

'How can you say that?' Jamie said.

'I told you I had dinner with him and his wife one night when you were in Boston with Anton, didn't I?'

'No. You didn't tell me.'

'I meant to.'

'How *could* you, Peter? That's so disloyal.'

'He kept on calling me, and I had nothing else to do, so we went to Elaine's.'

'What's his wife like?'

'Blonde, big overbite, enormous tits. Real, I think.'

'Ha!' Jamie scoffed. 'You guys *always* think they're real. Those kinds of girls *never* have real tits. They're man-made for sure.'

'You're being bitchy, sweetie.'

'Look,' she said, waving frantically, 'there's a cab – grab it!'

On the way home they necked in the back of the taxi while the driver pretended not to watch them in his rear-view mirror. Jamie was almost inclined to tell Peter that she'd been about to put a private detective on his tail. But then she thought he probably wouldn't appreciate it, so she managed to keep her mouth shut.

'What would you like to do tonight?' she asked when they reached their apartment. 'We have no plans.'

'That's what I like,' Peter said with a great big grin. 'No plans. My kind of evening.'

'We could send out for Chinese,' Jamie suggested. 'Rent a video.'

'Which one?'

'Anything with Brad Pitt.'

'And I'll watch anything with Charleze Theron.'

'Then we'll rent *two* videos, and order in *tons* of Chinese food. I'm starving. You do know we didn't even stop for lunch?'

'You wouldn't let us,' Peter pointed out. 'You were too busy buying out the store!'

Jamie waited until Peter was in his den, then she snuck into her bathroom and called Madison. The answering-machine picked up.

'Cancel the meeting on Monday,' Jamie whispered. 'I'll call you later. Or phone *us* when you get this message. Whatever you do, *don't* mention anything to Peter.'

* * *

Madison arrived home an hour later and picked up

Jamie's message. Goddamnit! Why had she volunteered to get involved in the first place? Jamie was like a yo-yo – up and down. One moment Peter was cheating, and the next he wasn't. Who gave a shit? Her life was falling to pieces, and all Jamie cared about was cancelling some appointment with a private detective.

Slammer greeted her as though she'd been away for a year. She sat on the floor next to him and rubbed his back. He immediately turned on to his side, legs akimbo, waiting for her to scratch his stomach – his favourite thing in the entire world.

'You're a funny old thing, aren't you?' she said.

Why hadn't Michael told her the truth when she was young?

Why had he forced Stella to live a lie?

Memories of the woman she'd thought was her mother kept flitting through her mind. Her first encounter with a boy – Stella hadn't wanted to discuss it. Her first bra – Stella had sent her out with the maid to buy one at Bloomingdale's. Her first crush when she was twelve – Stella had been totally uninterested.

Now it became clear why she'd had no real closeness with her mother, it was because Stella was *not* her mother, had no desire to *be* her mother, was probably jealous of Gloria and hated the connection.

Then there was Michael. So handsome and charming, always over-compensating, always ready to listen to anything she had to say and be on her side.

Now she knew why.

Guilt. Pure guilt.

She kept on going over the things he'd said.

They shot her.

Who were *they*? And why would anybody *want* to shoot Gloria?

Michael had said he was involved in something that wasn't so legitimate. What could that possibly have been? Did he have more secrets she didn't know about?

Obviously. And obviously he was pretty good at keeping them, since she'd never suspected any of this. It was all a terrible shock.

Having an analytical mind was a help; she grabbed a yellow legal pad and pen and started making a list of all the questions she planned to ask him. Were he and Gloria ever married? Did she have relatives? Were the people who shot her ever caught? Prosecuted? And if not, why not?

Oh, Jeez! There was so much she needed to know. This was almost like preparing for an interview, only this interview would be the most important one she'd ever conducted.

She decided that when Michael called she'd ask him to come by her apartment. When he arrived, she'd sit him down and very calmly find out everything. Full disclosure. No more secrets.

The truth would set her free. Only then would she be able to get on with her life.

Chapter Ten

Chas' latest girlfriend's professional name was Varoomba. She'd called herself that because of the amazing contortions she was able to perform with her outrageous bosom. A big, buxom girly girl with a squeaky voice and cheerful disposition, she was Chas' preferred type.

That afternoon he'd sent her to Bloomingdale's to buy a respectable dress. 'Not a tits-and-ass number,' he'd warned her sternly. 'Somethin' that covers the goods. An' while you're there, pick out a bra that squashes everythin' down.'

'What's the matter?' she'd said, blinking her heavily mascaraed eyes. 'You think I'm gonna disgrace you?'

'Naw, but I can't let my kids know I'm datin' a stripper.'

'Somethin' wrong with bein' a stripper?' she'd squeaked, quite insulted.

'It don't sit well,' Chas had growled. 'Not with *my* daughters. An' another thing, you'd better be nice to 'em 'cause they're very special girls.'

'How old are they?' Varoomba had asked, expecting him to say something like ten and twelve.

'Older than you,' he'd said.

Varoomba was smart enough to know that they would probably hate her. Most women did, especially when they found out she was dating their father.

Chas was busy trying to figure out how he was going to explain to Venice and Rosarita that his date was only twenty-three. 'If anybody asks,' he'd warned Varoomba, 'tell 'em you're thirty.'

'Thirty!' she'd shrieked in horror. 'You want my career to be over?'

'Nobody's gonna know who you are,' he'd said. 'We'll tell 'em you're a frienda mine. A nurse.'

'A nurse?' she'd repeated, shocked. 'You think I look like a nurse?'

'If ya wash off some of that goddamn makeup. An' drop the beehive – it don't suit you anyway.'

'What am I – auditioning for a soap opera?' she'd said, quite put out.

'Behave yourself, okay? If you behave, ya got a shot at stayin' around. An' if ya don't, well, y'know whatcha can do.'

'Thanks a lot,' she'd said huffily. 'You're one big bossy man.'

'Yeah, an' y' like it, doncha?' he'd said, grabbing a handful of her nicely rounded ass.

'I like *you*, Chas,' she'd answered coyly. 'I'd be good for you. I could be a mommy to your little girls.'

'Didn't I tell ya?' he said, irritated. 'You're a coupla years younger than the youngest one.'

'No, I'm not,' she'd said, widening her eyes. 'I'm thirty.'

One thing about Varoomba, she was a quick study.

* * *

Venice arrived first. Chas had named her for the romantic city in Italy where she'd been conceived.

Not exceptionally pretty, Venice had a look. Long, straight brown hair, nice eyes, nose slightly too long, lips too thin, but her husband, Eddie, thought she was a babe, and that was all that mattered.

Whereas Rosarita had changed everything about herself with plastic surgery, Venice was totally natural. She kissed her father on both cheeks. 'Are we the first to arrive?' she asked.

'Ya sure are, kiddo. So come inside an' meet my uh . . . friend.'

'Friend?' Venice said, teasingly. 'Don't you mean *girl*friend, Daddy?'

'It's this, uh, nurse I bin seein',' Chas explained. 'You're gonna get it in y' head that she's a bit younger than me. Forget it – she's older than she appears, so don't be shocked.'

'Daddy, I would *never* criticize anyone you're seeing,' Venice said. 'I've told you before – if this woman makes you happy, that's all that matters to me.'

Eddie, a nondescript-looking man, hovered in the background. Chas shook his son-in-law's hand and they all entered the living room, where Varoomba, rechristened Alice for the night, waited to greet them.

Chas threw a critical eye on her. She'd managed to squash her huge boobs into a high-necked orange dress. If she were smart, she would have chosen black because, to his annoyance, he could spot her nipples straining the orange material.

At least she'd toned down the makeup. However, in no way, shape or form did she resemble a nurse. She looked like she was about to appear on the Howard Stern TV show and strip off for one of his bizarre evaluations.

'This is my kid, Venice,' Chas said.

'Venice,' Varoomba repeated, in her high, squeaky voice, which irritated Chas now that he had to listen to it. In bed he was able to tell her to shut up, and she did. In his living room he had no such luck.

'Hi,' Venice said. 'What a pretty dress. That colour suits you.'

This immediately put Varoomba at ease. She winked at Chas as if to say, 'See, I've already charmed one of your daughters.'

Rosarita arrived twenty minutes later, completely lacking the ability to be on time. She marched into her father's house, Dexter behind her, his parents trailing after him.

'Mr Vincent,' Martha gushed, pushing her way in front of everyone, 'what a magnificent home you have. I've never been in a townhouse in New York before. This is *such* a treat!'

Oh, for God's sake, calm down, Rosarita thought.

'Thanks,' Chas said, gesturing to an overstuffed couch. 'Make yourself comfortable. Name your poison.'

Rosarita stopped short when she saw her sister. She and Venice were not the best of friends. Rosarita did not care for competition of any kind and, as far as she was concerned, Venice competed for their father's attention – not to mention his money. And it particularly infuriated her that Venice had two brawling brats, who would probably inherit plenty.

'Hello,' she said coolly. 'Nobody mentioned *you* were coming.'

Venice was never quite sure why her sister was so hostile towards her, but over the years she'd learned to accept it. Eddie had taught her patience. 'She's probably unhappy about something,' he'd told his wife when she got upset. 'Try to be nice and refuse to let her affect you.'

So that's exactly what Venice did. She smiled at her sister and greeted Dexter with a big hug. To Rosarita's constant irritation they got along exceptionally well – not that they saw each other much, but when they did it was as if they were on exactly the same wavelength.

'How *are* you?' Dexter said, patting her shoulder.

'Fine,' Venice replied.

'And the kids? We haven't seen them lately.'

'You're always welcome to drop by any time.'

'I know,' he said. 'Thing is, I've been so busy working on my soap that I never have time to do anything.'

'I've watched the show and you're terrific in it,' Venice said.

'You think so?' he said, pleased.

'It would be dull without you. Although I must say the character Silver Anderson plays is quite something.'

Privately, Dexter often thought he'd married the wrong sister. Venice was the caring, sweet one. A stranger would never believe that she and Rosarita came from the same parents.

While Rosarita was busy checking out Varoomba, Venice was making sure that Matt and Martha Cockranger were made to feel comfortable.

'What a gorgeous scarf!' she said to Martha.

'Yes, isn't it lovely?' Martha said, beaming. 'Rosarita bought it for me today.' She lowered her voice in awe. 'Do you know, it cost three hundred and fifty dollars?

I didn't want her to spend her money on it, but she insisted.'

'It's quite beautiful,' Venice said. 'Brings out the blue in your eyes.'

'Thank you,' Martha said, sparkling.

Rosarita veered back towards Venice. 'Who the fuck is the tramp with Dad?' she hissed.

'That's Alice. She's a nurse,' Venice said.

'If she's a fucking nurse, then I'm a fucking nuclear scientist,' Rosarita muttered.

Venice moved away.

All during dinner Rosarita vied with her sister for attention, which did not make for a pleasant evening for the rest of the guests. Every time Venice uttered a word, Rosarita contradicted her.

'Whassamatter with you tonight?' Chas said finally. 'You gotta be on everybody's case?'

Not everybody's, Rosarita wanted to say. *Just that sweet sister of mine who you think is such an angel. But I know the real truth. The only reason she had kids was so she could be sure of getting all your money.*

Half-way through dinner, Venice began passing around pictures of her two brats, which made Rosarita want to throw up.

Martha studied the photos and oohed and aahed in all the right places. 'What *adorable* children,' she raved. Then she looked straight at Chas and said, 'Matt and I are hoping that your little Rosarita will get pregnant next.'

Chas chuckled. His *little* Rosarita. Obviously they didn't know the real girl – the girl who'd come to him demanding that he knock off her husband, their precious son. Boy, would that make interesting dinner conversation!

He was angry with Rosarita. Who did she think he was? Some kind of killer? She lived in a fantasy world, and he didn't appreciate it. Dexter seemed perfectly okay to him. Good-looking guy, didn't screw around. He hadn't even eyeballed Varoomba's mammoth tits, whereas most men would have been drooling by this time. Chas noticed that Matt Cockranger had already managed a few surreptitious peeks. Jeez! The old guy probably hadn't got laid in years.

Varoomba was enjoying herself. She was not used to meeting her menfriends' families, and after she'd gulped down a couple of glasses of wine, Chas was having a hard time shutting her up. Any moment she was likely to hand out cards inviting them all down to the Boom Boom Club for a private performance.

Chas remembered his first look at her. He'd walked into the club, and there she was – working those giant titties like a mechanic operating the Big Dipper. That was some good memory.

'We've got to go now,' Rosarita said, when dinner came to an end.

'Do we have to?' Martha pleaded. 'I'm so enjoying myself.'

'Yes, we have to,' Rosarita said, through clenched teeth. 'Tomorrow is Dex's only day off. He likes to sleep in.'

'If he's planning to sleep late, why do you have to leave early?' Venice said innocently.

Rosarita wanted to slap her. 'Don't you get it?' she said nastily. 'He has to get twelve hours' sleep. So, if we go now, he gets it. But if we leave later, he'll only get eight.'

Dexter looked at her as if she was totally crazy – which, of course, he was beginning to realize she was.

'How about another fifteen minutes?' he suggested.

How about sticking it up your ass? 'Fine,' she muttered, her mouth tightening. *I really want to sit here with my prissy sister, your stupid parents, and Daddy's tramp of the week girlfriend.*

Chas, who was busy keeping a watchful eye on his two daughters, saw once again how different they were. Why couldn't Rosarita be more like Venice? He'd already decided that, although he loved them both equally, he'd leave the bulk of his money to Venice and her kids because she was the responsible one. If he left it to Rosarita, she'd probably pick up some fortune hunter who'd spend it instantly. Venice would make sure it wasn't squandered away. Besides, she'd always take care of Rosarita – in fact, he'd make sure that provision was put in his will. The best thing about his plan was that he wouldn't be around to listen to Rosarita's screaming.

'What are you smiling at, Daddy?' Rosarita said, suddenly reverting to her sweet side.

'Just thinkin' 'bout a thing or two,' he said.

Varoomba grabbed his hand. 'Your daddy has such a cute smile!' she exclaimed. 'I love it when he laughs, he's so adorable!'

Rosarita wanted to throw up again. This one was a big-titted, squeaky-voiced nightmare. And stupid with it.

'Don't go callin' me no names in front of my girls,' Chas hissed, highly embarrassed.

'Sorry, honeybunch,' Varoomba cooed.

So the evening wound to its natural conclusion, and Rosarita and her group went home at the same time as Venice and Eddie.

As soon as they were gone, Varoomba shook out her

mass of red hair, allowing it to fall around her face. Then she unzipped her orange dress, standing before Chas in a red, white and blue thong and nippleless bra. 'How'd I do, babykins?' she crooned. 'Was I the hit of the party?'

'C'mere,' he said, reaching out to tweak her enormous erect nipples. 'C'mere, an' lay those big bazookas all over me.'

So she did.

* * *

Meanwhile, across town, Joel Blaine was in the Boom Boom Club, complaining to the manager, 'Where's the broad with the big knockers? How come she's not here on a Saturday night?'

'She called in sick,' said the manager, a grim-faced man with patent leather hair and a permanent scowl.

'Sick, my ass,' Joel said. 'I want my money back.'

'I got a nice little Puerto Rican number blew in yesterday.'

'I don't do foreign.'

'How about Texas born and bred? That appeal to you?'

'Big tits?'

'Small, but nice.'

'Forget about it,' Joel said. 'I'll come back next week, and Miss Big Rack better be here.'

If he wanted small tits he could get them anywhere. Rosarita wasn't exactly stacked. She'd informed him they were her own, but he knew they weren't the real thing, he'd noticed the scars hidden underneath.

Honey, he'd wanted to say to her, *if you had 'em done, why couldn't you have had 'em done bigger?*

Instinctively he knew Rosarita was not the type who

took well to criticism. But maybe he'd see how far she'd go for him. 'Sugar, you got the greatest boobs in the world,' he'd tell her, 'but *I* like 'em bigger. Here's twenty thou – go get 'em done again.'

Was she worth twenty thousand bucks? No fucking way!

The only woman worth twenty thousand bucks in his mind was Madison Castelli. Now there was a *real* woman. It didn't matter that she wasn't stacked like some freako stripper, she had what it took in the brains department – and *that*'s what Joel was looking for. A touch of class.

Maybe he should do something about her. Turn on the charm. Launch into pursuit mode. At least call her.

Maybe he would.

Eventually.

* * *

'Thanks,' Dexter said.

'For what?' Rosarita said warily.

'For being nice to my parents. Ever since we had that talk you've been pretty damn good.'

'You think so?'

'Yes, I do.' He was lying on the bed with his hands behind his head, watching her undress. She was down to black panties and a lacy bra. 'Come lie beside me and we'll talk,' he suggested.

Hmm . . . Rosarita thought. Ever since she'd mentioned to him that they never had sex it had certainly made a difference. Yesterday he'd been quite enthusiastic. Now, tonight, she could see he was once again in the mood.

She bounced on to the bed beside him. 'You want I

should blow you?' she said, tantalizing him with her tongue, sticking it out and wagging it at him.

He hated her vulgarity. 'Can't we just lie here so I can hold you in my arms?' he said, ever the romantic.

'If you're sure that's all you want,' she said, caressing his half-erect dick.

Within seconds he was fully aroused, which didn't surprise her. 'I'll only be a sec,' she said, jumping off the bed and vanishing into the bathroom.

He counted to twenty and she was back.

Once more with feeling, he thought.

He had a hunch that tonight was the night he was going to get her pregnant.

Chapter Eleven

S lammer was limping and panting and drooling. In fact, he was doing everything possible to attract Madison's attention. His mistress had been tramping across Central Park for two hours now, and he'd had enough. As a pampered New York City apartment dog, he was anxious to go home. It was hot, and he could do with a drink of water and a lie-down. Pulling back on his leash, he looked up at Madison appealingly with his big brown eyes and gave a little whimper.

It was as if they communicated without words. 'Okay, okay.' She sighed. 'I'm taking you home.' Had she walked off enough frustration and fury? Had she got rid of the demons that were starting to plague her?

I'm twenty-nine years old, she thought. *I have no man to go home to. I have a father who's lied to me all my life. And I don't have a mother. No, that's wrong. The fact is, I have a dead mother who I never even knew.*

She had to talk to somebody, get it out of her system before she went crazy. Michael was not the right person. All she had for him were questions, and he'd better damn well answer them because she wasn't taking any more of his evasive shit.

She thought about dropping by Jamie's, but since it was Saturday Peter would be around, and that wouldn't do at all. Her other best friend, Natalie, was in Los Angeles. That would be a mammoth two-hour phone conversation, but surely it was worth it?

Back at her apartment the light on her answering-machine was blinking. Three calls. The first one was from Michael. 'We've got to talk,' he said, sounding tense and not at all like himself. 'I've checked into the Plaza. Won't go back to Connecticut until I've seen you. Call me.'

The second was from Victor. 'Got several ideas for your next victim,' he boomed, 'most of which you'll probably hate. Drop by the office Monday and we'll discuss it. If you're very good I'll buy you lunch.'

And the third message was a voice from her past. Jake Sica, a guy she'd met in L.A. when she was there on assignment at the beginning of the year. He was the brother of Natalie's ex co-anchor, Jimmy Sica.

'Hi,' he said. 'This is Jake – I'll be in New York for a few days next week, and I'd like it a lot if we could get together. Y'know, Madison, I think we –' The machine cut off.

'Damn!' she said, thinking about Jake for a moment, which was a welcome diversion from all the crap churning around in her head. He was an award-winning photographer with a casual attitude. As far as she could recall he had longish brown hair and laughing brown eyes. He favoured old leather jackets and denim shirts, and he had an easy-going laid-back manner.

She'd liked him a lot. But at the time they'd met

she'd been caught up in a murder case in L.A. and he'd been involved with a call-girl. Quite a convoluted situation. However, she'd persuaded Victor to use his photos in the magazine, and they'd stayed in touch sporadically until he'd moved back to Arizona several months ago and they'd lost contact. Now he was on his way to New York next week.

Hmmm . . . she thought. Jake might be the perfect person to talk to. Someone she hardly knew – somebody to whom she could pour out her heart. And he'd listen, because he was smart and intelligent and, most of all, he was nice.

But how was she supposed to contact him with no phone number?

Oh, well, that's the way things were going lately. She wasn't surprised.

She picked up the phone and called Natalie in L.A.

Natalie's brother, Cole, answered. 'Guess who?' she said.

'Don't have to,' Cole said. 'I'd know that sexy voice anywhere.'

'How're you doing?'

'Great.'

'Natalie tells me you're living with Mr Mogul, so how come you're there?'

'I drop by occasionally. Big sis is barely talkin' to me though – still pissed 'cause of me and Mr M. Keeps on waitin' for him to dump me so she can say, "I told you so"!'

Natalie did not approve of his current boyfriend – a much older mega-businessman whom she had unofficially christened Mr Mogul.

'Your relationship with this guy has lasted quite some time, hasn't it?'

'I get why she's worried,' Cole said. 'He's big-time, an' what do I do? Stretch people's muscles for a living. But, hey, we're havin' fun. How're you?'

'Getting by.'

'Comin' to L.A. any time soon?'

'That depends on Victor. If he sends me out on an assignment, I'll be there.'

'What happened to the movie deal on your piece about call-girls?'

'Two drafts later the studio passed. That's Hollywood, I guess. Anyway, I made a lot of money and met the great Alex Woods. Now *there*'s a character.'

'You gotta come out here again. We'll do the jogging thing – I know how you get off on physical activity.'

'Is that a dig?'

'You got it!'

They both laughed. Madison was extremely fond of Natalie's little brother. Not so little actually. He was a good-looking twenty-three-year-old with abs of steel and a great smile. Cole made his living working out the bodies of the rich and famous. He was one of the most in-demand fitness trainers in L.A.

Madison remembered how shocked she'd been when she'd re-encountered him earlier in the year in Los Angeles. Instead of the little brother she remembered – the horny teenager who was into rap, gangs and getting high – Mr Focused had emerged. Cole was gay, handsome and, as Natalie would say, had his shit together.

'Where *is* Natalie?' Madison asked.

'Probably at the studio,' Cole said. 'That girl is workin' hard, she's real into her new job.'

'I thought she was fed up with covering showbiz news?'

'That was before she got to anchor her own show.'

'Wasn't she anchoring the news with Jimmy Sica?'

'This is a much bigger baby.'

'Ask her to call me.'

'Will do.'

At least hearing from Jake Sica had taken her mind off Michael and his shattering revelations. She contemplated calling her father back, then decided to hell with him, she didn't feel like it. Instead she went into her bedroom, unplugged the phone, popped a sleeping pill from a bottle of Halcion David had left behind, and crawled under the covers with her clothes on.

Soon she fell into a deep sleep.

*   *   *

She was awakened the next morning by a hammering on her front door. It took a while for her to open her eyes. She wasn't used to taking any kind of pill, and the Halcion had knocked her out – which she supposed was the whole point.

Slammer crouched beside the bed barking and gazing up at her with his deep, soulful eyes as much as to say, 'How long do you expect me to hold it in?'

She reached for the clock, noting it was past ten. Damn! She'd passed out big-time.

She lurched out of bed, becoming aware that she'd slept in her clothes. The pounding on her door wasn't about to stop. There was also a pounding in her head to match, but that was probably the effect of the sleeping pill.

Christ! Who *was* it? And why didn't they go away?

She went to the front door. 'Yes?' she said, sounding as unfriendly as possible.

'It's me,' Michael said. 'Let me in, for Crissakes. I've been standing out here for ten minutes.'

What did *he* want? To tell her more stuff? Drive her even crazier?

She opened the door and he burst past her into the apartment. 'What the hell's wrong with you?' he said angrily. 'I called six times last night and three times this morning. Where were you?'

'Asleep,' she said coldly, turning her back on him. 'You don't mind if I sleep, do you?'

'What?' he said, unused to her sarcasm.

'I see you three times a year, and this time you take me out to brunch and inform me that my mother isn't my mother. That someone called Gloria *is*. Well, excuse me, *Dad*, but I'm confused and upset, so I took a sleeping pill and zoned out. Do you mind?'

'I'm sorry,' he said. 'I'm sick about this. I never thought it would happen.'

'What were you hoping, Michael?' she said coldly. 'That I *wouldn't* find out? That one day you and Stella would drop dead, and I'd say, "Isn't it sad? My parents have died," and I'd *never* know the truth. Was that your plan?' She stared at him full of hurt and frustration. 'I'm going to be thirty in a few weeks. I mean, I don't get it. *When* were you going to tell me? When I hit forty? Fifty?'

He shook his head. 'I didn't think it was necessary for you to know,' he muttered.

'You should have told me when I was like seven or eight,' she said accusingly. 'I could have accepted it then and gotten on with my life.'

'You're right.'

'Do you have any idea how cold Stella has always been to me?' she said, her anger bubbling to the surface. 'She never cuddled me, we never did the things girls were supposed to do with their mothers. Why do you think I couldn't have cared less when you didn't want me to live at home after college? I was *happy* to have my own apartment. Thrilled to get out.'

'You never told me.'

'What was I going to say? I can't stand my own mother. She's a cold bitch. She might be beautiful and everybody loves her, but I – don't – like – her.'

'How many times do you expect me to say I'm sorry?'

'Hey, listen, *I'm* sorry for *you*,' she said, her voice rising. 'It blew up in your face, didn't it?'

In some sick way it was quite satisfying watching him squirm. Michael, who was always in control. Michael, the perfect father, or so she'd thought.

'I'm making coffee,' she said abruptly. 'You want a cup?'

He nodded.

She marched into the kitchen and put on the coffee. Then she grabbed Slammer's leash and headed for the door. 'I'll be back,' she said shortly. 'While I'm out I'd appreciate you taking a look at the pad on the table. You'll find a list of questions. I expect an answer to all of them. And don't bullshit me, Michael, because it's about time I knew everything.'

Chapter Twelve

Dexter was already out jogging when Rosarita awoke. She lay in bed stretching, a half smile on her face. Way to go, Dex! He'd pumped her so hard last night she'd forgotten all about Joel for at least fifteen minutes. She hadn't known Dex to be like this since their honeymoon in the Bahamas, which Chas had paid for. Maybe having his parents in close proximity made him horny.

The trouble with Dex was that he didn't have any moves. He knew how to pump it, and that was about all. He had no clue how to kiss, never gave head, didn't seem to enjoy it when *she* obliged *him*, and his imagination never ventured beyond 'you lie there and I'll give it to you good.'

But still . . . sometimes a fuck was a fuck was a fuck. And she had to admit that he was quite a hunk of a man with his handsome face, broad shoulders and powerful physique.

She wondered if Matt and Martha had heard them going at it last night, she'd been screaming pretty loud. Her cries of delight had probably given Matt a thrill.

No doubt Martha slept with earplugs firmly stuffed in her suburban pink ears.

Oh, well, time to get up. Since Conchita didn't come in on Sundays, she hoped that Dex or his mom had put on the coffee. And maybe, if she smiled sweetly, Martha would fix her a plate of bacon and eggs. Martha was in the living room leafing through a copy of *Cosmopolitan*. 'Have a nice sleep, did you, dear?' she asked, putting the magazine down.

'Mmm . . .' Rosarita said, stretching. 'Where's Matt?'

'The boys have gone out jogging together,' Martha said. 'It's so nice to see Dick – I mean Dex,' she said, quickly correcting herself, 'with his daddy. When Dex was a little boy, Matt used to take him everywhere.'

'Really?' Rosarita said, bored already. 'Did anybody put on the coffee?'

'Shall *I* do it, dear?' Martha suggested, eager to please.

'Would you?' Rosarita said, as if it had only just occurred to her. 'I was hoping I'd have time for a shower.'

'Yes, certainly,' Martha said, obliging as ever.

'There's eggs and stuff in the fridge, if you want to fix something for when the boys come back. I'm sure they'll be hungry.'

'What a good idea,' Martha said, beaming. 'You don't mind if I use your kitchen?'

'Feel free. The orange-juice squeezer is on the side counter, and there's plenty of bread in the bin.'

'I'll get everything ready,' Martha said. 'Then the four of us can sit down and have a nice breakfast together.'

'Sounds good to me,' Rosarita said, hurrying back

into her bedroom and closing the door. On impulse she picked up the phone and dialled Joel's private number. His answering-machine picked up. Damn! He was probably still asleep.

She wondered if Honeysnatch, or whatever his girlfriend's name was, had noticed the mark on his neck. She tried to picture the scene.

Joel, how did you get that?

Got no clue, babe.

Joel, have you been seeing somebody else?

No way, babe.

I don't believe you. I'm leaving.

Rosarita laughed to herself. Then she phoned Chas. 'You awake, Daddy?' she asked sweetly.

'What is it now?' Chas said suspiciously.

'I want to thank you for dinner last night. It was so kind of you to have Dex and his parents over.'

'Don't mention it,' Chas said, wary of where she was going with this niceness shit that was so unlike her.

'Venice looked a little peaky.'

'Ya think?'

'Eddie doesn't look too good either. Of course,' she mused, 'he was never the most attractive guy in the world.'

'Gotta feelin' they need a vacation,' Chas said, purposely annoying her. 'Think I'll send 'em to Hawaii with the kids.'

'You mean you'll pay?' Rosarita said, quite put out.

'Why not? They're my grandkids, for Crissakes.'

She quickly changed the subject in the hope that he'd forget about Hawaii. 'Who was that woman with you last night?' she asked, her tone indicating her disapproval.

'None a ya business,' Chas growled.

'Daddy,' she said, reverting to the role of concerned daughter looking out for her father's welfare role. 'You shouldn't be with a woman who is so . . . you know, kind of cheap.'

'Whaddya mean, cheap?' he snapped. 'The broad's expensive. I gotta buy her presents all the time.'

'Oh, Daddy, you're impossible.'

'An' you're not?'

'Ever since I was a little girl you've dated unsuitable women. Always the same type – big and brassy-looking. What do you *see* in them?'

'I ain't in the fuckin' mood for your crap this morning,' Chas said, 'so quit with the criticism.'

'I'm merely calling to thank you for dinner.'

'Huh! I'll talk to you later,' he said, putting down the phone.

Rosarita was sure his bad humour was Venice's influence. Every time he saw that stupid sister of hers it put him in a miserable mood.

Rosarita had often tried to figure out what it was about Venice that irritated her so much. Was it that her sister had never had any plastic surgery and still looked good? Was it that Venice was a year younger than her and had managed to have two children already? Or was it that Eddie never looked at other women? His eyes hadn't even strayed towards that big-boobed freak last night, whereas she'd noticed Dex sneak a peek or two – not to mention Matt sitting there with drool on his face. At least that proved Dex had red blood coursing through his veins, which is more than she could say for Eddie – who was definitely a pussy-whipped wimp.

'I hate 'em all,' she muttered.

Then, just for fun, she tried Joel's number one more time.

* * *

'Did you do the dirty deed, son?' Matt asked, with a ribald wink, as they jogged side by side through Central Park.

'Dad!' Dexter said. 'You shouldn't ask me things like that. It's too personal.'

'What's too personal? That you did it? Or that you *didn't* do it?'

'Rosarita is my *wife*.'

'I know, son – I know. And I heard the screaming last night to prove it.'

Dexter turned his head away, staring out across the trees. He loved his dad, but sometimes Matt was too intrusive with his constant questions. There were certain things in life that were private, and although he'd revealed that Rosarita didn't want to have children, and Matt had advised him to play the diaphragm trick on her, he certainly wasn't about to discuss whether they'd had sex or not.

'When your mother was young –' Matt began.

Dexter held up his hand. 'Don't want to hear it, Dad,' he interrupted.

'Why not?' Matt said, put out. 'It's nothing dirty.'

'Some things should be private between you and Mom.'

'Why's that, son?'

'Because they just *should*,' Dexter said, exasperated.

'Talking's good,' Matt said. 'Getting everything out of your system.'

'For some people.'

'Did you punch holes in her diaphragm like I told you?'

'Dad!' Dexter said warningly. 'Leave it alone.'

'I'd enjoy being a grandfather before I'm too old,' Matt grumbled.

'Tell Rosarita, not me.'

A pretty girl jogged by, her small breasts bouncing up and down in a tight tank top. Matt actually stopped jogging and turned his head to ogle her.

'Jesus!' Dexter said. 'When do *your* hormones stop?'

'Viagra,' Matt boasted, with a self-satisfied smirk. 'Works like a dream. I take it every night. Only trouble is, your mother's not thrilled. She never really –'

'Please!' Dexter said. 'Whatever it is, I don't want to hear it.'

'Nice rack on that one,' Matt said, still watching the girl as she ran out of sight.

Dexter reminded himself to bring earplugs the next time he went jogging with his dad.

* * *

Back at the house Martha had put together a virtual feast. She'd fixed sausages, bacon, grilled tomatoes, scrambled eggs and a stack of French toast. The coffee bubbled in the pot, and a jug of freshly squeezed orange juice stood on the table.

'I can see that Rosarita hasn't been in the kitchen,' Dexter said, giving his mother a hug and a kiss.

'What a kitchen to cook in!' Martha exclaimed, her cheeks flushed.

'Where is Rosarita?' Dexter asked.

'Taking a shower.'

He entered the bedroom and found his wife relaxing on the bed, wrapped in a silk Chinese robe and reading *Women's Wear Daily*. 'Hi, honey,' she said, barely glancing up.

'I see you conned my mom into fixing everyone breakfast,' he said, stripping off his jogging clothes.

'She insisted,' Rosarita replied.

'Yeah, sure,' he said, standing before her, naked. 'I'll take a fast shower and meet you in the kitchen.'

'How about I meet you in the shower instead?' she suggested, unable to resist his fine physique. Not to mention his perfect cock.

Why not? he thought. *If I want to get her pregnant I'd better be prepared to go at it as many times as it takes.*

'Okay,' he said, surprising her. 'But we'd better be quick – my mother has everything ready.'

'I'm sure Mommy will wait for her baby boy,' Rosarita teased, jumping off the bed. 'And talking of baby boys . . .' Quick as a flash she cupped his balls in the palm of her hand.

'I'm all sweaty,' he said, backing off.

'Sometimes I like you sweaty,' she said, coming after him.

'*I* don't,' he said, pushing her away.

She sighed. It was tough teaching him anything. And the truth was, why bother? He wouldn't be around that long.

'Let's shower,' she said. 'I'll show you a trick with the shower-head that'll blow your sweaty balls all the way to heaven and back!'

Chapter Thirteen

Somehow Madison got through Sunday. After her long walk she returned to her apartment to find that Michael had not answered any of her written questions.

'I can't deal with this writing shit,' he said. 'Ask me anything you want.'

So she did, and hated sitting next to him listening to him trying to explain. He rambled on about how special Gloria was, how he'd definitely find pictures for her to see. But when it came to revealing details about why Gloria had been shot, he immediately began fudging. 'It was a small gambling debt,' he said, stony-faced. 'That's all.'

'They killed my mother over a small gambling debt?' she said, staring at him in disbelief.

He nodded, and refused to look her in the eye.

'It must have been bigger than you thought,' she said, studying him carefully.

'Who remembers? It was a long time ago.'

'Jesus, Michael,' she said, her voice rising. 'You're not giving me much information. Aren't I *entitled* to know?'

'I'm telling you everything I remember,' he said sharply. 'I owed money, they threatened me. I thought I had Gloria protected, and then they . . . shot her.'

'Who's they?' Madison asked accusingly.

'People,' he said evasively.

'*What* people?' she demanded.

'A gambling syndicate.'

'Run by?'

'Who the fuck knows.'

Madison was eager for details. Obviously he wasn't prepared to reveal them.

Who else knew the story? Who could she ask? Maybe Stella. After all, her so-called mother owed her an explanation.

'Where can I reach Stella?' she asked abruptly.

'I have no idea,' he replied, his tone hardening. 'She called me once, didn't say where she was. If you track her down I'd like to know.'

After a couple of hours of getting nowhere, she informed him she was tired and told him to go home.

'When will you come see me?' he said.

'Where?'

'In Connecticut.'

'You're staying in the house without Stella?'

'Haven't decided.'

'I need more time to digest all of this,' she said wearily. 'You're hardly telling me anything. I don't even know what my mother looked like.'

'She was beautiful, like you,' Michael said. 'I'll do my best to find a picture.'

Instinctively she knew he wouldn't.

After he left, she took Slammer for another marathon traipse through the park, her mind flying in a thousand different directions. What else was Michael hiding? He'd stonewalled her on everything she'd asked. She'd learned nothing about her mother. Just that Gloria was this mysterious twenty-one-year-old girl who'd been shot. A girl with apparently no relatives, no family at all.

Later in the day Natalie called her back from L.A. Madison wasn't in the mood to confide long distance – especially as she was still getting over the effect of the Halcion, which had made her groggy and bad-tempered. She listened as Natalie carried on about all the celebrities she'd recently interviewed, and what assholes some of the young actors were. 'Simply 'cause I'm up there in front of a camera,' Natalie complained, 'they think I'm all theirs. But, girl, *I* got *news* for them. They can take their arrogant little cocks and shove 'em elsewhere.'

'The important thing is you like what you're doing better than your last job,' Madison said.

'Yeah, I gotta admit *that*.'

'Then that's good.'

'When are you coming out here again?' Natalie asked. 'I miss you!'

'I'm seeing Victor tomorrow. Maybe one of his brilliant ideas will bring me back to L.A.'

'Let's hope it doesn't go down like last time.'

'Yes, that was a nightmare,' Madison said, remembering Salli T. Turner, the TV blonde who'd been murdered the evening after she'd interviewed her.

'Hey, at least it made fantastic copy,' Natalie said cheerfully. 'You wrote the crap out of it – did Salli proud.'

'Thanks.'

'So what's goin' on in the love stakes? You seein' anybody?'

'Like who?' Madison replied sourly. 'They're all morons.'

'*You*'re in a good mood. Is this your I-hate-men week?'

'How about you?' Madison said, ignoring the crack.

'No time,' Natalie said. 'I'm workin' my ass off on the new show.'

'What's your co-anchor like?'

'An older guy who is not thrilled to be working side by side with a black woman. And no way as friendly as Jimmy Sica.'

'I guess that means he's not lusting to get into your pants.'

'Right!' Natalie said, laughing. 'He's another married one. Besides, he'd sooner be sitting next to Barbara Walters or Diane Sawyer. Now *them* he could lust after!'

'I guess you miss working with Jimmy?'

'Ah, yes, he was my favourite married cheater. Always on the prowl.'

'His brother Jake called me.'

'No shit? You were kind of into him, weren't you? Only he was busy running after that hooker, Kristin something or other.'

'Thanks for reminding me.'

'Well, it's the truth.'

'Okay, I'll call you in a couple of days,' Madison said. 'Hopefully I'll have some news about my plans. Believe me, I'm in the mood to get away.'

* * *

Her doorbell rang at ten o'clock the next morning.

'Damn!' she said, almost tripping over Slammer on

her way to peering through the peep-hole.

An exceptionally tall person stood in the hall.

She opened the door. 'Good morning,' the tall person said. 'I'm Kimm Florian. We have an appointment.'

Slammer went into attack mode, growling viciously. Madison dragged him away by his collar.

Kimm Florian was a broad-faced Native American woman dressed in plain khaki slacks, a brown sweatshirt and running shoes. She wore no makeup and her jet black hair was plaited in a long braid down her back. She was not fat, merely large boned.

'Oh,' Madison said. She'd been so distracted that she'd forgotten to cancel the appointment. 'I'm so sorry – I meant to call you.'

'Problem?' Kimm said, standing there – an imposing presence.

'My friend changed her mind,' Madison said, thinking that Kimm Florian looked less like a private detective than anyone she could have imagined.

'She did?'

'Sorry.'

'Not your fault.'

Feeling guilty that Kimm had made the trip for nothing, Madison invited her in. 'Can I offer you a coffee, orange juice or something?' she said.

'Water will be fine,' Kimm said, entering the apartment.

'You don't look like a private detective,' Madison remarked.

'No?' Kimm answered, with the glimmer of an amused smile. 'What's a private detective *supposed* to look like?'

'I dunno,' Madison said vaguely. 'Don Johnson or something.'

'I'll see if I can summon up some of that stubble,' Kimm said drily, sitting on the couch. 'The good thing about me is that nobody ever suspects I'm watching them.'

'That's good,' Madison said, fetching a bottle of Evian from the kitchen and handing it to the tall woman.

'Tell me about your friend,' Kimm said.

'Well, uh, she was suspicious of her husband for about five minutes, then she realized she was making a mistake.'

'Women never make mistakes,' Kimm said knowledgeably. 'Instinct is everything. The first time a woman suspects her husband is screwing around, she's right.'

'How do you know *that*?'

'A hundred and fifty cases later I *should* know. Your friend will require my services. Maybe not now or next week, but she'll definitely be calling me again.'

'You seem pretty sure.'

'I'll give her a test to do.'

'What test?' Madison said, humoring the woman.

'Have her go to his wallet, take a look to see if he keeps a condom in it. Most men do, you know.'

'Not married men.'

'You'd be surprised.'

'Okay, she goes to his wallet, and to her amazement she discovers a condom. What then?'

'She marks the corner of the packet with a small dot. Then a week later she checks out his wallet again to see if the same packet is still there.'

'What will *that* prove?'

'If there's no dot, it's a new packet. And . . . if he's not using condoms with her . . .'

'That seems awfully simple.'

'It's the simple things that trip 'em up,' Kimm said, with a knowing nod.

'Really?' Madison said, and then she had a brilliant idea. 'Do you track *people* down?' she asked. 'You know, look into their past? Can you go back like twenty-nine years and find out about someone?'

'Certainly,' Kimm said.

'There's a man and a woman I'd like you to investigate.'

'Give me their names and all the information you have on them.'

'It's not much. The woman's name is Gloria Delagado. She was involved with a man called Michael Castelli. Apparently she was murdered. Shot.'

'Isn't Castelli *your* name?'

'Uh . . . yes.'

'Is Michael a relative?'

'He's my father.'

Kimm looked at her shrewdly. 'You want me to find out about your father?'

'Yes. I want to know everything about him, because I have this horrible feeling that I don't know him at all.'

'I can take care of it for you,' Kimm said. 'But you should be aware that if he's not giving you the information you need, you might not like what I discover.'

There was something reassuring about Kimm. She was strong and sympathetic, yet at the same time she exuded confidence. Madison had faith in her. 'I know,' she said. 'Go ahead and find out everything you can.'

* * *

By the time Madison arrived at the office it was past noon.

Victor greeted her with a hearty pat on the back. 'I have exactly two things to say to you,' he said, his voice louder than ever. 'And you, young lady, will like both of them.'

'Don't call me young lady,' she said irritably.

'Why?'

'It's patronizing.'

'So sorry,' he huffed, not sorry at all.

'Run it by me,' she said, all business.

'You've never interviewed a boxer, have you?'

'No.'

'There's a big fight coming up in Vegas. Antonio "The Panther" Lopez versus the champ, Bull Ali Jackson. I think the Panther's a fascinating subject.'

'That's 'cause you're a guy. What about our female readers?'

'You'll get into the personal aspect of his life, the same as you always do. You know, his women, clothes, social activities . . .'

'Is he married?'

'No. He's had three children with three different women, and he's only twenty-three. Is that interesting enough for you? The fight is in Vegas in six weeks. You'll be ringside.'

'Ringside!' she said disgustedly. 'Who wants to watch two assholes beating the crap out of each other?'

'You do. It'll be exciting.'

'Sometimes you're such a guy, Victor. Do you really think that's what excites women?'

'I *know* what excites women,' Victor said dourly. 'A new mink coat every winter. It certainly turns Evelyn on.'

'Haven't you told her that wearing fur is politically incorrect?'

'I've told her till I'm speechless. It makes no difference. She still expects me to buy her a new fur every year.'

'Don't,' Madison said sharply. 'You're supposed to be supporting the cause. What would you do if somebody threw a can of paint over her?'

Victor couldn't help smiling. 'I'd slip them a reward,' he said, chuckling to himself. 'A big reward.'

'So, you want me to go to Vegas?'

'How do you feel about that?'

'Not too bad – I was hoping to get away.'

'Why?'

'Just because . . .'

'You look tired,' Victor said, peering at her. 'Is everything all right?'

'Why wouldn't it be?'

'Another long, lonely weekend?'

'I do not have long, lonely weekends,' she said, irritated. 'First of all I have tons of friends, and secondly, I have a dog. Just because I'm not with a guy doesn't mean I don't have fun.'

'You miss David.'

'*Fuck* David!'

'Yes, you miss him. But I have the answer for you.'

'Can't wait,' she said, not at all anxious to hear what it was.

'We're having a dinner party. Evelyn insists you come.'

'And why is that?'

'Because my dear wife considers herself Manhattan's greatest matchmaker, and she has the perfect man for you.'

123

'No, Victor,' Madison groaned, 'not again. I've been through that too many times at your house. Let me see now, the last time the perfect guy was twenty-one and a nerd. And the time before that he was, like, eighty-six. I mean, with all due respect to Evelyn, she has no idea what I'm looking for. In fact, I'm not *looking* period. If I trip over it, fine, and if I don't, then I'm perfectly happy by myself.'

'I see,' Victor boomed.

'What *is* this whole deal about a woman always having to be with a man?'

'You can't turn us down this time,' Victor said. 'It's Evelyn's birthday.'

'Oh, God!'

'I take it that's a yes?'

'Okay, I'll come. I'll even bring a present. But *please*, *whatever* you do, no more fixing me up.'

Chapter Fourteen

'Come to my office,' Joel suggested. 'Be here around twelve forty-five.'

Rosarita didn't need asking twice. It was Tuesday, and she'd spent far too much time with her in-laws, although there had been a slight diversion – Dex getting into sex again was a mild bonus.

Chas hadn't mentioned a word to her since she'd requested that he get rid of her husband. Was it such a terrible thing to do? If Dex planned on screwing up her life, he had to be gotten rid of. There *was* no choice.

However, on the other hand, if he co-operated and gave her a divorce with no problems, perhaps she'd allow him a stay of execution.

Should he be difficult, she had alternative plans. If Chas wouldn't get with the programme, she'd be forced to hire a professional. A grim thought, but she'd definitely do it. No way would she allow herself to be trapped – tied to a clinging and unsatisfactory husband who wouldn't let her go.

She'd never been to Joel's office situated in the Blaine building – a magnificent shimmering tower of glass and concrete owned by his father. Joel had confided he was all set to take over the business. 'Leon's ready to retire,' he'd informed her. 'So I'm the man.'

Rosarita was surprised to discover that Joel's office was on the thirty-fifth floor because, according to what she'd found out, the place to be was on the thirty-sixth floor, where Leon Blaine kept his suite of personal offices.

Joel's assistant, Jewel, a skinny black girl with four-inch talon-like nails painted green, a massive amount of corn-rowed hair, and a belligerent attitude, was sitting behind a pale wood reception desk. 'Yes?' she said, in an unfriendly fashion, as Rosarita approached.

'I'm here to see Mr Joel Blaine,' Rosarita said haughtily.

'And who might you be?'

'Mr Blaine is expecting me,' Rosarita said.

'Then I guess you gotta have a name,' Jewel countered.

They locked eyeballs.

'Tell him Rosarita is here,' she said, through clenched teeth, realizing – and not for the first time – that she'd been stuck with a Mexican hooker's name because she'd been conceived while her parents were lolling on a beach in Puerto Vallarta.

'Rosarita,' Jewel repeated, giving her name an evil twist. 'I'll tell him. Take a seat, honey.'

Honey! Now Rosarita was seriously pissed off. She sat down in the reception area, picked up a copy of *People* magazine, and stared mindlessly at a picture of a half-naked Brad Pitt.

The girl with the green nails was now on the phone. A personal call. She was whispering and snickering, ignoring Rosarita's presence.

After ten minutes of this crap, Rosarita got up and approached the desk. 'Does Mr Blaine know I'm waiting?' she demanded, in a shrill voice.

'Oh,' Jewel said, unconcerned, 'he was on the phone when you got here. I'll check if he's free now.' She buzzed him, and said in a far too familiar fashion, 'Joel, some *lady* called Rosarita's waitin' out here. You want I should send her in?' A pause. 'Okay,' she said, giving Rosarita a long, insolent smirk, 'you can go in now.'

Rosarita marched into Joel's office, and was somewhat taken aback to find it was not the expansive suite of rooms she'd imagined. It was nice enough, with leather furniture and a big window overlooking the Avenue of the Americas, but it was hardly the luxury space she'd thought it would be.

Joel was sitting behind his desk, wearing a pink cashmere sweater and a welcoming smile. 'Hi, babe,' he said. 'Come on in, an' close the door behind you.'

She did as he asked. He stood up from behind his desk, walked around the side of it and came towards her. From the waist down he was totally bare-assed naked.

'Joel!' she shrieked, half shocked and half amused. 'I notice you're pleased to see me.'

'Thought I'd put a smile on your face,' he said, grinning.

She couldn't keep her eyes off his penis – it gave 'big' a whole new meaning. Rich *and* well hung, what more could a girl ask for?

'You're a rude boy,' she scolded. 'Rude and crude.'

'And you get off on it, don't you, babe?' He leered.

She glanced at the large expanse of window behind him. They were overlooked by another office building

127

across the street. Naturally his window blinds were open.

This immediately excited her. She knew there must be people watching, which is exactly the way he wanted it. 'How was your weekend?' she asked.

'Pretty laid-back,' he said, casually touching himself.

'What did you do?' she asked, taking a deep breath.

'What *didn't* I do.'

Instinct warned her not to question him further.

'Why doncha get on your knees an' gimme one of your specials?' he suggested, planting himself in front of her.

'Shouldn't we lock the door?' she said, knowing full well what his answer would be.

'What for? Nobody's gonna come in unless they knock.' He turned slightly so that his profile was in a direct line with the window.

Rosarita got down on her knees, feeling naughty and dirty and incredibly turned-on.

He put his hands behind his head, shoving his johnson in her mouth without so much as touching her.

She attempted to grab his magnificent eight-plus.

'No hands,' he commanded. 'Only your mouth, babe.'

A surge of excitement coursed through her veins.

'C'mon,' he urged. 'Do me the way you know I like it.'

So she did.

After he'd climaxed, she waited for him to reciprocate.

He didn't. He strolled back behind his desk, picked up his pants and pulled them on.

'What about me?' she demanded, getting off her knees.

'Come back tomorrow,' he said casually. 'I'm gonna spread you on my desk and eat you like I haven't had food in a week.'

She felt shudders of anticipation.

'Okay, babe,' he said, dismissing her with a wave of his hand. 'I got business to conduct. Same time tomorrow.'

Rosarita had never been treated in such an off-hand fashion. It was unbelievably exciting!

The girl at Reception gave her an arch look as she retreated from his office. Damn! She'd forgotten to complain about her.

No hurry. She'd do that tomorrow.

* * *

Across town, Dexter was having coffee with the star of *Dark Days*, Silver Anderson, a magnificent sixty-something-year-old woman who had ruled television for the last twenty years. Martha and Matt were also at the table, both of them in awe of the fabulous Silver.

'And so you see, darlings,' Silver said, in her exaggerated pseudo-British accent, 'I *adore* this business, and this business adores me. And when I get to work with young, upcoming actors like your son, it is pure pleasure. Observe the boy – isn't he a divine specimen of manhood?'

Dexter looked suitably modest.

'He certainly is,' Martha agreed, eyes shining.

Matt didn't say a word. He was mesmerized by this incredible woman, thinking back to the days when she was a huge movie star and he was a fourteen-year-old boy sitting in the back row of the local movie theatre jacking off over her image on the big screen. Silver

Anderson hadn't changed much, she was still magnificent.

After coffee, Dexter put his parents in a cab and sent them back to the apartment. Then he returned to the set. Silver was in her dressing room.

'Thanks for doing that,' he said, popping his head around her door.

'Dexter darling,' she drawled, 'any friend of yours is a friend of mine.'

'You don't know what a thrill it was for them to meet you. Especially when you agreed to have pictures taken with them.'

'Your father is *adorable*,' Silver said, peering at her reflection in her dressing-table mirror. 'By the way, Dexter, where's that wife of yours? How come *she* never visits the set?'

'Rosarita's always busy,' he said quickly.

'Does she work?'

'No, she has other stuff to do.'

'What *stuff?*'

'You know,' he said vaguely. 'Hair, nails, waxing.'

Silver gave a throaty laugh. 'She sounds like a Hollywood wife.'

'I'm trying to knock her up,' he confessed.

'Good idea,' Silver said, still studying her reflection. 'Barefoot and slaving in the kitchen, that's the way to keep a woman under control. Especially if she's out there spending your money.'

'Fortunately she's got a rich dad,' he revealed.

'The *worst* kind of girls.' Silver sighed, picking up a brush. 'Always running to Daddy with their problems. It *so* undermines your authority.'

Authority. Dexter liked that. He was Rosarita's husband. He had authority.

And the next time she brought up the subject of divorce, he was damn well going to hit her over the head with all the authority he could muster.

Chapter Fifteen

T he next few days passed quickly, which pleased
Madison because she had no desire to sit around
thinking about all the things she had learned.
After her meeting with Victor, she immediately got
into researching Antonio 'The Panther' Lopez. Only
twenty-three and a real comer, he'd never lost a
match. Now he was all set to fight the champion in
Vegas. It seemed he was quite a character, with a
colourful past for one so young.

Sitting in front of her computer, she decided it
would be good for her to get out of town. Vegas was
a crazy place. She hadn't been there in a couple of years
so it would be interesting to see how it had changed.

Wednesday night she had dinner with Jamie, Peter
and Anton. They went to their favourite Chinese
restaurant and ordered everything on the menu.

Anton was full of apologies. 'My dear,' he said,
waving his arms in the air. 'I would *never* put Joel
Blaine next to you at a dinner party. I would never
invite Joel Blaine to a dinner party. It was *Leon* I
invited. Joel simply took his place.'

'I should've guessed,' she said, taking a bite of her second duck pancake.

'Don't think I didn't phone his executive assistant to complain the next day,' Anton said, fussily. 'That boy is a joke, trading on his father's name whenever he can.'

'Don't worry about it,' she said, reaching for a honey-coated spare rib. 'I survived.'

'You always do,' Jamie interjected.

'If you're in the game, you gotta learn to play it,' Madison said, grinning.

'That's what I admire about you, dear,' Anton said. 'You do not hold a grudge.'

Half-way through the meal Jamie got up to go to the ladies' room. Madison accompanied her.

'Guess what?' Madison said, when they reached the sanctuary of the small room.

'What?' Jamie said.

'I forgot to cancel your detective. She turned up Monday morning.'

'*My* detective?'

'Well, you were the one who wanted Peter followed.'

'Shh . . .' Jamie said.

'Shush *what*? There's nobody in here.'

'You never know who's lurking.'

'This is *not* Ally McBeal.'

'Okay, okay,' Jamie said. 'It's all my fault, so I'll pay. How much is it?'

'Who's worried about the money?' Madison said. 'As it turns out she was an extremely interesting woman. A Native American. Oh, yes, and there's something she said you should do.'

'What?' said Jamie, staring in the mirror while applying a pale pink gloss to her luscious lips.

'Check out Peter's wallet, see if he's got a condom stashed there.'

Jamie burst out laughing. 'Why would Peter be carrying a *condom* in his wallet?'

'If everything's cool, he won't be,' Madison said. 'Only Kimm seems to think that once a wife suspects, that nagging inner voice is never wrong.'

'Charming!' Jamie exclaimed. 'I can assure you *I* was wrong. Peter has never been more loving.'

'So nothing lost if you take a look.'

'And what am I supposed to do if I find one?'

'Put a tiny mark on the corner of the package. Then look again in a week and see if the mark's still there. If it isn't and there's a new condom there, then you'll know he's cheating.'

'What a scam!' Jamie scoffed. 'And complicated too.'

'I think it's quite clever.'

'We don't use condoms,' Jamie pointed out.

'All the better. This way, if he's doing anything, you've got him busted. What can he say? That he was carrying it for a friend?'

'This is ridiculous,' Jamie said, brushing her short blonde hair a touch too vigorously.

'If it's so ridiculous, nothing lost by giving it a try.'

'We'll see,' Jamie said, putting her brush back in her purse. 'By the way, Peter met this guy at work he swears is exactly right for you.'

'*What* guy?' Madison groaned.

'A hot guy,' Jamie answered, spraying herself with a purse-size atomizer of Angel.

'I am so fed up with people trying to fix me up,' Madison said, frowning. 'If there's somebody out there who's right for me, I'll find him myself.'

'You're not doing a great job.'

'Thanks.'

'Well, it's true.'

'Anyway, Jake Sica called me.'

'Who's Jake Sica?'

'That guy I told you about – the one in L.A. who was lusting after some blonde call-girl, you know, the one who was busy getting involved with a total psycho.'

'Sounds like L.A.,' Jamie said crisply. 'What was it you called your trip?'

'The Magical Mystery Psycho Tour,' Madison said, remembering how she'd befriended Salli T. Turner, the sexy TV actress, on the plane out to L.A., and the next day Salli had been murdered. Madison had genuinely liked Salli – she'd possessed a sweetness and vulnerability that were irresistible to both men and women. The police had eventually caught the killer, who'd turned out to be TV talk show host Bo Deacon.

Pure Hollywood tragedy.

'What did this Jake guy call and say?' Jamie persisted.

'That he's coming out here this week. Unfortunately my machine cut off so I didn't get to hear the end of his message.'

'I hate machines. We're getting voicemail.'

'I'd miss that blinking red light.'

'You're such an old-fashioned girl at heart.'

'*Me?*'

'So, are you going to get together with him?'

'Of course.'

'Good,' Jamie said. 'But that doesn't mean you get out of meeting Peter's friend.'

'I'm not doing it.'

135

'We'll see,' Jamie said, smiling mysteriously.

'No, we *won't* see.'

'Peter says you'll like him a lot.'

'Peter doesn't know my taste.'

'What *is* your taste? It's been so long I've forgotten.'

'Hmm . . .' Madison said thoughtfully. 'Someone strong and truthful – oh, yes, and definitely faithful. And he has to have a finely tuned sense of humour plus a great butt!'

'Sounds *exactly* like Peter's friend,' Jamie said, grinning.

'Bullshit!'

'How do *you* know that he hasn't got a great butt?'

They both began to giggle.

'This reminds me of when we were in college,' Madison said. 'The mainstream of our conversation was –'

'Guys, guys, guys,' Jamie chimed in.

'Yeah, well, we didn't do too badly, did we? They were lining up outside *your* door.'

'And they would've been lining up outside *yours* if you'd let 'em,' Jamie said.

'No, I scored the nerds,' Madison said, grimacing. 'I was the brain, remember?'

'You also scored a few professors. I seem to recall a certain hunk who taught art history – did he have the hots for you!'

Madison smiled reflectively. 'He seemed so old to us then, didn't he?'

'He was.'

'The man was forty,' Madison exclaimed. 'Which reminds me, I'm going to be thirty in a few weeks.'

'I'm not far behind you,' Jamie remarked gloomily. 'Old, isn't it?'

'Not really,' Madison said. 'Thirty's old when you're twenty. When you're thirty, forty is old. And I guess when you're forty, *fifty* is old – and so on.'

'It sure beats the alternative,' Jamie said cheerfully.

'You got it,' Madison agreed.

'So,' Jamie said, 'are we on for dinner?'

'Don't *do* this to me,' Madison groaned.

'Why? You'll have a great time.'

'Says who?'

'Me.'

'Ha!'

'Tell you what,' Jamie said, 'meet this guy, and I'll do the condom thing for you. How's that for a deal?'

'Hey, let's get this straight. You're not doing the condom thing for *me*, you're doing it for yourself.'

'That's true, but –'

'Okay, I'll come to dinner, I'll meet the great guy with the perfect butt, and we'll get married and have six wonderful children. Does that make you happy?'

'Stranger things have happened.'

'Sure!'

They returned to the table, still laughing.

'What do you women *do* in there?' Peter complained. 'You've been an hour.'

'We have not,' Jamie said, playfully punching him on the chin. 'If you must know, we were talking about *you.*'

'Good choice,' Peter said. 'I'll be the first to admit that I'm a fascinating subject.'

'You certainly are,' Jamie said. 'And you *love* it when you know you're being discussed.' She nuzzled in next to him, giving him a long, intimate kiss on his earlobe.

'I find these public displays of affection quite sickening,' Anton complained.

'I know,' Madison agreed. 'You'd think they'd have something better to do with their time.'

'We do,' Peter said, with a dirty laugh. 'That's why I'm calling for the check.'

* * *

Back at her apartment Madison could hear the phone ringing as she unlocked her door. She burst inside at the exact moment her machine picked up. Slammer jumped all over her as she grabbed the receiver. 'Hi,' she said breathlessly, thinking it might be Michael, or maybe Kimm with some information.

'Gotcha!' Jake Sica said. 'I was about to hang up.'

She recognized his voice immediately. 'How are you?' she said, happy he'd called again. 'I got your message the other day. I would've phoned back, only you didn't leave a number.'

'That's because for the last few months I haven't *had* a number,' he explained. 'I've been roaming across America.'

'Sounds elusive.'

'You know how it is. I had to kind of . . . find myself.'

'I know *exactly* how it is.' A beat. 'Actually, I'm going through something difficult myself at the moment.'

'Difficult?'

'Nothing to be discussed on the phone,' she said, deciding now was definitely not the time to burden him with her problems.

'In that case I'd better take you to dinner or lunch or tea or breakfast. I'm in your city now, so what are you up for?'

Would it be too forward to say she was up for all of those things? 'Let's make it dinner,' she said. 'I'm free tomorrow night.'

'So am I. Haven't made any other plans.'

'I'm glad.'

'Hey,' he said, 'it's really good to hear your voice again.'

'You, too,' she said softly, feeling ridiculously pleased to hear from him.

'Where shall we go? Your choice, 'cause I'm not familiar with New York.'

'Do you like Chinese?' she asked, thinking of the restaurant she'd eaten at earlier.

'My favourite.'

'I'll give you my address and you can pick me up.'

'Sounds good.'

'Where are you staying?'

'Some fleabag hotel near Times Square. You know me – not into the fancy stuff.'

'What's the number? In case I break a leg or something.'

'You're not planning to, are you?'

'No.'

'Glad to hear it,' he said, clearing his throat. 'Hey – I just had a thought.'

'Is that unusual?' she teased.

'How about – naw,' he said, stopping himself, 'you wouldn't want to do that.'

'Do what?' she asked, a touch too quickly.

'You must've only just come home, so you've got to be dressed – right?'

'Oh, please,' she said. 'You're not about to ask me what I'm wearing, are you?'

'No,' he said, laughing. 'I was thinking how about if

we go out somewhere *now* and have a drink?'

'Now?' she repeated, sounding like an idiot.

'That's what I said.'

Well, uh . . . yeah, why not? she thought.

'Well, uh . . . yeah, why not?' she said.

'Great. I'll come by and get you.' She gave him her address and hung up feeling inexplicably flustered. This was crazy, she hardly knew the guy, and yet her heart was pounding. She must really be starved of decent male company.

Racing into the bathroom, she stopped and took a critical look in the mirror. She had on a white shirt, black jeans and a short black jacket. Jamie was always urging her to be a little more playful with her makeup, so with her friend's words in mind she grabbed a brush and added gloss to her full lips. Then she applied more mascara, and loosened her pulled-back hair. She'd always wished for long, straight hair, instead of which it was wild and curly. But tonight she had to admit it looked good as she fluffed it out with her fingers.

Slammer gazed up at her expectantly, as if to say, 'So? Are we hitting the streets or *what?*'

She buzzed down to Calvin, the doorman. 'Can you walk my dog?' she asked.

'Sure, Miss Castelli,' Calvin said. 'Anything for my favourite tenant.'

He had a mild crush, which came in useful when she needed anything.

'Thanks,' she said, nervously rushing back to the bathroom mirror.

Hmmm . . . don't like the white shirt – too severe, she thought, grabbing a red cashmere tank from her closet. She put it on. It looked sexy.

Do I want to look sexy?

Hell, yes.

Calvin rang her buzzer. He was a short, round-faced man with bright ginger hair and startled eyebrows. She handed over Slammer, who did not seem pleased. 'You look nice, Miss Castelli,' Calvin ventured, giving her a quick once-over. 'Like your hair.'

'Thanks,' she said, practically closing the door in his face.

Scent. She should put on some scent. A quick squirt of Jo Malone's Grapefruit. It used to drive David crazy. *Not crazy enough to stay*, she thought dourly.

His loss. Yes, definitely.

David should have realized that nobody would love him the way she had. Because when she loved she was totally loyal, and that wasn't easy to come by in a relationship.

The red tank looked great, emphasizing her bosom and narrow waist. She added some gold hoop earrings. She hadn't felt this good in a long time – in fact, she hadn't made this much of an effort in a long time.

The downstairs buzzer rang. 'Yes, Calvin?' she said, into the house phone.

'There's a gentleman here for you, Miss,' he said, not sounding very happy about it.

'Tell him I'll be right down.'

Jake must have been phoning her from around the corner, because it couldn't have been more than ten minutes since they'd spoken. She took one last look in the mirror, grabbed her purse and hurried out of the apartment.

The elevator seemed to take forever to reach the lobby. She stood totally still, attempting to compose herself. 'Hi, Jake,' she'd say. 'How nice to see you again. Oh, and by the way – how's that, uh, delightful call-girl you were lusting after?'

No, no, no – mustn't sound bitchy! Be cool. Be nice. 'Hi, Jake, great to see you again.'

Yes. That's it. Cool and friendly.

The elevator doors opened. He had his back to her. He was bending over playing with Slammer.

How nice, he likes dogs.

She walked over, casually tapping him on the shoulder. 'Hi there, stranger,' she said.

He stood up and turned round.

It was David.

Chapter Sixteen

Chas Vincent sometimes wished that he'd had a son. How come he'd got stuck with two daughters? The good seed and the bad seed. He loved them both, but Rosarita was definitely one big pain in the ass. Maybe it was all that hot Mexican sunshine when she was conceived.

Venice, on the other hand, was an angel, and so were her kids. Not that he saw much of them, but when he did, it pleased him to know that they were carrying on the Vincent bloodline, something that was important to him.

Chas Vincent had led a rip-roaring life, and he let no one forget it. He was ruler of his own particular roost. He had enemies, he had friends, but he sure was no killer, which Rosarita seemed to think he was. She was insane and deluded. How could she imagine he was capable of having a man whacked? Especially his own son-in-law.

Rosarita was in dire need of a shrink. And the sooner the better. He'd pay for it. He paid for everything else, so why not a shrink for his crazy daughter too?

143

It occurred to him that maybe he should talk to Dexter, warn him.

Naw! Nobody would believe that Rosarita would go to her own father to try to have her husband taken care of simply because the putz wouldn't co-operate on a divorce. No fuckin' way!

Varoomba was in the bathroom, doing whatever she did in there before she spent the night. She'd become a fixture ever since the family dinner. Having her around suited him for now – he'd even contemplated telling her to give up her job at the club and move in for a while. The trouble with that was the moment they moved in it was a bitch getting rid of 'em. And he didn't need that headache again.

His other thought was that he'd pay the rent on her apartment, that way she could stay over when he wanted her to, and go home when he'd had enough.

Varoomba emerged from the bathroom wearing the best Victoria's Secret had to offer. He got off on sexy lingerie, a fact she was well aware of.

'Lookin' hot, baby,' he remarked, lowering the volume on the TV.

'Thanks, Daddy,' she cooed.

Daddy! This was a new one. He wasn't sure he liked it.

'Don't call me that,' he said abruptly.

'Okay,' she said, absent-mindedly pinching her left nipple. 'But you told me yourself I'm younger than your two daughters. So, in a way, you could *be* my daddy.' She giggled coyly. 'My *sugar* daddy!'

Those words were enough to reduce his hard-on to nothing.

Why couldn't women learn to keep their dumb mouths shut?

* * *

Rosarita swept into the reception area of Joel's office as if she owned the place. The same black girl was sitting behind the desk filing those same atrocious green nails.

'Remember me?' Rosarita snapped.

'No,' Jewel said, surly as ever.

'Tell Mr Blaine I'm here. The name is Rosarita.'

'Oh, yeah,' Jewel said, snickering. 'Rosarita. Kind of an off-the-wall name for a non-Mexicana, huh?'

'What?' Rosarita said, outraged.

'You heard,' Jewel replied insolently, secure that Joel would never fire her – she knew too much.

Rosarita tapped her stiletto-heeled Gucci shoe impatiently on the marble floor. She'd had enough of this rude girl's shit. Why had she forgotten to tell Joel to get rid of the cretin?

Ignoring her, she strode past her towards Joel's office.

'Wait a minute,' Jewel said, scrambling out from behind her desk and chasing after her. 'You can't do that.'

'Try and stop me,' Rosarita said, flinging open his door.

Joel was standing in front of his desk, jerking off, large member in hand for all to see.

'Joel!' Rosarita exclaimed.

'Oops!' Jewel giggled, backing out of the door.

'What took you so long?' Joel questioned, a welcoming smirk on his fleshy face.

It occurred to Rosarita that she might be getting in over her head. Joel was definitely loco. But sexy with it.

'*What* are you doing?' she squealed.

'What does it *look* like I'm doing?' he replied, perfectly at ease.

'Couldn't you at least have waited for me?'

'Why waste a good head-start?' he said, right hand still in action.

Shutting the door behind her she ventured closer. 'Don't let me disturb you,' she said sarcastically.

'I can assure you, babe, you're not,' he answered, and then, grabbing a tissue, he groaned loudly and finished the job.

'Goddamn it, Joel!' she complained. 'What *is* going on? Why are you standing here by yourself jacking off?'

'*Am* I by myself?' he said, unconcerned as he zipped up. 'Thought *you* were here.'

'Yes, I am, and so was your so-called assistant.'

'Take no notice of Jewel, she's seen it all before.'

'You're not having sex with that – that tramp?' Rosarita asked, furious at the possibility.

'Get real, babe. I'm Joel Blaine. But y' know,' he added, with a cocky wink, 'when you spend a lot of time with someone, there ain't a lotta secrets between you.'

Rosarita was exasperated. This man was totally out there, and it excited the hell out of her.

'Move your ass over here an' stop nagging,' he ordered.

She sauntered towards his desk. 'My in-laws are still in town,' she said, as if he cared.

'Jump up on the desk, babe. I'm gonna show you some tongue action the like of which you've never experienced.'

Gingerly she perched on the edge of his desk.

He grinned and shoved her back so that her butt was firmly planted in the middle of the desk, while her legs dangled limply over the side.

'Raise your ass an' remove your panties,' he commanded.

'What makes you think I'm wearing any?' she said, in what she hoped was a provocative drawl.

'Oh, baby, baby,' he crooned, 'you and I, we're a pair made in heaven. An' *I*'m gonna show you what heaven's all about!'

* * *

'Where *were* you today?' Dexter asked, as soon as Rosarita arrived home.

'I had some errands to run,' she answered vaguely, trying not to think about Joel's talented tongue licking her dry. Was he the best or *what*?

'My mom thought you were taking her to the museum. She's disappointed.'

'I'll take her tomorrow,' Rosarita said, adding a snippy, 'I have a life, you know.'

'Your *life* is with me,' Dexter said.

That's what you think.

'Your sister called.'

'What did *she* want?'

'Maybe just to be sisterly. Has it ever occurred to you that it might be nice if you asked her over for tea? Martha would love to meet the kids.'

'Why is it that all you care about lately is making your goddamn mother happy?' she said.

'Don't start,' he said, throwing her a warning look.

'It's always about *you*,' she whined. 'Always about what *you* want. Sometimes you might consider what *I* want, and you *know* what that is.'

'What?'

'A divorce,' she said triumphantly.

'You promised me we wouldn't discuss it until my parents left,' he said, lowering his voice.

'*You*'re the one who's busy nagging me.'

'I'm sorry. I won't say anything else.' And he didn't.

That night he made love to her twice. He was determined to get her pregnant, and the way they were going, it shouldn't take much longer.

Chapter Seventeen

'W ow!' David exclaimed admiringly. 'You look sensational!'

'David?' She uttered his name like she didn't really believe it was him standing in front of her. 'David,' she repeated in shock. And then, as the reality set in, 'What the hell are *you* doing here?'

'I dropped by on the chance you'd be in,' he said casually, as if they saw each other all the time and this was no big deal.

Actually, it was an enormous deal. It was the first time she'd laid eyes on him since he'd walked out on her.

'I'm *not* in,' she said flatly. 'I'm on my way to dinner.'

'You are?' he said, surprised.

'Yes, I am,' she said.

'That's a helluva greeting,' he said, fixing her with a why-can't-you-be-nicer-to-me? look.

'Let me get this straight,' she said, struggling to recover her composure. 'Are you actually here to see *me*?'

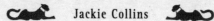

'Obviously.'

'Why?'

'I thought we should . . . talk.'

'You couldn't have picked up a phone?'

'Wasn't sure you'd speak to me.'

'I see,' she said icily. 'You got it in your head that it was better to come here at ten-thirty at night and confront me in person.'

'You look sensational,' he said, repeating himself.

'You've already told me that,' she answered, thrown by this new turn of events.

'So,' he said, conversationally, 'how have you been?'

'What *is* this crap?' she said, suddenly angry. 'Go home to your wife where you belong.'

'I've *left* my wife,' he announced. 'It's over between us.'

'What did you do – go out for cigarettes and forget to come back?'

David scowled. 'That doesn't make me feel good,' he muttered.

'I'm *sorry*. I fully intended it should make you feel great.'

'I hate it when you're sarcastic.'

'*You* are something else,' she said in amazement.

'Is this man bothering you, Miss Castelli?' Calvin inquired, stepping out from behind the porter's desk, a belligerent expression on his round face.

Slammer barked. He was straining on his leash to leave the building, and it was quite obvious that Calvin had no intention of taking him anywhere until he found out what was going on.

'No, Calvin, everything's fine,' she said quickly. 'This is not who I was expecting, and he's leaving anyway.'

'Uh-huh,' Calvin said, glaring at David.

She didn't know whether to stay in the lobby and risk Jake arriving, or return to her apartment.

'Where are you going for dinner?' David asked, as if he had a right to know.

'None of your business,' she answered. Was it her imagination or had he put on a pound or two? And his hair looked dry and lifeless – as if it needed a good conditioning.

'We had something so good together.' He sighed. 'Something so right.'

'We certainly did, David,' she replied calmly, watching Calvin and Slammer leave. 'That is, until *you* fucked it up. So, here's my suggestion. Do not come whining back to me simply because your marriage hasn't worked out. You see, quite frankly, I don't care.'

'Yes, you do,' he said quickly. 'I heard you haven't hooked up with anyone since we split. That means you *do* care.'

'No, it means I haven't found anybody I want to sleep with. There's a big difference.'

'I've got nowhere to stay tonight,' he said.

'Have you ever heard the word hotel?' she said caustically. 'They have them all over the city.'

A flicker of annoyance crossed his face. 'I wasn't expecting this kind of reaction from you,' he said.

'Really?' she answered coldly. 'What *were* you expecting?'

'I thought you'd have more compassion.'

'David,' she said patiently, 'the night you walked out on me, every bit of my compassion went with you. Get it?'

'Jesus, Madison, how many times do you want me to say I'm sorry?'

151

'As many as you like. It won't make any difference.'

'Have lunch with me tomorrow?'

'You've got to be out of your mind.'

'You're not giving me a crumb, nothing, huh?'

'I'm giving you what *you* gave me.'

'So that's it,' he said sulkily. 'I'm being punished.'

'Don't you *get* it, David?' she said, her voice rising in frustration. 'You're not being punished, you're not being anything. We had something you broke into a thousand pieces. Now it's over.'

'No,' he said stubbornly. 'It'll never be over.'

'Yes,' she countered. 'It's definitely over, and I'm going back upstairs, so you'd better leave.'

He shook his head as if he couldn't understand why she was dismissing him.

Please go, she urged him silently. *Please go before Jake arrives.*

And naturally, just as she was wishing David would leave, in walked Jake. And he looked good. He was a couple of inches taller than David, his hair was tousled and longer, and he had appealing brown eyes. He was sexy in a laid-back, street kind of way.

'Hey,' Jake said, unaware he was walking in on something.

'Hi,' she said, quickly grabbing the sleeve of his leather jacket and steering him back towards the door. 'I'm all ready, let's go.'

David started to follow, but she stopped him with a look that said, *Don't even think about it!*

'Did I interrupt something?' Jake asked, as they hit the street. 'You rushed me out of there like the building was on fire!'

'Actually you saved me,' she answered.

'From that guy? Who was he?'

'Someone I *used* to know.' A long, meaningful pause. 'I can safely say – not any more.'

'That's good.'

'Yes, it is.'

He gave her a quizzical look. 'New York suits you.'

'Are you saying L.A. didn't?' she responded.

'You looked pretty good in L.A., but as we both know, my mind was elsewhere. Jeez,' he grinned, 'I must've been blind.'

'I'm glad you're here,' she said.

'Why's that?'

''Cause I'm in desperate need of someone to talk to.'

'Is that the only reason?'

'One of them.'

'Then talk away.'

'First I need a drink. Then I want to know why you're in town, what your plans are, where you're heading next, and, uh . . . after that I'd simply like to have fun.'

He grinned again. He had a killer grin – she remembered it well.

'That's *exactly* what I had in mind,' he said. 'Fun . . . with you. A perfect night.'

* * *

Three hours later they were in bed in her apartment having recently finished making fast passionate love.

'I've never done this before.' She sighed, stretching luxuriously.

'Really?' he answered, with a playful laugh. 'So what you're telling me is that you were a twenty-nine-year-old virgin?'

'You know what I mean,' she said, smiling softly.

153

'I've never ended up in bed on a first date.' She paused for a moment, then added, 'Well, maybe once in college, and there was a quick one-nighter in Miami, but –'

'Hey,' he interrupted, touching her arm. 'I'm not here on a need-to-know basis. Anyway, this is our *second* date. Remember L.A.?'

'Of course.'

'I thought about you a lot since then.'

'I thought about you too,' she admitted.

He yawned and rolled over. 'I hope I'm not rebound guy 'cause your significant other turned up tonight.'

'David hasn't been my significant other for over a year,' she said, throwing her arms above her head. 'I barely recognized him.'

'Good,' he said, moving back towards her. Then he began kissing her neck, moving slowly down – very, very slowly.

She moaned in anticipation of what was to come. Being in bed with Jake was far better than she'd expected, a release that she'd desperately needed, and she was determined to relish every moment.

Earlier, over drinks at a nearby bar, she'd told him about Michael's revelations. He'd listened attentively and sympathized. She'd also told him about the private detective she'd hired to find information about her parents.

'Has she come up with anything?' he'd asked.

'I haven't heard from her since she was here.'

'If she's thorough, she'll wait until she can bring you everything.'

'What is everything? I don't know any more. It's like I'm completely lost.'

Now, lying in bed next to him, she didn't feel lost at all. She was in the right place at the right time, and that felt extremely satisfying. Plus the sex was great, natural and passionate, not as if it was their first time together at all.

His hands began exploring her body again, sending chills of excitement through her.

Oh, God, she loved the smell of him, the way his skin felt, the touch of his hands all over her. He was strong and comforting and loving and, most of all, he was there exactly when she needed him.

In the morning he was still in her bed. She propped herself up on one elbow and watched him sleep. He was handsome in an unaffected way. Not perfect like his anchorman brother in L.A., more edgy and casual. He was also an excellent lover although, she thought wryly, she was so out of practice she wouldn't know a bad lover from a good one.

She climbed out of bed without disturbing him and went into the living room. Slammer, who'd been shut out of the bedroom for the night, gave her a furious look and slunk over to the far corner as her punishment for locking him out.

She headed into the kitchen and put on the coffee, then slid back into the bedroom, threw on a shirt and jeans, grabbed Slammer's leash, left the apartment and ran him around the block.

When she got back, Jake was in the kitchen pouring coffee into two mugs.

'And *so*,' he said, killer grin going full force, 'she looks perfectly beautiful in the morning, too,'

'What are you – a poet?' she said, smiling.

'Last night was *very* special,' he said, handing her a cup of coffee. '*Exceptionally* special in fact.'

'How did it happen so fast?' she marvelled, perching on a high stool at the kitchen counter.

'Guess I'm irresistible,' he joked.

'Sure, that's it,' she joked back. 'Must've been those bony knees of yours that got me going!'

'My knees aren't bony,' he objected, sitting next to her. 'My knees are perfect.'

'Says who?'

'Me?'

'Okay, he has perfect knees. I'll accept that.'

'And *she* has a perfect mouth,' he responded.

'Anyway,' she said, becoming serious, 'it's no big deal, right?'

'What? My knees?'

'No. *Us.* Y'know, jumping into bed so quickly.'

'Right,' he agreed. 'After all, we've been friends for a while now, almost a year.'

'That's true, and as you said, this *is* our second date, so it wasn't like I threw myself into bed with you on our *first* date.'

'You worry about stupid details,' he said.

'I know,' she agreed. 'I'm trying to get over it.'

He smiled and sipped his coffee. 'How's work?'

'Same old grind. You know I wrote a piece for the magazine on call-girls in L.A.? I didn't quote your girlfriend since you asked me not to.'

'She wasn't my *girlfriend*,' he explained. 'She was a nice girl with whom I had a brief fling. And she only got into the business because she had to take care of her sister.'

'How compassionate.'

'Don't be bitchy.'

'Well . . . I do have to say,' Madison admitted grudgingly, 'she *was* very beautiful.'

156

'She was *pretty*,' he said, giving Madison a long, intense look. '*You*'re beautiful.'

'Thanks,' she said, feeling the burn of intimacy and not quite sure how to handle it. After David she was determined never to get hurt again. Casual was the name of the game from now on. No expectations. No disappointments. Simply fun.

'How about you?' she asked. 'What's going on with you work-wise?'

'Everything's good,' he said. 'I got back from Africa a week ago, where I was photographing cheetahs in the wild.'

'Oh, my God,' she said. 'I *love* cheetahs. They are *the* most beautiful animals.'

'You should watch them running. It has to be the most powerful sight you've ever witnessed.'

'Can I see your photographs?'

'Any time.'

'I'd like that.'

'And . . . I'd like to . . .'

'What?' she asked, breathlessly.

'I think you know what,' he said, leaning over and kissing her full on the mouth.

She could taste the coffee on his tongue and once more desire began coursing through her. She wanted him again, and there was absolutely no reason why she couldn't have him.

* * *

A week later he was gone. A long, lingering kiss at the door and then he was out of there on his way to an assignment in Paris. 'Come with me?' he suggested.

She knew it was too soon to start following him

around the world. 'I can't,' she said. 'I'm waiting to hear from the detective. I have work commitments, and I've got to talk to Stella.'

Excuses, excuses. She could go if she wanted to.

'I'll miss you,' he said. 'I'll miss everything about you.'

'How long will you be gone?'

'As long as it takes. You know me – not into making plans.'

She was beginning to understand that.

And so, after a week of complete togetherness, he vanished out of her life as quickly as he'd re-entered it.

Normal existence resumed. She checked out her answering-machine. It was jammed. For seven days she'd holed up with Jake and got lost in the experience. Now she had a list of people to call back and explain her absence to. Victor for one. Michael had phoned every day. Jamie, Natalie, Anton and David.

At least people cared whether she lived or died.

She called Victor first.

'And where exactly have *you* been?' he boomed. 'How dare you skip out of town and not tell anybody? You missed Evelyn's birthday. Even more important – you missed the date she arranged for you. Evelyn is mad, and that's not a pleasant sight.'

'Sorry, Victor. I fell in lust.'

'You *what?*'

'Caught up with an old friend.'

'You mean you had sex?'

'I really don't think that's any of your concern.'

'Ha!' Victor said loudly. 'You'd better think of a way to make it up to Evelyn. She is *not* pleased. Besides, it makes *me* look bad.'

'We never had a definite arrangement.'

'Of course we did,' he argued. 'You assured me you were coming.'

'How could I do that when I didn't even know what day your party was?'

'I left six messages on your machine.'

'I only listened this morning.'

'Ha!' he repeated. 'What if it had been an emergency?'

'It wasn't, was it?'

'You always have an answer.'

'You trained me well.'

'How's your research on the Panther coming along?'

'Pretty damn good,' she lied.

'You all set for Vegas?'

'I have a question,' she said, suddenly coming up with a great idea.

'Yes?'

'What photographer are you assigning?'

'Haven't thought about it yet. If the Panther wins, we'll do him as the cover, so I need the best.'

'And if he loses?'

'Tough shit.'

'You're such a charmer, Victor.'

'Thanks,' he said, his voice louder than ever.

She hesitated for a moment, then plunged ahead. 'Uh . . . remember Jake Sica? The photographer you hired in L.A.?'

'That's the guy who informed me he couldn't work for us any more. Had to go off and do other things. Likes photographing wildlife or something.'

'He's back.'

'In your bed?'

'Wouldn't *you* like to know?'

'In your bed,' Victor said, absolutely sure.

'I was thinking he could do a fine job. He's great with action shots. He might be the photographer to send to Vegas with me.'

'You don't have to hit me over the head with a block of plywood,' Victor said. 'I get it. Where can I contact him?'

'He's in Paris at the moment. I'll have *him* call *you*.'

'I've been meaning to ask, how's your book progressing? Still working hard?'

'Oh, my book,' she said guiltily – she hadn't worked on it in weeks. 'Yes, it's making progress,' she said, getting quite adept at lying to Victor. 'I promise you'll be the first to read it.'

'Good. Send Evelyn flowers.'

'No, *you* send Evelyn flowers, put my name on the card.'

'Cheapskate,' he muttered.

'*You*'re the one with the enormous expense account,' she pointed out. 'I'm merely an employee.'

She called Michael next.

He sounded even more tense than the last time they'd spoken. 'What is this?' he said. 'You leave town and don't even tell me where you are?'

'Why do you want to know?' she said, not prepared to offer any explanations.

'Because I've been trying to reach you for two days.'

Too bad, she thought, still trying to work out how she felt about him.

He's my father and I love him.

He's made my past meaningless and I hate him.

'What's so important?' she asked, wanting to punish him with her indifference.

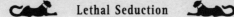

There was a long silence before he spoke. 'It's about Stella,' he said at last. 'She's . . . dead.' Another long, ominous pause. 'The funeral's tomorrow. I'd like you to be there.'

Chapter Eighteen

T hank God for Chas, was all Rosarita could say. As far as entertaining Matt and Martha Cockranger, he'd been a prince – she didn't know what she would have done without him. Probably thrown herself off the top of Barney's because anything was better than spending another minute with Dexter's boring parents.

The next night they all went to dinner at Le Cirque. Chas insisted on bringing his date, even though Rosarita begged him not to.

Her begging had put him in a bad mood. 'Somethin' wrong wit' Alice?' he demanded. 'She's a nurse, for Crissakes. Give her some respect.'

'Nurse, my ass,' Rosarita responded, acid tongue in action. 'She's a stripper with huge fake tits. Silicone has always been your weakness. Why can't you get over it?'

After that little exchange, Chas chose to ignore his annoying daughter, and palled up with Martha and Matt, who hung on his every word as if he were a movie star. Chas basked in the attention as he entertained them with a few of his outlandish stories.

Rosarita had managed to consume two martinis and a hefty steak – which she planned to regurgitate later – when she spotted Joel. He entered the restaurant with a long thin blonde draped all over him like a mink wrap. It made Rosarita *crazy*. She had realized that he had to have a life away from her because, after all, what could she offer him? She was married, so therefore she couldn't spend all her time with him. But actually to see him out on the town with a date – well, it wasn't very pleasant.

The girl had the kind of long, straight blonde hair you saw on models in the fashion magazines. And she had creamy skin and legs that went on for ever. And a flat chest, Rosarita was happy to note. She was taller than Joel. He probably didn't like that. Or maybe he did.

It occurred to Rosarita that she had not bothered to investigate all of Joel's likes and dislikes.

She gulped down the rest of her third martini and sat up straight. What was she supposed to do? Go over, wave, say hello? As far as Dex knew, she and Joel had barely met. She'd vaguely mentioned that she'd been introduced to both Leon Blaine and his son at a cocktail party. Dex hadn't taken much notice – he probably had no idea who Leon Blaine was.

She reached into her purse, took out her compact and a lipstick, examined her face in the compact mirror and decided that she looked miserable. She *was* miserable. Who wouldn't be, stuck next to Matt and Martha Cockranger every night? And Chas wasn't much help, what with insisting on bringing his latest tit-inflated bimbo. God! What a group to be seen with!

She watched Joel as the *maître d'* seated him. His

back was to her. Thank God he hadn't seen her. Now the only question was, did she go over or not?

Not. She didn't care to be introduced to that tall drink of water he was with. Why should she honour her with a hello?

'I'm tired,' she complained to Dexter.

'We haven't had dessert yet,' he said, studying the menu.

'I know, but I'm exhausted.'

'Then maybe you shouldn't have had three martinis,' he said, with a cutting edge to his voice.

'What're you doing – counting my drinks?' she said, belligerently.

'No. I simply happen to know how many you've had.'

'Now, now, children,' Martha interrupted, chuckling gaily, 'no bickering at the table.'

Chas guffawed. Varoomba gave a squeaky little giggle.

'What hospital do you work at, Alice dear?' asked Martha, paying Varoomba some attention. 'Is it one of those *ER* places, where you see all these emergencies, and handsome doctors running around? I *love* George Clooney.'

'What's *ER*?' Varoomba said blankly.

'Emergency room,' Chas said, kicking her under the table.

'Oh, yeah, emergency room,' Varoomba said. 'I'm a private nurse. I only give private service.'

'I see,' Martha said. 'So you go to people's homes?'

'Only if they pay me enough,' Varoomba said.

Chas threw her a *shut-the-fuck-up* look. So Varoomba shut the fuck up.

Rosarita ordered another martini while keeping a

well-trained eye on Joel's back. It seemed to her that his date was the one paying him all the attention. At one point she noticed the girl snake a long, thin arm around his shoulders, her hand making its way up to the back of his neck, where her fingers proceeded to do a little dance.

Skinny bitch!

She managed to leave the restaurant without Joel seeing her. So much for small favours.

The next morning the first thing she did was call him. His answering-machine picked up, so she tried him at his office.

'Joel won't be in for a few days,' said the girl with the green nails, or at least Rosarita assumed it was her.

'Is there anywhere I can reach him?'

'Who's calling?'

Oh, Christ! Here we go again, Rosarita thought. And she hung up.

Damn! Joel hadn't told her he was going away. But, then, why should he? They didn't have that kind of relationship. And the reason they didn't was because Dexter was in her way and refused to budge.

The sooner she got rid of him, the better off they'd all be.

* * *

The only good thing about them staying in the apartment was that it seemed to turn Dexter on.

'What *happened* to you?' she'd asked one night after a particularly vigorous love-making session.

'You're my wife,' he'd answered. 'I love you.'

'Sometimes love isn't enough,' she'd said.

'We'll see,' he'd replied.

165

Did he know something she didn't?

Martha was quite obviously entranced with Chas. Every word he uttered caused her to gaze at him with adoring eyes. *Major middle age crush*, Rosarita thought. How pathetic. Chas was hardly a matinée idol.

Chas, of course, got off on the attention. In the Cockrangers' eyes he was a big man living in a magnificent townhouse with a luscious girlfriend. He had many tales to tell about his colourful past in the construction business, and they ate it up. Especially Martha, while Matt couldn't take his eyes off Varoomba's tits – or Alice, as the family knew her. Mostly Rosarita ignored Chas's latest conquest. Her daddy might want to hang with trash, but there was no reason *she* had to be polite.

She hadn't been able to reach Joel for five days, which was pissing her off. Where was he? And, even more important, who was he with? When she finally did connect and asked him where he'd been, he was most uncooperative. 'Didn't know I had to check in,' he said, like she was nothing more than a casual acquaintance.

'I saw you the other night,' she said accusingly.

'Where'd you see me?'

'At Le Cirque with some skinny bitch.'

Joel chuckled. 'That skinny *bitch* happens to be a famous supermodel.'

'Famous, my ass.' Rosarita snorted. 'What's the difference between a supermodel and a showroom girl? No difference. Supermodel is merely a word the media made up. It means nothing. Anyway,' she added, finishing with the ultimate put-down, '*I*'ve never seen her before.'

Joel chuckled again. 'Don't go getting jealous,' he warned. 'She's too thin to be sexy. All bones and no tits.'

'Who's jealous?' Rosarita said, irritated that he would think she was.

'Wanna come by the office today?' he offered. 'Maybe around lunch-time?'

Yes, she did. But the last thing she needed was for him to think she was too eager. 'Depends what's on the menu,' she said casually.

'Who do *you* think should do all the eating today?' he asked. 'You or me?'

Now it was her turn to laugh. 'I *am* hungry,' she admitted.

'Then how about we go with a double-header?'

She was getting turned on already. 'In your office?'

'My desk. Your cute ass. Twelve thirty. I promise you a window-seat. Like that idea?'

Like it? She loved it. 'I'll be there,' she said. 'Only do me a favour and tell that moron working Reception to let me right in. I do not appreciate being kept waiting.'

'Jewel do something to offend you?'

'She needs firing.'

'See you later, babe.'

Rosarita quickly checked out the time. Ten thirty. Hmm . . . if she was going to indulge in a double-header, she *definitely* needed a bikini wax.

Shivering with anticipation, she called the Elizabeth Arden salon and made an immediate appointment.

* * *

'Have you heard the news?' Silver Anderson said, peering at Dexter with heavily made-up eyes.

'What news?' he said. He'd recently arrived at the studio and was waiting to go into Makeup.

'I hate to be the one to tell you,' Silver drawled, 'but you *should* know. You're one of my favourites, Dexter. You try hard and you look divine. You *will* be a star one of these days – mark my words.'

'What are you trying to say, Silver?'

'We're being cancelled.'

His stomach dropped. 'Cancelled?' he said, dismayed. 'When did you hear this?'

'I have my spies,' she said. 'And, naturally, being the star of the show, I hear everything first. They haven't made an official announcement, but I can assure you that within the next week you will get your pink slip. And, my dear, even though it seems positively ludicrous, so will I.'

'Jesus!' Dexter said, his stomach taking a further dive. 'I thought we were doing so well. I receive at least a hundred fan letters a week.'

'And *I* get thousands,' Silver said. 'However, it seems to make no difference. It's the executives at the network who make such foolish decisions, and unfortunately they're all mentally aged twelve. The fans mean nothing to them, they don't *care* what the audience wants.'

Dexter attempted to pull himself together and not look like this was the end of his world. 'What will they replace us with?' he asked.

'Who knows?' Silver said vaguely. 'Some boring teen drama full of pre-pubescent nobodies. It's shocking. And they're so lucky to have me, too.'

'I agree,' he said. 'You're such a star, Silver. You're so . . . so incredible. In fact,' he ventured, 'you're a legend in your own lifetime.'

She laughed. 'For a moment I thought you were about to say in your own mind.'

'What will you do?' he asked, trying to focus on her. 'Go back to L.A.?'

'I might,' she said. 'Or I could decide to stay in New York. I enjoy it here. Perhaps I'll even go to Europe. They positively *worship* older women in Europe. They understand that *we* are the ones who know all the secrets that make men very happy indeed.' She gave him a long, penetrating look. 'Does your wife make *you* very happy indeed, Dexter?'

He was embarrassed. He didn't care to discuss his sex-life with Silver Anderson, he admired and respected her too much.

'Yeah, we have a good . . . uh, satisfactory sex thing going,' he mumbled.

'I bet you do,' Silver trilled. 'You know, Dexter, darling,' she confided. 'In the old days I *always* slept with my leading men. It was a given.'

'You did?' He gulped.

'I considered it one of the perks of the business.' A low, throaty chuckle. 'And, believe me, so did they. However,' she sighed, 'things are different today.' She reached out a languid hand. 'Come over here, Dexter, come close to me.'

He felt like a deer caught in the sights of a particularly lethal rifle. Reluctantly he edged closer.

'Surely I don't scare you, do I?' Silver said, scaring the crap out of him.

'You're so . . . famous,' he blurted. 'Maybe I'm, uh, y'know, in awe of you.'

'You're a *very* attractive man,' Silver said, her voice getting deeper. 'And I've seen *many* attractive men in my time. Oh, I could tell you stories about some of the stars I've worked with. Burt Reynolds; William Shatner; even dear old Clint. But I've never been a believer in kissing and telling. I find that simply appalling. Although . . .' A naughty pause. 'If I *wanted* to tell, I'd have stories that would make Esther Williams's hair stand on end. Did you read her book? No, perhaps you didn't,' she said, gripping his hand firmly. 'You don't spend a lot of time reading, do you, Dexter?'

'Uh . . . no.'

She was making intricate little circles in his palm with her index finger.

In spite of himself, he felt a sudden and unexpected stirring in his pants.

'Lock the door, Dexter,' she said, in a low, sexy growl. 'It's time for your farewell gift.'

He tried to swallow but couldn't quite do so. Her hand was on his zipper. She was pulling it down.

Oh, God! If his dad could only see him now.

* * *

This time Rosarita was not prepared to take any crap. She swept into Joel's reception area, barely glancing at the girl with the green nails, who happened to be on the phone. 'Jewel, dear,' she said patronizingly, 'Joel's expecting me. He told me to go straight in.'

'He did?' Jewel said.

Rosarita smiled. She had lovely teeth, white and even; they'd cost Chas a fortune. 'Never mind, dear,' she said, and she was inside Joel's office before Jewel could give her one of her insolent looks.

Joel was on the phone, his feet propped up on the desk. He was actually fully dressed.

Rosarita slammed the door behind her. 'Welcome back,' she said, approaching his desk. 'Incidentally, where were you?'

He covered the mouthpiece with his hand. 'Fucking my brains out in Miami,' he said, with a lewd wink. 'Whyn't you sit down?' He went back to his conversation. 'Okay, babe,' he said, into the receiver. 'I'll see you later.'

Rosarita was dying to ask who was on the phone, but she was wise enough to keep her mouth firmly shut. It wouldn't be cool to push.

'How's it going?' he said, clicking off the phone.

'My in-laws are still in town,' she said. 'The moment they leave, Dex and I are going through with our divorce.'

He didn't exactly jump with enthusiasm. In fact, he didn't say anything. Instead he opened his desk drawer, took out a small glass vial of coke, tipped the powder on to the desk, arranged it in neat lines, handed her a short plastic straw and said, 'Take a snort, babe.'

It occurred to her that having people watch them have sex was one thing, but doing drugs with an audience across the street was quite another.

'Should we do this with people watching?' she said.

'What makes you think anyone's watching?' he countered.

'You walk around here most of the time with your crown jewels hanging out,' she said tartly. 'I'm sure you've got an avid audience.'

He roared with laughter. 'You're a trip.'

'So are you,' she retorted. And then she thought, *To hell with it, a little coke for lunch. Great for the figure. No food, just coke. Excellent choice.*

She took a delicate snort. He grinned at her and quickly snorted two lines. There was one line left.

'You or me?' he questioned.

'Go ahead,' she said graciously.

He did so. He had a big capacity. There was a little bit of white powder remaining on the desk top. Dampening his finger he placed it on the leftover powder and spread the residue on his gums.

'Take your clothes off, babe,' he said.

'Shouldn't we lock the –'

'How many times I gotta tell you?' he said, shaking his head. 'Nobody comes in here unless I invite 'em.'

Suddenly she was overcome with that same dirty feeling of excitement she always experienced around him. Quickly she unbuttoned her blouse and stepped out of her skirt. She'd worn a thong especially for him, and a lacy low-cut bra.

'You got any crotchless panties?' he asked.

'Of course,' she said, making a mental note to buy a few pairs.

'Wear 'em next time.'

She nodded, already anticipating his rough touch.

He stood up, dropped his pants and kicked them under the desk. 'Take it all off, babe, get up on the desk an' spread 'em,' he commanded.

Who was she to argue? She removed her bra, stepped out of her thong and climbed on to his desk.

'I *said* spread 'em, babe,' he said, parting her thighs. Then he crawled on top of her, employing the famous sixty-nine position.

And so the dance began.

Chapter Nineteen

Peter and Jamie drove Madison to the funeral in Connecticut. She was still in shock, struggling desperately to make sense of it all. 'It's surreal,' she mused, sitting in the back of Peter's BMW. 'I can't quite explain it – but it's like everything is happening in slow motion.'

'I know,' Jamie agreed, turning her blonde head to commiserate with her best friend.

'First of all, I find out Stella isn't my mother,' Madison continued, 'and before I even have a chance to talk to her, she's . . . she's gone.'

'What exactly did Michael tell you?' Jamie asked sympathetically.

'Not much. Apparently there was a robbery, and Stella and this guy she was living with were both shot. It's so . . . awful.'

'Goddamnit!' Peter muttered angrily. 'Nobody's safe any more.'

'Did they put up a fight?' Jamie asked.

'Who knows?' Madison said, thinking how strange Michael had sounded on the phone. There had been

173

something in his voice, a coldness she couldn't quite understand. Stella, his adored wife of over twenty-seven years was gone, and it was almost as if he'd completely disconnected.

Death affects people in different ways, she thought. *He'll probably fall to pieces at the funeral.* She wished for the hundredth time that she'd had an opportunity to talk to Stella, find out more about why she'd never been told the truth.

Too late now. There was no going back.

* * *

Michael greeted her at the door of the big country house. He was dressed in a black suit and appeared to be perfectly normal and at ease. She threw her arms around him and gave him a big hug. 'I'm so sorry,' she murmured, holding him tight, tears filling her eyes. 'It's such a tragedy.'

'I know,' he agreed, still sounding strange.

Before she could say anything else, he let go of her and turned to greet Jamie and Peter. She studied him for a moment, noticing that his eyes were not red-rimmed, which meant he hadn't been crying. Was it because Stella had left him for another man that he didn't seem upset? Could he be that cold?

She was beginning to wonder about the father she'd thought she'd known all these years. It was odd, but in many ways it was almost as if he was a total stranger.

A black limousine waited in the driveway to take them to the nearby church. Madison got in and sat next to Michael. He didn't say a word.

The funeral was a small affair, not more than two dozen people gathered in clusters. Victor had driven up from New York in a chauffeured car to show his respect. Embracing Madison, he murmured words of comfort. She thanked him and looked around, realizing that she knew hardly anyone. Most of the people there were the friends Michael and Stella had made in Connecticut. The only New Yorker she recognized was Stella's best friend, Warner Carlysle, a jewellery designer. Madison had known Warner since she was a kid, not intimately but well enough to be able to go over and exchange condolences. She wondered if Warner knew the truth about Stella not being her mother, and suspected that she did.

Warner was a tall, attractive woman, with short auburn hair and huge tinted shades. She seemed visibly distressed. 'I can't understand how this happened,' she said, obviously ill at ease. 'Why would anybody want to kill them?'

'It's all so crazy,' Madison agreed.

'Crazy is right,' Warner answered bitterly. 'Did they take her jewellery?'

'I have no idea,' Madison said, remembering Stella's magnificent collection of Art Deco treasures, and wondering why Warner would be worrying about that at a time like this. 'Stella was very security-conscious. I think she kept most of her good stuff in the bank.'

'Smart,' Warner said, adjusting her gold and emerald necklace.

'Uh . . . did you know the man she was living with?' Madison asked. 'Who was he?'

'Lucien Martin, an artist in his twenties,' Warner said, nervously fidgeting with her shades. 'The moment they met it was instant attraction, then a few weeks later she moved in with him.' Warner shook her head in disbelief. 'Now they're both gone.'

After the church service, everyone trooped out to the burial ground where there was another short ceremony. Then when that was over, there was a catered reception back at the house.

Warner was loading her plate at the buffet table when Madison approached her again. 'Was she *that* unhappy with Michael?' she asked.

'Your father never gave her the attention she craved,' Warner explained, piling more food on to her plate. 'Stella required constant assurance that she was the most beautiful creature on earth. After a time Michael got tired of telling her. Then she met Lucien, and he was there to tell her a thousand times a day.'

'What was he like?'

'A younger version of Michael,' Warner said shortly. 'And he adored her.' She walked over to the couch in the living room and sat down with her plate of food. Madison followed.

'Whatever you do, do *not* mention Lucien to Michael,' Warner said. 'Michael was very angry and bitter about Stella running off. In fact,' she paused for a long moment, nervously looking around, 'he even threatened her.'

'*Threatened* her?' Madison said, her heart beating fast.

'Yes, Stella was so scared that she and Lucien moved from his house into a high-security apartment. She shut herself off from Michael – didn't want anything from him, not his money, nothing. She was planning on moving to New York with Lucien to get away from him. Then Michael found out, and he was furious.'

Madison took a long, deep breath before speaking. 'You're – you're not saying he could have had anything to do with their deaths, are you?'

Warner stared at her with an impassive expression.

'We'll get together next week,' she said. 'I can't discuss it now.'

The woman's upset, Madison thought. *She doesn't know what she's talking about.*

'I found out the truth about Stella and me,' Madison blurted out, waiting for a reaction.

'The truth?' Warner said carefully, putting her plate down on the coffee table.

'Michael told me.'

'Oh, God, I thought he never would.'

'I guess you knew all along.'

'Yes,' Warner said. 'Stella and I were friends for over thirty years. I introduced her to Michael.'

'You did?'

'He was a friend of the man I was seeing then.'

'I had no idea they met through you.'

'Guilty, I'm afraid.'

'Here's my big regret.'

'What?'

'That I wasn't able to talk to Stella before this happened.'

'I'm sure it must be very difficult for you.'

'It is – especially as we were never really close. Stella was always kind of . . . I was about to say cold, but it was more like distanced, you know?'

'Yes, I do know, and that was because you weren't hers, and you never could be,' Warner explained. '*You* were the constant reminder that Michael had a great love before her. Stella needed to be number one in his life and she never felt she was.'

'How could she think that?' Madison said. 'Michael worshipped her.'

Warner nodded again. 'We have to talk, but this is not the place. I'll call you next week.'

'Please,' Madison said. 'I have so many questions I was hoping Stella could answer. Maybe you can answer some of them for me.'

'I'll try,' Warner said.

Somehow Madison got through the rest of the day. Then later, when most people had left, she asked Michael if he'd like her to stay the night. He said no. She didn't push it, instead she said goodbye and got into the car to return to New York with Jamie and Peter.

'Jesus!' Peter said, as they headed for the city. 'What a day.'

'Not one I'd want to repeat,' Madison said, with a weary sigh.

'How are you holding up?' Jamie asked.

'All I can say is thank God you both came with me,' she replied. 'I'm for ever grateful.'

'We wouldn't've let you go by yourself,' Jamie said.

'No way,' Peter added.

'It's so damn ironic,' Madison said, shaking her head. 'Today I buried a mother I never had. Isn't that something?'

Jamie nodded understandingly. 'You handled it well, as only you could.'

'Here's the thing,' Madison said softly. 'I love Michael very much, only right now I'm completely confused about everything. I have no clue who he is any more.'

'Come stay with us for a few days,' Jamie suggested. 'We're not crazy about leaving you alone in your apartment.'

'I'm *not* alone,' she said. 'I have a dog, and a doorman. Oh, yes, and David on the phone every day.'

'Scratch *him*.'

'And then, of course, there's Jake, who's somewhere in Paris and I have no idea where.'

'I hate to be mean,' Jamie said, 'but Jake sounds like a one-nighter.'

'Don't you mean a one-weeker?' Madison said wryly.

'I'm not saying he doesn't *like* you,' Jamie said quickly, 'only that he *does* seem to be Mr unreliable.'

'Why would you think that?'

'Well, wasn't he living with a call-girl in L.A.?'

'He wasn't *living* with her, it was a quick affair.'

'Listen, girls,' Peter interrupted, the voice of experience, 'any man who's sleeping with a call-girl is not exactly a winner in the love stakes. Because . . . if you have to pay for it –'

'He didn't *pay* for it,' Madison interrupted irritably. 'He wasn't aware that she was a working girl.'

'Oh, *please*,' Peter said, with a short, dry laugh. 'A man knows immediately.'

'How?' Jamie said, fixing him with a suspicious look.

'Those women have a certain technique,' Peter explained. 'It's all very professional.'

'How would *you* know?' Jamie persisted.

'I'm a man, aren't I?'

'A *married* man, Peter. And when did *you* ever pay for it?'

'Never did, darling.'

'Then how do you know all these things?' she asked accusingly.

'Bachelor parties,' he said, with a slight smirk.

'Bachelor parties!' Jamie and Madison exclaimed in unison. 'Didn't they go out in nineteen sixty-five?'

Peter laughed uncomfortably. 'You women,' he said, 'you'll never accept there's a double standard.'

'Bullshit!' Madison said.

'Crap!' Jamie said.

Later, when Peter pulled up his BMW outside Madison's apartment, Jamie was still worrying.

'I'll be fine,' Madison assured them. 'All I need is time and space to think things out.'

'Okay,' Jamie said. 'But don't forget, we're only a phone-call away.'

'Thanks,' Madison said, getting out of the car. 'It's pretty special to have friends I can rely on.'

'Love you,' Jamie said.

Calvin was delighted to welcome her back. 'Hope everything went all right, Miss,' he said, escorting her up to her apartment. 'I walked the dog about an hour ago, so he won't be needing to go out again.'

'Thanks, Calvin,' she said, letting herself in.

Slammer, out of the kindness of his heart, decided not to punish her. Instead he jumped all over her, thoroughly licking every inch of bare flesh he could find. She petted him for a minute, then went into the kitchen and threw him a treat. After that she did the usual ritual of checking out her answering-machine.

No Jake.

Plenty of David.

Damn! Where was Jake?

'Can we meet?' David's voice said. 'I think you owe me that.'

I owe you nothing, David, and I never will. Get over it!

The third call was from Kimm Florian. A cryptic 'Call me back immediately.'

So she did.

Kimm picked up on the first ring. 'I need to see you as soon as possible,' she said. 'I can come over now.'

Madison glanced at her watch, it was almost midnight. 'It'll have to be tomorrow,' she said. 'I just got back from a funeral and I'm out of it.'

'A funeral,' Kimm said slowly. 'Whose?'

'The woman who wasn't my mother.'

'*Stella* died?'

'I'm afraid so.'

'How did it happen?'

'The police said it was a home invasion. She and her boyfriend were shot.'

'Execution-style?'

'What does *that* mean?'

'Was it execution-style?' Kimm repeated.

'I don't know the details,' Madison replied. 'I only know they were both shot.'

'How early can you see me tomorrow?' Kimm asked, a certain urgency in her tone.

'Do you have news for me?'

'Yes, I do. And it's information you should hear at once.' A beat. 'I found out about Gloria.'

'What?' she said, her heart jumping. '*What* did you find out?'

'Can't tell you over the phone. I have to see you in person.'

'Come for breakfast.'

'I'll be there,' Kimm said. 'And, Madison, prepare yourself. You're not going to like what you hear.'

Chapter Twenty

Dexter was consumed with guilt, so much so that he could barely look at Rosarita. He was sitting at the table, pushing his fork around his plate without eating anything.

'What's the matter with you?' Rosarita finally said, irritated by his lacklustre attitude.

'Yes, dear,' Martha chimed in. 'You're awfully quiet tonight. Birdie got your tongue?'

'I, uh . . . heard something today,' he said, reluctant to share the news but unable to keep it to himself any longer.

'What was that, son?' asked Matt, chewing on a piece of steak.

'There's this rumour going around that they may be cancelling my show,' Dexter said glumly.

'Oh, my God!' Martha exclaimed in horror, her hand rushing to her mouth. 'They can't do that.'

'They can do whatever they want,' Dexter said, wishing his mother was right for once.

'Who told you?' Rosarita said, not revealing that

she'd been hearing the same rumour for the last couple of months.

'Silver Anderson.'

'Now *there*'s a fine woman,' Matt interjected, becoming quite starry-eyed. 'Hasn't aged a bit.'

'Of course she has,' snapped Martha, uncharacteristically bitchy. 'It's simply that your eyes have faded. You need glasses to see anything.'

Good for you, Rosarita thought. *You actually have a bit of spunk after all.*

'What will you do if the show's cancelled?' Matt asked, ignoring his wife's outburst.

'There's other opportunities,' Dexter said, moodily shoving his plate away. 'I have an agent. I'll talk to him.'

'Don't you think he should've talked to you first?' Rosarita said. 'If there's this rumour, why didn't *he* tell *you?*'

'I'm surprised he didn't,' Dexter admitted. 'It's not as if I'm unimportant at the agency. I have a lot of fans, you know. I receive hundreds of letters a week.'

'I'd love to read them, dear,' Martha said. 'What kind of things do people write?'

'They tell him all their sex fantasies,' Rosarita teased, a wicked glint in her eyes.

Dexter silenced her with a frown, then quickly looked away. Sex was a powerful weapon that women used, and Silver Anderson had used it on him. He couldn't stop thinking about what she'd done to him. God! He was a married man, and marriage was sacred. With all her faults, Rosarita would *never* dream of screwing around on him, yet he'd allowed himself to be used by Silver, and had done nothing to stop her. It was humiliating and demeaning.

Not that *he*'d touched *her*, but the fact that she'd

183

had his manhood in her mouth was enough to infuse him with overwhelming guilt. And he'd thought she was such a fine lady. *That* was a joke.

What would Rosarita say if she ever found out?

It didn't bear thinking about.

'When can we see Chas again?' Martha asked. 'I miss his smiling face.'

I bet you do, Rosarita thought. *I bet you'd like to get him in the sack. Only you're a little too old for him, dear. And your boobs droop.*

'We should plan a farewell dinner,' she said, thinking she couldn't wait until they got the hell out to Dodge. 'After all,' she added, smiling sweetly at Martha, 'you'll be leaving soon.'

Martha nodded sadly. 'I shall miss all the excitement,' she said. 'We're enjoying ourselves so much.'

'We certainly are,' Matt joined in, chewing on another piece of steak. 'Although I'm not happy with tonight's news.' He gave Dexter a penetrating look. 'What will you do next, son?'

'I told you,' Dexter said, thinking that as much as he loved his parents, this crisis was nobody's business except his own, 'my agent will have some ideas.'

'You should get into proper movies, dear,' Martha trilled, as if it were the easiest thing in the world. 'You could be another Harrison Ford. They *need* a younger Harrison Ford.'

'I'm sure my agent will know what to do,' Dexter assured them, wishing they'd all shut up. It was bad enough that he was about to be out of a job, he didn't need his family butting in.

After dinner, Matt and Martha settled in the living room to watch *Chicago Hope* on the big-screen TV. 'It's my favourite programme,' Martha admitted, a box

184

of chocolates by her side. 'Such a guilty pleasure. I wouldn't miss it for the world.'

'I told Mom I'd buy her a VCR for Christmas,' Dexter remarked, to no one in particular.

'That's all very well and good,' Martha said, downing two chocolates at once. 'The trouble is I'll never learn how to use it.'

'Dad'll get it going for you.'

'She knows I'm good with my hands,' Matt put in, with a lewd wink. 'And so she should, after all these years.'

Dexter wished his father would stop with the sexual innuendoes, it was unsettling to say the least.

More important, he didn't know how he was going to face Silver the next day. The show had not been officially cancelled yet, which meant that they'd probably be working together for weeks to come. How was he going to see her every single day? How was he going to live with the fact that he'd been unfaithful to Rosarita? Well . . . kind of. After all, President Clinton had publicly declared that a blow-job was not actually sex, so maybe things weren't as bad as he thought.

Perhaps he should tell Rosarita . . . confess . . .

No. That would be the worst thing he could do. She'd hold it against him, and then she'd definitely insist on going ahead with a divorce.

Every night he prayed to God that he'd knocked her up. If only things could stay the way they were until she discovered she was pregnant, he'd be safe.

As for Silver, he would just have to do his best to avoid her. He had no alternative.

* * *

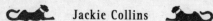

Varoomba turned up at the Boom Boom Club to collect her things. Chas had told her in no uncertain terms that he did not want her working there any more. And since he was prepared to set her up in an apartment and pay all her bills, he didn't want her working period.

Varoomba was delighted that she'd finally found a man who was ready to look after her. Sometimes Chas could be a little crass, but the thing she liked about him was that he was older, therefore he wasn't pawing her day and night like some of the younger guys she'd been with. One glimpse of her giant tits and it was usually non-stop action. Chas' action didn't last quite so long, which was a good thing, because Varoomba had experienced enough action to last several lifetimes.

She wasn't unhappy about leaving the club. There were too many freaks who came to watch her dance. Sometimes it was positively creepy the way they sat there like hypnotized zombies, dull, mesmerized eyes popping out of their sockets as she undulated in front of them. It was okay when it was some poor schmuck who was quietly admiring her body, and bachelor parties were okay too, but all too often there were sick perverts with strange and scary agendas.

Her boss, Mr Patent-leather Hair as the girls had christened him, was not happy she was quitting. 'Ya get a better offer?' he growled. 'If it's at another club, I'll top whatever they're givin' you.'

'No,' she said, busily packing up her makeup, wigs and various outfits. 'I've been seeing a gentleman friend who wants to have me all to himself.'

'*That*'ll last five minutes,' Mr Patent-leather Hair sneered.

'No it won't,' she said defensively. 'This man is very enamoured.'

'Enamoured!' Mr Patent-leather Hair bellowed. 'Enamour *me*, honey.' He coughed loudly, then said, 'I'll give ya an extra hundred to go out there and dance tonight, 'cause one of your fans has been comin' in all week, an' this dude's *desperate* t' see you shake it.'

'Who might that be?' she asked, curiously.

'That Joel guy.'

'Oh, *him*,' she said, wrinkling her nose. 'There's something freaky about him.'

'What's *your* beef?' Patent-leather Hair demanded. 'He's got plentya bucks to stick down your little titties.'

'*Little?*' Varoomba shrieked, quite insulted. 'That's the first time I've heard 'em called little!'

'I see you're gettin' a mouth now you're leavin'.'

Cramming a long black fall into her wig box, she thought about scoring some quick cash. 'How much did you say you'd pay if I dance for freako tonight?' she asked.

'An extra hundred.'

'Not enough,' she said, thinking that the more she managed to stash away the better. 'I gotta get outta here.'

'Okay – two hundred. That's as high as I'll go, an' you'll score a hefty tip from the schmuck.'

'Is he here now?'

'Yeah. Bin askin' for you all week.'

Two hundred cash. When her boobs dropped she'd better be prepared. 'Make it two fifty an' we got a deal,' she said.

'Jesus!' Mr Patent-leather Hair muttered in disgust. 'You hold yourself in high freakin' esteem for a stripper.'

'I certainly do,' she said, throwing him a haughty glare.

Mr Patent-leather Hair took off, while Varoomba tried to decide what outfit to dazzle them with for her farewell performance. How about her schoolgirl uniform? It was popular with all the guys. They got off on the crisp white shirt, red tie, blue pleated mini-skirt, proper cotton panties, white ankle socks and saddle shoes.

She put on the outfit and braided her hair in two cute pigtails. It was a look she should probably do for Chas one night – he'd be in heaven.

Well, there'd be lots of opportunities to show him plenty since she'd be taking all her costumes with her.

Mr Patent-leather Hair informed her that Joel was delighted to hear she was there, and had requested a private lap dance. She'd worked privately for him before. Last time he'd grabbed her tits, squeezing them so hard her nipples had been bruised for a week. *That* had cost him an extra hundred.

As soon as she entered the private cubicle she wagged a warning finger at him. 'No touching tonight,' she admonished. 'House policy.'

'Show me those big titties and shut the fuck up,' Joel replied, leaning back in his chair ready for a hot, lusty show.

'No bad language either,' Varoomba said, tugging on one of her pigtails. 'I'm a *good* girl. In fact, I'm a good little Catholic schoolgirl.'

And then she started to dance.

She had it down, moving to the music like the seasoned veteran she was, big tits swaying to the beat of Mariah Carey's 'Butterfly'.

Joel felt cheated because no one was watching

188

except him. Varoomba should be on public display for all to see. How could he get off without an audience?

He wondered how much it would cost to persuade her to come to his office at lunch-time.

Who cared about money? The question was, would she do it?

Yeah, she was a hooker. What other kind of girls got into the stripping business?

When she was down to her bra and panties, he asked her.

She swayed closer, shaking her boobs in his face. 'Sorry,' she said, allowing a large, dark nipple to graze his nose. 'I'm leavin' the business.'

'You don't wanna do that,' he said. 'You gotta get into private work, do special performances on your own time. Make some big bucks.' He sat up very straight. 'I'll pay you five hundred cash to come to my office tomorrow lunch-time.'

'Hmm . . .' she said, tempted by such a generous offer. 'Maybe I could do it later in the week. I'll let you know.'

'No sweat,' he said, grabbing her right boob. 'You gimme a call. An', babe, you will *not* regret it.'

Chapter Twenty-one

As tired as she was, Madison couldn't sleep. Kimm's call had disturbed her. *What* was she going to hear that she wouldn't like? What could it possibly be?

She lay in bed, tossing and turning, until eventually she switched on the light and made a half-hearted attempt to read.

Impossible, her concentration level was at zero. She clicked on the TV in the hope that it would work as a sleeping pill. No luck there. Damn! She refused to resort to David's bottle of Halcion, still sitting in her medicine cabinet. Drugs didn't do it for her.

Her mind was everywhere, it had been such a mixed-up few weeks and she found herself unable to calm down. David reappearing had not helped matters. What did he think? That she was going to rush back into his arms sighing, 'All is forgiven.'

Hell no. She would *never* forgive him.

And then there was Jake. What was *that* all about? Why hadn't he called? And, even more important, why did she care? After all, it was supposed to be casual sex.

No commitments. No promises.

But care she did, she simply couldn't help it.

She continued to toss and turn until five a.m., when she refused to struggle any more and finally got up, wondering if it was too early to call Kimm.

Yes, of course it was, so she didn't, although she was dying to. Instead she put on a thick sweater, jeans and boots, and took Slammer out for a marathon walk, stopping to buy bagels and cream cheese and two mugs of Starbucks coffee on her way home.

Picking up the *New York Times* from outside her door, she took it into her apartment, flopped on to the couch and started reading.

After a few minutes she realized there was no way the newspaper could hold her attention. Instead she kept thinking about the funeral and Warner and the things she'd said. Warner had indicated that Stella had been frightened of Michael, which seemed overly dramatic. It was understandable that Michael must've been pissed that Stella had run off with a guy half his age, but it was not in his makeup to frighten anyone, let alone threaten them.

Kimm's words kept running through her head too. *Were they shot execution-style?*

What the hell had she meant by *that*?

Madison got off the couch, toasted two bagels, spread them liberally with cream cheese and wolfed them both down. A great way to start the day. Very healthy. Thank God she never had to worry about her weight.

There was no way she was in the mood to do any research on Antonio 'The Panther' Lopez. Besides, she already knew plenty about him. How difficult was it to interview a boxer? He liked to fight, didn't he? He got off on beating up other men. Big deal.

If it wasn't for the fact that she was anxious to get away, she would've told Victor to have another writer cover the assignment.

Kimm arrived at eight-thirty. The tall, powerful, heavy-set woman was wearing a navy blue tracksuit and Nike running shoes, her broad face was devoid of makeup as usual, and her dark hair was braided down her back.

'I got you a Starbucks coffee,' Madison said, ushering her in. 'It's better than the crap I make. We can heat it up in the microwave.'

'Don't drink coffee,' Kimm said, rubbing Slammer's head. The dog seemed to have taken an instant liking to her. He started making happy sounds and Madison wondered if he knew something she didn't.

'Really? I can't live without it.'

'Water in the morning, juice in the afternoon, herbal tea at night.'

'Any alcohol in there somewhere?' Madison asked, half joking.

A faint smile flitted across Kimm's usually impassive face. 'Alcohol slows me down,' she said. 'So do tobacco and sugar. I've found that a healthy body creates a healthy mind.'

'Wish I could be that disciplined,' Madison said ruefully. 'It's not easy.'

'Nothing worth having is easy,' Kimm remarked.

Ah, a philosopher as well as a private eye, Madison thought. She hadn't made up her mind whether she liked Kimm or not: the woman did not exactly exude warmth.

'Let me get you a bottle of Evian,' she offered, walking into the kitchen.

'Room temperature will be fine,' Kimm called after her.

Abandoning the fridge, Madison reached into a lower cabinet and pulled out a bottle of water. 'It's been a while,' she said, coming back into the living room, handing it to Kimm. 'I thought I'd hear from you sooner than this.'

'Did your friend do the condom test?' Kimm asked, sitting down on the couch.

'You know, so much has been going on that I haven't asked.'

'Ask,' Kimm said. 'Make sure she does it.'

'Why?' Madison said, smiling. 'You need a new client?'

Kimm half smiled back. She had very large white teeth – not a cap among them. 'I never solicit new clients,' she said. 'They come to me on recommendations. Isn't that how *you* found me?'

'Yes,' Madison said, wishing she felt more alert. She hated not being able to sleep – it fuddled her brain. 'Now . . . uh . . . can we get down to business?' she said. 'You kind of unnerved me on the phone last night. Why did you say I'm not going to like what I hear?'

'Because I didn't want what I have to tell you to come as a shock,' Kimm said. 'Better prepared than not.'

'Prepared for *what?*' Madison asked, perplexed.

Kimm studied her gravely. 'I don't know you very well, although I *do* observe you to be a most together person. And observation is my business.'

'Thanks,' Madison said, not feeling at all together.

'So,' Kimm continued, 'do I sugar-coat it, or do I give it to you straight?'

'Straight,' Madison replied. *Straight before I go crazy!*

'I thought so,' Kimm said, getting up and walking across the room. 'I've read some of your interviews. I always think it's a good idea to know something about the person I'm working for.'

Get on with it! Madison's inner voice screamed.

'You're very insightful when it comes to other people,' Kimm continued, 'only you never investigated your own life.'

'Didn't know I had to,' Madison said flippantly, although – for some unknown reason – her stomach was busy doing flip-flops.

'What do you *know* about your father?' Kimm asked, giving her a long, steadfast look.

'That's a weird question.'

'It might be weird, but it's quite basic.'

'I suppose.'

'So?'

'Michael is a wonderful man,' she said slowly. 'And a terrific father.'

'What's his profession?'

'His profession?' Madison said, puzzled by this line of questioning. 'Well . . . he's actually retired, did that when he moved to Connecticut a few years ago. I know you're probably thinking he's too young to retire, but that was the whole point. He decided to enjoy himself while he was still young enough. You see, he and Stella – they like to travel, visit Europe, explore. They're always going somewhere – or, at least, they were. I guess Stella isn't going anywhere any more.'

'You're not telling me what your father's profession was.'

'Investments.'

'Sounds vague.'

'He made a lot of money.'

'I'm sure.'

'Lived extremely well. Still does.'

'I don't doubt it.'

'What are you getting at?' Madison asked, exasperated. 'Spit it out, Kimm, you're making me nervous.'

Kimm was silent for a moment before speaking. 'Your father was a hit man for the Mob,' she said at last.

'*Whaaat?*' The word fell out of Madison's mouth like a painful cry for help. 'That's – that's impossible.'

'Not impossible. A fact,' Kimm stated, her expression stoic.

Madison felt as if she were in the middle of some bizarre nightmare. *Wake up. Please wake up*, her inner voice urged.

No go, baby, this is actually happening.

'Why would you even say something like that?' she managed at last. 'It's – it's ludicrous, unthinkable, and totally untrue.'

'I'm afraid it's not,' Kimm replied, annoyingly calm and assured. 'Your father's real name is Vincenzio Michael Castellino. He changed it legally to Michael Castelli after the trial.'

'*What* trial?'

'The trial where he was accused of murdering your mother.' A long, ominous pause. 'And, oh, yes, her name wasn't Gloria. He lied to you about that too. It was Beth.' A short pause. 'I'm sorry to be the bearer of such devastating news, but unfortunately, this is the truth and . . . I have the evidence to prove it.'

Chapter Twenty-two

'I gotta surprise for everyone,' Chas announced.

Oh, no, Rosarita thought. *Chas and his surprises. What is he about to come up with now?*

She was in a good mood because this was the Cockrangers' farewell dinner.

Farewell, Matt.

Farewell, Martha.

And as soon as they were out of sight, farewell, Dex.

Chas had chosen to give them a dinner party at his house, where Varoomba, recently ensconced, was playing hostess.

What a joke, Rosarita thought. *How come he's allowed this big bimbo to move in with him? There's nothing more pathetic than an old guy with a young ding-bat. Especially a dummy like Varoomba with zonkers bigger than footballs.*

Chas had also invited Venice, Eddie and their two horrible little brats. Rosarita was less than pleased as she observed the action. Aunt material she was not.

When Martha wasn't playing flirty eyes with Chas,

she was busy fussing over Venice's kids. Matt, as usual, started drooling every time he sneaked a glimpse of Varoomba's voluptuous cleavage, and Dex seemed to be in a slump, which he'd been in ever since he'd had the official news of his show being cancelled.

It had not, Rosarita observed, affected his sexual prowess. What with her sessions with Joel a couple of times a week, and Dex every night, she was beginning to wonder if she had too much of a good thing going. There was only so much sex a girl could take.

'What's your surprise, Daddy?' Venice asked, all googoo-eyed and sugary as candy floss.

'For you,' he said magnanimously, 'it's a trip to Hawaii with the kids, all expenses covered.'

Rosarita's face fell. How dare he waste her inheritance in such a fashion? Venice didn't deserve shit. Certainly not a fabulous vacation.

'An' for you,' he said, turning to Rosarita, 'it's a trip to Vegas, 'cause I know how ya love it there.'

'Vegas?' she said blankly.

'Yeah, Vegas. I got us all tickets for the big fight. Whaddya think of *that*?'

What did she think of that? Not a lot.

'An' here's the kicker,' Chas continued. 'I'm throwin' in two ringside seats for Martha and Matt, 'cause Martha told me she's never bin to Vegas. An' if ya ain't seen Vegas, ya ain't lived.'

Martha clapped her hands together in ecstasy. 'Oh, my goodness!' she exclaimed. 'I'm *so* excited.'

Rosarita was dumbfounded. What the *hell* was going on? One minute she was telling Chas she wanted Dex knocked off, and the next he was inviting the whole gang to Vegas – *including* Dex and his stupid parents. She could happily *strangle* him.

Matt cleared his throat. 'I can't thank you enough,' he said. 'This is quite something.'

'Don't wantcha worryin' 'bout a thing,' Chas said. 'I know you're leavin' tomorra, an' the fight don't take place for another few weeks, so I'll be sendin' you plane tickets an' we'll all meet up in Vegas.'

For once Rosarita was speechless. She glanced at Dex to see how he was taking the news. He seemed oblivious, in his usual blue funk, damn him!

Hovering on the sidelines, Varoomba didn't say a word. She'd learned that when in Chas's company it was best to stay quiet, especially when his two daughters were around. Venice was okay, but the other one was a bitch on roller-skates, and Varoomba made sure to steer clear.

'So . . . whaddya think?' Chas said, beaming at the assorted company, getting off on playing big man on campus.

'Hawaii sounds dreamy,' Venice breathed. 'I've always wanted to go there.'

'Thanks, Chas,' Eddie said, brown-nosing as usual. 'We could all do with a vacation.'

'What about me?' Varoomba wanted to say, but she prudently kept quiet – not anxious to piss Chas off. If he *did* plan to take her to Vegas, it was probably best not to mention that she'd worked there at one time. In fact her grandmother, who used to be queen of the Strip, still lived there.

Rosarita couldn't wait to get her father alone. Oh, boy, was she going to give him a piece of her mind. On the way home she sulked in the car while Martha yammered on about what a fabulous evening they'd had, and how fantastic it was that they were all going to be meeting up in Vegas.

'*You* won't be able to come,' Rosarita said, shooting Dex a moody look.

'Why not?' he said.

'You'll be working.'

'No, I won't,' he said. 'This is my last week on the show. After Friday I'll be free to go wherever I want.'

'Oh, well, then,' she said sarcastically, 'I guess a nice little trip to Vegas is just what you need. Why *work*? Why not stand around *gambling* all day?'

'You're so goddamn negative. Why don't you shut the fuck up?' Dexter said, surprising everyone with his unexpected outburst.

'Are you *swearing* at me in front of your parents?' Rosarita responded furiously.

'Yes, dear,' Martha interjected, glaring at her son. 'It's not nice to use bad language. I thought I taught you that when you were a boy.'

'Yes, Dex, it's not nice,' Rosarita mocked.

'You know,' Martha said, oblivious to her son's bad mood, 'when Dickie was nine, he came home from school one day chanting the S word. I had to wash his mouth out with soap.'

'Did you now?' Rosarita said, enjoying every moment of Dexter's obvious embarrassment.

'We're all tired,' Matt said with a hearty yawn. 'It's been a hectic two weeks.'

'Actually, you mean *three* weeks,' Rosarita pointed out, silently adding that she'd counted every minute of every day, so she should know.

* * *

The next morning, as soon as she awoke, Rosarita was on the phone to Chas. 'What are you *thinking*?' she screeched.

'Huh?' Chas mumbled. 'Whassamatter?'

'I'm coming over to see you.' And before he could think of a way to stop her, she slammed the phone down.

Twenty minutes later she was at his house. Ignoring Varoomba, who was hovering in the front hall looking especially top heavy in a pink négligée, she swept past her into the library.

A few minutes later a reluctant Chas put in an appearance. He knew he was due for an ear-bashing and he also knew there was nothing he could do about it. When Rosarita was on a roll there was no stopping her.

'What is *wrong* with you?' Rosarita shouted, walking over and slamming the library door shut. 'I *told* you how I feel about Dex. How dare you invite him and his stupid parents to Vegas? I don't get it. You know what I asked you to do, and since you refused, I'll be forced to make other arrangements.'

'Shut your mouth with that bullshit crap,' Chas said, scowling. 'Do what everyone else does when they wanna divorce. Wait it out.'

'I'm not giving him half of everything,' she yelled. 'You bought *me* the Mercedes. The wedding presents are *mine*. The apartment is *mine*. He's getting *nothing!*'

'It's only money,' Chas said.

'Only money,' she said ominously. 'What happened to *you*? You used to be able to take care of things. *Now* look at you – you're turning into a senile old man.'

'Shut your damn mouth,' Chas repeated angrily, red in the face. 'Dexter's folks are decent people, an' even though he's a dumb actor he seems to be an okay guy. An' – more important, God help the poor bastard – he *loves* you. Where're you gonna find *that*? Most guys are assholes, an' you know it.'

She narrowed her eyes. 'What *you*'re saying is that *you* think I should sacrifice my chance of happiness and stay with Dex.'

'You could do worse.'

'And I could do better. And let me tell you . . .' A triumphant pause. 'I have.'

'Yeah?' he said, chewing his bottom lip.

'I wasn't going to tell you, Daddy, but I've been seeing somebody.'

'Dexter know about this?'

'Of course not,' she said, rolling her eyes at his stupidity. '*That*'s why I've got to get rid of him. Can't have him getting in my way, can I?'

'Who're you seein'?'

'I'm sure you've heard of Leon Blaine.'

Chas's mouth twitched. 'You screwin' that old fuck?'

'No,' she said scornfully. 'Not *him*. His son, Joel. He's crazy about me.'

'Joel Blaine is crazy 'bout you?' Chas repeated, certain his elder daughter was delusional.

'Don't sound so surprised, Daddy,' she said, slightly put out that he obviously didn't believe her. 'Men go wild for me, and since I have an opportunity to be with Leon Blaine's son, *I* think I should take it, and not be hindered in my quest to do so.'

'You . . . you're something else,' Chas said, shaking his head in wonderment.

'I'm not letting Joel Blaine slip out of my sight,' she said stubbornly. 'I have to do something fast.'

'You're talkin' crazy,' Chas said, scratching his chin. 'Crazier every day.'

'Fuck you!' she yelled, in frustration, because he simply didn't get it. 'You're no help. You're forcing me to deal with this myself. And I will. That's a goddamn promise!'

And before he could come up with a suitable answer, she slammed her way out of his house.

*   *   *

Joel waited for Varoomba to call him and keep their appointment. She didn't, which pissed him off because he'd had it all planned. He was going to have her dance for him on his desk, giving them a show across the street the likes of which they'd never seen. He was bored with Rosarita, he needed a new distraction, and Varoomba was it.

After a few days he contacted the manager at the Boom Boom Club, who informed him he had no idea where Varoomba had gone.

Jewel buzzed him at his desk. 'That woman's been on the phone again, the one with the Mexican name,' she said. 'What'll I tell her?'

'That I'm out,' he said shortly. '*Permanently* out to her.'

'Sure,' Jewel said, used to the way he treated women. They came. They went. They lasted a few weeks, then it was bye-bye and on to the next.

She was well aware of what went on in his office, but it didn't bother her, as long as *he* didn't bother her. And he never did, because as far as she could tell Joel Blaine sat in his office all day jerking off, which suited her fine. No e-mails, no faxes, no filing. Joel didn't know what work was. Besides, everyone knew that his daddy was the man with the power: Leon Blaine controlled everything. Poor old Joel was lucky if he got him on the phone once a week.

* * *

Meanwhile, Dexter was doing his best to avoid all contact with Silver Anderson. This was not easy since they were working together, and sometimes they had scenes to perform side by side.

The day after their show was officially cancelled, Silver had finally cornered him. 'You've been staying out of my way, you bad boy,' she'd scolded, wagging a beringed finger at him.

'N-not true,' he'd stammered.

'Yes, you have,' she'd admonished him. 'And I know why. It's because you are uneasy about putting me in a compromising position.' A pause. A smile. 'Actually, I think that's very gentlemanly.'

He wasn't sure what she meant, but went along with it anyway. 'You're right, Silver,' he'd said. 'I'd never want to see you hurt. And, as you know, I *am* a married man.'

'I understand, darling, and it makes no difference to me because I have absolutely *no* desire to steal you away from your wife.' A naughty giggle. 'All I did was suck your cock. No need for a melt-down.'

Dexter was shocked. How could a woman of her age and dignity talk in such a base fashion? If it meant he never had to see her again, then he was relieved the show was cancelled.

He'd called his agent two days previously. The man had failed to get back to him, which was not a good sign. But Dexter had confidence, he *knew* that something else would come along. He was quite sure

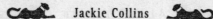

he was destined to be far more than one of the leads of a cancelled soap.

Yes, there were big things waiting for him, and when they came, he'd be ready to seize the opportunities.

Dexter Falcon was prepared for bigger and better.

Chapter Twenty-three

M adison had lived with the news for a week, one long nightmare week. She'd holed up in her apartment, not speaking to anyone, becoming a recluse, even turning the sound down on her answering-machine so she wouldn't have to listen to anyone's pleas to return their calls.

Kimm's information had shaken her to the very core. If she'd thought she was upset before, it was nothing to how she felt now.

Kimm had left behind a briefcase of documentation – old newspaper clippings, magazine articles, some video-tape of the trial. For several days Madison refused to go near it, but finally she'd given in and opened it, devouring everything it contained.

She'd soon found out that Kimm had been right. Michael *had* been arrested, tried and acquitted for her mother's murder. The facts were there in black and white, copies of numerous newspaper clippings full of allegations about Michael's past and the people he was rumoured to be involved with – including his lawyer, reportedly one of the best, hired for him by the man he allegedly worked for, the infamous Don Carlo Giovanni of the notorious Giovanni family.

She read the reports of the trial carefully. Michael and Beth had lived together in a house in Queens. While Michael was out one night, someone had broken in, shot Beth in the back of her head and fled. Madison – nine months old at the time – was asleep in her crib.

On the day of Michael's acquittal the newspapers were filled once more with the news, and his photograph standing on the courtroom steps making a victory sign with his right hand.

She studied the photos for a long time. Her daddy. Michael. He was so young, and he looked so different with his long, slicked-back hair, seventies-style suit and dark shades. He was still unbelievably handsome.

The first time she saw her mother's face was a photograph in the *New York Post*. Beth's innocent beauty took her breath away.

Later that night she'd stared at her reflection in the mirror and realized she was a combination of both her parents: it was uncanny – she was truly their child.

Kimm had asked her what Michael's profession was and she'd told her investments. Sure. That was vague enough. And she'd never questioned what he did. How naïve she was to have always believed him.

Kimm was right. How come she always found out everything she needed to know about her interview subjects and yet it had never occurred to her to investigate her own family? Why would she?

She was hurt, angry and confused.

Was it possible that she could ever face Michael now that she knew the truth?

Did she care?

No. He was lying scum and she hated him.

And yet . . . he was still her father.

As far back as she could remember Michael had always told her that neither he nor Stella had any immediate family. According to him, his parents had perished in a fire when he was a teenager, and he'd been raised by different sets of foster-parents, some of whom had abused him. Stella's story was that she'd run away from home when she was sixteen and had not contacted her family since that time.

So Madison had grown up accepting that she had no grandparents, no cousins, no relatives at all. Just Michael and Stella. Her loving parents. Or so she'd thought. What a sham!

She'd been raised in a New York apartment with either a maid or a nanny for company. At a very young age she'd been sent away to boarding school, while vacations were usually spent at summer camp. But there were times she *was* home, and she remembered them well. Sometimes Michael would go on business trips that lasted anywhere from a few days to a week. That's when Stella would lock herself in her bedroom and play classical music, telling Madison that she wasn't allowed to disturb her.

When Michael came home, he'd always bring her presents, teddy bears or dolls. As she grew older the presents were books, jewellery, gold pens – anything she wanted. She looked forward to him leaving because every time he came back it was like Christmas.

It was a lonely childhood, but since she didn't know any other kind, she'd assumed it was normal. Growing up that way, she'd learned to be satisfied with her own company. An avid reader, she'd always done well in composition at school and genuinely enjoyed learning.

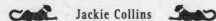

It wasn't until she'd gone away to college that she'd finally made friends. There she'd met Jamie and Natalie, and they'd become like the sisters she'd never had.

'I'm sorry to be the bearer of such bad news,' Kimm had said, before she'd left. 'Think about everything. I know you'll have more questions, so I'll come back when you're ready.'

She'd thought about it all right. She'd done nothing *but* think about it.

Your father was a hit man for the Mob.

Your father was accused of murdering your mother.

Your mother's name wasn't Gloria, it was Beth.

Kimm's words kept coming back to haunt her, she couldn't shake them.

She knew why Michael had said her mother's name was Gloria – he didn't want her digging and trying to learn more. Of course, he'd never expected that she would, but he'd done it just in case. Michael was a man who covered his tracks.

She needed to talk to Kimm again, meet with her to discuss everything, because Kimm was the only person who could possibly understand. They both had unspoken questions. Who was responsible for Stella's death? Was it Michael? Had he gone to Stella's apartment and shot her and her lover?

It was too horrifying to consider.

Another thought: should they inform the detectives investigating the double homicide of who Michael really was? Or would they figure it out for themselves?

Probably not. Why would they? He had invented a new identity for himself. His trial was almost thirty years behind him.

Sensing her distress, Slammer stayed nearby,

sleeping on her bed, gazing up at her with sympathetic doggy eyes, only slouching from the apartment when Calvin came to fetch him.

'I've got flu,' she explained to the concerned doorman. 'You'll have to walk Slammer for me until I feel better.'

'Sure, Miss Castelli,' Calvin said, only too happy to oblige.

The first thing she did when she started to emerge from the fog was call Kimm. 'I have to know more,' she said.

'I understand,' Kimm answered quietly.

'Can you come over?'

'I'll be there in an hour.'

Kimm, as usual, arrived on time. Striding into the apartment she took in Madison's appearance, which was dishevelled to say the least, and immediately asked, 'Have you been eating? You're about ten pounds thinner than the last time I saw you.'

'Would *you* be eating if you were me?' Madison said listlessly. 'For God's sake, everything I ever knew about my parents was a lie. I'm totally alone in the world, and that's the way it's been for the last week.'

'You're not alone,' Kimm said calmly.

'Maybe I'm having a nervous breakdown,' Madison worried, pushing a hand through her uncombed hair.

'You need help,' Kimm said briskly. 'Not to mention a shower.'

'What kind of help?'

'Do you see a shrink?'

'Don't believe in them.'

'I'm with you on that, but you *should* talk to someone.'

'I'm talking to you, aren't I?' she said testily. 'At

least *you* understand what I'm going through. I can't explain it to anyone else. And I don't intend to.'

Kimm nodded. 'Where's my water?' she asked. 'Room temperature, remember?'

'You're awfully bossy,' Madison said, managing a wan smile as she fetched Kimm a bottle of water.

'I know,' Kimm said, glancing around the apartment, zeroing in on the answering-machine. 'Are you aware you have sixteen messages waiting to be heard?'

'Would you be one of them?'

'No,' Kimm said, 'I expected you to phone me when you were ready.'

'Then don't worry about it,' Madison said, not interested in knowing who'd called her. 'I'm not in the mood to speak to anyone.' She stared at Kimm defiantly. 'That's my prerogative – right?'

'Hey,' Kimm said, holding out her hand to ward off bad vibes, 'do not take your nasty mood out on me. I'm merely here to try and help.'

'How *can* you help?' Madison demanded. 'How can you change what's happened to me?'

'Let's analyse the situation,' Kimm said, forever calm. 'What *has* happened to you? You were unaware of what your father did for a living, your mother wasn't your mother, your real mom was murdered, and your father was accused of the crime.'

'Great!' Madison interjected. 'I belong on Jerry Springer.'

'You're an adult,' Kimm continued. 'You can handle it. I always say that we can handle anything God hands us.'

'Here you go with your philosophy again.' Madison sighed. 'Where do you get these sayings?'

'You don't like my philosophy?' Kimm said. 'Maybe

you'd prefer to hear about *my* background.'

'Why?' Madison challenged. 'Is it worse than mine?'

'It's pretty out there,' Kimm said. 'You're a beautiful, successful woman with a great job, good health, everything going for you. I'm a six-foot-tall American Indian lesbian female, who could lose a pound or two. I was raped by my uncle when I was seven, knocked down by a car when I was ten and told I would never walk again. And when I was twelve I was raped by my brother, who then freaked out and murdered my entire family. He's now in a mental institution.' She paused before continuing. 'But I think you'll agree that I've done pretty well for myself. I have a successful business of my own – I don't have to answer to a soul. And although I'm not in a relationship at the moment, I've had some pretty good ones in my time. So here I am, a living, walking testament that you cannot spend every moment worrying about what's happened in your past, you have to get on with the future.'

'Jesus!' Madison said. 'Talk about a depressing story.'

'And I survived,' Kimm said.

'You certainly did.'

'Moving on,' Kimm said, matter-of-factly. 'It's the only way.' She took a long swig of Evian from the bottle. 'Have you talked to your dad?'

'No. And I don't intend to.'

'Okay,' Kimm said carefully. 'If that's the way you want it.'

'I do. He deserves to be punished for lying to me all these years.'

'If that's how you feel.'

'It's *exactly* how I feel.'

'Then you must follow your instincts.'

'You know,' Madison said hesitantly, 'we haven't discussed it, but about Stella and her boyfriend.' She paused, it was difficult voicing her fears, saying the words aloud made her feel weak and vulnerable – emotions she was not used to and didn't like. 'You, uh, don't think Michael could've had anything to do with their deaths, do you?'

Kimm was silent for a moment. 'It's possible,' she said. 'I have a friend who was able to check out the police report. There *was* a break-in. They were both shot execution-style – in exactly the same way your real mom was murdered.'

'Oh, God!' Madison groaned. 'This is insane.'

Kimm put a comforting hand on her arm. 'Distance yourself,' she said. 'Let it go. That's what I had to do.' A long beat. 'I'm warning you, if you can't do that, you'll be pulled under and drowned.'

'What do you have on your office door?' Madison asked wryly. 'Private eye slash shrink?'

'I have no office door,' Kimm replied, with a faint smile. 'I work out of my apartment. It's more discreet that way.'

'Of course,' Madison said. 'You do everything your way.'

'And why not?' Kimm responded. 'It works for me.'

'Here's the thing,' Madison said. 'Do we tell the detectives what we know?'

'No point in rushing to do anything you might regret,' Kimm said thoughtfully. 'After all, what *do* you know? Nothing concrete.'

Madison nodded her agreement. 'So,' she said. 'What do you have for me today? More good news?'

'Maybe,' Kimm said, taking another long swig of

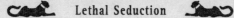

water. 'I've found out that your mom had a twin sister. I've got her phone number. She lives in Miami. I thought you might want to speak with her.'

'God, yes!' Madison said, and found that she could barely breathe.

Chapter Twenty-four

Wearing dark glasses and a cashmere scarf over
her tell-tale red hair, Rosarita met with a man
in a coffee shop who'd been recommended
by her dentist as a person who could take care of
anything. Of course, her dentist had not known what
she wanted taking care of, and neither did the man – a
sorry specimen in a grubby raincoat, with coarse,
flyaway hair and a bad facial tic. She loathed him on
sight.

'What can you do for me?' she said, choosing her
words carefully in case he turned out to be an
undercover cop.

'Anythin' you be wantin', ma'am,' the creature said.
'Garbage disposal, pet clean-up, gutters, drains, roofs.'

'What's pet clean-up?' she asked, thinking it
sounded kind of promising.

'If you got animals who done messed up your rug –
that kinda thing,' he said, facial tic going full force. 'I
be your man t' take care of it.'

'How about,' she said, speaking very slowly and
precisely, trying to make sure he understood what she

was getting at, 'if I had a . . . *dead* animal?'

'We can be removing the body, ma'am,' he said, oblivious to her hint.

She laughed, trying to keep it light. 'And . . . if it was a dead . . . *person?*'

His facial tic accelerated. 'Oh, no, no, wouldn't be dealin' with that kinda thing,' he said. 'That be work for an undertaker.'

Rosarita slammed down some money for the coffee, got up and left. It was obvious that her dentist had had no idea what she was looking for. *Damn!* How did you go about hiring a hit man when your father refused to help? She was very mad at Chas. He could take care of her problem with no trouble at all. So why wouldn't he? Bastard!

That afternoon she had an appointment with her gynaecologist. Not her favourite way of spending the day, but a boring necessity.

Dr Shipp was a distinguished-looking man with silvery sideburns and a gentle touch. Rosarita was sure that he found her extremely attractive. Well, why wouldn't he, when she was lying with her feet in the stirrups and he was getting a bird's-eye view of Paradise?

'How are you feeling today, Rosarita?' Dr Shipp inquired, entering the examining room, his prissy-faced nurse hovering discreetly by his side.

'How would *you* feel, Doc, if *you* were lying here with your feet up in stirrups exposed for all to see?'

'I would be glad that I had such an understanding doctor,' he said, putting on a pair of thin rubber gloves.

She wondered if he could tell by examining her that she'd been indulging in a flurry of activity. Husband every night, boyfriend every other day – although for the last week she hadn't heard from Joel and had been unable to reach him, which was pissing her off.

'You look a touch inflamed down there,' Dr Shipp said, probing and poking with his rubber-covered fingers.

'I have a very enthusiastic husband,' she replied, with a saucy wink.

'I'll prescribe some cream,' he said, ignoring her comment. 'Make sure that whenever you have sex you're always fully lubricated. It's most important.'

Oh, he should only know!

After a few more minutes Dr Shipp was finished with his examination. 'Let's take a look at those breasts of yours,' he said. 'Any unusual lumps?'

Yes, Joel's balls, she wanted to say. *Two little lumps of sugar, which I love trying to cram into my mouth. And I miss them.*

'No, Doctor, everything's fine,' she said, as he palpated her perky man-made breasts. 'Although I have been feeling tired. It's probably because my in-laws were in town driving me totally nuts. Extremely demanding people.'

'That could be it,' Dr Shipp said. 'I'll take a urine sample anyway, check what's going on.' He left the room while she dressed.

Outside his office, she used her cellphone to call Joel.

'Not in,' snapped Jewel. 'Won't be back today.'

'Have you given him my messages?' Rosarita demanded, wondering where the hell he was.

'Sure have,' Jewel replied.

Rosarita didn't believe her. The girl was a bitch. That was obvious to anyone.

She hurried out of the building, hailed a cab, and sulked all the way home.

* * *

'That was your Mexicana honey again,' Jewel announced, hovering in the doorway of Joel's office, her corn-rowed hair newly blonde in the front. 'She doesn't give up, does she?'

'Keep saying I'm out. She'll go away,' Joel said. 'I had to change my home phone number.'

'I know,' Jewel said, tapping her lethal nails against the door jamb. 'You forgot to give it to me.'

'Has Varoomba called?'

'Varoomba?' Jewel shrieked, pencilled eyebrows shooting up. 'What kind've a name is *that*?'

'You heard,' Joel replied. 'Did she call?'

'Not as far as *I* know.'

'If she does, put her right through.'

'Yes, *sir*,' Jewel said, returning to her post.

As soon as she was gone, Joel opened his desk drawer and took out a small glassine envelope of coke. Emptying out the contents, he arranged the white powder neatly on his desk-top. Then he snorted it line by line.

He couldn't believe that some dumb stripper was giving him a hard time. Varoomba had promised she'd call and come to his office. He'd offered her five hundred dollars to do so. So where was the bitch?

Joel was unused to women letting him down. He picked up the phone and spoke to one of his super-model girlfriends. If they weren't away on some highly paid modelling gig, one or other of his harem of supermodels was usually available. They liked to be seen as much as *he* liked to be seen with them. It was a mutual let's-get-our-photo-in-the-gossip-columns society. And they got off on the coke and champagne and all the other perks of going out with Joel Blaine. Frankly, he found most of them sexually unexciting – too stick thin and certainly not into public sex. Try fucking a supermodel in the back of your Rolls with an avid audience and you'd get exactly nowhere. Plus they *never* gave head – they considered themselves far too famous and pretty.

There *were* exceptions. Joel knew most of them.

He fixed up a date with an anorexic brunette for that evening, then decided to leave early.

Jewel was sitting at her desk outside his office painting her alarming nails in intricate red and white stripes.

'If anybody needs me, I've gone to a meeting,' he said, thinking that any guy who got his cock within two feet of those lethal nails needed serious therapy.

'Sure, Joel,' Jewel said, thinking, *Who is he kidding?* The last legitimate meeting he'd attended had been months ago.

Joel pressed the elevator button and waited impatiently for it to arrive while trying to make up his mind how to spend the rest of the afternoon. He had choices. He could drop in on a weekly poker game with the guys, or he could go work out at the gym – *not* one of his main priorities. Then again he could drive straight home, settle down on his oversize couch in front of his oversize TV and watch sports; maybe place a few bets with his bookie.

As these thoughts went through his head, the elevator doors opened and there stood his most unfavourite person in the world – Marika, his father's significant other.

Marika was a very tall, very thin Asian woman with ebony hair pulled back into a severe bun, deadly slanted eyes, thinly pencilled eyebrows and the expression of a sphinx. She and Leon Blaine had lived together for several years, ever since Leon had dumped his wife of thirty-five years, giving her almost a billion dollars and the opportunity to start anew. Joel's mother had promptly hot-footed it to New Zealand where she'd shacked up with a farmer, and was currently living happily ever after.

Joel had visited his mother once. Once had been more than enough.

'Hello, Joel,' said Marika, barely cracking a smile.

'Hello, Marika,' he replied, stepping into the elevator.

'Going down?' she said.

Oh, did he have an answer for her!

He nodded.

'Your father and I were discussing you this morning,' Marika said, snapdragon eyes boring right through him.

'Really?' Joel answered. He hadn't run into Leon for a few weeks, and he certainly didn't miss him. 'What were you saying?'

'Your father has decided to go to Vegas for the upcoming championship fight. He'd like you to accompany him.'

Shit! Joel thought. What the hell was *Leon* going to Vegas for? Joel already had his ringside ticket for the fight, and plans to spend time with the guys – not to mention hitting all the casinos and strip clubs. Now, if Leon wanted company, he'd have to be there for him. What a goddamn *waste!*

That was the problem with having a rich and

powerful father: if he wished to inherit he had to jump – exactly like the girls he dated. Trouble was, he'd been jumping ever since he could remember, and he was getting tired of it.

'Sounds good,' he mumbled, attempting to summon up a modicum of enthusiasm.

'We'll take the plane early,' Marika said, still staring. 'That way we can have dinner and see a show.'

We, Joel thought. Was Leon dragging along the prison guard? Well, if that was the case – 'Should I bring someone?' he said.

'Do you have someone . . . suitable?'

Boy, would he like to ram it to this cunt! She was so fucking rude he couldn't stand it. 'How about Carrie Hanlon?' he said, naming the top supermodel of the moment.

'Are *you* dating Carrie Hanlon?' Marika asked, barely able to conceal her surprise that he could score such a prize.

'No big deal,' Joel said casually. 'Carrie and me, we see each other on a fairly steady basis.'

'Does Leon know?'

'Dunno.'

'She's very pretty,' Marika allowed, her tone indicating that she was amazed that a successful supermodel like Carrie Hanlon would choose him.

'Yeah, she is and, uh . . . nice, too.'

The truth of the matter was that he had met Carrie Hanlon once at a party, and she was an utter bitch. She'd turned down his offer of a date, and a movie-actor friend of his who'd taken her out on two occasions had told him she gave 'balls-breaker' a whole new meaning. But, still, every woman had her price . . . and it shouldn't be too difficult to find out what Carrie Hanlon's was.

'I'll tell your father it's all arranged,' Marika said, as the elevator reached ground level and she swept out. 'He'll be pleased.'

Marika, of course, had a chauffeured car waiting outside the building. Joel had not managed to score such a perk although he *did* drive a Maserati, which his mother had bought him for his last birthday.

'Goodbye, Marika,' he muttered, as the elevator continued down to the parking level. 'Always a pleasure.'

Now he had to work on getting Carrie Hanlon for the Vegas trip.

Oh, well, at least it gave him something to do.

* * *

Two days later Rosarita awoke with a feeling of deep gloom. She hated having Dex home all day, hated seeing his handsome face lying beside her in bed when she woke up, abhorred having to eat every meal with him.

'I'm staying in bed today,' she announced. 'I'm not feeling well.'

'What's the matter?' he asked.

'I have a headache,' she said, 'and my stomach's queasy. It was that Chinese food last night.' She glared at him accusingly. '*You* picked the restaurant. I *told* you it was shit.'

'No, Rosarita,' he said patiently. '*You* picked the restaurant.'

'Well,' she said truculently, refusing to let him off the hook, '*you* took me there.'

'I'm sorry you're not feeling good,' he said. 'Is there anything I can get you?'

221

'Some juice,' she said, pulling the sheet to her chin.

'That's not good for your stomach. Too much acid.'

'Then don't ask me if I want anything,' she said peevishly.

'I'll have Conchita make you a cup of herbal tea and some toast,' he said, wishing she could be a little nicer to him. Right now he needed love and support, not constant bitching.

'Sounds *very* appetizing,' she sneered, stepping out of bed, grabbing her silk robe and marching into the bathroom before him.

The reason she was in such a bad mood was because it had started to occur to her that Joel was never going to accept her calls again. He was being utterly unfair, although she knew why he was doing it. Joel was obviously furious that she was still married and hadn't dumped Dex. He'd had enough. And rightly so. If the situation were reversed she would feel exactly the same way.

One thing she knew for sure, she was *not* letting Joel Blaine slip away: he was far too important a catch.

She, Rosarita Vincent Falcon, was going to be the first Mrs Joel Blaine – even if it killed her.

Chapter Twenty-five

'I don't get it,' Victor boomed, his deep voice louder than ever. 'It's not like you to drop out of sight. And now you've done it twice.'

'I've had personal problems,' Madison explained, hoping that he'd let it go at that, sure that he wouldn't because Victor was one of those people who had to know everything.

'Something to do with the detective you wanted to hire?' he asked.

'No, Victor,' she said brusquely. 'Nothing to do with that.'

'Then what?'

'Hey, listen,' she said, her voice rising. 'Aren't my personal problems mine? Isn't that the way things are supposed to work?'

'Is it David?' Victor asked, determined to find out.

'No, it's not David,' she said, hanging on to her patience by a thread. 'When will you get it into your head that David is my past?'

'No need to get snippy.'

'Anyway,' she sighed, 'thought I'd check in, because

I know you get panicked when you don't hear from me. I've been researching the boxer – he'll be an interesting interview. And I haven't talked to Jake Sica, but I will.'

'No need,' Victor said. 'He already called me.'

'*He* called *you?*' she said, thinking, *Oh that's great, isn't it? I sleep with the guy and it's Victor he calls. What the hell is the matter with him? Are all men totally into themselves?*

'He phoned from Paris to find out if the magazine wanted to use him again,' Victor said. 'I told him we both thought it was a good idea for him to cover the Vegas fight with you.'

'You did, huh?' she said evenly.

'That's what you wanted, isn't it?'

'It's what I wanted a week ago. I'm not so sure now.'

'Why?' Victor said, prying as usual. 'Haven't you heard from him?'

'Of course I've heard from him,' she lied, although the truth was that when she'd played back her sixteen messages, there hadn't been one from Jake. And that was something else to add to her pile of woes. 'Am I supposed to see him in Vegas, or is he coming through New York?' she asked, all business.

'Said he'll let me know. Or you. Whichever one of us gets lucky. And from what I can tell,' a crafty chuckle, '*you*'ve already gotten lucky.'

'Drop it, Victor,' she said coldly. 'As I've told you before, I really do not appreciate you messing in my private affairs.'

'You're very testy, Madison.'

'And *you*'re very nosy.'

'I sent Evelyn flowers from you. Orchids, in case

you're interested. She was delighted, wants to set a new date.'

'Oh, for Crissakes, I'm not in the mood for dates.'

'Evelyn insists.'

'Tell Evelyn to shove it up her ass.'

'Madison!'

'Sorry, Victor,' she said, with a sigh, putting down the phone.

At least she'd taken care of business. She couldn't let her career go south while she worried about everything else.

She'd taken a trip to the photo shop around the corner and had the newspaper photo of her mother blown up and laminated. Now it stood on her dresser, this picture of a beautiful woman with soulful eyes and clouds of black, curly hair. This beautiful woman who was her mother.

We have the same hair, she thought. *The same cheekbones, the same eyes. We look exactly alike, except Beth is prettier than me.*

There were messages from Michael on the machine, and from David, who was obviously intent on calling her until she gave in and met up with him – which she had no intention of doing. There were other business calls. And several entreaties from Jamie to please phone back immediately because she and Peter were worried about her.

She hadn't planned on returning any calls, only Victor's, but Jamie was important to her, and it wasn't fair to shut her out, so she picked up the phone. 'Before you say anything,' she said quickly, as soon as Jamie answered, 'I'm sorry, sorry, sorry.'

'I understand you feel like shit,' Jamie said, a tad

uptight, 'but couldn't you at least let your friends know you're still alive?'

'Jamie, please understand. There's so much going on, more than I can tell you over the phone. It's really bad.'

'What?' Jamie said, sounding alarmed. 'Are you sick?'

'No, it's . . . more things about my past.'

'Bad things?'

'Remember the detective who was supposed to work for you? I had her kind of check out some stuff for me, and what she's come up with is . . . oh, God, it's impossible to talk about now.'

'Anything I can do?'

'Nothing, except be there when I need you.'

'I'm always here, so is Peter, but please don't shut us out. It makes me nervous.'

'I promise.'

'And the next time you ignore your phone for days on end, I'm coming by and breaking down the door. Is that understood?'

'Absolutely.'

'As a matter of fact,' Jamie said, 'I called your doorman, the one with the crush on you. He informed me you had flu and didn't want to see anybody. I told him to go to the deli and buy you chicken soup. Did he?'

'Yes,' Madison said, laughing softly. 'And he wouldn't let me pay for it.'

'Good,' Jamie said.

'Not good. It puts me in his debt, and I hate that.'

'It's only chicken soup, Maddy.'

'Okay, okay, you're right.'

'Now,' Jamie said, 'when can we get together?'

'In a few days.'

'Don't you think talking about things will help?'

Madison realized it probably would, only right now she wasn't in the mood. 'Not yet, okay?' she said, hoping Jamie would understand.

Fortunately – good friend that she was – Jamie did. 'Fine,' she said. 'But don't forget, whenever you're ready, I'm here.'

* * *

As soon as she hung up, Jamie called Peter at his office. 'I finally heard from Madison,' she announced.

'Thank God!' he responded. 'Now you can stop worrying.'

'*You* were worried too, you have to admit it.'

'Only until we talked to her doorman.'

'Don't you think it's strange that she didn't pick up her phone or call me? After all, she *is* my best friend.'

'I imagine the funeral took it out of her.'

'I'm sure it did.' A beat, then Jamie moved right on. 'Anyway,' she said, bubbling with enthusiasm, 'I've come up with a fantastic idea.'

'What now?' he said, always wary of his wife's fantastic ideas.

'Natalie will be in Vegas for the fight. And Madison's on assignment for her magazine interviewing one of the boxers.'

'So?'

'So if I was there too,' she said quickly, 'it would be like a real reunion. We'd all be together for Maddy's birthday, and we could throw her a surprise party on the night of the big fight. Doesn't that sound like a terrific idea?'

'Haven't you forgotten something?' Peter said.

'What?'

'Vegas is my most unfavourite place in the world and, much as I love you, my darling, I do *not* plan on spending one single minute there.'

'Oh, Peter – *please*. It would be such a great surprise for her.'

'No, honey,' he said, mind made up. 'Anywhere else but Vegas. That place makes me nauseous, I can't do it.'

'*Peter!*'

'I *said* no. I do most things you want, but not this.'

Peter had a strong stubborn streak, so Jamie knew there was no point in pushing any further. 'It was just an idea,' she said dejectedly. 'I thought it would be fun to surprise Maddy, especially as she's so down. All of us being there would make her birthday special.'

'We'll send her flowers,' he said. 'We'll buy her a present at Tiffany's – we'll even have a party for her when she gets back *and* fly Natalie in. How's that?'

'I guess,' Jamie said, barely able to conceal her disappointment. *Hmm*, she thought. *What's so terrible about Vegas that he can't make an effort to spend a couple of days there?*

Peter was a wonderful husband and lover, but sometimes he could be downright selfish, and this was obviously one of those times.

That night, when Peter arrived home, she tried persuading him again, but soon realized it was a no-go situation.

Later, when he wanted to make love, she informed him she had a headache, and rolled across the bed putting space between them. Then she picked up a copy of *In Style* and began to read.

'Okay,' Peter said, not sounding too upset. 'Reject your husband.' And he clicked on the TV, immediately channel-surfing to a ball game.

Ten minutes later he was asleep, the clicker clutched firmly in his hand.

Jamie put down her magazine and gently tried to extract his precious clicker from his hand. Since every man considers the clicker an extension of his penis, this was not an easy task. Even in his sleep Peter held firm. 'I'm watching,' he mumbled.

Ha! she thought. *You won't go to Vegas to make your wife happy. You won't even let me watch what I want. Why can't you be generous and giving, like me?*

She wasn't about to stay in bed staring at a stupid ball game, so she got up and went into the spacious walk-in closet they shared.

The first thing she noticed was Peter's wallet sitting on top of his dresser.

It occurred to her that she'd never done the detective's little test. It seemed so foolish. Why would Peter be carrying a condom when they never *used* condoms? The whole thing was ridiculous.

However . . . what did she have to lose?

Nothing to gain either, but still . . . It was too tempting to resist so she reached for his wallet, an expensive black alligator number she'd bought him at Gucci two Christmases ago, and felt guilty because early on in their marriage they'd agreed never to invade each other's privacy.

Gingerly she opened the wallet. Credit cards. Money. A photo of the two of them on their honeymoon. And a condom.

A CONDOM!

She could hardly believe her eyes. A condom in his

wallet, exactly as the detective had suspected there would be.

Oh, my God! she thought. *This is totally bad.*

Her first instinct was to race into the bedroom, shake him awake, and say, 'What in God's name are you doing with a *condom* in your wallet?'

But she didn't. She stayed calm, remembering what Madison had said. She fetched a felt-tip pen from the study, went into the dressing room and made a tiny mark on the corner of the package. Then she put it back exactly where she'd found it, leaving his wallet in the same place.

Seething with fury, she climbed into bed, only to discover that Peter was snoring, a half-smile on his face.

Damn him! What if Madison and the detective were right? What if when she looked again the condom was replaced with a fresh packet?

She'd kill him, that's what she'd do. She'd cut off his precious dick, slice it off just like Lorena Bobbitt. Only she wouldn't throw it out of a car window, she'd stuff it down the waste-disposal where it belonged.

Revenge had no fury like Jamie – the perfect stylish blonde.

* * *

Madison and Kimm were eating lunch in a small Italian restaurant on Lexington. Over spaghetti bolognese and large mixed green salads, Kimm filled her in on Beth's sister, whom she'd managed to locate by phone. According to Kimm, the woman was Beth's twin, and refused to have anything to do with Michael. She was especially concerned that he did not find out where she was.

'I told her it was you who wanted to meet her, but

she was adamant, wants to completely forget her past.'

'I'm her niece,' Madison said, frustrated. 'How can she say she doesn't want to meet me?'

'That's how it is,' Kimm said, shrugging.

'She's the only clue to what really happened,' Madison said, frowning. 'The only person other than Michael who can tell me anything about my mother.'

'Perhaps you should confront Michael,' Kimm suggested. 'Tell *him* what you know. That way he'll be forced to open up.'

'No,' Madison said. 'He may be my father, but he's a liar, and I need to find out the real truth, not a bunch of bullshit. I'm flying to Miami. She *has* to see me.'

'You're sure you want to take a chance that she will?'

'Positive.'

'Then I guess I'm coming with you.'

'You don't have to.'

'Sure I do,' Kimm said. 'Knowing you, you'll arrive at the airport and get lost.'

'I'm *very* together,' Madison said. 'You told me that yourself.'

'You *were* together. This whole thing has affected you. God sent me to look after you.'

'Oh, please,' Madison groaned.

'Don't worry,' Kimm said, with a rare smile. 'I'm not about to hit on you. I keep my lesbian tendencies to myself unless I'm sure they'll be reciprocated.'

'That's a relief,' Madison said drily.

The two women exchanged smiles of friendship. They had discovered something that bound them together, and it made for a closeness that was new to both of them.

'We'll fly there tomorrow,' Madison decided, the very thought making her stronger. 'I'll organize everything.'

Chapter Twenty-six

'Y ou're pregnant.'

'I'm *what?*' Rosarita shrieked.

'Pregnant, Mrs Falcon,' Dr Shipp, her gynaecologist replied, his phone manner congenial.

'Are you *sure?*'

'I wouldn't be telling you if I wasn't,' Dr Shipp said, clearing his throat. 'I'd like you to make an appointment for next week. We'll discuss everything then.'

Rosarita was in shock. *Pregnant!* This was impossible. She always wore her diaphragm – never had sex without it.

'You must have made a mistake,' she said, into the phone.

'No mistake,' the doctor said cheerfully. 'I'll see you next week, Mrs Falcon. Congratulations.'

She hung up, still in a state of shock.

This was impossible news. She hated babies, scrawny little things with scrunched-up faces who screamed all night. Plus if she was pregnant, she would *definitely* lose her figure. And the pain of childbirth – she'd heard about the horror of it from some of her friends.

No! No! No! This wasn't happening to her.

Abortion. The word slid into her mind immediately. A quick, convenient abortion.

Then she remembered, the first time she'd got together with Joel in his car she had not been wearing her diaphragm. Which could only mean one thing: this baby was Joel's because she'd never had sex with Dex *without* using her diaphragm.

I'm pregnant with Joel Blaine's child, she thought. *Leon Blaine's grandchild. Leon Blaine, the billionaire.*

OH . . . MY . . . GOD!

This solved some of her problems. Although it didn't get rid of Dex, and he was the biggest problem of all. Right now he was out meeting with his agent and would not be back for a while.

Rosarita took to her bed to think things through. Being pregnant with Joel's child changed everything. It gave her enormous power. In fact, it was a stroke of genius because it meant that her position was secured for life.

That old cliché was true . . . Sometimes God works in mysterious ways.

She buzzed Conchita and requested orange juice, freshly brewed coffee and eggs over easy. Then she clicked on the TV to watch the women on *The View* – a daily habit. Star Jones always amused her with her raunchy take on everything. So did the others, especially Barbara Walters when she was in one of her feisty moods.

Today Rosarita found herself unable to concentrate. Today she felt like a million dollars – no, a *billion* dollars. She was destined to be one of the richest women in the world. She was having a baby. And not just any baby: Joel Blaine's baby.

It made her feel safe and secure. Now there was no hurry to cement the deal with Joel, because once she told him he was destined to be a father, he would be one very happy man indeed. Not only would it validate his manhood, it would also prove how much she cared for him.

All she had to do was get rid of Dex. Then everything would be perfect.

* * *

Dexter's agent, a fast-speaking man with a severe Marine crew-cut and a brown Brooks Brothers suit, informed Dexter he was leaving the agency. 'Got a gig out on the Coast,' he explained. 'Goin' into indie prod – had enough of this agenting shit.'

'Indie prod?' Dexter questioned, still something of a virgin when it came to showbiz terminology.

'Independent production,' the man replied, giving Dexter a *what are you – a moron?* look.

'What about *me?*' Dexter said, a frown creasing his leading-man forehead.

'I've taken care of you, dude,' his agent said. 'Put you together with a gal you're gonna love. Annie Cattatori. She's a doll.'

'I don't need a doll,' Dexter said, asserting himself. 'What I *need* is a good agent.'

'Did I say she wasn't good? Annie's the best. Follow me, I'll take you to her office an' introduce you.'

Dexter was disappointed. Not only was he out of a job, now he had to start with a new agent. It wasn't the way things should be going.

Annie Cattatori, an extremely fat woman in her late thirties, was ensconced behind her desk. Her baby-doll prettiness was lost in a sea of double chins and chubby cheeks, but she had a winning smile and big, pale blue eyes. Around her neck hung a long gold chain with a pair of rhinestone-studded glasses attached.

'Meet Dexter Falcon,' his almost ex-agent said. 'I'm sure you've seen him on *Dark Days*.'

'Seen him? I jerk off over him,' Annie joked, standing up from behind her desk, revealing even more of her huge bulk. 'Come over here, soap boy, an' gimme a hug. We're gonna be close friends.'

The last thing Dexter needed was a close friend. What he needed was a hot agent, and somehow he didn't think Annie Cattatori was the one.

He hugged her anyway, because how could he not? She smelled of mothballs, lilac and garlic, and she hugged pretty damn hard, almost crushing his ribcage.

'Here's what we're gonna do,' she said, sitting back down behind her desk. 'We gotta get t' know each other.'

'Okay, kiddos,' his former agent said, backing towards the door. 'I'll leave you two together.'

Annie waited until the other agent had left the room, then she said, '*I*'m gonna make you a movie star, soap boy. How'd you like them *cojones?*'

I've heard that before, he wanted to say. *I heard it when I auditioned for Scorsese. I heard it when I almost landed a Clint Eastwood movie, and I heard it when I just missed being Gwyneth Paltrow's lover in a Miramax film.*

'Wouldja *like* that?' Annie said, reaching for a cigarette from an open package on her desk.

'Who wouldn't?' Dexter said, sitting in a worn leather chair across from her, thinking that he did not appreciate being called soap boy and he'd better tell her up-front.

'I can do it for you,' Annie promised, crinkling her blue eyes. 'I'm good. I'm very, very good.'

'Who do you represent?' he asked, hoping that Ben Affleck or Matt Damon might be part of her client list.

'Plenty of talent,' she answered. 'Don't expect a resumé,' she added, putting on her glasses and peering at him. '*You*'re comin' to *me*. *You*'re the only one that *matters* when you're in my office.'

'Excellent,' he said.

'*I*'m working for *you* – remember that,' she continued, 'so don't go givin' me any bull, soap boy, an' you and I will get along fine.' She lit up and drew deeply. 'You married?'

'Yes,' he said, wondering what that had to do with anything.

'Don't advertise. Women prefer their leading men single.'

'They do?'

'Whaddya think we're all sittin' in the movies for? We wanna *fuck* you, not picture you screwin' the little woman.' Another deep drag on her cigarette. 'Any chance of dumping the old lady?'

'I'm *happily* married,' he said, realizing as he uttered the words that it wasn't strictly true.

'Okay, okay, only asking,' Annie said, blowing a stream of smoke across her desk into his face. 'Tell me about your bad habits. You do drugs?'

'No.'

'Drink?'

'No.'

'Screw around?'

'No.'

She removed her glasses. 'What are you – perfect or something?'

236

'My wife thinks so.'

'She must be one lucky gal.'

'*I*'m lucky,' Dexter said, wishing it were true. He'd like nothing more than a happy marriage with a woman who genuinely loved him.

'*That*'s what I like t' hear,' Annie said. 'In this business we can use all the luck we can get.'

'You're right,' he said quickly. 'Luck and talent. I've got both.'

'I'm puttin' you together with an acting coach,' she said, regarding him shrewdly. 'You're gonna be more than just another pretty face on a hot body. We got pretty faces knee deep from New York to L.A. Everyone wants to be the next Brendan Fraser or Jude Law. But you,' she said, blowing an impressive smoke-ring, 'you got more than the average Joe. You got the looks, the body, the height, and let's see if we can give you the talent.'

He wasn't pleased that she appeared to be knocking his acting. Hadn't he just told her he *had* the talent? 'The producers liked my work on *Dark Days*,' he said stiffly. 'I never got any complaints.'

'Yeah, honey.' She sniffed. 'They liked it so much they cancelled you.' She reached for a Kleenex and blew her nose. 'Listen to me, I'm puttin' you together with a real smart acting coach. You'll work your dick off, then we'll see. I'm not sending you out on anything until you've done some real studying. Understand?'

'But I need to work,' he protested.

'Who pays your rent?' she said. 'You? Or were you smart enough to marry a rich broad?'

'My wife has some money,' he admitted, albeit reluctantly.

'Then *use* it, honey. Let *her* support you now, and

when you make it, she can bleed you for every cent you've got.' Cackling uproariously at her own humour, Annie added, 'Don't forget you heard it here first. *I* am gonna make you a star, soap boy. If you trust Little Orphan Annie, one day your balls will be enshrined in cement on Hollywood Boulevard.'

Who was he to argue with *that*?

* * *

Finding out where Carrie Hanlon was shooting a cover for *Allure* magazine was no big deal for Joel. He knew most of the bookers, encouraging the friendships by regularly sending them chocolates and small gifts. That way, whenever a new girl came into town he was the first to know.

Fortunately for him, Carrie was shooting with a friend of his – Testio Ramata, a playboy in his own right. Testio was also an extraordinarily talented and much in demand photographer. All the girls loved working with Testio because he made them look sexy, fuckable and beyond gorgeous. He and Joel had paired up on many an occasion on double dates – usually somewhere exotic like Sardinia or Corsica, where Joel would join Testio on one of his assignments and they'd party all week long.

They hadn't got together in a while because their last meeting had not been exactly friendly: Joel had inadvertently stolen one of Testio's girlfriends, an angular Danish model Testio appeared to be getting serious about.

Months had passed. The Danish model was long gone, so Joel felt no compunction about dropping by Testio's studio uninvited.

He could tell his friend was hard at work because he

could hear the sound of the Rolling Stones coming from the studio. Testio swore he got some of his best shots when Mick Jagger was crooning 'Satisfaction', and he had the girl's clothes off and her eyes were fixed on his camera lens. Mick Jagger's throaty growl seemed to turn them on every time.

Joel strolled into the outer studio and up to the reception desk, where Testio's efficient assistant, Debbie, stopped him.

'Haven't seen you in a while, Joel,' Debbie said, removing her fashionable eyeglasses.

'Been busy. You know how it is,' he answered, leaning on her desk. 'Who's the master shooting today?'

'Carrie Hanlon. You'd better not go in unless I announce you. She's *very* temperamental.'

'I know Carrie,' Joel said. 'She won't mind.'

'Sorry, Joel, you'll have to wait out here.'

'You're kidding me, right?'

'No, I'm not. Testio will kill me if you ruin the shoot.'

'Why would *I* ruin anything?'

'Carrie Hanlon is a bitch,' Debbie said, lowering her voice. 'She's got an entourage in there like you wouldn't believe, and she refuses to have strangers watch her when she's shooting.'

'I told you,' Joel said airily. 'I know her.'

'Yes,' Debbie argued briskly. 'And *I* know my instructions.'

'Okay, okay,' he said, glancing at his watch, noting it was past three. 'Have they broken for lunch yet?'

'Any minute now.'

'Good. Then I'll join my friends Testio and Carrie for a glass of wine – that way I won't be disturbing the

shoot. Tell Testio I'll be back in ten minutes.'

He left the studio, walked to the corner flower shop and purchased three dozen pink roses.

Bitch or no bitch, women were suckers for flowers. And Carrie was a woman, wasn't she? A supermodel woman, but he had a hunch that it would work with her just like all the rest. Roses would signal the beginning of a beautiful relationship.

Chapter Twenty-seven

Miami was in the midst of a heatwave even though it was way past summer. The airport was crowded and noisy, filled with people of all nationalities rushing in different directions.

Madison looked around to see if she could spot a chauffeur holding up a card with her name on it.

'Why did you book a limo?' Kimm asked, as they made their way through the crowd. 'The less anyone knows, the better.'

'I've always found that when arriving in a town I'm not familiar with, a driver is the way to go. Otherwise we could end up in the wrong place at the wrong time – y' know, like in *Bonfire of the Vanities*.'

'I can look after myself,' Kimm said, staunchly confident.

'*You* might be able to,' Madison countered. 'But I'm not so sure about me. Lately I've been thinking of buying a handgun.'

'Don't go that route unless you know what you're doing,' Kimm warned.

'I know what I'm doing.'

241

'Well,' Kimm said, 'also consider taking karate lessons. A woman must always be prepared to defend herself.'

'I'd defend myself, all right,' Madison said, with a short, humourless laugh. 'I'd go right for the balls.'

'Very effective if executed in the right way,' Kimm said. 'I'll give you a few pointers. I'm an expert.'

'No – what you *are* is an amazing woman,' Madison said. 'I'm glad to know you.'

'Thanks,' Kimm said awkwardly, unused to compliments.

'Of course,' Madison added. 'I'm not happy about the things you've found out, but then again, I guess I should be – 'cause there I was blithely going along thinking that everything was great, and it wasn't, not at all. So, yeah, maybe God did send you to teach me what's important.'

'You must be nervous,' Kimm said.

'I don't *get* nervous,' Madison answered, still glancing around to see if she could spot their driver. 'As a matter of fact, I'm calmer today than I've been for a while. The idea of meeting my mother's twin sister is scary, yet at the same time exciting.'

'You might not get to meet her,' Kimm pointed out. 'We could turn up at her front door only to have it slammed in our faces.'

'God, I hope not.'

'You have to be prepared,' Kimm said, the voice of reason. 'The woman is obviously afraid of Michael. She ran when her sister was murdered – even changed her name.'

'What *is* her name now?' Madison said, realizing it was the one question she hadn't asked.

'Catherine Lione,' Kimm said. 'That's all the

information I have – her name and an address.'

'Then let's go find her,' Madison said, finally spotting a uniformed chauffeur holding aloft a big white card with her name on it. 'She'll talk to me. I'm sure of it.'

* * *

Jamie was taking an early-morning shower when Peter slid into the glass enclosure, surprising her.

'Peter,' she objected. 'I'm all slippery.'

'Slippery when wet, huh?' he said, lasciviously. 'Exactly the way I like you.'

'And I'm not in the mood,' she said, as his hands began caressing her breasts.

'Last night you had a headache, now this morning you're not in the mood,' he said, fingering her nipples in the way he knew drove her a little bit crazy. 'What's going on?'

'Am I supposed to always be ready and available?' she said, trying not to let his practised touch affect her.

'You're my wife, aren't you?' he said, squeezing an already erect nipple between his thumb and forefinger.

'Yes,' she said, shivering as his hands skimmed their way down her body.

'Glad we got that straight,' he said, moving behind her so she could feel his hardness pressing into the small of her back.

'Peter,' she murmured, suddenly flooded with desire.

'What is it, my sweet?' he asked, nibbling her ear.

'We're happy, aren't we?'

'Very happy,' he said, gently stroking the inside of her thighs.

'You love me, don't you?' she said, turning around so that she faced him.

He placed her hands at the back of his neck, then hoisting her legs around his waist, he entered her with a ferocity she was not expecting. 'You know I love you,' he grunted. 'Can't get enough.'

'Love is more than sex,' she gasped, throwing back her head.

'Stop talking,' he commanded.

'You'd never be unfaithful to me, would you?' she murmured.

'Are you *nuts?*' he said loudly. 'How could you think like that?'

And as he rocked her back and forth, the memory of the condom in his wallet faded into oblivion.

* * *

'This can't be right,' Madison said, as their car pulled up in front of a restaurant club along the gaudy strip of ice-cream-coloured buildings in South Beach.

'We're at the address you gave me, ma'am,' their driver said.

Madison looked at Kimm. 'It's a restaurant,' she said.

'I can see that,' Kimm replied. 'Take a look at the sign. It's called Lione's.'

'You didn't know this?' Madison asked.

'I guess I'm slipping in my old age,' Kimm said drily, as they both got out of the car.

'Driver, please wait,' Madison said. 'I'm not sure how long we'll be.'

The man nodded.

'At least if she doesn't want to meet you, we'll get a

decent cup of Cuban coffee,' Kimm remarked, as they approached the open terrace, where people were sitting around tables sipping drinks and enjoying the loud salsa music coming from inside. It was four o'clock in the afternoon.

'Here's the way we should play it,' Kimm said decisively. 'We're customers. We'll sit down, order something and check out what's going on. Maybe we'll see *her* before she sees *us*.'

'*This* is making me nervous,' Madison said, biting her lower lip.

'I thought you didn't get nervous.'

'I wasn't expecting a restaurant. I thought we were on our way to her house.'

'She probably lives here,' Kimm said, as they made their way to a vacant table.

A snake-hipped young waiter, clad in tight black leather pants and a white T-shirt, swayed over to them bearing menus. 'You ladies here for tea?' he said. 'Or how about something stronger? I can recommend the house margarita.'

'I'll have one,' Madison said, ready for a drink.

'Make mine water,' Kimm said.

'Ah,' the waiter said, staring straight at Madison, 'the beautiful lady likes to live dangerously.'

'Huh?' Madison said, meeting his direct gaze. He was all of nineteen, but full of confidence.

'I am Juan,' he announced. 'Anything you need, call for me.'

'This is an interesting place,' Madison said. 'I love the Art Deco theme. Who owns it?'

'Another beautiful lady,' Juan said, flashing his exceptionally white teeth marred by one gold filling in the front. 'She's older, but women are like wine . . .

they only get sweeter and more precious.'

'Come *on*,' Madison said, laughing. 'You're not going to tell us those lines actually work?'

'Ah, yes,' he said with a wide grin. 'Especially in the tourist season. Are you ladies tourists?'

Kimm was unamused by this banter. 'No, we're not,' she snapped. 'We're here on business.'

'Sorry to insult you, serious lady,' Juan said. 'I will fetch your drinks.'

'What's with the serious-lady crap?' Kimm said, as he walked off. 'I could kick his skinny little tight ass.'

'Don't get pissed,' Madison said. 'He might be the one to tell us about Catherine.'

'Or her husband.'

'No,' Madison said. 'He told us this place is owned by a woman, so since it's called Lione's, that must be Catherine, right?'

'It's a helluva place to hide if her plan was to get away from Michael,' Kimm said. 'What makes her think he'd never come to Miami? Especially with South Beach being so popular.'

'Who knows?' Madison said, shrugging. 'I like it here. There's something free and sexy and kind of . . . welcoming. I'm starting to feel a lot better.'

'No, you're not,' Kimm argued. 'You're starting to imagine that your aunt is going to appear, open up her arms, and say, "Madison, I've waited for you all these years, come live here with me and I will be your real family." Your imagination is shifting into overdrive.'

'Get real,' Madison said tartly. 'Do you honestly think I'm that stupid?'

'You're not stupid at all,' Kimm said. 'You are merely experiencing a fact of nature. We all yearn for family, people who care about us no matter what we do. Now that you've found out about Michael, and that your mother is dead, you feel you have no one, so you're reaching out. And, right now, Catherine is the only person you feel you can reach out to.'

'All I want is to meet her,' Madison said defiantly, 'so she can tell me something about my heritage. I know *nothing* about my mother. I don't even have a clue where she was born.'

'Now's your chance to find out,' Kimm said. 'I think this might be Catherine heading our way.'

Madison glanced up and caught her breath. Coming towards them was a woman the absolute image of Beth in the photo. The same black curly hair, delicate, high-cheekboned face, full lips and seductive eyes. She was slim, wearing a scarlet dress and very high heels. She was in her early forties.

Quickly, Madison figured it out. She was twenty-nine, so if Beth had given birth to her when she was seventeen, that would make her twin sister forty-six.

The woman walked straight past them to the next table, where she stopped to greet a fat man in a white suit and a Panama hat. They kissed each other on both cheeks and began chatting. 'I am so happy to see you,' the woman enthused. 'I have missed your smiling face.'

Madison was startled to hear that she had a slight accent.

'She's Cuban,' Kimm said, in a low voice.

'How do you know?'

'The accent.'

'Oh, my God,' Madison exclaimed. 'Does that mean I'm half Cuban? That I'm not American?'

'Your mother probably came here from Cuba before you were born. You're American, all right.'

'But does it mean I have Cuban heritage?' she said excitedly. 'This is something I didn't know about.'

'There's probably a lot you didn't know about,' Kimm said. 'How's your dancing?'

'Pretty damn good.'

'Now you know why.'

'Ah . . . not only is she an excellent detective, she has a sense of humour too. Although I have to admit that she keeps it well hidden.'

Kimm flashed a smile. 'You're returning to your normal self. I like that.'

'You don't *know* my normal self.'

'I can only imagine. Tough with a soft heart. Intelligent. Loyal friend. Hates stupidity and dumb people. Am I on the right track?'

'I hope so. I sound nice.'

They both laughed.

'I am delighted to see that you ladies are having a good time,' Juan said, returning with their drinks.

'Actually,' Madison said, '*we are* kind of tourists in a way – but not really. You see, I work for a travel magazine, and they've sent me and my colleague to check out South Beach. Y' know, root out the hottest restaurants, clubs, that kind of thing. I was wondering if you could help us.'

'I'm your man,' Juan said with a proud smile. 'There is nothing I do not know about Miami.'

'When do you get off?'

'I have a four-hour break at six. Then at ten I am back to deal with the chaos.'

'What chaos?' Madison questioned.

'You are sitting in one of the hottest places in South Beach,' Juan boasted.

'We are?'

'Yes.'

'And you say Lione's is owned by a woman?'

'Madam is over there,' Juan said, indicating the woman sitting with the man in the white suit.

'Can I meet her?'

'Miz Lione does no personal publicity. Write about the restaurant, not her.'

'So, this is where it all happens, huh?'

Kimm was silently shaking her head, her expression saying, *What do you think you're doing?*

Madison winked at her. She had a strong hunch this was exactly the right way to approach the situation. 'I'll tell you what, Juan, for a hundred bucks can you give us a tour of the place and some of the history?'

'You mean when I get off?'

'We were planning on flying back to New York tonight, but I'm sure we could stay over for one night.'

'I can recommend a hotel for you,' Juan said. 'If you're writing about the night life in South Beach you have to live it. I will tell you exactly where to go, and I will make sure you are welcomed in every place.'

'That's very accommodating of you,' Madison said, 'but I'd prefer to concentrate on here. Can you book us a table for dinner?'

'Of course,' Juan said. 'You and your . . . uh . . . friend. Will there be any gentlemen with you?'

'No, this trip is strictly business.'

'There is no lack of gentlemen who would be happy to spend the evening with you,' Juan suggested slyly.

'We're not looking for company,' Madison said, patting Kimm's hand. 'We're perfectly happy . . . together.'

'Ah, I see,' Juan said, rolling his eyes at his own stupidity. 'You are a couple.'

'Right,' Madison said, smiling. 'A couple.'

Kimm threw her a furious glare.

A woman at a nearby table began calling for her check.

'I'll be back,' Juan said, tight leather pants taking off.

'What are you doing?' Kimm demanded, as soon as he'd left.

'Giving us background,' Madison said. 'This way we'll get to meet Catherine casually, and later I'll tell her.'

'So we *are* staying the night?'

'Yes.'

'Oh, good,' Kimm said, full of sarcasm. 'Have Juan book us a cosy double since we're a couple.'

'Hey, I only told him that so we're not bothered by unwanted attention.'

'Just two dykes on the road. Is that it?'

'Don't get touchy. Anyway, if it's action you're after, it's always easier to cruise if you're with someone. This way all your options are open.'

'Madison,' Kimm said, shaking her head in wonderment. 'I'm seeing a whole new you since we left New York. You're kind of . . . a changed person.'

'No, I'm not,' Madison said firmly. 'I'm a survivor. I was thinking about what you said, and you're absolutely right – I have to let go to continue. This devastating news is not going to slow me down. I'm my own person. I always have been. I've never believed in those people who blame everything on their parents – you know, I'm a fuck-up because my father was a fuck-up. Or I'm a drunk because my mother was an alcoholic.' She took a deep breath. 'So my father was a hit man? *Maybe.* So he murdered my mother? *Maybe.* I don't know any of these things for a fact. But I'm accepting them, and I'm beginning to realize they're not part of who *I* am.'

'Okay,' Kimm said. 'We'll do this your way.'

'Thanks,' Madison said. 'And who knows? You might end up meeting the woman of your dreams.'

'I'm not looking.'

'Trust me,' Madison said, smiling. 'That's exactly when it happens.'

Juan returned, filled with enthusiasm. 'Ladies,' he said. 'I will make this night totally memorable. You will not regret staying over. Juan – he is in charge of everything.'

Chapter Twenty-eight

'How was your meeting?' Rosarita asked, not particularly interested but vaguely aware that she had to keep up some kind of front.

'My agent quit,' Dexter said, his handsome face glum.

'Quit *you?*' Rosarita said, not surprised because his so-called career was going exactly nowhere.

'No. Quit the agency.'

'What now?'

'I have a new agent. A woman.'

'Oh. Attractive?'

'She seems nice.'

'Dynamic?'

'No idea. She talks a good game.'

'That's what you need, Dex. Someone who talks a good game.'

'You look rested,' he said, fully aware that she'd been in bed all day because Conchita had told him so on his way in. He considered it a good sign – maybe her body was trying to tell her something. 'Did you only just get up?' he asked.

'As a matter of fact, I did,' she replied, yawning. 'I'm still recovering from that Chinese restaurant you insisted we eat at the other night.'

He was not in the mood to remind her again that it was a restaurant *she* had chosen.

'Annie wants me to study with an acting coach,' he said. 'What do *you* think?'

'Who's Annie?'

'My new agent.'

'It's not a *bad* idea,' Rosarita said, thinking she couldn't care less what he did. Having spent the day in bed, she'd come up with a plan. And the plan was – poison!

She smiled to herself. It was all so simple, why hadn't she thought of it before? She didn't need a hit man, she didn't need her father. Why allow other people to have something on her? No, this was a project she could undertake all by herself.

The idea had occurred to her while she was flipping TV channels and had come across an old Bette Davis movie. Poison. The ideal solution.

She was planning to poison Dexter, and she was going to do it in Las Vegas!

* * *

Carrie Hanlon was surrounded by a makeup artist, a *body* makeup person, two hairdressers, three stylists, an editor, an assistant from the magazine and a journalist who was writing a profile on her. Carrie Hanlon gave great entourage.

Carrie, supermodel that she was, seemed unimpressed with Joel's roses. She glanced at him as if he was a creature from outer space, and threw them to one of her minions.

For a moment Joel was intimidated. But then he thought, *The hell with this bitch. I'm the son of one of the richest men in the world. Why shouldn't she sit up and take notice like all the rest?*

Testio – a manic-looking Italian American the same age as Joel, with long, greasy hair and several gold stud earrings – was pleased to see him. 'This is like old times,' he said, flinging his arm around Joel's shoulders. 'Haven't *seen* you, haven't *heard* from you. Where you bin hiding, man?'

'Whatever happened to Miss Denmark?' Joel asked, hoping there was no bad blood between them. It was stupid to fall out over a woman when there were certainly enough of them to go around.

'Oh, *her*,' Testio said, obviously out of love. 'She turned out to be the same as all the rest. Went back to Denmark and married a farmer.'

'Who're you talking about?' Carrie asked, sitting in the midst of her entourage at the long trestle table.

'Dagmar, remember her?' Testio said.

'Not really,' Carrie replied, picking up a lettuce leaf and nibbling at it. 'She can't have been anybody.'

Carrie Hanlon was a magnificent specimen of womanhood. She was five feet ten inches tall, with a mane of tawny hair, large eyes, full lips, a straight nose, and the kind of body every red-blooded American boy *wished* lived next door.

'It's been a while, Carrie,' Joel said, finding a place for himself at the table as close to her as possible.

'Have we met before?' Carrie inquired, prompting a sly under-the-table giggle from her bisexual stylist.

'Surely you remember?' Joel said. 'Or maybe you were too stoned that night.'

'I don't do drugs,' Carrie said, causing her other

stylist to break into insane laughter. 'Coke isn't drugs,' she muttered irritably. 'Coke clears the sinuses. I have very bad sinuses. Anyway, I don't do it.'

The interviewer, a thin, bespectacled man, perked up considerably. 'You don't do what?' he asked, tape-recorder in hand.

'Any kind of drugs,' Carrie said, widening her eyes. 'I take vitamins. They keep me full of energy and make me look good.'

'No, *I* make her look so good,' muttered the Chinese makeup artist sitting at the other end of the table.

'How come you're here today?' Testio asked Joel, passing him a bottle of red wine.

'I was in the neighbourhood,' Joel said, pouring himself a glass. 'Figured it had been too long. Had no idea you were working with Carrie.'

'She's not easy,' Testio muttered in his ear. 'But she's worth it.'

'I hope you're talking about the photos,' Carrie said, enjoying being the centre of attention, although quite used to it at this stage of her career. She'd been a star model since she was fifteen.

'No,' Testio teased. 'I was talking about sex.'

'I don't have sex,' Carrie said, glancing at her interviewer. 'I'm saving myself for marriage.'

Testio roared with laughter.

The interviewer said, 'Is that true?'

Carrie smiled her all-American-girl smile. 'That's what you're going to print,' she said sweetly. 'Isn't it?'

The man nodded. He was in the presence of true beauty and it was making him a nervous wreck.

'I have a business proposition I'd like to discuss with you, Carrie,' Joel said, pouring her some wine.

'Talk to my agent,' Carrie answered, dismissing him with a wave of her hand.

'It's personal,' Joel persisted.

'I have no secrets from my agent,' Carrie said, licking her full, glossy lips with a wickedly pink tongue.

'You might want to listen to me first. Why pay ten per cent when you don't have to?'

'Fifteen per cent,' Carrie corrected, as if paying more was a badge of honour. 'And the *reason* I pay fifteen per cent is because my agent gets me the best deals in town.'

'And I thought you were smart,' Joel said, not endearing himself to her, but unable to stop.

Carrie tossed her mane of hair, turned to one of her hairdressers and began talking about a recent Beck concert she'd attended.

Joel realized he was being dismissed. He glanced at Testio, who pulled a face.

'Come into my office,' Testio said, getting up. 'There's something I wanna show you.'

The two men left the table and walked into Testio's private office. The photographer shut and locked the door.

'Supercunt is some trip, huh?' Testio remarked.

'She certainly is,' Joel agreed. 'Thing is, I need her for something.'

'Yeah? Lots of luck,' Testio said, absent-mindedly stroking his crotch.

'No, I'm serious. My father is under the impression I'm bringing her to Vegas for the upcoming championship fight. I'll look like a dumb ass if I don't show up with her. What am I gonna do?'

Testio shrugged. 'Your problem, not mine. Wanna do some blow?'

'Why not?' Joel said, although he wasn't in the mood.

'I've got a thought,' Testio said, going for his stash, which he kept in a locked black-leather Gucci overnight bag. 'There *is* one thing that our Carrie likes better than anything.'

'What's that?'

'Boys.'

'Boys?'

'Yeah, her scene is fifteen-year-old boys.'

'You gotta be shittin' me.'

'I know – it's crazy,' Testio said, putting down several lines. 'There you have this incredibly gorgeous twenty-three-year-old supercunt, and she only gets off on fifteen-year-old boys. I had this teenage intern working for me last summer – thought Carrie was gonna slice him up and eat him for dinner. So here's your answer. All you gotta do is find her a hot fifteen-year-old. And, oh, yeah, I forgot, she likes 'em to be Puerto Rican and built like a brick shit-house.'

'I don't fucking believe this,' Joel said.

'Believe it,' Testio said, snorting a line of coke. 'Carrie's been successful for so long she lives her life like a man. Knows what she wants and goes after it. So get her what she wants, an' I'm sure you can persuade her to go with you.'

'You make it all sound easy,' Joel said, nonplussed. 'Where am I supposed to find a horny, good-looking fifteen-year-old Puerto Rican *boy*?'

'Try Madam Sylvia's,' Testio said casually.

'Who's Madam Sylvia?'

'Where have *you* been?' Testio said, snorting a second line of coke. 'Madam Sylvia's is an escort service for rich women. If you've got the cash, they've got the kid.'

'Then how come Carrie doesn't go straight to this Madam Sylvia?'

''Cause she can't. Too famous. Somebody has to do it for her,' Testio explained, snorting a third line. 'I'm telling you, Joel, this is what she wants. Find it for her and, believe me, she's all yours.'

* * *

Now that Dexter was home, Rosarita decided to go out. She had no desire to sit around making conversation with the husband she was soon going to be rid of.

'Where are you going?' Dexter asked.

'Barney's,' she said, although her plan was to visit a few bookstores and start doing research on various poisons. She'd decided that a hotel in Vegas, where they'd be surrounded by people, was the perfect place for her to do the deed. She had in mind something simple like arsenic or strychnine, a poison that would work fast and not throw suspicion on her. In Vegas anything could happen.

'I'll come with you,' Dexter offered.

'No, you won't,' she answered quickly. 'I'm choosing outfits for Vegas, and you'll get in the way.'

'I'd like to see what you're planning to wear.'

'You will. When I've decided. Right now I'm only at the looking stage.'

Rosarita was a big spender. Because of this Chas took care of her credit card bills. 'I don't make the kind of money you're used to,' Dexter had told her early on in their marriage.

'I know that,' she'd snapped back at him. 'I'll get my father to pay.'

So Chas still continued to settle her sometimes exorbitant credit card bills.

Rosarita swept from the apartment, claiming she'd be back in an hour.

Dexter was well aware that this meant at least three hours. Now that he did not have the studio to go to every day, he was at a loss. He missed the camaraderie of shooting a TV series. He missed being treated like a star on the set. And he especially missed the reassuring presence of Silver Anderson, who'd given him the sense that he was at least working with a true professional. Even though she'd behaved in such a vulgar way at the end, he still couldn't *help* missing her.

He wandered around the spacious apartment, thinking about his future and what it held. Annie had assured him she would call him later with the address and number of the acting coach she had in mind. 'Go see him,' she'd said. 'Do what Johnny Depp did, study and study hard. Now Johnny Depp is considered a *real* actor, not just another pretty face. And *that*'s because he studied his craft with a *professional*.'

When the phone rang, he grabbed it before Conchita could pick up.

'May I speak to Mrs Falcon?' a female voice said.

'She's not in right now,' Dexter replied. 'Can I take a message?'

'This is Dr Shipp's secretary. The doctor asked me to call and make an appointment for Mrs Falcon next week.'

'What does she need to see him about?' Dexter asked.

'Excuse me?'

'Uh . . . this is Mr Falcon. I was wondering what the appointment was about.'

'Oh, Mr Falcon, what a treat!' the secretary gushed. 'Congratulations. It's wonderful news.'

'Thanks,' he said – and then a shot in the dark – 'You mean about the baby?'

'We're so excited for both of you. I'm sure Mrs Falcon has been longing to get pregnant. And, may I say, I love you on *Dark Days*. I set my VCR so I can watch it when I get home. I'm *such* a fan.'

'Thanks,' he said, always happy to hear from someone who thought he was great, because he sure as hell never heard it from Rosarita. 'I'll have Mrs Falcon call to make an appointment.'

He put down the phone and was suddenly overcome with a wild desire to dance around the apartment, yelling triumphantly.

He'd gotten Rosarita pregnant!

His wife was knocked up!

No wonder she'd stayed in bed all day.

This news was the answer to all his prayers.

Now he didn't have to worry about his marriage.

All he had to worry about was his sinking career.

Chapter Twenty-nine

'Now what?' said Kimm, hands on her solid hips as she and Madison stood side by side in the double room Juan had booked for them.

'Guess I'll have to sleep on the floor,' Madison said, straight-faced.

'This is a ridiculous situation,' Kimm snapped.

'But you have to admit,' Madison said, 'it *is* funny. And, oh, boy, was I ready for a laugh. Besides,' she added thoughtfully, 'since we're a couple, we won't have a ton of guys hitting on us tonight.'

'And what makes you think there'd be a ton of guys hitting on you?' Kimm said.

'*Us*,' Madison corrected. 'Because, as I'm sure you're aware, once men see women out alone, their dicks go into overdrive.'

'I don't find this situation at all amusing,' Kimm said, poker-faced. 'This new you, full of light-hearted cracks. Do you regard being a lesbian as some kind of joke?'

'Not at all,' Madison protested. 'It's just that I've never had a close relationship with a gay woman before, so maybe I'm not behaving in the correct fashion. Am I supposed to ignore that you're gay and never mention it?'

'You're not supposed to *ignore* it,' Kimm said, frowning, 'but you don't go around telling everyone you're my companion because you think that will protect you from all the men who'll be chasing after you. God,' she snorted, 'you must've led a spoiled life.'

'I'm sorry if I've offended you in any way,' Madison said, truly not understanding why Kimm seemed so upset. 'I'll go down to the desk and get us another room. I figured this wasn't a problem.'

'It's not a *problem*,' Kimm said, still on cold alert. 'I'm sure I can manage to keep my hands off you for one night.'

'Oh, now it's your turn to be funny.'

'Anyway,' Kimm said truculently, 'I have other clients who need my attention. So if you want to meet your aunt you'd better do it tonight, because I'm out of here and back to New York first thing tomorrow.'

'I fully intend to meet her,' Madison said. 'And meeting her this way means she *can't* slam the door in my face.'

'And what exactly is your plan?' Kimm asked. 'To sneak up on her and say, "Oh, by the way, I'm the niece you don't want to see?"'

'I'll figure it out as I go,' Madison said, refusing to be put off.

'Good,' Kimm said, sitting down on the edge of the bed. 'Then basically you don't need me, so I'll stay in the hotel.'

'I *do* need you,' Madison insisted. 'I feel more secure with you around.'

'Why?'

'I just do.'

'Okay,' Kimm said reluctantly, sighing. 'If you absolutely insist.'

'I do,' Madison said. 'And since neither of us came dressed for a night on the town, I suggest we go shopping. My treat.'

'I hate shopping,' Kimm grumbled. 'Nothing ever fits me. And I'm perfectly comfortable in my tracksuit – it's my uniform.'

'No, no, no,' Madison said. 'We're in Miami. We have to look good. Besides, I've never seen you in a dress.'

'And you're not likely to,' Kimm muttered.

*   *   *

Lione's at night was a sight to behold. Throbbing Cuban music was being played by a live group. Exotic creatures were everywhere: fantastic-looking women and handsome, sexy men, all as snake-hipped as Juan, and everyone ready to party.

'Jesus,' Madison breathed, glancing around at the throng. 'And I thought South Beach was simply media hype. Seems I was wrong.'

It was ten o'clock and Juan, who greeted them at the door, informed them the real action didn't start until after midnight.

'Can't wait to see what the real action looks like,' Madison dead-panned.

'Dancing, drinking, smoking . . . fucking,' Juan ventured, giving a naughty-little-boy grin. 'Did I say something wrong?' he added innocently.

'Not at all,' Madison replied coolly. 'I've done a little of all of them in my time.'

Kimm threw her a quick glance as if to say, *Don't encourage him*.

'Where do we sit?' Madison inquired. 'I'd appreciate a prime position.'

She was wearing a skimpy black dress that clung to her body like a second skin. Her hair was long and wild. Gypsy gold hoops hung from her ears, and she'd even put on makeup.

Heads turned. She didn't care. She felt different, more free. She didn't know why. What she did know was that she was in desperate need of a drink to bolster her courage.

Kimm was dressed in *her* new outfit – black-leather pants, boots, a red shirt, and a long black leather coat. Madison had insisted on buying the clothes for her in spite of Kimm's hearty protestations. 'We're not going to a fashion show,' Kimm had grumbled.

'We have to look the part,' Madison had insisted. 'Anyway, I feel like spending money, and black leather suits you admirably.'

Reluctantly Kimm had agreed to the purchase. In spite of her height and heavy build, she was a good-looking woman, powerful and strong with attractive features emphasizing her Native American heritage. Madison had a feeling that if her own sexual inclination travelled in a different direction, Kimm might be the perfect choice. That's if k.d. lang wasn't available.

Earlier she'd called Jamie. '*What* are you doing in Miami?' Jamie had asked, perplexed. 'I thought you were going through some kind of crisis.'

'I am,' she'd replied. 'This is part of it.'

'Miami is part of your crisis,' Jamie had said, like it was the most ridiculous thing she'd ever heard.

'I'll be back tomorrow and explain everything.'

'You'd better.'

Juan led them towards a centre table. 'May I say that you two ladies look very beautiful tonight,' he crooned. 'It is a shame you are . . . involved.'

Kimm threw Madison another warning glance. *Do not even go there*, it said.

'How about you, Juan?' Madison asked. 'Do you have a girlfriend?'

'One, two, three.' He grinned again. 'I have many.'

'Why is it that I'm not surprised?' Madison said, as they reached a key table near the already crowded dance-floor.

She sat down, looked around again, ordered a margarita and wondered what the hell had happened to her in such a short period of time. She'd thought she was so together, and then everything she was so sure of had crumbled. But she would get through it, she was a true survivor. And tonight was only the beginning.

An hour and three margaritas later she was feeling no pain. Even Kimm was starting to relax as the sensual beat of the music and the hedonistic atmosphere swept over them. While not exactly drunk, Madison was aware that she was not totally in control. She'd been trying to spot Catherine, but so far her aunt had not put in an appearance.

Finally, when Kimm went off to the ladies' room, she asked Juan where the owner was.

'I told you,' he said, 'she will not be interviewed.'

'If I don't use the interview, surely I can speak to her?' Madison persisted.

'Why would you want to speak to her if you will not use it?'

'Because Lione's is *her* creation, and it's obviously

very successful. Did she open this place by herself, or does she have a husband or maybe a business partner?'

'You ask a lot of questions,' Juan said, a wary look in his eyes.

'I'm a journalist,' she said. 'That's what we're supposed to do.'

'Miz Lione does not care for journalists,' Juan said, his young face hardening.

'Surely she wants publicity for Lione's?' Madison said. 'I've never heard of a restaurant/club-owner who doesn't.'

'The restaurant speaks for itself,' Juan said woodenly. 'Miz Lione *never* does publicity.'

'Then let me speak to her husband.'

'There is no husband.'

'Where is he?'

'Not around.'

'If I promise not to mention that she owns this place, will you introduce me?'

'Why are you so anxious to meet her?' he asked, staring at Madison suspiciously.

''Cause I think it's fascinating a woman has created all of this. It's not usual. I'm sure you've never heard of it, but there's a restaurant in New York called Elaine's that's owned and run by a woman. And then there's Regine's in Paris. Two exceptions. Not a lot of women create this kind of sensation. Your boss should be proud.'

'You think I am stupid?' Juan said haughtily. 'Of course I have heard of Elaine's and Regine's. When I first came to America, I worked as a bus boy at Le Cirque in New York. I know much about restaurants.'

'When *did* you first come here?'

'I came from Havana when I was thirteen. My mother sent for me.'

'What does your mother do?' Madison asked.

Before he could reply, Kimm returned from the ladies' room, and Juan retreated into the throng.

'What's going on?' Kimm said, sitting down and peering at her. 'I think you should order a black coffee. You're starting to look glassy-eyed.'

'I'm not,' Madison protested. 'I'm having fun – something I don't get to do too often.'

'You're drunk.'

'Bullshit,' Madison said. 'Merely relaxing.'

'Ha!' Kimm responded, not believing her, and rightly so.

'Don't you drink at all?' Madison demanded.

'Surely you know?' Kimm said, with a sarcastic edge. 'We can't hold our liquor very well.'

'Who's *we?*'

'Native Americans.'

'Oh, please, what kind of crap is that?'

'I prefer not to put it to the test,' Kimm said. 'Anyway, my goal is to keep a clear mind.'

'Yeah, well, while you're keeping a clear mind, you might have missed the beautiful black creature sitting over there who's been eyeing you for the last half hour.'

'Excuse me?' Kimm said, immediately blushing.

'Take a look,' Madison said, indicating the corner table.

Kimm glanced over. Sure enough there was a very tall black girl in a long blonde wig and skimpy gold dress. The girl smiled at Kimm and raised her glass.

'Methinks somebody might be getting lucky tonight,' Madison sing-songed. 'And unfortunately it's *not* me.'

'You know,' Kimm said slowly, 'it's okay for straight people to sleep around, but contrary to popular belief, the gay community is a touch more discriminating.'

Madison burst out laughing. 'That's the biggest bullshit I've ever heard,' she said. 'I have gay friends who think nothing of doing three guys a night.'

'That was before AIDS,' Kimm pointed out. 'Things have changed.'

'Maybe at first,' Madison said, 'but now everyone's gone back to their good old ways.'

'You have no idea what you're talking about,' Kimm said. 'You're half drunk and completely hopeless.'

At which point, the black girl got up and slinked her way over. 'Wanna dance?' she said, standing directly in front of Kimm.

Kimm was just about to say no, when Madison gave her a prod and answered for her. 'She'd love to.'

Reluctantly, Kimm got to her feet. It was at that moment that Madison observed Catherine entering the room. She was accompanied by the man in the white suit from earlier.

Madison jumped up. 'I'll be back,' she said.

She manoeuvred her way around the edge of the dance-floor, trying to avoid the pulsating, swaying figures. Without hesitating she hurried over to Catherine. 'Excuse me,' she said excitedly, totally blowing her cool, 'I've been waiting to meet you all night. I'm writing about Lione's for a magazine, and although I've been made aware you don't do personal publicity, I wanted to shake your hand and say, uh, this is an amazing place.'

Catherine stared at her for a long, silent moment, her face very still. 'You are my niece, aren't you?' she said, without a trace of emotion. 'I told the woman who phoned that I did not wish to see you, so why are you here?'

'Because,' Madison said sadly, as the room began to spin, 'I don't know who I am any more, and you're probably the only person who can help me find out.'

Chapter Thirty

'Hi, honey, how are you feeling?'

Rosarita gave Dex a wary look. Why was he acting all concerned? 'I'm feeling fine, thank you,' she said, although she wasn't, having had an extremely frustrating trip to several bookstores – it wasn't easy digging up information about poisons. However, she'd managed to do *some* research: strychnine, she'd discovered, increased reflexes, caused jumping of the muscles when touched, followed by painful spasms, dilated pupils and asphyxia cyanosis – which did not tell her a lot. Arsenic was not much better than strychnine: heat and irritation in the throat, vomiting, cramps and restlessness, even convulsions, prostration and fainting.

How was she going to find a nice quiet poison that would seep into his system and kill him within an hour? An hour would give her time to send him out to the casino where he would conveniently collapse and die while she was nowhere in sight. She didn't need him having fits and delirium and all of that. She had her alibi all planned. She would be somewhere public with

Chas and her parents-in-law. Cast iron. No arguing with *that*.

Goddamnit! Even poisoning somebody wasn't easy.

'Can we talk?' Dexter said, taking her by the arm and leading her into the bedroom.

Oh, God, what now? Had Joel called and revealed everything?

'What is it, Dex?' she said irritably. 'I just got in. I'd like to relax and have a cup of coffee before you come to me with all your problems.'

'No problems, honey,' he said in that same smooth, incredibly aggravating tone. 'I know you were probably waiting to tell me later, only I found out, and I can't keep it to myself. Now, don't be mad at me – 'cause I've already called my parents and told them.'

'Told them *what?*' she said, alarmed at his sudden concern.

'You're such a clever girl,' he said. 'I'm so proud of you.'

Clever girl? Proud of her? What the hell was he on about?

'Dex, will you kindly explain what you're talking about,' she said, speaking slowly.

'The baby,' he said, beaming. '*Our* baby.'

Oh, my God! Somehow or other he's found out I'm pregnant. This is all I need!

She sat down on the edge of the bed, her stomach fluttering. 'How do you know?'

'Dr Shipp's secretary called to make an appointment for you. I had a hunch, so I asked her.' He moved in front of her, taking her hands in his. 'Why didn't you tell me, honey?'

'I – I only found out myself this afternoon,' she

stammered, caught off-guard. 'I was planning on telling you tonight.'

'It's great news, Rosarita,' he said, pulling her up and enveloping her in a hug. 'I'm so happy.'

'I suppose it is,' she said, still trying to collect her thoughts. It was probably a good thing he knew, because to the world they'd now be this loving and united couple. United, married and having a baby – so that when he dropped dead she would not be a suspect. Instead people would feel sorry for her. The bereaved widow. The *pregnant* bereaved widow. A part she could play to perfection.

How would all this sit with Joel? Should she run it by him?

Absolutely not. He might not condone murder as the answer to her marital woes.

'I'm glad you're happy, Dex,' she said, deciding to go with it. 'It came as a shock to me because, as you well know, I always use my diaphragm, and uh . . . I can't understand how this happened.'

'Protection is never one hundred per cent,' he said. 'Besides, I *wanted* us to start a family.'

Thank God he was understanding. Another man might have said, 'Since you always use your diaphragm, how could this be? Have you been sleeping around?'

'I'm sorry this had to happen while you're out of a job,' Rosarita said. 'It seems a pity to burden you with further problems.'

'You can be so thoughtful,' Dexter said. 'Much as you try to keep your sweet side hidden, it's always there – underneath the tough-cookie act. *That*'s why I married you, 'cause *I* know the real you.'

'Thank you,' she said demurely.

'You're welcome.'

'What did your parents say?'

'They were excited. I was thinking, if it's a boy, can we name him Dexter?'

'Of course.'

'And how about Rosarita for a girl?'

'Whatever you want, darling.'

'I'm planning to treat you like a princess,' he promised. 'You can have anything you want.'

'Thank you, Dex, but perhaps you shouldn't make too big a fuss. Let's wait until we get back from Vegas and tell people then.'

'I'm wondering if you should still take that trip.'

'What are you talking about?' she said quickly. 'I'm pregnant, not an invalid.'

'Do you really think it's wise?'

'I *love* Vegas. All that shopping. I can take Martha shopping, and Matt too. In fact, I'll take everybody shopping. You know I'm a world-class shopper.'

He smiled. 'Yes, I know that. And I promise you, Rosarita, I'll get another job that'll be better than the soap. I'm planning to be the star you always wanted. Will you trust me on that?'

'Yes, Dex,' she said, nodding. 'I know you won't let me down.'

* * *

'Madam Sylvia?'

A suspicious 'Who wants her?'

'I'm calling to speak to Madam Sylvia. I was given this number by Testio Ramata.'

'Never heard of him.'

Oh, Christ, Joel thought. *What am I doing? This isn't going to work.*

273

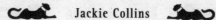

'Testio Ramata, the photographer,' he said. 'Put Madam Sylvia on.'

'Wait a minute,' the voice said, and went away.

A few moments later the phone was picked up again. 'This is Madam Sylvia. Can I help you?'

'Yeah, um . . . Testio told me to call you. He said you'd have what I want.'

'And the password is . . . ?'

'I don't know any fucking password,' he growled, beginning to lose it.

'Then I'm afraid I can't help you.'

'Do you know who I am?' he demanded.

'No.'

'Joel Blaine – Leon Blaine's son.'

'Give me your number, Mr Blaine, and I'll call you back.'

'Is that necessary?'

'It is. If your secretary picks up I'll use the alias Mrs Brown.'

'Don't bother. I'll give you my private number.'

He did so and waited impatiently by the phone. Within seconds she called back. 'I'm sorry, Mr Blaine, can't be too careful.'

'I understand,' he said, although he didn't.

'Did Testio tell you that this is an escort agency for women only? I do not supply gay companions. I supply straight men for straight women, so I really don't see how I can help you.'

'I have this, uh, problem,' Joel said. 'It's something I feel uncomfortable talking about on the phone. Can we meet?'

'That's most unusual. Generally I do not meet potential clients.'

'Listen,' Joel said. 'I've told you who I am. I'm not

likely to turn up with a wire attached to my chest and a couple of cops trailing me.'

She chuckled politely. 'I didn't think so, because I *do* have our conversation on tape, and I'm sure you wouldn't want it made public – just as *I* wouldn't want anything *I* say made public.'

'Then can we meet?'

'Very well,' she said. 'How about the bar at the Four Seasons Hotel at seven?'

'How will I know you?'

'If you're who you say you are, I'll know *you*.'

Joel slammed down the phone, feeling foolish and inept. He'd got himself into this situation because of Marika, the Asian cunt. Damn her! Why had he told her he was bringing Carrie Hanlon, the most difficult girl to nail in New York, to Vegas?

He walked across to the window of his apartment and stared at Central Park spread out before him. Unfortunately for him, there were no other apartments in sight. Sometimes, when he was desperate for an audience, he booked a high-rise suite at the Four Seasons, invited a girl over and made love to her in front of the bedroom window, which was conveniently overlooked by the hotel next door. That was always a kick. Tourists staying in the other hotel must really think New York was a hot place. Joel chuckled at his fond memories.

Maybe he should do that with Rosarita. He hadn't seen her in a while and she was probably pissed at him, but so what? He was sure that once he said, 'Meet me,' she'd come running. Married women were the best kind, because if you treated them like shit, there was nothing they could do about it.

Rosarita had always warned him, 'Don't call me, I'll

call you.' But since he'd been giving her the brush, he knew if he wanted to see her again he'd have to make the effort.

Damn! All he needed was the husband answering. That big ox of a handsome TV guy with birdseed for brains. Joel kind of got off on the thought that she preferred fucking *him* to the pretty-boy husband. And why not? Joel had the goods *and* the money. When his father dropped he'd be mega-rich. Leon Blaine was almost seventy. How much longer did the old cocker have?

On a sudden impulse he looked up her number in his little black book and picked up the phone. A female voice answered. 'Rosarita?' he said.

'Joel?' she whispered, sounding panicky. 'I told you never to call me here. Where have you *been*? Oh, God, let me call you back.'

'I'm at my apartment,' he said. 'I have a new number.'

'I know,' she said. 'It's unlisted. I couldn't get hold of it. Your bitch secretary wouldn't give it to me. What is it? Quickly.'

He told her the number and hung up. Mistake. He should never have given her his new number – the reason he'd changed it was because of her.

But, then again, she was certainly the most adventurous woman he'd ever come across, and she wasn't a hooker. It was one thing for a hooker to be adventurous, but to get a normal woman to do the things he liked to do . . . well, that made it all the more exciting. *And* she gave the greatest head *he*'d ever had.

A beat of ten and his phone rang. He grabbed it. 'Meet me at the Four Seasons Hotel in half an hour,' he said.

'I can't do that,' she said, still sounding panicky.

'Why not?'

'I have a husband at home.'

'Tell him you gotta go out.'

'Where would I be going at six in the evening?'

'I thought you ran your own life. Isn't he working on a soap?'

'It's been cancelled. He's home, in the other room. You made a mistake calling me here, he could have picked up the phone.'

'Well, he didn't, so quit bitchin'.'

'I can't have him finding out about you, Joel.'

'Why?'

'I told you, he'll soon be history.'

'Yeah, yeah – you've been saying that for ever. Can you meet me or not?'

'Well . . .'

He knew he had her. 'Four Seasons, the lobby. Don't be late. I haven't got a lot of time.'

'Is there anything special you want to tell me?' she said, waiting for him to say something nice.

'What do *you* think?'

'How do I know *what* to think? I've been trying to reach you for weeks, now you call me out of nowhere and insist I meet you immediately.'

Women! Why did they always have to talk? Why couldn't they just shut the fuck up? 'Did you get those crotchless panties?' he asked.

'Yes,' she said breathlessly.

'Wear 'em. I'll see you soon.'

* * *

'Who was that on the phone?' Dexter asked, as she ventured into the den where he was watching TV.

'It was Chas,' she said. 'He needs to see me. I think it's about that woman he's living with. The one he *pretends* is a nurse.'

'Why does he have to see you?'

'It's a family thing,' she said vaguely. 'I must go over there.'

'I'll come with you,' Dexter said, clicking off the TV.

'No,' she said quickly. 'He wants to see me by myself. Mumbled something about it being private.'

'If it's family business, maybe I *should* be there,' Dexter said. 'Anyway, now that you're pregnant, I can't have you running around town by yourself.'

'Don't get paranoid, Dex, I'll be back in an hour.'

Rosarita had never been the best of liars, but she seemed to have pulled this one off because Dexter stopped objecting and switched the TV back on.

She hurried into the bedroom, went straight to her lingerie drawer, opened it and inspected the supply of crotchless panties she'd purchased in every colour imaginable. They were stuffed in the back of the drawer so that Dexter wouldn't come across them by mistake. Not that he searched through her lingerie, but she could never be sure. Choosing a scarlet pair with black-lace trim, she rushed into the bathroom, locked the door and slipped them on. Then she touched up her makeup and reached Chas on her cellphone.

'Daddy, this is important,' she said, speaking fast. 'I'm coming over to see you, but not really. If Dex calls, tell him I'm on my way. If he asks for me, say I've just left. Okay?'

'What the fuck's goin' on now?' Chas grumbled.

'Nothing to concern yourself with. I have some

private business to conduct, and Dex is determined to stalk my every step.'

'You doin' somethin' you shouldn't?' Chas asked suspiciously.

'What do you *mean?*' she said innocently.

'You'd better not screw around on him,' Chas growled. 'He's likely to beat the shit outta you.'

'Daddy, you're so dramatic,' she said, with a heavy sigh. 'Now remember, if he asks, I'm there, or I'm on my way there, or I've just left. Got it?'

'Whaddya think I am? A moron? I got it.'

'Thanks, Daddy.'

She clicked off the phone, took one last look in the mirror and slipped from the apartment.

* * *

Fortunately for Joel, the hotel was able to oblige him with the suite he requested. Thirty-eighth floor, on the left side, overlooked by the hotel next door.

He waited in the ultra-modern lobby until Rosarita put in an appearance. When he finally saw her, he realized that, in a strange way, he'd kind of missed her. He gave her a quick peck on the cheek.

'You're lucky I'm here,' she said, slightly out of breath.

'Yeah? What makes me so lucky?'

'Because you haven't been treating me very nicely,' she scolded. 'I know me being married upsets you, but you could at least treat me a little nicer.'

'How can I treat you any way at all while you're still married?' he complained. 'What am I supposed to do? Come over to your place an' hold hands with your husband?'

'Don't be silly, Joel.'

'I got a surprise for you,' he said, taking her hand.

'What is it?' she asked, excited to see him.

'You'll see,' he said, leading her over to the elevator. They travelled in silence to the thirty-eighth floor. When they got out he walked her towards the suite.

She wondered if she should tell him about her pregnancy.

Too soon, a voice warned her. *Much too soon*.

He opened the door of the suite and ushered her in. 'Straight into the bedroom,' he said, patting her on the ass, 'and open all the blinds.'

'I can't stay the night,' she said. 'I got out for an hour. That's all I can manage.'

'An hour will do,' he said. 'It's ten after six. I have a meeting downstairs at seven. You'll be safely outta here by that time.'

'What are we doing?' she asked curiously.

'What do you *think* we're doing?' he said, with a dirty laugh. 'We're about to entertain the folks next door.'

And as she opened the blinds on the side window, she saw exactly what he had in mind.

'Lights on,' he commanded. 'Clothes off. We're givin' the out-of-towners a show the likes of which they'll never see on Broadway. Get to it, babe! This is a take!'

Chapter Thirty-one

Reluctantly Catherine Lione agreed to speak to her. Madison followed the dark-haired woman into a comfortable private office in the back of the restaurant, where there were video monitors on the wall and speakers playing music.

Catherine switched everything off, stared at Madison for a moment, then gave a deep sigh. 'I knew who you were when I saw you this afternoon,' she said in her soft, slightly accented voice. 'It was smart of you to find me. Although I suppose I'm not that difficult to find if one starts looking.'

'My detective found you,' Madison said restlessly.

'I see,' Catherine said, sitting down on a long Art Deco couch.

Unsteady on her feet, Madison sat down next to her.

Catherine gave another long, drawn-out sigh. 'You see, Madison,' she began, 'after my sister's murder I had to get away from Michael and his evil, so I fled to Miami and married a man who was good to me. My husband put up the money to start this place, then later he was killed in an accident. Lione's began small, then after the big earthquake in L.A. everyone began flocking here. Photographers, models, designers – they all discovered South Beach with a vengeance. At first I was worried, I thought the publicity might put me on the front pages. But the people who cared about me knew I did not desire personal publicity, so Lione's became a force on its own, and I stayed in the background.'

'I'm not interested in the history of your restaurant,' Madison interrupted fiercely. 'I'm interested in *you* and what you can tell me.'

'I see,' Catherine said quietly.

Madison got up and began pacing. 'Recently I discovered that the woman I believed was my mother all these years was not,' she said, watching Catherine for a reaction. 'You might have read that she and her boyfriend were murdered.'

'I know,' Catherine said, her face very still. 'Stella was shot in the same way as my sister.'

Madison ran her hands through her long hair, wishing she felt more together and able to handle this. But unfortunately too many margaritas had fogged her brain, and she knew she wasn't thinking as clearly as she should. 'Are you saying you . . . you think *Michael* could have done it?'

Catherine regarded her carefully. 'What do you know about your father, Madison? Did he tell you everything?'

'No,' she said quickly. 'As soon as I discovered Stella wasn't my mother, I hired a private detective. She's here with me tonight. Kimm did some investigating, came up with the press clippings, informed me that Michael . . . Oh, God, I still can't believe it.'

'*What* did she tell you?' Catherine asked gently.

'She – she said that Michael was once a hit man for

someone in the Mob.' Her eyes met Catherine's, and she stared at her hopefully. 'That's completely crazy, isn't it?'

'It must seem crazy to you,' Catherine murmured. 'To me, it's something I always knew. From the very beginning I warned Beth she was playing a dangerous game, but she loved Michael and there was nothing I could say to change her mind.'

'Did you try?' Madison asked, sitting down again.

'Many times.'

'And she wouldn't listen?'

'Beth and I came here as teenagers from Cuba. We lived with an aunt who died shortly after we arrived. Beth met Michael when we were still in high school – they became inseparable.' Another long sigh. 'For a while, Michael took care of both of us. He paid the rent on our apartment, and even after Beth moved in with him, he still supported me.' She paused for a moment before continuing. 'There was a time when I loved him like a brother. I loved him because he loved Beth so much. But when he murdered her . . .' She trailed off, tears filling her eyes.

'So . . . you *do* think he killed her?' Madison said, hardly able to get the words out.

Catherine laughed bitterly. 'I don't *think* anything,' she said. 'I *know* he's guilty. He got off because he had a powerful attorney – paid for by his Mafia boss.'

'Oh, God!' Madison said, her heart pounding. 'So it *is* true?'

'I tried to take you away from him – he wouldn't let me. Michael had the power, the money, the lawyers. Me, I had nothing.'

'*Why?*' Madison demanded. '*Why* did he do it?'

'He thought she had taken a lover. It wasn't so.'

'I don't believe it,' Madison said sadly, reluctant to face the truth. 'It's the same story as Stella.'

Catherine shrugged. 'Michael is aware I know the truth about him. He could find me if he wanted to. When he was acquitted, I knew I was probably safe, there was no necessity for him to come after me. But just in case, I keep a loaded gun beside my bed.'

'I don't understand,' Madison said, trying to hold back the tears that threatened to engulf her. 'Why didn't you want to see me?'

Catherine shook her head. 'It's too painful,' she said abruptly. Her voice softened. 'My sister was everything to me. You – I'm sorry, but you're somebody I don't know. You're Michael's daughter.'

'No. I'm *Beth*'s daughter,' Madison said, her voice rising. 'And I've only just found out all of this. Doesn't that mean *anything* to you?'

'I know it should,' Catherine said, her voice a flat monotone. 'However, I cannot bring back the memories that haunt me.'

'How can you *say* that?'

'I wish you luck, Madison, but Michael is your family.'

'So you're saying you don't want anything to do with me?'

'No,' Catherine said. 'I'm *saying* that I can't allow Michael back into my life, and if I accept you, then Michael will follow. I know him, he is filled with enormous jealousy. If he thought you and I were close, his ego couldn't take it. I don't know what it is with him – when he possesses somebody, they have to be his all the way.'

'He doesn't possess me,' Madison said vehemently. 'I'm his daughter, but he's always left me free to do my own thing.'

'He's allowed you to *think* that.'

'I really am a journalist – I work for *Manhattan Style*.'

'I know,' Catherine said. 'I've followed your career.'

'You have?' Madison said, surprised. 'How did you know who I was?'

'I have friends,' Catherine said. 'They've kept me informed. I know you were raised thinking Stella was your mother, and when she was murdered – well, I expected you to come searching for the truth. I'm surprised Michael told you. It must be his punishment to Stella.'

'Listen,' Madison said, 'I'm only here for one night, but I'd love to come back and spend some time with you.'

'No,' Catherine said sharply. 'This is impossible for me. You must understand.'

'I need to know more.'

'Then you'll have to find it out elsewhere,' Catherine said, standing up. 'I must go, my guests are waiting. Please, Madison, do *not* tell Michael we have spoken or where I am, because if you do, he will try to ruin everything I've worked for.'

'I'd never do that.'

'I wish you luck, Madison.'

'That's *it*?' she said disbelievingly.

Catherine nodded, her dark eyes full of sorrow. 'I'm afraid that's all I can offer you.'

Angrily Madison got up, left the room and returned to her table. The first thing she noticed was that Kimm was taking risks on the dance-floor locked in a close embrace with the black woman who'd been coming on to her earlier.

'They look good together, huh?' Juan said, sidling up next to her. 'Jealous?'

'No way,' Madison answered recklessly. 'Get me another margarita, Juan, then I want to dance. With you.'

'With me?' he said, grinning confidently.

'Yeah,' she said, fixing him with a look. 'You're it tonight.'

He fetched her another drink and she tossed it back fast. Her head was spinning, spinning, spinning. This was all too much. She'd found her mother's sister who did not want to be her friend, did not want anything at all to do with her.

So be it.

She could take it.

She could take anything that was dished out.

And yet . . . she was enveloped in a cloak of sadness. What had happened to her perfect life?

She grabbed Juan and hit the floor, soon finding out that he was an accomplished and sensual dancer. The last margarita had made her into a wonderful dancer too, for suddenly she was swaying and twirling to the beat of the music, all else forgotten.

She remembered her last visit to Miami – the sexy male model, their passionate one-night stand.

That's what she wanted more than anything – another one-nighter. Another incredible night of hot, unforgettable sex.

Dangerous sex.

Dangerous anything.

She had an unquenchable desire to get out of her body and into somebody else's.

'What time do you finish here?' she murmured, clinging to Juan as he spun her around, making her even dizzier than she was before.

'Any time I want. Miz Lione told me to make sure you are happy. She is pleased you are here.'

'No, she's not,' Madison said, holding back sudden tears. 'But it doesn't matter. Nothing matters any more.'

'She enjoyed your company,' Juan insisted. 'Said you are an excellent journalist. And as long as you don't write her name, she is pleased to help you.'

'*Help* me?' Madison said, laughing derisively. 'She didn't help me. *You*'re the one who's helping me.' And then they were kissing, their lips pressed hard against each other, his tongue exploring her mouth with a great deal of fiery passion.

'Let's get out of here,' she gasped, when they finally parted.

'What about your friend?'

She glanced over at Kimm on the dance-floor, still entwined with the black woman. 'My *friend* will be perfectly fine,' she said. 'Let's go before I change my mind.'

He put his arm around her, guiding her toward the door. 'You are sure?'

The hot salsa music and the effect of all the margaritas she'd consumed swept over her. Juan was a conduit to forgetting everything. And he was right there beside her. 'Oh, yes,' she murmured. 'I'm *very* sure.'

And everything was still spinning, spinning, spinning.

And she knew things would never be the same.

Chapter Thirty-two

Joel wanted it all – the whole nine yards – and Rosarita was so happy to see him, and so psyched by the knowledge of her pregnancy that she was prepared to go along with anything he suggested.

With the lights blazing in the bedroom, and the blinds wide open, the hotel guests next door were certainly getting an eyeful. There was Rosarita in crotchless panties, posed on the bed, legs spread. There was Joel, parading up and down in front of the window with a full erection. There were the two of them going at it in front of the window.

Joel got off on every show-off moment. This was his time in the sun. He was indulging in an activity his father could *never* top.

Joel Blaine – exhibitionist.

Joel Blaine – number one.

Yeah. He liked this action a lot.

Occasionally he glanced at the digital clock beside the bed. Had to keep an eye on the time, it wouldn't do to keep Madam Sylvia waiting.

'I've missed you, Joel,' Rosarita gasped, as he thrust

in and out of her. 'Have you missed me?'

'Sure have, baby,' he lied, sweat beading his upper lip as he exerted himself.

'Then how come you changed your phone number without telling me?'

What was it with women? Why did they have to fuck and talk at the same time? Couldn't they shut up for once?

'Whyn't you quit with the small-talk, honey, an' concentrate?' he muttered, changing positions. 'Here's what I'd like you t' do.'

'Yes, Joel?' she said obediently.

'Get down on all fours,' he said. 'We're gonna do it doggy-style.'

Okay with her. He was Joel Blaine, Leon Blaine's son. He was also the father of her unborn child, so she was prepared to co-operate all the way. Besides, doggy-style was a turn-on.

She tried to imagine his face when she gifted him with the good news about their baby, but first she had to get rid of Dex. Then, after a few weeks of mourning, she'd tell him.

He grunted.

She came.

Getting together again was better than a day at the spa.

By the time she left the hotel she felt like she'd experienced a vigorous work-out, which in fact she had. She reminded herself to ask Dr Shipp if too much sex was bad for the baby. Perhaps she shouldn't be *quite* so adventurous.

The hotel doorman hailed her a cab. She sat in the back seat touching up her makeup. Sex with Joel was a trip. Sex with Dex was not nearly as much fun. Either a guy had it or he didn't. Dex didn't. And you would think that he would, what with all the experience he'd had in the modelling world.

Hmm . . . Maybe he was secretly gay. He never got down-and-dirty the way Joel did. Yes, maybe Dex had gay tendencies he hadn't faced up to. After all, he'd been discovered by Mortimer Marcel, and nobody was gayer than Mr Marcel.

Whatever . . .

She didn't care . . . all she wanted was Dex gone.

* * *

As soon as Joel entered the bar, Madam Sylvia waved him over to her table. She was not at all what he'd expected. He'd imagined worldly sophistication. Instead he was confronted by a short, dumpy woman with a heavily lined face, hardly any makeup, reddish, thinning hair and a complacent expression. She was wearing an ordinary moss-green suit and unobtrusive matching earrings. She looked like a housewife from the suburbs, not a notorious madam.

'*You*'re Madam Sylvia?' he said, hardly able to conceal the surprise in his voice.

'Yes,' she answered. 'What were you expecting? A glamour-puss?'

'Hadn't thought about it,' he lied. 'You hardly look like you're in the madam business.'

'That's the whole point,' she said, cackling heartily. 'Nobody would ever suspect me, would they? I can hardly see *me* being hauled off for pandering, unlike – who was that girl in California?'

'Heidi Fleiss.'

'Ah, yes,' she said, nodding knowingly. 'Well, you see, the smart ones – like me and the late Madam Alex, one of the greats – *never* flaunt ourselves. We keep a discreet low profile.'

'That's nice to know.'

A smug smile. 'It pleases our clients.'

'I'm sure it does.'

'Sit down, Mr Blaine, and tell me what I can do for you.'

'It's like this,' he said, pulling up a chair and getting right to it. 'There's a woman I'm interested in, and I think she's interested in me too. But she has a little . . . uh, indiscretion that she's into playing out.'

'Indiscretions are my specialty,' Madam Sylvia said, with a superior smirk.

'That's what I've heard,' Joel said, clicking his fingers for a waiter and ordering a Dewar's on the rocks.

'Then maybe you'd better tell me what it is,' Madam Sylvia said.

'She, uh . . .' he glanced around the spacious room, making sure there was no one within earshot '. . . likes 'em young.'

'How young?' Madam Sylvia said, matter-of-factly. 'I won't go below twelve.'

'Not that young,' he said. 'Fifteen, sixteen will do. Puerto Rican. Hot-looking. Kind of a junior Ricky Martin.'

Madam Sylvia repeated her knowing nod. 'It'll be expensive,' she said.

'I can deal with that,' Joel said, eyeballing a tall, thin blonde on her way to the bar.

'When do you require this?'

'Gotta get back to you with the dates. I have t' be sure you can supply the goods.'

'I'll need twenty-four hours' notice.'

'I understand,' he said, as the waiter brought his drink.

'Do you want the price now?' Madam Sylvia inquired.

He took a couple of fast gulps of Scotch. 'Makes no difference to me,' he said, wondering why she would even bother to ask.

'Ah, yes, I forgot,' Madam Sylvia said. 'Can't scare a rich kid, isn't that right?'

Joel laughed and took another mouthful of Scotch. 'So, tell me,' he said, warming to this dumpy woman, 'who're some of your clients?'

Madam Sylvia smiled mysteriously. 'Wouldn't *you* like to know?' she said. 'And wouldn't *you* be surprised if you did.'

'Truth is, I'd never heard of you till Testio filled me in,' Joel said. 'Had no idea this kind of service existed for women.'

'Why shouldn't it? There are respectable women in this town married to powerful, hard-working men – men who simply have no time for them. And there are certain things the husbands refuse to do to their wives sexually. So the wives use *my* service to satisfy their needs.'

'Doesn't that make them – ?'

'*What*, Mr Blaine?' Madam Sylvia interrupted.

'Whores,' he said, before he could stop himself.

'No, it makes them female johns,' she said, with a tight little smile. 'I'm sure you find nothing wrong with *male* johns, do you?'

'That's different.'

'Not at all. Women desire the same amenities as men. And *I* make sure they get them.'

'So your service is for women only?'

Another mysterious smile. 'Yes. And, believe me, Mr Blaine, I am *very* much in demand.'

* * *

'I wish ya wouldn't do that,' Chas grumbled, glaring at Varoomba, who was beginning to annoy him.

'What?' she asked innocently.

'Cut your freakin' toenails in the bedroom.'

'Somethin' wrong with my toenails?'

'It ain't a very ladylike thing t' do.'

'Oh crap,' she snapped, fed up with his constant criticism. 'You've not got me livin' with you 'cause I'm ladylike, Chas.'

'No,' he agreed. 'But if ya do somethin' that pisses me off, I gotta tell ya, right?'

'What pisses you off about me cuttin' my toenails, for Crissakes?' she said, waving her foot at him.

He could see he was getting nowhere with this argument. 'Do it in the bathroom,' he said gruffly. 'That's an order.'

'Huh!' she said, jumping off the bed, her huge breasts shaking with indignation. 'Any other orders you'd like me to take care of today? Such as suckin' your big fat cock?'

His eyebrows shot up in surprise at her rudeness. '*What* didja say?'

'You heard,' she answered insolently.

It occurred to him that this relationship might not be working out. Varoomba was getting on his nerves, and even though he appreciated her incredible assets, enough was enough.

How to get rid of her, that was the problem. Unfortunately that was *always* the problem. Especially with this one, as he'd persuaded her to give up her job and move out of her apartment. Some dumb mistake *that* was. Now he was stuck with her, and that wasn't good.

But he had a plan. Chas always had a plan. Vegas was coming up. She'd asked him the other night if he was taking her and he'd said yes. She'd been excited because, she'd informed him, her grandmother lived there. Bingo! They'd go to Vegas, and while they were away he'd have his housekeeper pack up her things and transfer them to a rented apartment. By the time they got back, she'd be moved out. He'd buy her a mink coat, hand her a few thou in cash, take care of her rent for three months, and it would be goodbye Varoomba. Nobody could ever accuse Chas Vincent of not being a sport.

On the other hand, if Varoomba wasn't around he'd have to find himself another woman, because he couldn't take being alone – constant silence drove him nuts. Besides, he slept badly when there wasn't a warm body lying next to him. And he had a thing about tits. Big, warm, comforting tits.

Why couldn't he find a woman who behaved herself and didn't get aggravating?

Why couldn't he find a girl who was more like his daughter, Venice?

Now Venice was a peach. Whereas all *he* ended up with were sour plums.

It occurred to him that maybe he was looking in all the wrong places. It might be a good idea to broaden his horizons, move out of the bars and strip clubs and get into the real world.

No, he thought glumly. In his experience, real-world women weren't any better and, even more important, they didn't have the tits to get a man *really* hot.

* * *

When Rosarita arrived home, Dexter was on his way out. Now it was her turn to question him. 'Where are *you* off to?' she asked.

'Got a call from Silver Anderson,' he said. 'She says she has to see me.'

'Silver Anderson?' Rosarita said. 'What does *that* old bag want?'

'She mentioned something about a script.'

'Not another of those dreary soaps, I hope,' Rosarita said, trying to conceal a satisfied yawn.

'Who knows?' Dexter said. 'It's worth finding out.'

'Well, try not to be long 'cause I'm starving.'

'Everything okay with Chas?'

'Who?'

'Your dad.'

'Oh, yes,' she said quickly, remembering her excuse. 'Everything's fine.'

'You look flushed.'

'I hate riding in cabs. All those stupid foreigners drive like maniacs. They should send every one of them back to where they came from.'

'For God's sake, it's not nice to say things like that.'

She threw him a look. Dex was such a tight-ass, she couldn't wait to never have to see him again.

'I'll be back soon,' he said. 'Get into bed, rest and look after yourself.'

'I plan to,' Rosarita said, wishing he'd leave. 'I plan to look after myself all the way.'

* * *

A Filipino houseman came to the door of Silver's apartment and ushered Dexter in. 'Follow me, please,' he said, leading Dexter into a large living room where Silver lolled on a brocade-covered *chaise-longue*. She was clad in a pale peach négligée trimmed with dyed-to-match fox fur. On her feet were high-heeled silver mules.

Dexter's stomach dropped – it was definitely an out-to-seduce outfit, and he had no intention of allowing himself to be seduced again. Especially as somewhere in the future he was going to become a daddy.

'Hi, Silver,' he said, hovering in the doorway.

'Dexter, darling, *do* come in and sit down,' she said, waving a languid arm in his direction.

He'd never visited her apartment before. He entered the living room tentatively and glanced around, noting that it was luxurious in the diva style. There were enormous white couches, leopard throws, and a great many ornate silver frames with pictures of Silver cosying up to various celebrities – not to mention a president or two. He couldn't help being impressed as he settled down on the vast couch opposite her.

'Drink?' she offered.

'I'll pass,' he said.

'How about a glass of champagne to celebrate?'

'Celebrate what?'

She picked up a bound script from the marble coffee table and tossed it over to him. 'Our new project, darling,' she drawled. 'Forget about agents and managers. *I*'m the one who'll make you a star! *I*'m the one to whom you're going to be very grateful indeed.'

And he believed her.

Why shouldn't he?

Chapter Thirty-three

Madison and Kimm were sitting side by side on the plane, but there was no talking going on. Madison had a hangover from hell: her head was ready to explode. She gazed out of the window as the plane prepared for take-off. God! What a way to handle things – getting drunk and laid. Big answer. Very smart.

She was mad at herself, and Kimm was mad at her because she hadn't got back to the hotel until six a.m. 'Did it ever occur to you that I might be worried out of my mind about you?' Kimm had said.

'Sorry,' she'd mumbled, heading straight for the bathroom.

Standing in the shower for almost an hour, letting the cold water bring her back to reality, she'd thought about everything going on in her life and it wasn't pleasant.

'Anyway,' she'd said, when she'd finally emerged, 'I was under the impression you were too busy having fun.'

'I was,' Kimm admitted. 'Not a one-night stand – just fun.'

'Okay,' Madison had said. 'No lectures. I know what I did. I fucked up. I had an opportunity to convince my aunt we could mean something to each other and I blew it. I sat in her office in a drunken haze, listening to everything she had to say and hardly reacting at all. Then I ran off with Juan and indulged in a night of mindless sex. Good move, huh?'

Kimm had shaken her head disapprovingly.

'Hey, listen, I've got this theory,' Madison had said. 'Sometimes a person has to blast off, otherwise they'll explode. I blasted off, now I can go home and attempt to cope with things.'

Kimm had nodded, noncommittal to the end. 'If that's your way of handling it.'

Now they sat on the plane in silence.

Sipping a tomato juice, Madison decided what she would do when they got back. Concentrate on her career, that was for sure. She'd leave Michael on a back burner for now, because there was no way she could deal with seeing him. He was a liar and a fraud. Maybe even a killer.

Michael. Her father. Daddy. The betrayer.

She shuddered at the thought of what he might be.

Once the plane was in the air she fell asleep, awakening shortly before landing.

'I suppose this concludes our business together,' Kimm said, busily tightening her seatbelt. 'It's been an interesting experience.'

'It certainly has,' Madison replied. 'And I want you to know that I appreciate everything you've done.'

'Do you?' Kimm said. 'Maybe you'd be happier if I *hadn't* found out some of the things I did.'

'No,' Madison said. 'I'm one of those people who prefers to know everything, and now I do.' She took a sip of her tomato juice. 'And thanks for coming to Miami with me. I couldn't have done it without you.'

'Wish I could've been more help.'

'Like how?' Madison said. 'Stopped me from making a fool of myself?'

'You didn't make a fool of yourself,' Kimm said, sensible as ever. 'You slept with a very attractive young man. It's understandable.'

'Young's the operative word,' Madison responded ruefully. 'But what the heck? I'm free to do what I please – big fucking deal.'

Easy enough to say, she thought. Inside she was cringing. A one-night stand with a baby. How humiliating! She hadn't wanted it to be that way, but she'd had no one else to hang on to. If only Jake had been in her corner, things might have been different. But no. Jake was exactly like all the rest. He'd proved that she was nothing more than a sexual interlude to him and it hurt. How foolish of her to have imagined it was more.

She had no desire to see Jake again, therefore she had to call Victor and tell him to assign another photographer for the Vegas gig. Jake was yesterday's news, and the last thing she wanted was to work with him.

'Well,' she said, turning to Kimm, who, she'd noticed, was a white-knuckle flyer, 'did you at least enjoy yourself a little bit?'

'I relaxed,' Kimm said, 'and I got a new outfit.'

'You *looked* like you were having fun. I saw you on the dance-floor.'

'There's something very energizing about that place,' Kimm said, with the glimmer of a smile. 'I got caught up in the moment.'

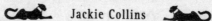

'Tell me about it,' Madison said wryly.

Outside the airport they hailed a cab and shared it into the city. The driver – a talkative Armenian – dropped Madison off first.

Standing on the kerb in front of her building she suggested to Kimm that they get together for lunch before she left for Vegas.

'Call me,' Kimm said, raising the window as the cab took off.

But they both knew she probably wouldn't. This was a phase of her life she was anxious to forget, and Kimm would always be a painful reminder.

Slammer, fed up with her absences, went totally berserk when he saw her, barking and drooling with excitement.

'I'm not very fair to you, am I?' she said, collapsing on the floor next to him and rubbing his stomach. 'I dump on you all the time. No more nice long walks. I'm always miserable. But it's going to change, I promise. Things are definitely returning to normal.'

Slammer barked as if he understood. He probably did: he was one smart dog.

She jumped up and played back the messages on her answering machine. The usual suspects: David, who was obviously never giving up; Jamie; Victor, wanting to know how far she'd progressed on her research; and Michael – damn him. Right now she wanted nothing to do with him. Even speaking to him would be an ordeal.

She took her second shower of the day, her mind drifting back to the night before. Already it seemed as if South Beach was another place, another time.

Kimm had said there was something about the atmosphere there, and she was right. Some kind of sexual buzz had taken over, rendering her helpless.

After getting dressed, she headed for the office.

* * *

Victor greeted her with exaggerated enthusiasm. 'Ah, my star reporter has decided to put in an appearance,' he boomed. 'What an exciting occasion!'

'I had business in Miami,' she explained.

'*Miami?*' His jowls quivered. 'Why would anybody go there?'

'You should take your wife to South Beach, Victor,' Madison said. 'It'll loosen her up, get the plug out of her ass.'

Victor's bushy eyebrows shot up. '*Excuse* me?' he said.

Madison laughed. 'You heard. It's a very laid-back place.'

'Ah,' Victor said. 'I can tell *somebody* got lucky.'

'Lucky, unlucky, it doesn't matter,' she murmured. 'Oh, and by the way, I'd like you to assign another photographer to the Vegas gig. Jake Sica isn't right for the job.'

'Too late,' Victor said loudly. 'I've already hired him. Besides, his work is excellent.'

'Damn!' she muttered.

'Is there a problem?'

'I was hoping you might break into your piggy bank and hire Annie Leibovitz. Her photographs are awesome.'

'That would please *Vanity Fair*,' he said drily. 'She's theirs.'

'I thought it would be a good change to work with a woman,' she said. Victor was notorious for employing mostly male staff, which she was always complaining about.

'Why?' he said.

'Why not?' she said, challenging him. 'You're so sexist, Victor. Lighten up.'

'Me? Sexist?' he said, offended.

'Okay, boss, don't go getting your balls in an uproar.'

'You leave my balls alone.'

She grinned. '*That*'s a promise.'

'By the way,' Victor said, 'it's about time we started lining up your next victim.'

'Now?'

'I was thinking Bruce Willis.'

'Bruce Willis?'

'He's an extremely underrated actor. And with the divorce thing behind him, and the fact that he's such a macho kind of man – not to mention one of the highest-paid movie stars in the world – I'm sure people will be salivating to read your take on him.'

'What's this thing you have about movie stars?'

'They generate heat and big news-stand sales.'

'Give me another choice?'

'Charlie Dollar.'

'Trouble in waiting.'

'Nothing wrong with trouble. Isn't that your forte?'

'What you're trying to tell me is that you want another boring Hollywood cover.'

'Exactly.'

'Then how about Lucky Santangelo? Titan of Panther Studios?'

'She'd be a real coup,' Victor said enthusiastically. 'However, I understand she doesn't do publicity.'

'Maybe *I* can persuade her.'

'How?'

'Woman to woman. She's an incredible character. She's done a lot for women, and I'm sure I could get to her. I'm vaguely friendly with Alex Woods – remember? He nearly did my call-girl project, and I understand he's quite close to her. Send me out to the Coast for a while and I'll see what I can pull off.'

'Do I sense you're anxious to get away from New York?'

'I've had a lot of personal problems to deal with. I need a change.'

'Ah, yes,' Victor said. 'The death of your mother was a terrible tragedy.'

'It's more than that,' she said, thinking *If he only knew.* 'Things I can't talk about now.'

'Are you sure?' Victor said, shooting her a penetrating stare. 'I have an extremely sympathetic ear.'

'Someday, when I've gotten used to the situation.'

He looked concerned. 'Whatever it is, Madison, you know I'm always here for you.'

'That's the one good thing,' she said. 'I've discovered that I really do have wonderfully loyal friends.'

'And so you should,' Victor said pompously. 'A person gets the friends they deserve. And you, my dear, deserve only the best.'

* * *

Madison left the office, hit Lexington, and immediately heard someone calling her name. She stopped and looked round. Running down the street towards her was Jake Sica. 'Hey,' he yelled, reaching her side, 'I *thought* it was you.'

'Well, well, well,' she said, cool as ice. 'The travelling photographer. Hello, stranger.'

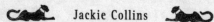

'Stranger?' He looked at her quizzically. 'Two weeks and I'm a stranger?'

'Did you have a good time in Paris?' she asked, still on the icy side. 'I guess you must have, because *I* sure as hell didn't hear from you.'

'You didn't hear from me 'cause I hate those damn answering-machines.'

'So you're telling me you phoned and omitted to leave a message?'

'Nope,' he said, rubbing his hands together. 'I didn't phone 'cause I know your machine's always on. I figured I'd see you when I got back.'

'Really.'

'Right now I'm on my way to visit Victor. How about you?'

'I just left him.'

'Wanna come with me and surprise him?'

The surprise will be on you, she thought. *If Victor has the balls, he'll cancel you off the Vegas job, and it'll be goodbye, Jake.*

'No, thanks,' she said, faking a bored expression.

'You look tired,' he said. 'Everything okay?'

Screw you, Jake Sica! I am not tired – I am hung-over. Plus I have a sex hangover too, because the sex I had last night was amazing – better than the sex we had. And you have no idea what I've been through since you left. So fuck you big-time.

'I only got back from Miami this morning,' she said, trying not to sound too uptight. 'I was covering a few of the clubs in South Beach. Up all night, you know how it is.'

'Miami, huh?' he said. 'You must've had a good time.'

'Naturally,' she said. 'Wouldn't waste it.'

He leaned in a little closer. 'Are you *sure* everything's all right?'

'You keep on asking me that,' she said, backing away. 'I'm fine.'

'I understand we're covering the fight in Vegas together.'

'We are?' she said, as if it was the first she'd heard of it.

'Victor mentioned you requested me. Thanks.'

I don't want to work with you, Jake. I don't want to sleep with you again either. You're exactly like all the rest.

'You'll have to excuse me,' she said, pointedly glancing at her watch. 'I've got an appointment and I can't be late. Work first. Everything else second.'

'Can I see you tonight?'

Was he dense or what? 'Let me ask you one question,' she said, unable to hold back any longer, 'do you want to see me because you happened to run into me, or were you planning on calling me later?'

'Oh, I get it,' he said. 'You're pissed, aren't you?'

'Why would I be pissed?' she said quickly.

'Oh, yeah, you're pissed all right.'

'No, I'm not,' she said, hating him for having any kind of effect on her.

'Yes, you are.'

'Okay,' she admitted, fed up with playing games. 'Maybe I am. We were together for a week, had a perfectly great time, then *you* take off to Paris, and not another word until I bump into you a few minutes ago. Tell me, Jake, why the hell *shouldn't* I be pissed?'

'You could've called *me*,' he said, infuriating her even more.

'I could've. Only one minor problem – you didn't

give me your phone number or tell me where you were staying.'

'Yeah,' he admitted sheepishly. 'That *would* be a problem.'

'So, you will excuse me, won't you?' she said. 'I *am* pissed, and I do not wish to discuss it.'

Without waiting for his reply, she took off, striding down the street without looking back.

Who the hell did he think he was? Just another selfish jerk with bedroom eyes and a great body. *Screw him*.

She stopped at the nearest coffee shop, went straight to the pay-phone in the back and called Jamie. 'I'm here,' she announced. 'And ready to talk.'

'Thank God for that,' Jamie exclaimed. 'I can't keep up with you any more.'

'Guess who I bumped into on the street?'

'Who?'

'Jake,' she said flatly. 'Can you believe it? *And* the son-of-a-bitch acted as if nothing happened.'

'What do you mean?'

'You *know* what I mean. The prick doesn't call me after spending a week at my apartment. What does he expect? That I'll jump into his arms? I don't think so. I fucking *hate* him.'

'You need a therapy session,' Jamie said calmly.

'Oh, Christ! If one more person tells me I need a shrink, I'll go totally stone cold crazy.'

'I'm not saying you need a shrink. What I'm *saying* is you need a therapy session – with *me*.'

'Bullshit.'

'No. Talking it out helps. Are you free for lunch?'

'Yes.'

'Then let's meet.'

'If you insist.'

'I do.'

'Okay, where?'

'Somewhere we can talk.'

* * *

They met for lunch in the refurbished Russian Tea Room, and over borscht, blinis and several Black Russians, Madison let it all out.

Jamie listened sympathetically, interjecting only when it was absolutely necessary. 'If this were a plot for a movie,' she said, when Madison had finished her long story, 'I wouldn't believe it.'

'I know,' Madison agreed. 'I'm still in shock myself. That's why I got drunk last night. And laid.'

'Was he any good?' Jamie asked slyly.

'What do *you* think?' Madison said, sipping her drink. 'He was nineteen years old, for Crissakes. I felt like an old lady ravishing a young boy's body.'

'Hmm . . . Well, you know what they say – guys are at their hottest when they're nineteen.'

'Trust me,' Madison said, grinning, 'it's true.'

Jamie laughed softly. 'I'll have to give that a try one day.'

'*That*'ll go down well with Peter. By the way, how *are* things?'

'They're actually great,' Jamie said slowly. 'Although something did happen.'

'What?'

'Remember what your detective lady told you to have me do?'

'Yes?'

'I did it. I looked in his wallet and found a condom.'

'No shit?'

307

'Maybe it's a male thing – like the clicker. You know, they don't feel safe unless they've got a clicker in one hand and a condom in their wallet. Not that he'd ever use it.'

'So you marked it?'

'I felt stupid but, yes, I did.'

'And?'

'And nothing. Everything's been so good that I haven't had a chance to look. And anyway, checking out his wallet makes me feel like a sneak.'

'You didn't feel sneaky when you thought he was cheating on you,' Madison pointed out, in a decidedly better mood after a couple of drinks.

Jamie brushed a delicate hand through her short blonde hair. 'I don't *want* to look,' she said.

'Could that be because you're frightened of what you'll find out?'

'No,' Jamie said stubbornly.

'Then do it.'

'Okay, I will,' Jamie said, with a big sigh. 'I'll take a peek as soon as he goes to sleep tonight.'

'What else has been happening?' Madison asked. 'Have I missed anything?'

'Anton had another party.'

'Was Kris Phoenix there?'

'No.'

'Disappointed, huh?'

'No,' Jamie said, giggling softly.

'You wouldn't have done anything with him anyway.'

'I would if I'd caught Peter.'

'Maybe you *will* catch Peter. So then Kris Phoenix can be number one on your hit list.'

'You know, Maddy,' Jamie said sternly, 'you're not a good influence.'

'Agreed. I'm not. I'm angry and wired up and all I want to do is scream. I feel like I had a family – you know, a mother and a father – then it all turned to shit before my eyes. And on top of that there's a strong possibility that Michael, the man I've looked up to all my life, is some kind of . . . Christ, I can barely say it.'

'What?'

'Killer, murderer, hit man. Who the fuck knows? It's insane.'

'I wish I could do something,' Jamie murmured.

'A wise woman advised me how to handle it,' Madison said. 'I have to let go and regard this as just another story. I have to be strong and make my own way.'

'You always *were* a bit of a loner,' Jamie remarked. 'I remember college vacations, we never went to your house, you always came to stay with my family, or we'd go to Natalie's. I can only recall meeting Stella twice. And your father at graduation, well, it was almost like he didn't want to be there. He kind of sat in the auditorium all stiff-backed, while Stella was glammed to the max and every boy in the place was busy eyeballing her tits. Neither of them seemed very parent-like. They didn't take photos or give you flowers, none of that. You've forgotten, haven't you?'

'I've blocked it, I guess,' Madison said sadly.

'*Big* surprise.'

'The funny thing is I still love Michael,' she said wistfully. 'But that doesn't mean I have to like him.'

'What'll you do now?' Jamie asked. 'Tell him you know all this stuff?'

'Maybe, one day. Right now I'm into researching my next interview. I'll go to Vegas, write a hell of a story, then perhaps I'll stay in L.A. for a while. I have to get my head together before I confront him.'

'Sounds like a plan.'

'I'm also thinking of going back to Miami and talking to Catherine. If she sat down with me once, that means she *will* talk to me again. And this time I'll make sure I'm sober and together. Oh, yes, and this time I am *not* planning on getting laid by some juvenile stud. The sole purpose of my trip will be to find out more about my unknown past.'

They left the restaurant and by mutual agreement strolled down to Bergdorf's, where they did some therapeutic shopping. Madison bought a sleeveless cashmere turtleneck sweater, and a pair of dense black Dolce and Gabbana sunglasses. 'After all,' she said, smiling ruefully, 'I *am* going to Vegas. Got to look the part.'

Jamie was frustrated that there was nothing she could do for her friend to make her feel good again. If only Peter would relent and agree to go to Vegas, but she knew he wouldn't.

They parted outside the store and Madison flagged down a cab.

'Come by for dinner later?' Jamie suggested. 'We'll send for Chinese, rent a video . . .'

'Thanks for the offer, but no,' Madison said, climbing into the taxi. 'I'm a recovering alcoholic from last night. For somebody who usually doesn't drink, believe me, I put away plenty. Besides, I have a date with my computer, and I promised my dog I'd stay home.'

'*Your* dog?' Jamie said, raising an eyebrow.

'That's right.'

'He's not even yours.'

'He is by adoption.'

'Okay, crazy girl, we'll talk tomorrow.'

'It's a deal.'

Chapter Thirty-four

Rosarita didn't tell Chas, Martha Cockranger did. She had the balls to call Chas from wherever it was in the boondocks that she lived and inform him that his own daughter was pregnant.

Chas got on the phone to Rosarita immediately. 'Why the hell didn't ya tell me?' he exploded. 'What the frig is this? I gotta hear it from some old broad I barely know?'

'What do you mean, barely know?' Rosarita said, outraged that he'd found out before *she*'d had a chance to tell him. 'Martha Cockranger looks at you like she's discovered the second coming of George Clooney!'

Chas calmed down and chuckled. 'Can I help it if I got that effect on broads?'

'Daddy, stop it,' Rosarita said, bad-temperedly. Her father always *had* been a conceited son-of-a-bitch, and as he grew older his ego seemed to be getting bigger than ever.

'So,' Chas said, 'you're knocked up, kiddo. Ya gotta bun in the box. This'll make things right between you an' Dex.'

No, it won't, she thought grimly. *But then again, I'd better play it cool. After all, Chas knows my original plan, and since he isn't prepared to co-operate, I can't let him in on what I'm about to do next. Let it all come as one big surprise.*

'Ya given Venice the good news?' he inquired.

'I wasn't planning on making a public announcement,' she answered testily. 'I don't want anybody knowing until we get back from Vegas.'

'Whyzatt?' Chas demanded.

'Because my doctor insists I should take it easy and keep it to myself. In case you're unaware, the first few weeks of pregnancy are an extremely delicate time.' Her voice rose. 'Call that Cockranger bitch and warn her to shut her big fat mouth.'

'Too late for that,' Chas wheezed, indulging in a short coughing fit. 'Ya better talk to your old man.'

'Fine,' Rosarita said, happy to place the blame on Dex. 'It's all *his* fault.'

Where *was* her soon-to-be-deceased husband anyway? She hadn't seen him, which could be because she was still in bed and had no intention of getting up any time soon. She was allowed to pamper herself, wasn't she?

After saying goodbye to Chas, she buzzed Conchita.

'Is Mr Falcon around?' she asked, when Conchita entered the bedroom.

'Out jogging, Miss,' Conchita said, diligently straightening the drapes.

'Tell him when he comes in that I'd like to see him. And bring me some toast and . . . I think I'll have hot chocolate today.'

'Ah, very good for the baby,' Conchita said, with a knowing smirk.

'*Excuse* me?' Rosarita said haughtily. 'What do you mean, the baby?'

'Madam is pregnant.'

'How do *you* know?'

'Mister told me.'

Oh, God, she was going to ream Dex's ass when he came home – his big, dumb, soap-opera ass.

How had she ever gotten stuck with such a jerk? He honestly thought it was *his* baby she was carrying, and now – the idiot – was announcing it to anyone who'd listen.

No fucking way. She was carrying Joel Blaine's baby, and one day she'd be free to tell the world.

* * *

Dexter did double duty on his jogging time. Now that he didn't have to report to the studio every morning he could concentrate on other things, such as health and fitness. His physical appearance was number one on his list, as it had to be – after all, the way he looked was his biggest asset. Matt had developed a large gut, and Dex considered it disgusting. He would *never* allow himself to go to seed the way his dad had. He hoped it didn't run in the family – he'd sooner kill himself than look like that.

He thought about Silver and her script. She'd announced that *she* would make him a star. He wished he had a dollar for everyone who'd promised him that.

Not quite believing her, he'd taken her script and hurried home to his pregnant wife.

'What did the old witch want?' Rosarita had asked.

'Nothing important,' he'd said, and later, when Rosarita was in bed drooling over Don Johnson in

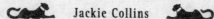

Nash Bridges on TV, he'd gone into the living room, settled into a comfortable armchair and read Silver's script in one sitting.

It was pure genius! It had everything! Love, sex, violence, tragedy. And at the core of it all, a passionate love triangle involving a man and two women.

Silver was right: the role of Lance Rich was a star-maker. Dexter wanted in.

He was so excited that he'd immediately decided to phone Silver and ask her what the deal was. Did she own it? Was she planning on producing? Was it a movie-movie, or a TV deal?

So many questions. But by the time he'd finished reading and was ready to ask, he realized it was too late to call.

He'd rushed into the bedroom to share his excitement with Rosarita, only to find her snoring soundly, the TV still playing.

Now it was morning and he was out jogging, pounding his way through Central Park, sweating profusely, fired up with enthusiasm. He couldn't wait to get home and call Silver. She must think he was right for the script, otherwise she wouldn't have given it to him to read. But he had to know the deal. *Did* she have the power to give him the role? That was the burning question.

No point in calling his agent yet, he'd have to wait and see.

Yes. Slow and easy – that was definitely the way to play it.

* * *

Meanwhile, back at the apartment, Rosarita kicked the

duvet off the bed, and lay there staring at the ceiling, fondly remembering her previous day's tryst with the oversexed Mr Blaine. God, he was a horn-dog! He knew how to do it to her like no other man ever had.

While she was being serviced by Joel in front of the window, in a suite at the Four Seasons, she could have sworn she'd spotted a group of people gathered in one of the rooms across the way. Of course, they *would* gather, wouldn't they? She and Joel put on a show like no other.

The truth was, they were perfectly matched. Oh yes, she knew that when they weren't together he dated supermodels and actresses, she'd read all about him in the gossip columns. But what did that matter when he'd met his soulmate? And she *was* his soulmate. No doubt about it.

Conchita brought her hot chocolate and dry toast on a tray. 'Couldn't you have put jam on it?' she complained, sitting up, a frown on her face.

'Too much sugar not good for Missus now that Missus pregnant,' Conchita said.

'When I want your opinion, I'll ask for it,' Rosarita snapped.

Conchita muttered something rude in Spanish under her breath and marched from the room.

Shortly after that little exchange Dexter returned home. Rosarita had to admit that he looked ruggedly handsome in his red tracksuit and Nike running shoes. Shame he was such a loser.

'Morning,' he said, a great big smile plastered all over his face.

'Hi, Dex,' she answered.

He bent over to kiss her. 'Don't,' she said, turning her cheek. 'You're all sweaty. Go take a shower.'

He was dying to share his news about the script, but he decided to shower first and tell her after.

He stood in the shower, singing loudly as he soaped his body. He was happy. Why shouldn't he be?

Finally he emerged from the bathroom, a towel knotted loosely around his narrow waist, still smiling.

'What are *you* so cheerful about?' Rosarita inquired, biting into a slice of unappetizing dry toast.

'I'm going to be a daddy, aren't I?' he said excitedly. 'It's the greatest news I can think of!'

So intent had she been on reliving her sexual encounter with Joel that for a moment she'd forgotten about the baby growing in her stomach. 'Oh, yes,' she said, with a distinct lack of enthusiasm. 'I have to talk to you about that.'

'You do?'

'For God's sake,' she said irritably, 'don't go telling the world.'

'I told my mom,' he said, surprised she didn't want it shouted from the top of the Empire State Building. 'Is that so terrible?'

'*You* told Martha, *she* told Chas, and *he*'s fucking *furious*.'

'Why's that?' Dexter asked, sensing big trouble ahead.

'Shouldn't *I* be the one to tell him? I was under the impression this is *my* exciting news.'

'Ours,' he said quietly.

Ignoring his comment she pushed her tray away and said, 'Go phone Martha right now and tell her to shut her stupid fat mouth.'

'Don't talk about my mom like that,' he said indignantly.

'Then stop her from broadcasting the news of my

pregnancy as if it's hers to broadcast.'

'If you feel so strongly —'

'And another thing,' she interrupted, not prepared to listen to his lame excuses.

'What?'

'How does Conchita know?'

'She *should* know. Conchita's the one who'll be looking after you.'

'Oh, for God's sake, Dex,' she yelled. 'Get it into your head — I am *not* an invalid. *Nobody* has to look after me, and certainly not my maid.' An angry glare. 'How *dare* you reveal my personal secrets to the maid?'

'Rosarita, honey, it's no secret,' he said, attempting to calm her down. 'It's something we should be proud of. I'm so excited *and* — on top of everything else, Silver's script is the real deal, it's sensational, and she wants *me* to be in the movie.'

'What script? You didn't mention a script.'

'Silver gave me a script to read. And, uh, well,' he said, managing to look modest, 'she assures me it's the part that'll make me a star.'

Rosarita laughed derisively. 'How many times have we heard *that*?' she said, in her best put-down voice.

'Exactly what *I* thought,' he said. 'But this script is dynamite.'

Oh, yes, Rosarita thought. *Like Dex would know a dynamite script if it fell in his lap.* 'Is it for a theatrical movie? Or a movie-of-the-week TV crap thing?'

'I have to call Silver and find out. I'm contemplating whether I should contact my agent and fill her in.'

'Of course you should. Let's see if she knows what she's doing. Anyway, *she* should be the one to call dear old Silver. And remember, you are *not* working for nothing. You'd better get that into your head, *and* your agent's.'

'Silver and I haven't discussed business,' Dexter said. 'She only gave me the script last night.'

'Fine,' Rosarita said, losing interest. 'Go call your mother before she does any more damage.'

'Let me put on some clothes first.'

While Dexter was in the bathroom getting dressed, Venice phoned.

'I'm so happy for you and Dexter,' she trilled. 'It's such a special time for both of you.'

Rosarita prickled with indignation. How *dare* Chas tell Venice? Especially when she'd warned him not to. 'I suppose Daddy told you,' she said, making a half-hearted attempt to be nice.

'No, Dexter's mom contacted me. Isn't that sweet of her?'

Sweet! SWEET! What bullshit!

'Very sweet,' Rosarita said, almost choking on the words, her eyes narrowing with fury. Enough was enough. 'Dex!' she screamed, slamming down the phone. 'Get in here before I go mad! Your mother is about to drive me fucking crazy!'

* * *

Silver Anderson was busy putting on her face when Dexter phoned. 'Good morning, dear boy,' she said, balancing the phone in one hand as she continued to apply dramatic black eyeliner. 'And what can I do for you?'

'You can tell me more about that script,' he said. 'It's sensational!'

'You like it, do you?' she said, sounding amused.

'What actor wouldn't?'

'I rather thought you would,' she said smugly.

'Does it belong to you?'

'It was written by a young man who sent it to me through the mail. He thinks I'm the perfect star for his film.'

'Then what's the deal?' Dexter asked.

'I've optioned the property,' Silver said crisply, 'and I need an investor. A nice, rich person who will stay in the background and put up the money to make *our* movie. And by today's standards it's comparatively low-budget. Ten million dollars should do it, and that – *quelle surprise* – includes *my* fee. I'm having a detailed budget prepared even as we speak.'

'You mean it'll be a theatrical movie?'

'Naturally. I've had enough of boring television. Silver Anderson must be back on the big screen where she belongs.'

'Do you have any investors in mind?'

'I was hoping that *you* might be able to come up with someone.'

'Me?' he said, surprised and a little bit flattered.

'How about your wife's father? I understand he's quite well off.'

'I – I don't know,' Dexter stammered. 'He's never invested in anything *I've* heard about.'

'There's always a first time,' Silver drawled. 'And if he's of a certain age I'm positive he's had a lifelong crush on me. How about bringing him to meet me so I can *charm* the money out of him.'

'What you're saying,' Dexter ventured, 'is that if *I* bring you someone who'll put up the money, then *I* get the role of Lance Rich.'

'Oh, darling, you'll get the role anyway,' she said

off-handedly. 'You're perfect for it. I thought of you the moment I read it.' A meaningful pause. 'Although, if we're *forced* to go to a studio, they'll probably *insist* upon a star. Naturally I'll fight for you all the way, but you know how they are.'

'Yes,' Dexter said, immediately realizing the studios would want Brad Pitt or Ben Affleck. He had to do something radical to secure the role for himself.

'My other idea was how about that divine man you used to work for? Remember when you had that billboard up in . . . where was it?'

'Times Square.'

'The one where you were posing in your tiny little briefs looking rather naughty. I'm sure that's why they cast you in *Dark Days*. What was that designer's name?'

'Mortimer Marcel.'

'Ah, yes, Mortimer Marcel. He must be *very* rich, and most likely *loves* you. Arrange a meeting with him also.'

Dexter was getting the picture. 'Let me see what I can do,' he said. 'I'll get back to you as soon as I've put something together.'

'Good boy,' Silver purred. 'This is an opportunity neither of us can afford to let slip by.'

'I know,' Dexter said. 'Leave it to me.'

Chapter Thirty-five

Making up for lost time, Madison went to work with a vengeance. She thoroughly researched Antonio 'The Panther' Lopez, also looking into the career of his opponent, the champ. Then, on a roll, she managed to write two chapters of her novel; attend a few yoga classes because she thought it would help relieve her tension; phone Stella's best friend, Warner Carlysle, who never returned her call; had a couple more lunches with Jamie; wrote a long letter to Michael, saying she did not wish to see him for a while and would contact him when she was ready; spoke to Natalie on the phone at length; attended one of Victor's incredibly boring dinner parties at which she almost insulted the blind date that Evelyn sat next to her; and finally agreed to have lunch with David, because his incessant phone calls were driving her nuts.

'If I have lunch with you, will you leave me alone?' she demanded, on the phone.

'You have my word,' he promised.

Yeah, well, David's word was about as trustworthy as a recovering sex addict at an orgy. This could be because he was a producer of an early morning news show and, as such, knew plenty about manoeuvring his way out of difficult situations.

She walked to the Italian restaurant he'd chosen, thinking that she couldn't wait to get out of town. A change of scene was exactly what she needed, and the sooner the better. Victor, the coward, had not cancelled Jake, so that was the only downer: *he* would be in Vegas. But she'd made up her mind – no more getting involved, however Jake decided to play it.

Relationships were a bitch. Who could figure anything out? Smart as she was, *she* certainly couldn't. She was still confused about the way Jake had behaved. She'd thought they were at the start of something special. He apparently had not.

The first words David said to her when she sat down at the cosy corner table he'd chosen were, 'Have you met somebody else?'

'If I *were* to meet somebody else,' she said, immediately uptight, 'that would mean there was somebody in my life in the first place and, believe me, David, you've been long gone.'

'You know what I mean,' he said, pouring her a glass of her favourite red wine, which he'd prudently ordered ahead of time.

'No, I don't,' she retaliated, pushing her wine-glass away. 'And I'm not drinking today, so don't bother.'

'Okay, I'll rephrase it,' he said. 'Have you met somebody?'

'No, David,' she answered patiently, trying to keep her anger under control. 'I have not met anybody. And I do not want to. Right now, I'm off men.'

'That sounds bitter,' he said, making a face.

'Actually,' she said, messing with his head because

322

deep down David was a pure chauvinist *and* a closet homophobic – two things she'd always hated about him, 'I was thinking of changing tracks.'

His eyebrows shot up. 'Changing tracks?'

'Maybe I'll get myself a girlfriend,' she continued, pushing his buttons. 'Y'know, a sensitive *woman* who'll cater to my every need.'

'You're full of shit,' he said with a disbelieving snort. 'You love sex.'

'I love sex with someone special,' she shot back. 'I *thought* you were someone special. Turns out I was wrong.'

The waiter appeared by their table with menus. He handed them over, then reeled off a list of the day's specials. Madison ordered lightly grilled sea bass and a mixed green salad. David went for the house recommendation – seafood lasagne and a small Caesar.

'Listen to me,' he said, when the waiter had left, 'the one who was wrong was me.' He fixed her with one of his intent looks. 'I made a huge mistake.'

'You know what, David?' she said restlessly, wishing she hadn't agreed to come. 'It wasn't a mistake as far as I'm concerned, because it proved to me what kind of person you are. If you're capable of doing that to me, then you're capable of anything.'

'Thanks,' he said sulkily.

'The truth is a bitch, right?'

He stared at her angrily. 'Don't you have any compassion?' he said. 'You *do* know I'm getting a divorce?'

Ha! she thought. *Like I care. What kind of a door-mat does he think I am?*

'No, I didn't know,' she said evenly. 'And I'm sorry to hear it, because I'm sure you must have had a delightful marriage. However, I have no intention of turning into your shrink and listening to your problems.'

'I'm not asking you to.'

'Yes, you are, David. And *I'm* making it quite clear that the *only* reason I met you for lunch is because *I* want you to leave me alone – and I mean it.'

'That's impossible,' he said, attempting to place his hand over hers.

'Oh, *please*,' she said angrily, snatching her hand away. 'I don't need this shit.'

Realizing he was on shaky ground, he quickly changed tactics. 'I read about your mother,' he said. 'I know the two of you weren't always close, but it was such a terrible thing the way it happened. What's the story? Has there been an arrest?'

Madison frowned. He was trying to be intimate in every way he knew how, and she wasn't having it. He'd switched into his investigative-producer mode, and she was not about to start revealing what had taken place. 'I appreciate your concern,' she said – she could look at him now and experience no feelings at all, 'but it's over, and I don't care to talk about it.'

'I can respect that.'

Can you? she thought. *You have no idea what respect is.*

'How about this for an idea?' he said, as the waiter returned and began serving their salads. 'You and I spend a weekend in Montauk. A friend of mine leases a house there, and he's offered to lend it to me next weekend.' He gazed at her with his *I'm-the-most-sincere-guy-in-the-world* expression. 'Say yes, sweetheart. We shouldn't let the two years we spent together go to waste.'

She couldn't help laughing. He really thought he was going to talk his way back in. 'Let *what* go to waste? We're *over*, David. Can't you understand that? You walked out on me. Remember?'

'That's just it,' he said quickly. 'I walked out, now I'm back and truly sorry.'

'No, you're not,' she said, picking up her fork.

'It wasn't like we had closure,' he said, beginning to sound whiny.

'We had closure all right,' she said heatedly. '*You* married someone else.'

'It was a mistake, so let's spend the weekend together, talk it out, and see if we can put everything back together.'

Typical David. His marriage didn't work out so he thought he could step right back into her life and pick up where they had left off.

Think again, asshole.

'We can't,' she said coolly. 'Because here's the thing, David – I can never trust you again. And without trust there's nothing.'

'I never cheated on you when we were together,' he said, as if it were an award-winning feat.

She shook her head in amazement. 'What do you want? A bouquet of roses?'

'That's *something*, isn't it?' he persisted. 'Most guys cheat all the time.'

She'd had enough of his painful excuses; it was getting boring. 'For God's sake,' she said, 'you're only making this worse. Why don't you go find yourself a beauty queen with big tits? Or a school-teacher. *Anyone* who isn't me.'

'That's nice talk.'

'Whatever you do,' she continued, 'I couldn't care

325

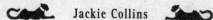

less. And yes,' she added, thinking this was the perfect lie to get rid of him once and for all, 'if you really want to know, there *is* someone else.'

He jumped on that one. 'The guy you were with in the lobby of your apartment building?'

'No, not him.'

'Then who?'

'None of your goddamn business.'

He shook his head in a hard-done-by fashion. 'Jesus, Madison, you're cold.'

'*I'm* cold?' she said, refusing to hold her anger in any longer. 'Fuck you, David! Fuck you big time.' She stood up from the table and glared at him. 'Don't call me again, or come by my apartment building. This is it, so get it into your thick head – it's over.' And with that she strode out of the restaurant.

Saying goodbye for the final time felt extraordinarily good. It was as if he was fully exorcized and she could put him behind her once and for all.

S'long, David. It wasn't fun.

* * *

While Madison was busy getting her life back on track and throwing herself into her work, Jamie was making slow progress. Every night after Peter fell asleep she decided it was time to check out his wallet again. But somehow or other she couldn't bring herself to do it. She found it too dishonourable. Besides, there was *no way* he was screwing around on her. He made love to her every day, treated her like a queen. Okay, so he was stubborn about going to Las Vegas, but the rest of the time she could get more or less anything she wanted from him.

326

Monday night he called her from the office and informed her he'd be home late. She reminded him they were due to attend a dinner at Anton's.

'Shit!' he said. 'I forgot. Don't worry, though, I'll meet you there.'

'Aren't you coming home to shower and change clothes?' she asked.

'I'll take a shower at the office. No need to change, I look pretty good today.'

'You *always* look pretty good,' she said, agreeable as ever. 'Damn!' she added wistfully. 'I hate going without you.'

'Call Maddy, she'll go with you.'

'Maddy passed on the invite. She's too swamped with work.'

'I won't be late,' he promised. 'You know Anton's cocktail hour always goes on too long. I'll be there in time for dinner.'

Jamie never liked walking in anywhere on her own, and she especially didn't like taking cabs by herself at night. So, after thinking about it for a few minutes, she decided what the hell – she'd be late along with Peter. All she had to do was alert Anton not to expect them for drinks before dinner.

She called Peter back at his office. The phone rang and rang, but there was no answer. Remembering the main switchboard shut down at a certain time, she tried him on his cell phone. An electronic voice requested her to leave a message.

Warning signals immediately went off in her head. If Peter was at his office, why wasn't he answering his phone?

Damn him! Now she felt suspicious again. Tonight she would definitely check out his wallet and see if the stupid condom was still there with her mark on the packet.

The moment she arrived at Anton's, he could sense her nervousness. 'What's the matter, Princess?' he asked. 'Something wrong?'

'Nothing,' she answered vaguely. 'I was thinking about that job we have to finish in the Hamptons. Maybe *you* should take it over.'

'Why would you suggest that?'

'Because I was there two days last week, and I'm not into leaving Peter alone.'

'Pray, why?' Anton said, chuckling. 'Think he'll be a bad boy?'

'Of course not,' she said sharply.

'*Sorry,*' Anton said.

Now she started thinking about the previous week, when she'd spent two days in the Hamptons moving clients into their new house – which, she had to admit, looked amazing, and already was due to be photographed by *Architectural Digest*. Every night she'd called Peter at the same time, and every night he'd been at home. But how did she know that the moment she hung up he hadn't slipped out? How did she know he didn't have a girlfriend on the side?

True to his promise, Peter arrived before everyone sat down to dinner. Putting his arm around his wife, he nuzzled her ear. 'Hi, gorgeous,' he whispered. 'Miss me?'

'I always miss you,' she said. 'In fact, I called you back, but there was no answer.'

'You know the switchboard closes down at six.'

'I tried your cellphone, no answer there either.'

He patted his pocket, not taking a beat. 'The battery must be dead.'

328

'Then how come the service picked up?'

'I'll have to check into it,' he said. 'Battery could need recharging. You know what,' he whispered in her ear, 'at the same time, I'll recharge you. I'll recharge you all over our apartment.'

'Shush!' she said, giggling nervously. 'Somebody'll hear.'

'Oh, yeah, that'd be a shock, wouldn't it? Two married people talking about sex.'

She laughed softly. It was all her imagination, she knew it. And yet, deep down, she had this nagging feeling of unease.

Later, when they got home, they made love, and it was as good as it had ever been.

Tonight, though, she waited until Peter fell asleep, then she slipped out of their bed and went into the dressing room.

His wallet was in its usual place. She took it off the dresser, opened it, checked out the contents and, to her chagrin, discovered there was no condom packet.

NO GODDAMN CONDOM IN HIS WALLET.

Where was it? What had he done with it? Had the son-of-a-bitch *used* it?

The fact that it wasn't there blew her mind. This wasn't the way things should be. She was furious, her suspicions were correct.

THE BASTARD WAS SCREWING AROUND ON HER.

She hurried into the bathroom and opened the clothes hamper. Burrowing around in it she took out the shirt he'd had on. She picked it up and pressed it to her nose.

Yes, she could swear there was a trace of perfume, and it certainly wasn't hers.

Damn him!

I've got to play this cool, she thought. *I cannot accuse him unless I know for sure.*

It was too late to call Madison, yet she was desperate for her advice.

Nothing she could do until the morning, so eventually she got back into bed and fell into a troubled sleep.

In the morning, as far as Peter was concerned, she was her normal self.

As soon as he left for the office she called Madison. 'Remember that detective you hired?' she said. 'I need to meet her. And I need to meet her today.'

Chapter Thirty-six

I t took Dexter a few days, but eventually he was able to secure a meeting with Mortimer Marcel. Mortimer, who kept luxurious offices on Park Avenue, suggested he drop by at five to see him.

Dexter arrived on time. Mortimer greeted him sitting behind his elegant antique desk. Stationed beside him was his faithful black lover, Jefferson, who obviously did not trust his paramour to be alone in Dexter's company. There had always been an edgy atmosphere between them. Jefferson was extremely jealous of Dexter, whom he considered a rival of sorts.

Dexter greeted them both, and they all exchanged the usual you're-looking-wonderfuls.

'I hear your soap has been cancelled,' Jefferson couldn't wait to say. 'Does that mean you're coming back to try to score another underwear campaign?'

Dexter managed a smile. 'I got so many other things going on,' he said. 'My new agent is confident we're about to sign on for something big.'

'Excellent news,' Mortimer said, while Jefferson merely glared. 'Now, what can I do for you?' he asked,

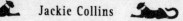

sitting up straight, looking every inch the fashion maven in a pale blue sports shirt with a crisp white collar and impeccably pressed beige linen pants.

'Well . . .' Dexter began. 'I'm sure you've heard of Silver Anderson.'

'Who hasn't?' Jefferson sniffed, running a hand over his shiny bald head.

'I actually had the honour of working with her on my soap,' Dexter said.

'The one that was just cancelled?' Jefferson interjected.

'That's right,' Dexter said, wishing that Jefferson would butt out or get lost. It was painfully obvious that Mortimer's boyfriend was not pleased to have Dexter back on the scene.

'What *about* Silver Anderson?' Mortimer asked, his Adam's apple bobbing up and down as he spoke.

'As I'm sure you know,' Dexter said smoothly, 'Silver Anderson is a legend in her own lifetime.'

'She's also an old drama queen,' Jefferson snorted, 'well past her sell date.'

'Age doesn't make any difference,' Dexter said, maintaining his cool. 'Silver's still a great beauty, with a world-famous name.'

'I get your point,' Mortimer said impatiently. 'Now, enlighten me about this meeting.'

'Silver has a script she's optioned.'

'We're not interested,' Jefferson said, rolling his eyes.

Mortimer shot him a dirty look. 'Continue,' he said to Dexter.

'She has this script, and it's quite something,' Dexter said, nervous now. 'She gave it to me to read, and I suggested that maybe I could come up with an investor rather than her taking it to a studio.'

'Bullshit,' Jefferson screeched. 'What you mean is the studio won't put up the money – right?'

'Silver wants to keep control of this project,' Dexter said, ignoring his enemy. 'It's a very special script, so she's decided to look for an investor who'll come up with the money to get the film made.'

'How does that involve me?' Mortimer inquired, vaguely interested. 'Does she want me to design the clothes?'

'No,' Dexter said, 'although that's a terrific idea. And with Silver in the movie, imagine the publicity.'

'Ha!' Jefferson sneered. 'The last thing Mortimer Marcel needs is publicity. He's as famous as Calvin Klein, Ralph Lauren *and* Tommy Hilfiger put together. Publicity – I hardly think so.'

'It occurred to me,' Dexter said, still ignoring Jefferson and directing all his energy and enthusiasm toward Mortimer, 'that it might be a way for you to branch out into the film business, which I'm sure has always intrigued you.'

'The movie business is shit,' Jefferson offered. 'You put money into *that* cesspool and you gotta have brain surgery.'

'Will you shut the fuck up?' Mortimer said, finally snapping. 'This is *my* meeting, Jefferson. *Mine*, not yours. So be quiet – or if you can't manage that, go and do something useful.'

Jefferson scowled.

'Would you be prepared to meet Silver Anderson?' Dexter asked, pressing on. 'Allow her to outline what she has in mind?'

'I don't see why not,' Mortimer said. 'I'm surprised she isn't a client.' He tapped his fingers together. 'I could design her something wonderful. Bob Mackie, move over!'

'Bob Mackie!' Jefferson screeched in horror. 'Puleese!'

'Set it up, Dexter,' Mortimer said, favouring his lover with a spiteful look, because *nobody* told Mortimer Marcel what to do. 'And we'll see where it goes from there.'

* * *

Meanwhile, across town in the underground parking lot of the Federal Building, Rosarita and Joel made fast, reckless love.

'You realize what would happen if we were caught?' Rosarita said, enjoying every decadent minute as she lay spreadeagled and half naked on the back seat of Joel's Bentley.

'Yeah, I'd be headline news,' Joel said, bare-assed and happy as he pumped away.

'What about me?' Rosarita said, wriggling into a more comfortable position. 'I'm married to a celebrity.'

Joel roared with laughter. 'Come *on*,' he spluttered. 'You're not calling that hunk of meat you're married to a celebrity, are you?'

'He was on a soap for almost a year,' Rosarita said huffily. 'He has a well-known face.'

'Gimme a break,' Joel said, almost at the point of orgasm.

'It's too dark here,' Rosarita said, once again shifting her hips on the back seat. 'Nobody can see us.'

'Next time we'll take it out into the open,' Joel promised. 'I thought there'd be more traffic. Apparently not.' He let out a loud grunt, followed by,

'Oh, yeah, baby, baby, baby!' as he finished the job.

Rosarita was pleased to note that Joel was no longer avoiding her calls. Ever since he'd summoned her to meet him at the Four Seasons, they'd been seeing each other most days. She had not told him she was shortly flying to Vegas. Instead she'd decided to let him wonder where she was. It would do him good to find out that she was not always available.

Apart from having regular public sex with Joel, Rosarita had not been idle. She'd been researching everything she could get her hands on regarding ways to poison someone. Ways that could not be traced. She'd finally settled on an obscure weed-killer from Holland, banned in America, that she'd read about on a somewhat scary Internet site – a site she'd stumbled upon by accident. The poison was exactly what she was looking for. A colourless, tasteless, odourless liquid that could be poured into a drink, and took about an hour to do its dirty deed.

Rosarita was triumphant. The only problem was that she didn't know how to get it. But, after continued probing, she'd finally found the address of the manufacturing company in Amsterdam. Knowing she could hardly order it under her own name, she'd opened a post-office box in SoHo under an assumed name, and sent the manufacturer of the poison a cash payment.

Now she was waiting for delivery, and since she would be leaving for Vegas in three days, she was becoming anxious in case it didn't arrive in time.

Too bad if it didn't, because that would ruin everything.

'You ever gotten fucked in the back row of a movie?' Joel asked, clumsily pulling on his pants.

'When I was a teenager,' she said, groping around on the leather seat for her thong. 'Well, not exactly fucked, but I had this boyfriend – he used to take the bottom out of his carton of popcorn, so every time I put my hand in, what did I get?'

'A hot dick!' Joel said, laughing lewdly. 'Oldest trick around.'

'Exactly,' Rosarita said. 'And nobody was any the wiser, *including* my math teacher, who happened to sit next to us one day.'

'You know somethin'?' Joel said. '*We* should do it in the back row of a movie theatre. Bring back our teenage years.'

'Isn't that rather risky?' Rosarita said, loving the idea.

'Risky is where it's at, babe.'

'But what if we were caught?'

'How we gonna get caught?'

Rosarita considered the scenario if they were. She shuddered. It would not be a good thing.

* * *

Joel, meanwhile, had all his plans in place. Madam Sylvia had come up with the perfect specimen: Eduardo, a teenage Puerto Rican boy who was so darkly handsome that Joel almost fancied him himself!

He'd consulted with Testio, who'd agreed to bring Carrie Hanlon to Joel's apartment that night for a small dinner. Joel had gathered together a few friends and arranged for the boy to be there too. He had it all planned. When Carrie spotted him, Testio would refer her to Joel, the boy would come on to her, then Joel would suggest the Vegas trip, luring her with the bait that Eduardo would meet her there.

It was a foolproof plan if what Testio had said about Carrie was true.

Meanwhile, Joel had not spoken to his father regarding Vegas. Marika, the Asian cunt, was the one who'd made all the arrangements. He and Carrie were supposed to meet them on Thursday morning and fly to Vegas on Leon's Gulfstream jet.

'Tell Carrie to bring plenty of changes of clothes,' Marika had informed him. 'There'll be many parties, and Leon is in a party mood.'

Sure, Joel had thought. *That'll be the day.*

He decided not to tell Rosarita that he would be away for a few days. Let her wonder where he was, it would do her good.

There was nothing like a little *where-the-hell-is-he?* to build the sexual tension.

Chapter Thirty-seven

Jamie was a wreck. It took Madison and Kimm twenty minutes to calm her down.

'I can't believe the bastard has done this to me,' she shrieked, pacing agitatedly around Madison's apartment. 'I thought we were so *happy*. What *is* it with men and their travelling dicks? Tell me,' she demanded, her voice rising. 'I want to know.'

'Take it easy,' Madison said soothingly. 'You're not sure of anything.'

'She knows for sure the condom is gone,' Kimm said, stoic as ever.

'That doesn't necessarily mean he used it,' Madison argued.

'I hate to say this, but I'm usually right,' Kimm said. 'We'll investigate Peter in the same way I handle all my cases.'

'What does that mean you'll do?' Jamie asked, still pacing.

'We'll have him followed, take photographs,' Kimm explained. 'I'll get a full report within forty-eight hours.'

'Christ!' Jamie snapped. 'This is the worst.'

'You wanted to know, didn't you?' Madison said.

'Hell, yes!' Jamie said adamantly. 'Because if he *is* screwing around, I'm leaving the son-of-a-bitch.'

'Some women like to know, then they do nothing about it,' Kimm commented. 'They prefer to stay in the marriage with the knowledge.'

'Why would they do that?' Jamie demanded. 'What are they? Idiots?'

'The knowledge gives them power.'

'Who wants power?' Jamie scoffed. 'All *I* want is a faithful husband.'

'You know what Peter's like,' Madison said, trying to be helpful. 'When he's had a few drinks –'

'Yes?' Jamie said, aquamarine eyes flashing.

'Well,' Madison said, treading carefully, 'when he's had a few drinks he can sometimes get a little lecherous.'

'How do *you* know?'

Oh, Christ! Madison thought. *Now I've started something. She's not letting this drop.* 'The truth is he . . . uh . . . comes on to all your friends.'

'He does *what?*'

'Only when he's had too much to drink,' Madison said hastily.

'Has he come on to you?' Jamie asked accusingly.

'Not in a way that makes me think he means it.'

'For God's sake,' Jamie snapped. Then she turned to Kimm and said sharply, 'When can you start?'

'I'll need his social security number, work address, phone numbers – cell phone included. I'll make out a list for you.'

'Is it really so terrible having somebody followed?' Jamie asked, turning back to Madison. 'I mean, what if he's totally innocent and I'm simply being a jealous bitch?'

'At least you'll know,' Madison said.

'Yeah, I'll know,' Jamie said bitterly. 'But I'll still feel shitty about myself. Spying on him – it doesn't feel right.'

'He'll never find out,' Madison assured her.

'You know me,' Jamie wailed, thinking of the consequences, 'I'm not good at keeping secrets. In a moment of weakness I'm likely to tell him.'

'That's your prerogative. Nobody can advise you except yourself.'

'You're hired,' Jamie said to Kimm. 'Please start immediately.'

'Unfortunately I can't handle it myself as I have a full workload at the moment,' Kimm explained, 'but there are other competent people I use.'

'No, no,' Jamie said, vigorously shaking her blonde head. 'I must have you.'

'Can't do it,' Kimm said.

'You've got to,' Jamie insisted.

'It's not possible.'

'Maybe as a personal favour,' Madison interjected quickly. 'For me.'

'You and your personal favours,' Kimm said dourly.

'Thanks,' Madison said. 'I'll buy you another leather coat.'

Kimm allowed herself a small smile. 'Exactly what I *don't* need.'

'*Now* what happens?' Jamie asked, agitated.

Kimm fished in her large purse and handed her a pad and pencil. 'Write down all the relevant information,' she said. 'If he has family, include their addresses. And the names of his parents, his assistant, anyone he works closely with.'

'Why would you need that?'

'As I said before, knowledge is power.'

Later, after Kimm left, armed with all the information, Jamie said, 'Is she okay? I mean, she's, like, a bit odd, isn't she?'

'Why would you say that?'

''Cause maybe I'd be better off using a man.'

'Really?' Madison said slowly. 'Would that be because you think men make better detectives?'

'You know what I mean,' Jamie said, flustered. 'Men kind of get the job done faster. She's a tall, big woman, with an aggressive attitude.'

'That's a very sexist, bigoted remark,' Madison scolded. 'I'm glad Natalie can't hear you talking like this. She'd be shocked.'

'I didn't mean anything *bad*. It's just that . . . well, I don't know *what* it is. I simply didn't expect her to be the way she is.'

'Are you talking about her sexuality?'

'I'm not interested in her sex-life.'

'You obviously figured out she's gay.'

'I didn't, and I wish you hadn't told me. That makes it even worse.'

'Jesus, Jamie, if she does a great job, why would her being gay bother you?'

'It doesn't *bother* me.'

'Yes, it does.'

'No,' Jamie said fiercely. 'Peter *bothers* me. He bothers the hell out of me. I've tried so hard to be a great wife, and there he is fucking his bloody secretary for all I know.'

'That would be too much of a cliché,' Madison

observed. 'If Peter's in bed with somebody, it won't be a woman who works for him.'

'How do *you* know?'

'C'mon, you've got to admit, Peter's a major snob. It'll be someone he considers to be on his level.'

'Oh, you mean like my best friend?' Jamie said shrewdly.

'*I*'m your best friend,' Madison pointed out.

'He's not in bed with *you*, is he?'

'I think I'd know if he was.'

'How will that Kimm person contact me?' Jamie asked, flopping down on the couch. 'She can't call me at home.'

'Kimm will get in touch with me,' Madison said. 'Then I'll set up another meeting.'

'But you're leaving for Vegas.'

'Not for another couple of days.'

'I'm sorry to burden you with this.' Jamie sighed. 'In comparison to what you're going through, my problems seem insignificant.'

'Of course they're not,' Madison said. 'There's no way you can stay with a guy if he's cheating. You're too special for that – too beautiful and smart.'

'Wow! It's nice to have friends to fuel one's ego.'

'Everything's ahead of you, Jamie. You can do anything, have anybody. If Peter's guilty, I suggest you bail. Look what happened with David and me.'

'At least you didn't catch him screwing around.'

'No, he walked. That's even worse.' She didn't add that he was now begging to resume their relationship – it didn't seem the appropriate time.

'Okay, enough of this drama,' Jamie said, jumping up. 'My plan is to try and forget about it until your detective comes back and tells me it's all my imagination.'

'That's the best thing you can do.'

'How about dropping by the office with me?' Jamie suggested. 'We'll kidnap Anton for lunch.'

'You're not planning on telling him, are you?'

'You've *got* to be kidding. Anton? The eyes and ears of the world? No way! Besides, I have nothing to tell – yet.'

'Okay,' Madison said, deciding it might do her good to get out. 'Let me grab my coat and we'll go.'

*　*　*

After lunch with Jamie and Anton, which turned out to be relaxing and fun because Anton, as always, was full of the most outrageous gossip, Madison decided to pay a surprise visit to Stella's friend, Warner Carlysle. She wanted to talk to her, even though ever since the funeral Warner had been avoiding her calls. She was determined that before she left for Vegas they would get together, so she took a cab to Warner's showroom in the hope that she'd catch her.

The place was crowded, but Madison knew how to get action. She walked up to the girl at Reception and said, 'Hi, I'm Madison Castelli from *Manhattan Style*. Warner's expecting me – is she in her office?'

'Yes,' the girl said, harassed because several people were on her case at once. 'I'll buzz her.'

'That's okay,' Madison said. 'I know my way.'

Warner was on the phone, sitting behind a huge glass-topped desk in her cluttered office. She looked up and registered shock when she saw Madison.

Madison gave a little wave, walked over to the couch

in the corner, sat down and picked up a magazine.

'Uh . . . can I call you back?' Warner said into the receiver. Obviously the person at the other end said yes, because Warner quickly hung up. 'Madison!' she exclaimed. 'What a surprise.'

'I was in the neighbourhood,' Madison said, putting down the magazine, 'and since you haven't returned my calls, I thought I'd drop by to see if you're okay.'

'I'm so sorry – it's fashion time,' Warner explained. 'I've been *extra* busy. Everyone's *screaming* for their jewellery.'

'I'm sure.'

'Anyway, it's nice to see you,' Warner said.

Is it? Madison thought. *I've got a strong suspicion there's something you don't want to talk to me about.*

'Unfortunately,' Warner continued, 'this is not the greatest of times for us to get together because I have an appointment.' She glanced at her watch. 'In exactly five minutes. Then, after that, I'm taking a buyer from Houston to dinner.'

'Can we make a date?' Madison said. 'I'm leaving on a trip Friday morning and I'd like to get together before.'

'Bad timing,' Warner said regretfully. 'As I mentioned before, this is the busiest time of the year for me.'

'You can't clear an hour for us to sit down and talk?'

'I know it seems foolish,' Warner said apologetically, 'it's simply that I'm running from one buyer to the next, my designers are driving me crazy . . . and, uh, my spring line of silver and turquoise is not yet finished. Oh, yes, and if that isn't enough, the factory in Hong Kong is behaving badly. Can our meeting wait until you get back?'

'You're giving me no choice,' Madison replied coolly.

'I knew you'd understand,' Warner said, standing up. 'I'll call you or *you* call me. This time I promise I'll get back to you. By then my desk should be clear – not to mention my head.'

Madison nodded, walked towards the door, then stopped. 'By the way, Warner,' she said, on impulse, 'did you ever sleep with Michael?'

'What?' Warner said, paling.

Madison fixed her with a long, steady stare. '*Did* you?'

'I . . . I don't understand that question,' Warner stammered, losing her cool – but only for a moment.

'It's very simple,' Madison said, speaking slowly. 'A yes or a no would do nicely.'

'No,' Warner said, her mouth tightening into a thin line. 'Goodbye, Madison.'

'Goodbye, Warner.'

Madison hit the street not knowing why she'd asked, but it had occurred to her that Warner had something to hide. What could it be after all these years? Had Michael gotten to her? Warned her not to talk?

When she got back from Vegas, she was definitely getting into it further. She was also planning on persuading Victor to allow her to write an investigative piece on the old crime families of New York. If she was legitimately researching a story, she could find out plenty. And why not find out about the Giovanni family? Especially Don Carlo Giovanni – the man Michael had supposedly worked for. Maybe that way she could discover the truth about her father.

And when she had all the answers, that would be the time to sit down with Michael and listen to exactly what he had to say.

Chapter Thirty-eight

Joel's dinner party was a blast. Testio certainly knew how to get things going. Not only did he bring the delectable Carrie, he also had a couple of other supermodels in tow, both of whom Joel had been anxious to get acquainted with.

Joel himself had invited a young, sexy singing sensation of the Latin persuasion, two other models and a card-playing friend of his.

The ratio of guests was not exactly to Carrie's liking – six girls to three men. In the middle of complaining to Testio, she spotted Eduardo, and her mood improved. 'Who's the pretty boy?' she whispered.

Testio shrugged. 'Dunno,' he said, playing his part well. 'You'd better ask Joel.'

'Do I have to?' she groaned.

Testio looked at her quizzically. 'What's this thing you got against Joel?'

Carrie wrinkled her nose. 'He's so . . . *crass*.'

'Nah, he's okay once you get to know him.'

'I don't *want* to get to know him.'

'Yeah, well, you should. His old man's one of the richest dudes in New York.'

'That's his father, not him.'

'I know Joel likes you.'

'All men like me,' she said with an exaggerated sigh, followed by a superior smile.

Man, Testio thought, *this one brings conceit to a new level.*

Joel had hired one of the best chefs in New York to cook dinner. He had taken the trouble to find out Carrie's favourite foods, and he'd made sure they were all served.

He introduced Eduardo as his nephew from Puerto Rico. 'My mother's side of the family,' he said, with a wink. Then he sat Eduardo on one side of Carrie at the dinner table, and himself on the other.

Before long, Carrie and the boy were engaged in animated conversation.

Testio signalled Joel across the table, mouthing, 'I told you so.'

Soon Carrie began to relax. Several glasses of her favourite wine, followed by the exquisite Château d' Yquem, another of her favourites, then peach brandy.

Eduardo played his part to perfection. Although he looked no more than a well-built fifteen, he was actually nineteen. When Madam Sylvia employed someone she had them expertly trained before she sent them out on a job and Eduardo was well versed on his mission.

Joel was paying handsomely to make sure Eduardo made Carrie Hanlon very happy indeed. Only not too soon. He had to persuade her to come away with him first.

After dinner he got his opportunity. 'I'm flying to

Vegas on Thursday for the big fight Saturday night,' he said, with full-on Joel Blaine sincerity. 'I'd love it if you'd accompany me. Separate suites at the hotel, everything straight up. We'll fly there on my father's plane.'

'Why would I go to Vegas with you?' Carrie asked, tossing back her third peach brandy.

'Maybe 'cause Eduardo will be there,' Joel said slyly. 'I know *he*'d like you to come, only you'd better not mention him to my old man. As I said, he's from my mother's side of the family – an indiscreet, illegitimate fling.'

Carrie smiled her all-American-girl-next-door-by-way-of-Julia-Roberts-smile. 'Wish I had a joint.' She sighed.

Joel, ever the magnanimous host, said, 'You can have whatever you want.'

'Then I'll take a hit of your best stuff,' she said, stretching luxuriously.

'Is that a yes to Vegas?' he said, nailing her decision down. 'I'll have a limo pick you up at your apartment. There'll be plenty of press and some great parties. Leon's very generous when it comes to giving money to the ladies to gamble – not that you need it, but it's kind of a kick that he hands out thousands of dollars just so you can lose on his behalf.'

'Hmm . . .' Carrie said languidly. 'And you say Eduardo will definitely be there?'

'Waiting in your suite if you want,' Joel said, puzzled as to why she'd prefer to fuck a fifteen-year-old when she could have him.

'Well,' Carrie said, dazzling him with a smile, 'you *do* make things tempting.'

'I try to please,' Joel said.

'Maybe I was wrong about you,' Carrie mused. 'I always heard you were like this model-chaser, you know – every new girl in town and Joel Blaine's the first to score.'

'That's for publicity purposes only,' Joel said, kind of getting off on his new respectable image. 'Truth is, I have a steady girlfriend.'

'You do?' Carrie said, surprised.

'Yeah, but once again, I can't tell my old man about her. Sure I'm old enough to know better, but, uh . . . I gotta play by his rules, 'cause when I inherit the billions – and, baby, I plan to – I'll be free to do whatever I want.'

'Who's your girlfriend?' Carrie asked, amused.

'Privileged information,' he answered. 'She's, uh . . . married.'

God, if Rosarita could hear his lies she'd be creaming her skimpy little thong thinking he meant it!

Carrie seemed intrigued by his stories. By the end of the evening she'd agreed to the trip.

'Can I trust her?' Joel asked Testio.

Testio, who was completely stoned, mumbled, 'Sure, man, s'long as you got Eduardo on alert.'

'It's all taken care of.'

Before Carrie left his apartment, Joel spotted her in the bathroom with Eduardo, snorting coke and grabbing a quick feel.

Fortunately, Eduardo knew the rules. No way was he allowed to give it up until Vegas.

* * *

Rosarita visited her post-office box twice daily, even though the man behind the counter assured her there was only one delivery a day. While it was a drag traipsing all the way to SoHo, she still felt it was important to make the trek. Whenever she went there she wore a clever disguise – huge, black wraparound sunglasses, a long coat and a floppy hat. God, she would have made a fantastic spy! How clever she was at covering her tracks.

'I'm expecting something from Holland,' she informed the man three days in a row. 'It could arrive at any moment.'

'Fine, lady,' he answered, fed up with her pestering. 'But I keep on tellin' ya, you is wastin' your time. It'll take a coupla weeks.'

Just when she was about to give up hope, the package was sitting there – in a box marked TULIP BULBS: HANDLE WITH CARE.

She had a large Gucci bag with her, and she quickly threw the package inside without opening it. Then she marched up to the man at the counter and closed her account.

As soon as she got home she hurried into her bathroom, locked the door and opened the package. They'd sent one small bottle of the stuff. She picked it up, handling it gingerly. It didn't look so lethal. The bottle was accompanied by a list of instructions in Dutch, which meant nothing to her. It didn't matter, she knew what she had to do. Slip it in his drink and goodbye Dex. That's all there was to it.

She spent an hour in the bathroom shredding the instructions and flushing them down the toilet, then trying to dispose of the cardboard box in the same way. It wasn't easy: she had to soak the cardboard in hot water, then get rid of it piece by piece. Finally, all that was left was the small bottle of lethal poison.

She took a plastic bottle of bath oil from the

bathroom cabinet, emptied out the contents and rinsed the bottle thoroughly until there was no odour left. Then, slipping on a pair of Conchita's rubber work gloves that she found stashed under the sink, she transferred the poison into the empty plastic bottle.

Next she wrapped the bottle in layers of Kleenex and placed it carefully at the bottom of her travel vanity case, which she then shut and locked.

A job well done, she thought, when everything was completed.

Soon . . . soon . . .

* * *

Dexter sat in Annie Cattatori's office and scowled. The fat woman was not being very co-operative. He told her about Silver's script, that Silver had asked him to raise money, and Annie laughed rudely in his face.

'That's a ridiculous idea,' she scoffed. 'Don't you *dare* get involved. She's trying to use you.'

'How is she trying to use me?' Dexter asked, perplexed.

'She wants *you* to raise the money for her, then she'll take that money and run with it. Honey, you've got no chance of being in her movie. Besides, who do you think's going to put up big bucks for *her*?'

'Thanks, Annie,' he said. 'It's nice to have an agent with confidence in me.'

'Merely being realistic,' Annie said, playing with an oversized gold earring attached to her rather plump earlobe.

'I'm not an idiot,' Dexter said heatedly. 'I'd get a lawyer to draw up a legal agreement saying that if *I* find the money, *I* appear in the film.'

'Jesus!' Annie exclaimed. 'You're so naïve.' She

groped for a cigarette. 'How you've survived in this business as long as you have I don't know.'

'I haven't,' he said sulkily. 'I got canned, remember?'

'Did my acting coach call you?' she asked, lighting up her cigarette.

'No.'

'Then *you* call *him*. No use sitting around. Forget about Silver Anderson and start taking acting classes. *That*'s important. Do that, and before you know it, you'll be working again.'

'That's what I like about you, Annie.'

'What?' she said, blowing smoke-rings across her desk.

'Your enthusiasm.'

'Enthusiasm, *and* I know what I'm doing,' she said, with a pleased smirk. 'Listen to me, soap boy, and we'll get you somewhere big.'

He had no intention of listening to Annie. Silver's script was too exciting an opportunity to blow. Besides, she'd better quit calling him soap boy, or he'd be quitting *her*.

As soon as he left her office, he contacted his father-in-law from a pay-phone. 'I'd like to come see you about something,' he said.

Oh, Christ, Chas thought. *The schmuck's havin' a kid so now he wants a loan*. 'Yeah, yeah, I'm at my office,' he growled.

'Where's that?' Dexter asked.

'Queens. Ya wanna make the trip, or ya wanna wait till later?'

'I'll make the trip,' Dexter said, deciding his mission was too important to wait. 'This is business.'

'Business, huh?' Chas said, scratching his balls.

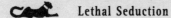

'Yes,' Dexter said firmly. 'I have a proposition for you.'

Christ! Chas thought. *Dumb soap-opera son-in-law with a proposition.*

Nothing he liked less.

Chapter Thirty-nine

'He's doing it, all right,' Kimm announced over the phone.

'Oh, shit!' Madison said. It was the day before her Vegas gig, and she was busy packing. 'Does this mean you've got proof?'

'Unfortunately,' Kimm said. 'Shall I come over?'

'You'd better,' Madison said, hoping she'd be able to catch Jamie at her office before she left.

'I'll be there in an hour,' Kimm said, and hung up.

Although Madison had suspected it was true, this was still not good news. Jamie would be devastated, and unfortunately Madison wasn't going to be around to help keep her together. Damn! Bad timing. Jamie would need her friends, because in a way she'd led such a sheltered life: always the beautiful one; the girl who married the boy of her dreams and supposedly lived happily ever after.

Jamie and Peter. The golden couple.

Obviously they were not to be.

She abandoned her packing and called Jamie at her office.

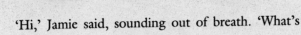

'Hi,' Jamie said, sounding out of breath. 'What's up?'

'What're you doing?'

'Coming up with a design concept for – can you believe it? – Kris Phoenix.'

'Kris Phoenix!' Madison exclaimed. 'When did *he* reappear?'

'Hmm,' Jamie said sheepishly. 'I didn't tell you this, but he never actually went away. He kind of called me after Anton's dinner, told me he was buying a penthouse in New York, and would I be interested in designing the interior.'

'How come you never mentioned it?'

'It's not like I've been dealing with *him*. I get to confer with his manager and a couple of executive assistants. If I were dealing with Kris I would've told you. Besides, *you*'re the one who'll see him next – he's performing in Las Vegas.'

'How do you know that?' Madison asked suspiciously.

'I kind of spoke to him on the phone once,' Jamie admitted. 'He . . . sort of invited me to his show.'

'Interesting you never mentioned this.'

'There's been so much else going on, and I'm not about to start behaving like a giggling schoolgirl – y'know, running to my best friend every time a guy calls me.'

'*Every* time?'

'Don't be silly.'

'Kimm wants to see you. Can you make it to my apartment now?'

'*Right* now?' Jamie said, sounding alarmed. 'Is it *that* urgent?'

'I'm leaving early in the morning, and I thought I should be at the meeting.'

'Why? Is it bad news?'

'Let's see what Kimm has to say.'

'Oh, God,' Jamie groaned. 'How can I face up to bad news? I love Peter, and I'm positive he loves me.' Suddenly she lowered her voice to a whisper. 'Can't discuss it now, Anton's lurking.'

'So jump in a cab and get over here.'

'I'll be there ASAP.'

* * *

Kimm was wearing the black leather coat Madison had bought her in Miami, and a modicum of makeup.

'You look nice,' Madison said, ushering her in. Slammer immediately began sniffing at her legs. The tall woman stooped to pet him.

'I have Evian water, *not* on ice,' Madison said, 'and I see Slammer is pleased you're here.'

Kimm rubbed the dog's head. 'I'm sorry I come bearing bad news,' she said. 'Had a hunch it would turn out this way. Once a wife is suspicious – forget about it, it's over.'

'Jamie will not take this well,' Madison said, thoughtfully. 'She's not strong like me, she's much more delicate.'

'I can tell.'

'Y' see,' Madison explained, 'because of her looks people have always spoiled her. She's treated like this blonde, blue-eyed goddess – the kind of woman men always fall desperately in love with. Not lust, love. So she's always been somewhat protected.'

'Nice for her,' Kimm said drily.

'She met Peter straight out of college. They've been married three years and are – *were* – extremely happy. This will destroy her.'

'She'll be even more upset when she sees the photographs,' Kimm remarked.

'Why? Is the girl he's with very beautiful?'

'It's best if we wait until Jamie arrives.'

'Right,' Madison agreed, hating every moment of this. 'It's her business, not mine. Maybe I shouldn't even be in on this.'

'Didn't mean it that way,' Kimm said shortly. 'I'd sooner not go through it twice, that's all.'

'I understand.'

Slammer began barking, signalling Jamie's arrival. Madison hurried over and threw open the front door.

'Hi,' Jamie said, looking prettier than ever in a long blue cashmere trenchcoat. 'That was quick. I didn't even have to ring the bell.'

'I have my own personal dog radar.'

'Yes,' Jamie said sternly, 'and you're getting too attached to him. What're you going to do when you have to give him back?'

'His owner is never coming home from Australia,' Madison said firmly. 'And if he does, I'll simply inform him, too bad, he's lost custody.'

'You're funny,' Jamie said, running a hand through her short blonde hair. 'I can remember when you used to be petrified of big dogs.'

'He's a better companion than a man any day,' Madison joked. 'Faithful, loving and always there!'

As if he was aware they were talking about him, Slammer threw himself down in the centre of the room, rolled on to his back and lifted his legs in the air.

'Just like a guy,' Jamie said, grinning. 'Showing off the goods and proud of 'em.'

'It's nice to see you again, Jamie,' Kimm said.

'I *hope* it's nice to see you again too,' Jamie replied,

staring at the detective. 'What exactly do you have for me?'

'A surprise,' Kimm said.

'I used to love surprises,' Jamie remarked, shrugging off her coat.

'Maybe not this one,' Madison said.

'So what is it?' Jamie asked, steeling herself for the inevitable.

'Photographs,' Kimm said. 'And tape recordings of his cellphone conversations.'

'Are you allowed to do that?'

'It's not a question of whether I *can*, I *do*.'

'Right,' Jamie said, her expression becoming sombre.

'Hey, listen,' Madison said. 'I'll be in the other room if you need me.'

'No,' Jamie said sharply. 'I *do* need you. You'll stay here with me.'

Kimm opened her briefcase. 'You might want to look at the photos first,' she suggested, her wide face serious.

'This is torture,' Jamie moaned. 'You look at them for me, Maddy – I can't do it.'

'Yes, you can.'

'*No*, I *can't*. What if she's someone I know?'

'You've got to do it yourself,' Madison insisted.

A reluctant Jamie accepted the photos with shaking hands. She studied them for a moment, her classically beautiful face impassive. 'What *is* this?' she said at last, thrusting the photos at Madison. 'What the hell *is* this?'

Madison inspected the photographs. The first one showed Peter on the street talking to another man. The second photo was more intimate as the two men leaned closer together. In the third photo they were embracing. And in the fourth, they were entering a hotel arm in arm.

'Oh, Jesus!' Madison said, feeling sick for her friend.

There were a few moments of silence before anyone said anything. 'I'm sorry,' Kimm said finally, 'but I suppose you had to find out some time.'

'Find out *what?*' Jamie demanded, the colour draining from her cheeks.

'It's pretty obvious,' Madison ventured.

'*What?*' Jamie yelled. 'Tell me! *What?*'

Madison and Kimm exchanged glances, and Madison gave an imperceptible nod, giving Kimm permission to say the words aloud.

'Your husband's having an affair with a man,' Kimm said.

And then there was silence.

Chapter Forty

Rosarita was all set for Vegas. She visited Barney's, purchasing a couple of expensive designer outfits before making a trip to one of her favourite places in New York, the Bigelow Apothecaries store on Sixth Avenue. Rosarita was a makeup freak and in Bigelow she went crazy, buying CE nail polish in red glitter, a selection of Laura Mercier lipsticks, several Portuguese soaps from Klaus Porto and, finally, a tube of glycolic acid skin lightening lotion from Peter Thomas Roth – her favourite skin-care line.

After paying for her purchases on the credit card Chas always settled, she took a cab home.

Now that I'm pregnant, she thought, *maybe Daddy will spring for a chauffeured car to drive me around. It's not right that I should be struggling on the cold New York streets climbing in and out of cabs.*

She decided to take it up with him in Vegas, pre-ferably in front of Martha, who she was sure would agree with her.

Back at the apartment she packed her new makeup purchases carefully in her vanity case, making sure that the plastic bottle of poison was still well hidden at the bottom.

She was uncharacteristically nervous, but also excited. Vegas was finally coming up, and, if all went according to plan, soon she would be a free woman.

Wouldn't *that* be something to celebrate.

* * *

Across town, Dexter arrived at his first acting class full of enthusiasm. He'd had a few good days. Both Chas and Mortimer had agreed to meet with Silver Anderson, and the moment he returned from Vegas he was setting a time and a place. When he'd told Silver, she was delighted. 'Put me in the same room with a potential investor, darling,' she'd drawled, 'and the money is practically ours.' A throaty laugh. 'I'm *very* persuasive.'

Yes, he knew that.

The acting coach Annie had recommended was a tall, thin, pale man with narrow eyes, a mean slash of a mouth and yellow Dracula teeth. His name was Finian Price and he was a small-time character actor in big-time movies. Dexter recognized him immediately. 'It's an honour to meet you, sir,' he said, walking over and introducing himself.

Finian dismissed him with a snarly look. 'Enough with the sir shit,' he said. 'Go sit over there,' he added, indicating the end of a row of straight-backed wooden chairs.

Dexter had expected a more friendly greeting, considering Annie had assured him she'd called the guy personally. Obviously Finian had other things on his mind.

The class was filling up with students. There were about twenty people, most of them quite young.

Dexter looked around and wondered if any of them were working actors like him. He didn't recognize anyone, so he went and sat down where Finian had told him to go.

A girl looked up as he approached, a petite natural blonde with flowing hair that reached below her waist, an innocent face, wide eyes, full lips and an adorable snub nose. She was slender and possessed a beauteous smile, with which she honoured him as she put out her hand. 'Hi,' she said, in a soft, lilting voice. 'I'm Gem.'

There and then Dexter fell truly in love for the first time in his life.

'Uh . . . Dexter Falcon,' he said, shaking her hand.

'Nice to meet you, Dexter,' she murmured. 'Are you new here?'

'As a matter of fact, yes,' he said, entranced by this angel.

'Oh, good,' she said, relieved. 'So am I, and I'm *so* nervous.'

'Don't worry,' he found himself saying. 'I'll look out for you.'

'You will?' she said hopefully.

'Course I will,' he said, experiencing an over-whelming need to protect her.

'I only arrived in New York last week,' she confided. 'From Indiana. A friend told me about this class, and I knew this was where I had to be, even though enrolling used up almost all my savings.'

'I hear the teacher is excellent,' Dexter said.

'I hope so,' she said. 'I only have enough money to support myself for three months. If I can't make it in that time, I'll be on a bus headed back home. I was wondering,' she added tentatively, 'should I be looking for an agent?'

She sounded like him when he'd first arrived in town, naive and trusting – the things you shouldn't be in a city as hard-edged as New York.

He'd been lucky. Somebody would have to make sure she was lucky too.

'How about some *quiet* around here?' Finian thundered, planting himself at the front of the class. 'Concentrate, for God's sake.'

A murmur of assent echoed around the room.

'Today we're going to discuss the movie *The Fight Club*,' Finian announced. 'We'll analyse who those characters are and how you relate to them. At the same time we'll attempt to discover *why* you poor sods want to be actors in the first place because, God knows, it's hardly an easy profession and very few of you will make it. *I* did,' he boasted, 'but *I*'m one of the lucky ones. And today *you*'re the lucky ones, because today I'm sharing some of my hard-earned knowledge with you.'

'He's a famous actor, isn't he?' Gem whispered, obviously impressed. 'I've seen him in movies.'

'Not a star, if that's what you mean,' Dexter said in a low voice. 'Although, according to my agent, he's an excellent teacher.'

'Oh,' Gem murmured, even more impressed, 'you have an agent?'

'Yeah, well, you see, I'm a working actor,' Dex explained, hoping it didn't sound as if he was showing off. 'I'm only here to gain a few extra pointers.'

'You've appeared in movies too?' she said in her soft melodious voice, so unlike Rosarita's strident shriek.

'TV,' he said. 'I was on a soap, *Dark Days.*'

'How exciting,' she breathed. 'Unfortunately I

never have time to watch TV 'cause I'm always at work. Back home I was a checker at the local supermarket.'

'Not you?'

'Yes, me,' she said, with an endearing smile.

'Lucky customers.'

'Thanks,' she said, lowering her eyes. Then, 'I've been saving for three years to come to New York,' she revealed. 'Ever since I was sixteen.'

'Shut up over there,' Finian yelled harshly. 'What are you morons paying for? To watch? Or to listen? Go to the movies if you want to *watch* me. If you wish to listen and learn, then *do so*, for Crissakes! It's bad enough teaching a bunch of amateurs like you, but if you're planning on talking throughout my class, I simply refuse to continue.'

Dexter was shocked at how rude Finian was. He was also shocked that Annie would send him to a class that was quite obviously for beginners. He was no beginner, he'd been on *Dark Days* for a year, making him an experienced actor. Anyone who knew anything at all about the business realized that performing on a soap was a crash course in gaining experience. Every day there were pages and pages of dialogue to memorize, and he'd excelled at being word-perfect, able to function at the speed of light. Damn Annie! This eight-week course was costing him fifteen hundred dollars, which seemed exorbitant.

'Sorry,' Gem murmured under her breath. 'It's my fault he's cross.'

Dexter couldn't stop looking at her. She was so pretty. And so innocent. 'Don't worry,' he whispered back. 'Bullies never bother me.'

Finian spent the rest of the hour-long class putting

people down. He'd summon a student to the front, instruct them to read a scene, then, when they were finished, proceed to pull their performance to pieces. While he was at it he also managed to trash the entire cast of *The Fight Club*, proclaiming that Edward Norton was dull, Helena Bonham Carter was far too dramatic, and Brad Pitt was an overrated sexy dud.

Jesus, this is one bitter guy, Dexter thought. *Got a strong hunch this is not the place to be. Better call Annie and tell her.*

He could see Gem was completely in awe of Finian, and he was sorry she'd wasted her hard-earned money. *He* could afford it. *She* certainly couldn't.

When the class was dismissed they walked out together. 'How about grabbing a coffee?' he suggested.

She nodded. 'Okay,' she said softly.

'Good,' he said, ridiculously pleased that she'd accepted.

'I feel so insignificant,' she said, with a sigh, as they left the building. 'Insignificant and totally inadequate. I'm sure he hates all of us.'

'No, he doesn't,' Dexter assured her. 'He's a frustrated actor who never made it to the top, so now he's taking it out on us. It's his way of hitting back.'

'How can somebody like that teach acting?'

'Beats me,' he said, shrugging.

'And I was so looking forward to his class.'

'Maybe he'll improve.'

'I hope so.' She tilted her chin. 'How long have *you* been an actor, Dexter?'

'Not that long,' he admitted. 'I was a model before – the Mortimer Marcel boy.' He gave an embarrassed laugh. 'Jeez, that sounds terrible, doesn't it?'

'Not at all.'

'I did most of Marcel's ad campaigns. Had a billboard in Times Square.'

'You did?' she said, gazing up at him with adoring eyes. 'How fantastic.'

In the entire time he'd been married to Rosarita, she'd never looked at him the way Gem did.

Suddenly he was jolted back to reality with a vengeance. What was he *doing*? His wife was pregnant, and here he was having thoughts about this girl. It was all wrong, he had to stop immediately.

'Uh, listen, Gem, about that coffee,' he said. 'I just remembered, I've, uh, got an appointment.'

'Oh,' she said, obviously disappointed. 'That's all right, I understand.'

'So I'll see you next week in class?'

'Yes,' she said, gazing at him expectantly.

He knew she was waiting for him to ask for her number, but he didn't, couldn't. 'You'd better watch out,' he said. 'This city can be brutal.'

'I know,' she said, nodding determinedly. 'But at least I've got a job waitressing.'

'Where?'

'At a restaurant in TriBeCa. So . . . as long as I'm making survival money, I can keep chasing my dream.'

A girl with a dream.

How refreshing.

* * *

All packed for the upcoming trip to Vegas, Varoomba called her grandmother. It took several attempts before she reached her, Renee being a very busy woman indeed, running a highly successful phone-sex service. Although Renee had raised Varoomba after her mom died of a drug overdose, she was hardly the nurturing grandmother type.

'Hi,' Varoomba said.

'Who's this?' Renee answered suspiciously.

'It's me, Grams. Surely you recognize my voice?'

'Oh, *you*,' Renee said grumpily.

'I'm on my way to Vegas, Grams, an' I was kinda thinkin' that it might be a good thing if you could like dress down and come meet me and my boyfriend,' Varoomba said hopefully.

'What boyfriend is this?'

'He's a keeper, an' I'm hopin' he'll marry me.' A wild giggle. 'Who knows? Perhaps we'll get t' do it while we're there.'

'An' where do I come in?' Renee asked.

'Chas is into family. It'd be nice for him to know I got one of my own, that I'm not just another dumb stripper.'

'You mean he loves you for your family?' Renee jeered. 'Not your big tits?'

'Grams! Please!'

'All right, all right. Phone me when you get here. An' bring money, 'cause you ain't sent nothin' for months.'

'I will, Grams, I promise. Only one thing – when you meet us, you can't be drunk.'

'Ha!' Renee said. 'What makes you think I'm still drinkin'?'

Oh, Varoomba thought, *perhaps it's 'cause ever since I was a kid I've never seen you without a drink in your hand.*

'This is important to me, Grams,' she said, almost pleading. 'It could mean a lot of money for us both – this one's rich.'

'*Finally* the girl gets smart.'

'We're flyin' in for the big fight. I'll call you as soon as we check in.'

Varoomba had a plan, one that she'd decided was the way to get to Chas. It was quite obvious he was a man who honoured family, what with his two daughters always coming over. And it was also apparent that he genuinely loved the one with the kids, so if only her grandma would co-operate, behave herself and, most of all, stay sober, Renee would definitely make a good impression.

Varoomba knew it was about time she settled down, and right now Mrs Chas Vincent sounded pretty damn good to her.

* * *

'Hi, honey,' Dexter said, giving Rosarita a perfunctory peck on the cheek.

'Hi, honey,' she responded, mirroring his tone. Wouldn't do to cause any waves right now.

'Get all your shopping done?' he asked.

'I certainly did. Bought two great outfits. Am I gonna look hot!'

Dexter managed a weak smile, although he didn't think it was appropriate for a mother-to-be to choose sexy outfits. Gem would never do that.

'How was the acting thingie?' Rosarita said, examining her perfect French manicure.

'Okay,' he answered carefully. *Better than okay. I met the girl of my dreams. And I can't stop thinking about her.*

'Just okay?' she said, stifling a yawn. 'Didn't he tell you that you were the second coming of Harrison Ford?'

''Fraid not.'

'Shame,' she said, a slight mocking tone in her voice. 'Maybe you should show him some of your tapes, let him see you in action.'

Sometimes Dexter couldn't help wondering why Rosarita went out of her way to be so bitchy. There was always a put-down in everything she said.

He turned away and thought about Gem. That's exactly what she was – a gem, a beauty, the girl he *should* have married.

How did he know?

He just did.

Several months ago Rosarita had requested a divorce and he'd said no. Too late now. Like an idiot he'd followed his dad's advice and knocked her up. Now there was no way he'd ever ask her to get rid of their baby. As his mother would say, 'You've made your bed, Dick Cockranger, now you've got to lie in it for eternity.'

'Want to go out for dinner tonight?' he suggested, having no desire to sit around the apartment thinking about what might have been.

'Good idea,' Rosarita answered, having no desire to sit around the apartment thinking about what might have been.

Dexter flexed his muscles and kept thinking of Gem. 'What time do we leave tomorrow?' he asked.

'Chas is picking us up around nine.'

'You're *sure* you want to go?' he said, hoping she might change her mind.

She fixed him with a long penetrating look. 'Wouldn't miss it, Dex. This trip will be unforgettable. And *that*'s a promise.'

BOOK TWO
LAS VEGAS

Chapter Forty-one

Antonio 'The Panther' Lopez had greased-back dark hair, a cocky grin, several prominent gold teeth, and a full-of-confidence attitude.

'The champ ain't got no chance wit' me,' he said, sitting with Madison on a bench at his training camp, his manager and handlers hovering nearby.

'Why's that?' she asked, studying his sharply chiselled face, thick bull neck and muscled shoulders, mentally preparing the way she would describe him.

''Cause I'm gonna kick his sorry ass like it ain't never bin kicked before,' Antonio boasted.

'Really?'

'Ya got it.'

'Childhood dream to be champion?'

He screwed up his face. 'Never had no freakin' childhood.'

'How come?'

'My old man didn't think I needed one.'

'Why?'

''Cause he kept me workin' wit' him.'

'And he was . . . ?'

'A freakin' handyman to rich assholes in Mexico City.'

'You didn't enjoy working with your dad?'

'I was freakin' *ten*, for Crissakes.'

'Tough life, huh?'

'That's how I learned t' kick any mothafucker's ass.'

'Tonio,' said his manager, a fat, middle-aged man in a crumpled suit, hurriedly stepping nearer, 'take it easy. This is a nice lady from a classy magazine.'

'Fuck nice!' Antonio said fiercely. 'Bein' nice never got me nothin' but dog-shit!'

'Tonio!' his manager pleaded, sweat dripping from his brow. 'Calm. Relaxed. Save the anger for tomorrow night.'

Antonio gave a crafty grin, stood up and stretched. He wore striped green shorts, a loose tank top and silver running shoes. Around his neck there were several gold chains: two had diamond-studded medallions hanging from them. 'She don't mind,' he said. 'She be cool. Right, lady?'

'Right,' Madison agreed, glancing around to see if Jake had arrived. It was about time he got there because he was missing out on some good shots. Besides, even though she'd decided to have nothing more to do with him, she was still waiting to see what he had to say.

Better concentrate on Antonio, she thought. *Better not let my mind wander.*

She had a strong suspicion that if Antonio *did* win the title, he'd soon become impossible to deal with. He was a true character – the man who would be champ. There was no doubt that the fame and attention would go to his head and explode. The time to get to him was now, *before* the explosion.

She'd arrived in Vegas late the previous night, taken a cab from the airport to her hotel and fallen straight into bed, ready for an early-morning interview at the Panther's training camp.

Jamie was on her mind. After Kimm's departure they'd sat up all night talking. 'What am I going to *do?*' Jamie had wailed over and over. 'What *the hell* am I going to do?'

'Confront him,' Madison had suggested. 'Go home and tell him that you know everything. Then give him a chance to explain.'

'Explain *what?*' Jamie had yelled angrily. 'That he's fucking a *guy?*'

'Show him the photos.'

'He'll only deny it.'

'But you have all the proof you could ever need.'

'I can't take a confrontation. All I want is out.'

'C'mon, Jamie, you still have to face him.'

'*Why?*'

'Because you share a life together. An apartment. Possessions. Everything. You must go home and make him understand it's over – if you're absolutely sure that's what you want.'

'No,' Jamie had said sarcastically. 'I'm *longing* to continue sharing my husband with a man.' And then she'd burst into tears. 'Fuck him! I hate the prick! I *never* want to see him again.'

She'd stayed the night at Madison's, and when Peter had called looking for her, they'd let the answering-machine pick up. Madison had taken off for the airport the next morning, leaving Jamie in her apartment.

'You gonna bet on me tonight?' Antonio inquired, squinting at her, intruding on her thoughts. ''Cause if you do, you better bet big.'

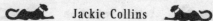

'I don't bet.'

'Howzatt?'

'Only losers gamble.'

Antonio roared with laughter, gold teeth catching the sunlight. 'Bullcrap, baby! Bet on me an' you gonna be a winner.'

'Thanks, but no thanks,' she said, thinking that she'd better get on with the interview.

She never prepared set questions, preferring to let her subject take her wherever they wanted to go. Which is why she liked to conduct interviews over several sessions – that way the subjects became comfortable with her and subsequently let their guard down. It seemed Antonio didn't need any persuading to do that: he was all mouth.

He peered at her, narrowing his eyes. 'You got a reputation, lady.'

'So have you,' she countered.

'My manager checked you out.'

'Likewise.'

'An' what you find out?' he said, challenging her to come up with something new.

'That you're twenty-three years old and already have three children by three different women. And that you don't plan on marrying any of them.'

'Marriage is shit,' he said, looking disgusted.

'Why?'

'You're a smart lady, you gotta *know* why.'

'Tell me.'

'Things get stale.'

'Really? How would you know that?'

A sly grin. 'Who wants ta fuck the same woman night after night?'

His manager groaned audibly.

'Were your parents happy?'

'Happy. *Shee-it*,' he said. 'My mama worked her ass inta the grave, an' my old man did the nasty wit' anyone he could.'

'So it seems that their relationship coloured your view of marriage?'

'Huh?' he said blankly.

She changed direction. 'What about love?' she asked coolly.

'Love?' Antonio laughed derisively. 'That's somethin' wimmen made up. Like some big freakin' fake trip.'

'So you've never been in love?'

'I love my kids,' he said indignantly. 'They part of me.'

'The good part?'

'Mebbe,' he said, throwing her a suspicious glare.

Out of the corner of her eye she observed Jake pulling up in his truck. He had a girl with him, a young blonde with a body to die for and cute little pigtails. The girl jumped out of the truck and began unloading camera equipment.

Antonio took one look at her and over-exaggeratedly licked his thick lips. 'Momma! Momma!' he crooned. 'Who's the foxy cooze in the ass huggers?'

Never one to miss out on a pertinent question, Madison quickly asked, 'Do you prefer your women black or white?'

'Long as they got a cunt,' Antonio snickered.

Nice quote. She would use it.

'Hey,' Jake said, strolling over and zeroing in on her, 'you came without me. Thought we were supposed to do this together?'

'Sorry,' she answered vaguely. 'I was under the impression you'd be arriving earlier.'

'Why?'

'I just was.' And before she could help herself she found herself saying, 'Who's the girl?'

'Oh, Trinee, she's my temporary assistant. Daughter of a friend of mine. It's her first job.'

'How nice,' she said, thinking, *Trust Jake to hire an assistant with a body that belongs in* Playboy.

'Don't tell me you're jealous?' he said, grinning. 'She's just a kid.'

'Are you insane?'

Before he could answer, Antonio's manager stepped between them. 'You the photographer?' he inquired. Jake nodded. 'Make sure there are no right-profile shots,' the manager ordered, still sweating profusely. 'Catch him from the left. And no crotch shots.'

'Excuse me?' Jake said.

'He's over-endowed in that area,' the manager explained, *sotto voce*. 'Let's not emphasize it.'

'Of course,' Jake said, winking at Madison, letting her know exactly what shot he'd go for, and when Antonio saw it he'd probably love it.

'Hey, cutie,' Antonio said, attempting to make time with the pigtailed blonde, who was now busy stacking film. 'How'd you like to play sucky face wit' the future champ?'

The girl blushed, a genuine pink-cheeked blush.

'I could show you things you ain't *never* gonna see through a camera,' Antonio continued, with a lewd wink. The blonde blushed a deeper red; she couldn't have been more than seventeen.

'Antonio,' Jake said, introducing himself to the young boxer, 'I'm Jake Sica, taking photos for *Manhattan Style*. Any objection if I just keep snapping away while you talk? Then maybe we can plan a more

378

formal shot for later today.'

'Yeah, man, go for it,' Antonio said, beaming. 'I got that photogenic thing goin'. Even my ass look good.'

'How fortunate for you,' Madison interjected drily, thinking that this was turning out not to be such an ordinary interview after all. Antonio was setting *himself* up – *she* wasn't putting the words in his mouth.

By noon she had more outrageous quotes than she could handle. And Jake was capturing some interesting shots as Antonio went about his business – flirting outrageously with the pigtailed blonde, working out with a sparring partner in the outdoor ring, jogging around the property with two of his handlers, then eating a hearty late breakfast of steak, eggs, and a mountain of fruit.

After a while, Antonio's manager suggested that Madison and Jake return later. 'He's in training for the biggest fight of his life,' the man explained. 'Gotta make sure he concentrates.'

'He doesn't seem to think he'll have any problem winning,' Madison remarked.

'My boy's had thirty-three fights an' never lost,' the manager said proudly. 'Knocked his opponent out every time. This kid's like a meteor rising. He's gonna make it all the way.'

'Well, I'm very flattered you allowed us to be here today,' Madison said.

'Come back around four,' the manager said. 'You can talk to him some more while your photographer gets the cover shot.'

Hmm . . . Madison thought. *Victor has promised them a cover. Well, the way Antonio's talking, there's no doubt that's what it will be – winner take all, including the cover.*

While Jake's cute assistant was packing up, he made his way over to Madison. In spite of herself she liked the way he looked – lean and lanky and sexy. *No*, she told herself sternly. *Don't even think about it.*

'Where are you off to now?' he asked.

'Meeting Natalie for lunch,' she said, trying to avoid contact with his appealing brown eyes.

'Natalie's here?'

'She's covering the fight for her show. Right now she's over at the champ's training compound.'

'Can I join you for lunch?'

'I don't think so, Jake,' she said. 'Natalie and I have a lot of catching up to do.'

'I'm still being punished, huh?' he said.

She threw him a quizzical look. 'Punished?' she said. 'For what?'

'I know how mad you were the other day. And you're right, we *did* have a great time together. And maybe *that*'s why I didn't call.'

'Excuse me?'

'It's difficult, Madison,' he said restlessly. 'Every time I get close to somebody, something bad happens. And I don't want anything bad happening to you.'

'Oh,' she said coolly. 'That's a new one. Usually it's "I can't see you again because you're too good for me." How come you didn't use *that* one?'

'Listen to me,' he said. 'I'm sorry I left, even sorrier I didn't call. I know I made a big mistake. How about we get together for dinner tonight and talk about it?'

For a moment she was flustered. Her immediate desire was to say yes, but every instinct warned her not to. 'Look,' she said finally, 'we'll meet back here later and discuss it then.'

'I guess that's a no,' he said ruefully.

'It's a maybe,' she countered.

He stared at her intently. 'How do I turn a maybe into a yes?'

'You had your chance, Jake.'

'Yeah, I know, and I had a chance in L.A. too, and blew it. How about making Vegas the lucky charm?'

'We'll see,' she said, getting into her rental car, thinking that he had no chance because she wasn't about to get hurt a second time. And he *would* hurt her. He was obviously that kind of guy.

'I'll see you later,' he said.

'Sure,' she said, with a dry smile, adding a silent, *I won't hold my breath*.

*   *   *

Jamie bestowed one of her special smiles on the portly man behind the reservations desk, and even though the flight to L.A. was overbooked, he managed to find her a seat.

'Thank you,' she murmured graciously, a vision in her long blue cashmere coat with faintly tousled short blonde hair and luminescent skin.

The man wondered what it would be like to bed this modern-day princess with the high cheekbones and luscious full lips. He watched her walk away, realizing sadly that he would never find out.

Jamie boarded the plane and found herself sitting next to a black woman, who was engrossed in a book on supernatural powers. She was relieved, for she knew without a doubt that had it been a man seated next to her, he would have come up with some lame excuse to talk to her all the way to California.

Yes. She was on her way to Vegas. And Peter didn't

know. Peter had no clue. Peter, without whom she hadn't made a move since they were married, was in for an enormous shock.

She'd stayed in Madison's apartment after Madison had left. Peter had called several times looking for her, but she'd ignored his messages on the answering-machine. Let him sweat. She didn't care, she was too furious to care. He was such a lying, cheating, dishonest son-of-a-bitch! And she couldn't care less if she never saw him again.

Not only had Kimm supplied photographs: there were tape recordings of his intimate cell phone conversations with his male lover who, she'd found out, was an up-and-coming young Wall Street broker named Brian.

As soon as she'd made up her mind what her next move was, she'd called Anton at the office.

'Where *are* you, dear heart?' he'd said. 'Peter is having a cow. I understand you did not go home last night, you naughty little girl.'

'Tell Peter,' she'd said slowly, 'that maybe his good friend *Brian* will be able to find out where I am. And you can also tell him that he'll be hearing from my lawyers.'

'*What is* going on?' Anton had asked, ears lighting up.

'I'm taking a leave of absence,' she'd replied. 'Don't expect me back in the office for a while.'

'But, darling –' Anton had started to object.

'Trust me,' she'd said firmly, because nobody was changing her mind. 'I need this break.'

Now, as she sat on the plane, she knew exactly what the break was going to consist of: one wild weekend in Vegas, where she'd celebrate Madison's birthday *and*,

when she was finished partying, she would fuck Kris Phoenix.

Jamie was a girl who *knew* how to get the perfect revenge.

Chapter Forty-two

Rosarita stared at the girl in the blue cashmere coat sitting across the aisle from her on the American Airlines plane, and hated her. She was the kind of blonde who really considered herself hot shit. The kind of blonde Joel might like to hang with.

The thing that infuriated Rosarita more than anything was that the girl was obviously a natural blonde. *Bitch!*

Rosarita picked up her glass of champagne and orange juice and downed it. Then she buzzed the flight attendant to bring her another one. Dexter was snoozing beside her. How could he sleep on a plane? Didn't he know it could *crash*, hurtling them all to a fiery and unwelcome death? What a moron. She'd be so glad to be rid of him.

Chas and Varoomba were sitting two seats in front of them. How dumb of Chas to bring his stupid live-in stripper slut. Didn't he know Vegas was jam-packed with strippers? Bringing Varoomba was like taking a Hershey bar to a chocolate factory.

Dumb! Dumb! Dumb!

They were stopping off in L.A. because Chas had decided he wanted to spend the night there and have dinner at the fabled Spago in Beverly Hills.

'There's a Spago in Las Vegas,' Rosarita had pointed out.

'Not the same,' Chas had replied. 'In Beverly Hills we're gonna see movie stars.'

Big fucking deal. Rosarita didn't need to see movie stars: she'd already bagged the son of one of the richest men in America.

She wondered what Joel was doing now. Missing her? He probably hadn't even noticed she'd left.

But he would. And when she returned to New York – if all went according to plan – she'd finally be a free woman. And then she could *really* start living.

* * *

Joel sat in the limo, grinding his teeth with frustration, waiting for Carrie Hanlon to put in an appearance. Twenty-five fucking minutes he'd sat there, waiting patiently like schmuck of the year.

He'd made his driver buzz her apartment three times, and each time the same answer came, 'I'll be right down.'

When she finally appeared, it was worth the wait. Miss All-American Sexy Supermodel – with the mane of shining auburn hair, glowing skin, long limbs and big white teeth.

Passers-by on the street stopped to stare. Joel felt a frisson of pride. She was hot and she was with him.

Only temporarily. Soon she would be with some teenage delinquent stud. No accounting for some women's taste.

'Hi, Jack,' she said, climbing into the back of the limo.

Jack! Was she fucking kidding? Jack! Jesus H. Christ, the stuck-up bitch couldn't even remember his fucking *name*. What kind of shit action was *this*?

'Joel,' he said, through clenched teeth.

'Whatever,' she said, exploring the stash of liquor in the side compartment. 'No champagne?' she complained, a small frown creasing her smooth forehead.

'It's nine in the morning,' he said.

'So?' she said.

'You want champagne?'

'Cristal.'

Joel tapped on the tinted-glass partition separating them from the driver, and told the man to stop at the next liquor store. If the spoiled bitch wanted Cristal, that's what she'd get.

* * *

'Baby!' Natalie's wide grin lit up the outside patio of Spago in Caesar's Palace.

Madison gave her a big hug. Natalie squealed with delight. She was a vivacious five-foot-two-inch black woman with glowing skin and wide brown eyes. 'Man, you look *great!*' she exclaimed, stepping back.

'So do you,' Madison said.

'Yeah, well, I wasn't expecting *you* to look so good,' Natalie said. 'From what I hear, things are pretty down.'

'That's true,' Madison said, shrugging. 'But you know me – always the survivor.'

'Come on,' Natalie said, grabbing her by the arm. 'I got us a table inside.'

'I'd sooner sit outside and watch the passing crowds.

Vegas is a circus. I love the action.'

'Oh, good. Does that mean we can hit the blackjack tables later?' Natalie said, approaching the *maître d'* and organizing a table for two on the patio.

'I'll watch,' Madison said. 'Given the way my luck's been running . . .' She trailed off.

They sat down and Natalie clicked her fingers for a waiter.

'Drinks, ladies?' he asked. He was a would-be actor with tousled mud-brown hair and a boyish grin.

'Perrier,' Madison said.

'Same,' Natalie said, smiling up at him. 'And bring us a couple of your delicious pizzas.'

'You got it.'

'Hmm . . . not bad,' Natalie said, watching him as he retreated. 'Nice ass.'

'Do you ever think about anything other than sex?'

Natalie smiled mischievously. '*Is* there anything else?'

'Cute.'

'So, how was Antonio "The Panther" or whatever his name is?'

'Major sexist asshole.'

'Figures. While *you* were with him, *I* was interviewing the champ. Although I gotta say, your one's more of a babe.'

'He's not *my* one,' Madison objected. 'And he's not a babe, he's a dummy. You should *hear* the crap that spews out of his mouth. I mean, where do guys learn such bad behaviour?'

'Hey – he must be all of twenty,' Natalie said. 'At that age guys think with their dicks, an' since this one makes a living with his fists, what did you expect, girl – Einstein?'

'Right,' Madison agreed, with a dry laugh. 'I keep

forgetting how young he is. Young and full of himself. He's convinced he'll win.'

'Whatever gets him through the day.'

The waiter returned with their drinks, and Natalie bestowed another big smile on him.

'Flirt!' Madison admonished her, after he left.

'Can't help it.' Natalie giggled. 'It comes naturally.'

'Tell me about the champ,' Madison said, picking up her Perrier and sipping it.

'Busy black boy doing his Muhammad Ali shtick,' Natalie said, waving at an acquaintance.

'Did he come on to you?'

'*No!*' Natalie exclaimed. 'He's a Muslim with a knock-out babe of a wife who sits silently in the background, completely calm, watching everything. Man, that woman's got dagger eyes. He wouldn't *dare* look at another female – she'd have his balls for breakfast, sprinkled with sugar.'

'So eloquent,' Madison said, laughing again.

'I try.'

'And how *is* the complicated and always interesting love-life of Miz Natalie De Barge? You still seeing the football player?'

Natalie grinned. 'Big Luther. Sure, when he's around.' A succinct pause. 'He comes, he goes, if you get my subtle drift.'

'Your *not* so subtle drift.'

'And you?' Natalie inquired. 'Anything new and exciting in the love stakes?'

'Remember I told you Jake Sica called me?'

'*And?*'

'He was in New York recently and we . . . had a little interlude. Actually, it was more like a week-long interlude.'

'Girl!' Natalie yelled. 'Don't tell me you finally did it?'

'Shout a little louder,' Madison said, frowning. 'I think there's a couple in the corner who didn't quite hear.'

'Thank God!' Natalie exclaimed. 'I thought we'd *never* get you laid again!'

'You're so crude.'

'Never said I wasn't.'

'Jesus!'

'Of course,' Natalie mused, waving at another acquaintance, 'you two *always* had chemistry.'

'Oh, yeah, there was chemistry all right,' Madison said wryly. 'After seven great inseparable days and nights, *he* took off for Paris, and that's the last I heard from him until I ran into him on the street. Unfortunately, I'd already suggested him for this job, so he's here in Vegas, and he wants to have dinner with me tonight. Naturally I told him no.'

The waiter returned with two pizzas. 'May I say that I love your show,' he said to Natalie, a lock of tousled hair falling appealingly on his forehead.

She grinned, pleased. 'You may.'

'Are you here for the fight?'

'Isn't everyone?'

'Bruce Willis was in last night,' he confided. 'So was Leonardo.'

'Cool.'

'Will you be interviewing either of them?'

'Maybe.'

'I'll be watching.'

'I think he likes you,' Madison said, as the waiter departed.

'Cute guy with taste,' Natalie said, grinning again.

'Now back to you – here's the thing.'

'What?'

'When it comes to men you're too particular.'

'And what exactly does *that* mean?'

'It means you gotta loosen up, girl. The poor guy is probably scared shitless of you. A week in your company is enough to scare anybody.'

'Ah, compliments,' Madison said drily. 'Exactly what I'm craving.'

'I'm sorry to say this, Maddy, 'cause you know how much I love you, but your extreme smarts intimidate people – *especially* guys who can't live up to you.'

'Hmm . . .' Madison drawled sarcastically. 'Maybe I should try to appear dumber.'

'Jake probably figured he couldn't compete. So he took off rather than try.'

'Christ, Natalie! Am I *that* bad?'

'Like David,' Natalie said, on an unstoppable roll. 'You see, basically David *knew* he wasn't as smart as you, so he ran into the arms of the first dumb blonde he could find.'

'She was his childhood sweetheart,' Madison pointed out.

'Doesn't make her any smarter.'

Madison sighed, she'd had enough of Natalie's dime-store philosophy. 'And I suppose *that*'s why he's begging to come back?' she said.

'David?' Natalie questioned, eyebrows shooting up.

'Yes, *David*. Believe me, I haven't even begun to tell you all the stuff that's been going on.'

'Well, girl,' Natalie said, leaning back in her chair. 'Enough of this Perrier crap. I think it's time I ordered myself a long, cool martini, then I'm chillin' out and listening to *everything* you have to say.'

* * *

Carrie managed to irritate Joel all the way to the private air-strip where Leon's G-4 waited, sitting on the tarmac like a huge, gleaming predatory bird.

He'd had the driver stop the limo and purchase a bottle of Cristal. Then he'd opened it, inadvertently spilling it all over his Armani sports jacket. After that little mishap, he'd filled a glass for her and the bitch had taken barely a sip. Instead she'd gazed out of the window as if bored, ignoring his valiant attempts at conversation. The problem was, in the limo – with only the two of them as witnesses, it was okay. But how about on the plane when he had to impress his god-damn father? Not to mention the Asian prison guard.

Carrie Hanlon had to shape up and put on some kind of show, or he was royally fucked.

He considered the situation. She had her own money, plenty of adulation, a hot career. What could he possibly offer her that she didn't already possess?

Of course, there was always Eduardo. But he was a done deal. Paid for and waiting in a luxurious suite at the hotel.

What to offer the bitch, that was the question.

And then it came to him. A movie career. Yes! Every supermodel he'd ever known had lusted after a movie career. They all fancied themselves as the next Cameron Diaz.

'Carrie,' he said slowly, as the limo drew to a halt, 'you ever met Marty Scorsese?'

'No,' she said, not really interested.

'The reason I ask,' he said, persevering, 'is 'cause he'll be at the fight, an' he happens to be a very good friend of mine.'

She considered his words for a minute.

'A very, *very* good friend,' he added, in case she hadn't gotten it the first time.

'Hmm . . .' she said, licking her full lips with a surprisingly pointed pink tongue. 'I've already done a movie.'

'A flop,' he said, remembering her début in a tits-and-ass débâcle, in which the producers had her running around in a barely there T-shirt cavorting with a lacklustre co-star.

'It was an action-adventure film,' Carrie said, a touch huffy.

'No, darling,' Joel corrected, quite pleased with himself. 'It was a genuine piece of crap.'

'That's *your* opinion,' she muttered.

'And every reviewer's in America,' he said, guessing accurately. 'You see, Carrie, the way to make it in the movies is with an A number one director.'

'Like Scorsese,' she said, the thought of meeting the talented director finally sinking in.

'He did it for Sharon Stone.'

'She had to show her snatch.'

'Not for Scorsese. For him she got nominated for an Oscar.'

'Really?'

'*Casino*.'

'Oh.'

'Somethin', huh?'

'My agent says –'

'Forget about agents,' he interrupted. 'They don't know shit. What *you* need is to meet one of these big-time directors on a *personal* level.'

'I can meet anyone I want,' she said defiantly.

'Sure you can,' he answered soothingly. 'But, you

gotta realize, meeting them at the right time in the right place, it means a lot. And what with Marty being such a close friend of the family . . .' He trailed off, allowing her time to think about it – which she did.

'Introduce me,' she said.

'Be nice to me in front of my old man and I will.'

And so they made a bargain. And Joel wondered how the hell he was going to pull *this* one off, on account of the fact that he didn't even *know* Martin Scorsese, let alone have any idea if the director was in Vegas.

He'd find a way. He always did.

* * *

'Did Jamie call you?' Madison asked, sampling a piece of irresistible apple pie sent to their table by the dessert chef.

'Was she supposed to?' Natalie said.

'I guess you'll hear,' Madison ventured. 'Only I wanted it to come from her first.'

'Hear *what?*'

'About her and Peter.'

'What about them?'

'Things are not good. She put a detective on him and it's really bad.'

'Don't tell me,' Natalie groaned. 'Not Jamie and Peter, my dream couple.'

'I'm sorry to say the dream couple are about to hit a brick wall.'

'Is he gettin' it on with someone else?'

'You could say that.'

'Somebody Jamie knows?'

'It's not for me to say.'

'Why not?' Natalie demanded, determined to know everything.

'Because I'd sooner she told you herself.'

'*Why?*'

'If you can make the time, it wouldn't be a bad idea for you to fly to New York. Right now she needs her friends around her.'

'When are *you* going back?'

Madison took a deep breath. The very *thought* of going back was a total turn-off. Go back to what? Michael and his lies? No. She could do without her father for a while. He was a man she didn't know any more, and merely thinking about him gave her a creepy feeling.

'Uh . . . I was hoping to stop off in L.A. for a few weeks,' she said vaguely.

'I'd love *that*,' Natalie said excitedly. 'So would Cole. Baby bro is crazy about you.'

'It's mutual.'

'Shame he's gay,' Natalie mused. 'The two of you would've made a lovely couple.'

'You are about the most unrealistic person I know,' Madison said, shaking her head in wonderment.

Natalie giggled. 'It's more fun that way.'

'I guess.' Madison sighed, thinking about the events of the last few months. 'After everything *I*'ve been through, I could do with a little fantasy. Y' know, I was saying to Jamie the other day – I think I belong on *The Jerry Springer Show*.'

'*You?*' Natalie said, raising a sceptical eyebrow. 'Miss Classy Boots?'

'Don't give me that crap,' Madison said, pushing the tempting dessert away. 'How is Cole, anyway?'

'Doing okay. He and Mr Mogul seem to be couple of the year.'

'I thought you hated Mr Mogul?'

'I did. But at least he's kept Cole close for a while, so that makes me feel more secure. The man has a reputation for dumping the prettiest boys in town.'

'Cole's a great guy. And smart. Why would anyone dump him?'

'Hey, I'm just the critical sister who only wants the best for baby bro.'

Madison nodded. She enjoyed being with Natalie – like Jamie, Natalie was the sister she'd never had. Telling her everything over lunch had been a cathartic experience, but now it was time to return to work. She glanced at her watch. 'I'd better get moving,' she said. 'The man who would be champ is waiting – *not!*'

'Me too,' Natalie agreed. 'I'm doing a sit-down with Jimmy Smits, and that I *do not* want to be late for.'

'Lucky you,' Madison said. 'I get stuck with a boxer when I'd sooner be in Washington talking to a politician.'

'Politicians are *way* worse than boxers,' Natalie said knowledgeably. 'They're so horny it's pathetic! I interviewed a senator last week, and practically had to jump ten feet in the air when he stuck his goddamn *hand* up my skirt!'

'Ah,' Madison said with a grim smile. 'The Clinton legacy.'

'My cameraman was falling down laughing.'

'What did *you* do?'

'Continued the interview. What else? Hey –' She grinned. 'Nobody can *ever* accuse me of not being professional.'

'You're something, Natalie.'

'Yeah, tell me about it.'

Madison snapped her fingers for the check.

'*My* check,' Natalie insisted, as the waiter appeared at their table.

'No, mine,' Madison argued. 'The magazine will pay.'

'It's all taken care of,' their waiter said, a cowlick of mud-brown hair drifting on his forehead. 'Compliments of Wolfgang.' A sly wink directed toward Natalie. 'He watches your show too.'

'Why thanks,' Natalie said, wide smile springing into action. 'And your name is . . .'

'Willem.'

'You deserve a tip, Willem.'

'It's not necessary,' he said.

'Yes, it is,' Natalie answered crisply. 'Change your name – it's the best tip you'll ever get.'

Chapter Forty-three

'Fuckin' a woman is like eatin' a meal,' Antonio proclaimed, bare-chested in a pair of orange shorts, thick white socks and brown lace-up boots.

'And why would that be?' Madison asked, keeping her voice neutral.

''Cause y'see,' Antonio explained, creasing his forehead as if he'd given the subject a great deal of serious thought. 'You got all types a wimmen, an' all kinda food. Yeah,' he nodded to himself, pleased with his speech, 'like you can get a hot dog or a steak. A burrito or a pizza. Get it?'

'No,' Madison said. 'Tell me what you mean.'

He regarded her as if she were extremely dense, then launched into his philosophy. Fortunately his manager was out of earshot.

'You order a steak,' he said patiently. 'Like you'd compare a steak to one of them movie actresses or a dancer or singer – they're somethin' special. Then you got your everyday burrito – a quick snack – you eat 'em an' take off.' He guffawed heartily. 'Sometime you eat 'em an' wanna throw up.' Another guffaw.

'And currently . . .' Madison said '. . . you are eating . . . ?'

'Prime rump,' he boasted. 'Ass on her better than Jennifer Lopez!'

'Any relation?'

'Naw,' Antonio crowed cheerfully. 'But I'm gonna fuck her one of these days.'

Madison rolled her eyes. She'd had enough of Antonio and his dumb sexist rhetoric. She had her story, it was time to move on. 'Thanks,' she said, standing up and looking around for Jake. He was conferring with his young assistant, preparing for the cover shot. Since returning to Antonio's training compound she'd had no chance at all to speak with Jake. It was obvious that when he was working he became totally immersed in what he was doing. Occasionally she'd glanced over, observing him behind his camera, his face alert and concentrated. Anyone could see he was very into what he did – creating pictures, images that captured the imagination, although she knew that photographing celebrities was not his favourite work.

She waved at Antonio's manager. 'I'm leaving,' she called out. 'See you tomorrow night.'

'You're gonna be watchin' a winner tomorrow,' Antonio bragged, flexing his arm muscles. 'Better make sure you do what I tell you, lady – put yourself on line for a big bet.'

'I told you,' she said, wishing he'd shut up, 'I don't bet.'

'You gotta – for me,' Antonio said, his gold teeth catching the light. 'It bring me plentya luck.'

The manager escorted her over to her rental car. 'Y'know, sometimes Tonio says things he don't really mean,' he confided. 'But I can see you're a nice, honest gal. You wouldn't print nothing to make Tonio come over stupid, would you?'

'I print the truth,' she answered calmly. 'I don't make things up.'

'No, no, honey, it's not that we don't trust you,' he said, speaking much too fast. 'Only sometimes Tonio says things about women that, you know, some people could find disrespectful. But that's Tonio – he loves women too much.'

'Glad to hear it.'

'So, uh . . . you'll come by the dressing room tomorrow before the fight? The place'll be crazy, but you'll sit in the corner, stay quiet, take a few notes . . . that kinda thing. It's what you do, huh?'

'Yes,' Madison said. 'It's what I do.'

Jake didn't even notice she was leaving. Hmm . . . So much for their supposed dinner plans. Not that she'd considered saying yes but it would have been nice if he'd repeated his invitation.

Damn him! How come he was on her mind so much?

Well, why shouldn't he be? They'd had such a great time together – so why did it have to end up like this?

Now she had nothing to do later, although Natalie had promised to call, and Natalie *always* had plans. 'There's a million parties in town,' Natalie had assured her, 'and I'm gonna hit all of 'em. And there's also the Kris Phoenix concert, which I'm supposed to be covering. So . . . if you don't go to dinner with Jake, you'll come with me.'

The last thing Madison was in the mood to do was party. *Natalie* was the party girl. *She* preferred staying home. And she certainly didn't care to tag along while

Natalie interviewed Kris Phoenix. Ageing rockers were not her thing.

However, sitting alone in a hotel room wasn't exactly tempting either, so maybe she *would* join Natalie.

Why not? It wasn't like she had anything else to do.

* * *

Rosarita was talking non-stop in the limo taking them to the Beverly Hills Hotel, but Dexter wasn't really listening. His mind was on Gem. He was thinking about how he'd finally met the girl of his dreams, yet he was trapped in a marriage his wife had repeatedly told him she didn't want. Because even though Rosarita was pregnant, deep down he knew she didn't care to stay married to him. And now that he'd met Gem, he was inclined to feel the same way.

But Rosarita was carrying his baby, so therefore they were both stuck. But how could he tell his mind to stop thinking about Gem – the wonderful girl with the innocent face?

'This is *stupid*,' Rosarita announced, in her shrieky voice.

'What's stupid now?' Chas growled.

'Stopping off in L.A.,' Rosarita complained. 'I mean, if I wanted to come to Beverly Hills, I'd certainly plan on spending more than one night here.'

'You're lucky we're here at all,' Chas said. 'An' I got another surprise – I arranged for Matt and Martha to meet us. We're *all* having dinner at Spago.'

'Shit!' Rosarita yelled, startling their limo driver, who immediately slowed down in case of trouble. 'Why did you do *that*?'

'What do you mean, why did he do that?' Dexter said, affronted that she would object to his parents meeting them in L.A.

'I thought they wanted to see Vegas,' she said sulkily. 'Wasn't that the whole idea?'

'I'm treatin' 'em to a trip to Beverly Hills, too,' Chas said. 'You don't *mind*, do you?'

'Of course not,' she said stiffly. 'It's just that it seems foolish. I would have liked to have spent the day shopping on Rodeo Drive but, no, we have to rush to the hotel, rush to dinner, then rush back to the airport tomorrow morning.'

'Ya got time t' shop,' Chas said.

'Not enough,' Rosarita replied, sulking.

'Anybody ever told you you're spoiled?' Chas said.

'I may be spoiled,' Rosarita responded, pouting, 'but guess who made me that way?'

'I spent a week in Beverly Hills once,' Varoomba offered, joining in the conversation.

Nobody took any notice, nobody was particularly interested.

The limousine pulled up in front of the Beverly Hills Hotel, and they all piled out.

'This is where I stayed,' Varoomba chirped. 'In a bungalow.' She thought it prudent not to add that she'd been with two Saudi princes who'd won her in a poker game. But that was another story.

Dexter took a deep breath. California – it smelt different from New York. He gazed at the palm trees and lush foliage surrounding the front of the luxurious hotel. *Yeah*, he thought, *I could get used to this. And I bet Gem would love it.*

'We got dinner reservations at seven o'clock,' Chas announced.

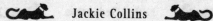

'Seven o'clock?' Rosarita screeched. 'Why so early?'

''Cause that's the only time I could get a table at Spago.'

'Not if you know someone,' Rosarita said. 'You should've let *me* do it.'

'Ya wanna call an' see if you can make it for eight?'

'Too late now,' she snapped. 'Anyway, that'll give me time to do *some* shopping.'

'I'll come with you,' Dexter said. 'I've always wanted to take a walk down Rodeo Drive.'

'No, Dex,' she said sharply. 'You spend time with your parents. That's the whole idea, isn't it?'

'Can *I* come with you?' Varoomba ventured, anxious to get on Rosarita's good side. 'I know all the best stores.'

'That's very kind of you, dear,' Rosarita said, dismissing Stripper Slut with a wave of her hand, 'but nobody has *ever* had to help *me* find the best stores. *I* put the S in shopping.'

* * *

Joel had to hand it to her, when Carrie Hanlon cared to put on the charm, she dazzled. And right now she was busy dazzling Leon Blaine, who was not the easiest man in the world to impress. Even Marika had perked up considerably, especially when she and Carrie had got into a spirited discussion about several Paris designers and their sexual foibles.

It was the first time Joel had ever seen Marika crack a smile.

'This girl is charming,' Marika said, catching him by the buffet table on Leon's plane where he was loading a plate with bagels, smoked salmon and cream cheese.

'Yeah, well, I told you she was a regular girl,' he said, savouring his triumph.

'She's more than a regular girl,' Marika said imperiously. 'She is a beauty.'

'Glad you like her,' Joel said. Frankly, he couldn't give a piss what Marika thought, it was Leon he was out to impress.

'Yes, Carrie is delightful,' Marika added, still full of praise. 'I only hope you'll be able to hang on to her.'

Hang on to her? What the hell did that mean?

Marika was a cunt, a definite cunt. In fact, she gave the word a whole new meaning.

He glowered silently.

* * *

'Hi,' Jamie said, smiling softly at the desk clerk, who immediately fell in love with the classy blonde in the long blue cashmere coat. 'I wonder if you can help me?'

Help her? He'd walk over hot coals if it would assist him in getting closer. 'Yes, ma'am,' he said, clearing his throat. 'What can I do for you?'

'It's like this,' she said, gazing appealingly at him with her wide aquamarine eyes. 'I flew in unexpectedly to surprise a friend on her birthday, and I was so busy getting out of town in a hurry that I forgot to make a reservation.'

'We're booked out, ma'am,' he said regretfully. 'It's the big fight tomorrow night, and every room is taken.'

'I'm sure,' she said. 'But, you see, my friend who's having the birthday is Madison Castelli. She's here interviewing Antonio Lopez for *Manhattan Style*.

And the other friend I'm meeting is Natalie De Barge – the TV reporter. So . . . I was thinking that you probably have emergency accommodation available for last minute VIP arrivals. And although I'm not a VIP, I'm sure that you *can* help me, can't you?'

He'd recently turned away a six-foot-three Texan who'd offered him two thousand bucks cash if he could give him a room for one night. However, money wasn't everything, and this delectable beauty was right, there were always VIP rooms available, although by tomorrow afternoon they'd all be gone.

'Uh . . . can you wait here a minute?' he said. 'I'll see what I can do.'

'You're the best,' she murmured.

Last night his wife had informed him he was the worst – lover, that is. Now this gorgeous blonde was telling him he was the best.

The best what?

Who cared? He'd score her a room if it killed him.

Chapter Forty-four

'Hi.' It was Natalie on the phone, cheery as ever. 'How'd it go?'

'Fine,' Madison said. 'He was his usual sexist self.'

'The boxer or Jake?'

'Ha ha, very funny.'

'So, seriously, did you work anything out with Jake?'

'No. He was too busy photographing Antonio.'

'Okay, okay. So I guess you're not readying yourself for a long, lustful night of great sex.'

'I guess not.'

'Then, honey, *you* are coming with me to the Kris Phoenix concert.'

'Do I have to?'

'Yeah, I think you do. You told me you had fun in Miami, why not Vegas too?'

'Because getting drunk and getting laid by some juvenile is *not* a great idea.'

'I thought the guy in Miami sounded wild.'

'He was nineteen, Nat. More your type than mine.'

Natalie raised an amused eyebrow. 'Are you sayin' I'm a slut, girl?'

'We all *know* you're a slut. Let's call it like it is – you've been one ever since college.'

'Ha! If I was a guy you'd admire me. I'm just using *them* the way *they* use us.'

'I wish *I* had half your attitude,' Madison said. 'You know I'd love to be a slut too, but somehow or other I just can't seem to cut it.'

'Bitch!' Natalie said, laughing.

'Takes one to know one.'

'Okay, okay. Enough talk – I'm meeting my camera crew downstairs in approximately half an hour, and you'd better be there dressed to party 'cause we're coverin' everything tonight.'

'I'll think about it,' Madison said, changing her mind, because maybe sitting alone in her hotel room *was* better than hitting the town with an uncontrollable Natalie.

'Forget that,' Natalie said firmly. 'You're coming whether you like it or not. Downstairs in half an hour. Look spectacular.'

* * *

Spago, Beverly Hills, was big, noisy, crowded and full of activity.

Chas slipped the girl at the reception desk a twenty to make sure they got good service. She favoured him with a fleeting smile and said, 'Sorry, you'll have to wait at the bar. Your table won't be ready for another fifteen minutes.' Then, just as she was finishing her sentence, she noticed Dexter and her attitude changed. 'Mr Falcon,' she gushed, 'how *nice* to welcome you to

406

Spago. I don't think we've seen you here before. Are you with the Vincent party?'

'Uh, yeah,' Dexter said, modestly pleased to be recognized.

'Your table's almost ready. Let me check.'

'Huh!' said Rosarita. 'Seems that being an actor – however minor – counts in Hollywood.'

Trust her to be bitchy, Dexter thought.

The girl returned a few minutes later with a gracious smile. 'Follow me, Mr Falcon,' she said, leading them out to a table on the terrace.

'Not bad,' Chas said, looking around as they all sat down. 'I like this place already. It's got class.'

'Notice any movie stars?' Rosarita asked, a tad sarcastically.

'Yeah,' Chas replied. 'Isn't that Tony Curtis walkin' in?'

They all turned to stare at the ageing actor and his tall, blonde, buxom wife, clad in a gold lamé dress that quit at the top of her thighs. Tony was wearing a velvet smoking jacket and a proud smile: it was glaringly obvious he got off on all the staring that was going on.

'Now *that*'s what I call a movie star,' Chas said admiringly. 'Been around since God knows when and still looks hot. Gotta young broad for a wife. *That's* a movie star, an' *that*'s why we stopped off in Beverly Hills.'

'Really?' Rosarita said, bored. She couldn't take much more of this: she was too anxious about Vegas and her plans for Dexter's demise. Now that the time was drawing close, she realized what a radical move this was. Poor Dexter. He could have been a movie star too, instead of which he was on his way to becoming a corpse.

After their arrival at the hotel, she'd taken off to Rodeo Drive and spent several thousand dollars in the space of an hour – all on her father's credit card. He wouldn't get the bill for several weeks, so what did she care? Spending someone else's money was one of life's small pleasures.

Due to their plane being delayed, Matt and Martha arrived at the restaurant twenty minutes late. 'Oh, my goodness,' Martha exclaimed, flustered, 'our flight was so bumpy I thought we might *crash*.' She threw her arms around Dexter's manly shoulders. 'How's my baby boy?'

He squirmed away from his overly affectionate mother. 'Don't *do* that,' he muttered, embarrassed.

'It was quite a flight,' Matt said, eyes immediately peering down Varoomba's voluptuous cleavage. 'Frightened the bejesus out of me. 'Scuse my language.'

'Well, you're here now,' Chas said, ever the magnanimous host. 'At the famous Spago. Whaddya think?'

'Exciting!' Martha said, sitting down. 'Oh, my goodness, do I spy Tony Curtis?'

'You bet your pretty little rump,' Chas said, as if he'd personally arranged for the movie star to be there.

Martha fluttered her eyelashes. 'I *love* Tony Curtis,' she said reverently. 'I always have.'

'Mom, get a hold of yourself,' Dexter said, in a stern voice.

'Would it be all right if I went over and asked him for his autograph?' Martha inquired.

'No,' Rosarita said quickly, putting a stop to such nonsense. 'You want us to look like a bunch of dumb tourists?'

'Isn't that what we are?' Matt questioned cheerfully.

Rosarita shot him a filthy look.

Chas perused the menu. 'Everythin' looks good enough to eat,' he said, with a bawdy chuckle.

'You're so funny,' Varoomba trilled, snuggling closer to him, almost falling off her chair.

Oh, for God's sake! Rosarita thought. *Don't be so obvious, it's pathetic.*

'I'm cold,' she complained, pulling her new seven-hundred-dollar pashmina wrap around her bare shoulders.

'Stop with the naggin',' Chas said. 'Everywhere we go ya gotta nag. Whassa *matter* with you?'

'I told you,' she said tartly. 'I'm spoiled. And *you* did it to me, so don't start bitching about it now, it's a little too late.'

'What do you recommend?' Dexter asked the waiter who was hovering by their table looking bored.

'Everything's good, sir,' the waiter replied, springing to attention.

'Enough with the menu crap,' Chas said, shoving his menu at the startled waiter. 'Bring out plenty of your best starter stuff.'

'Can I have a smoked-salmon pizza?' Varoomba piped up. She had dressed for the occasion in a buttercup yellow plunging-neckline girly dress and very high heels.

'What's a smoked-salmon pizza?' Chas demanded.

'We call it the Jewish pizza, sir,' the waiter explained. 'Smoked salmon, cream cheese, with just a touch of caviar.'

'Never heard such crap,' Chas growled. 'A pizza is a pizza – cheese, tomato an' pepperoni.'

'You've got to try this one,' Varoomba encouraged. 'I had it last time I was here.'

'You mean ya bin here before?' Chas said, not pleased. 'In this restaurant?'

'I told you I was in Beverly Hills for a week,' she murmured, thinking how nice it would be if he ever listened to a word she said.

'Yeah? Who with?'

'Just a friend,' she replied evasively. Wouldn't do to tell Chas *too* much about her somewhat colourful past.

And so the evening progressed.

Rosarita was thinking, *The sooner I get to Vegas the sooner I can get the deed done, and the sooner I'll be a free woman.*

Dexter was thinking, *I wonder what Gem is doing now. Do I cross her mind at all? Does she even realize what an incredible connection we had?*

Chas was thinking, *I hope my dumb maid has packed up Varoomba's things, 'cause she's really gettin' on my ass. Tits or no tits, this broad is history.*

Varoomba was thinking, *Grams better behave herself in Vegas, 'cause if she does, I got a good chance of getting Chas to make it legal. And about time too.*

Martha was thinking, *Tony Curtis, Tony Curtis, Tony Curtis. Oh my God! He used to be so handsome, and he still is.*

Matt was thinking, *I wonder if Varoomba sucks Chas' dick? Yeah, she looks like the kind of bad girl who does a dirty thing like that.*

And then it was pizza all round.

* * *

Joel didn't know whether to be pissed or pleased. Carrie had bonded so well with Leon that the two of them had not stopped talking the entire journey. At first Marika had been delighted. Here she was in the presence of a world-famous supermodel, who was being charming to both her and Leon. But after a while it occurred to her that most of Carrie's attention was directed towards the multi-billionaire, and that she and Joel were out in the cold. This seemed to amuse Joel, but by the time they landed in Vegas, Marika was furious.

'These stupid young girls,' she hissed at Joel, her new-found ally. 'They think they're such superstars.'

'Well, Marika,' Joel replied, as innocently as he could, 'I guess they are, 'cause they're treated like goddesses wherever they go, and it's obvious Leon likes her – I haven't seen him this happy in a long time.'

Marika's eyes narrowed to thin slits. She was livid that Joel now had something over her.

Meanwhile, Carrie was enjoying the lifestyle. Private planes were definitely for her. And so were multi-billionaires. She found Leon Blaine quite interesting, in spite of his being old. He was nut brown, thin and fit – thanks to daily tennis. Extreme power made up for youth: she'd discovered *that* early on in her career.

Yes, she'd take Leon over Joel any day. But for *real* pleasure she'd take Eduardo. Oh, how she *loved* the smell of a very young body. To her it was the ultimate turn-on.

She got off the plane, helped down the steps by Leon. Joel and Marika trailed behind.

Two limos waited on the tarmac.

'Carrie, you'll come with me,' Leon commanded, contented as only an old billionaire can be when in the company of a luscious young supermodel. 'Marika, you and Joel ride together.'

Fuck, Joel thought. *My old man is falling in lust!*

There had to be some way of using this to his advantage.

Marika was not a happy prison guard as she climbed into the second limo and positioned herself stiffly next to Joel. 'Your father,' she snapped. 'Always swayed by a pretty face. Perhaps he's under the impression you'll marry this one. Are you planning to, Joel?'

'Hey,' Joel answered, as casually as he could, 'you and my dad never married, and as far as I'm concerned, you've got the right idea. So why would *I* do it?'

Marika glared at him even harder. Marriage to Leon Blaine was her ultimate goal. Being Leon's mistress did not carry quite the same cachet as being his wife.

The two limos separated on their drive into town, and by the time Joel and Marika reached the hotel, Leon and Carrie were nowhere to be seen.

Joel checked in at the reservation desk. 'We're with the Blaine party,' he said.

'Ah, yes, sir,' the reservation clerk said, practically bowing. 'Mr Blaine has already arrived. I'll have somebody show you to your accommodation.'

If he'd thought Marika was livid before, now she showed her true wrath. 'This is rude,' she hissed, her mouth a tight, scarlet line of disapproval. 'Leon should have waited.'

'It's just Leon being himself,' Joel said, shrugging. 'He's always been a selfish son-of-a-bitch. Mom used to complain about him all the time.'

'I'm not your mother,' Marika said coldly.

'Not even my step-mom,' Joel agreed.

She threw another glare in his direction, and as he turned round to conceal a self-satisfied smirk he spotted Madison Castelli walking towards him.

'Well, well,' he exclaimed, delighted to see her.

'What are *you* doing here?'

It took her a second before she realized who it was. 'Oh, hi,' she said, thinking, *Just my luck to run into this moron*. 'I'm, uh, here on business.'

'What kind of business goes on in Vegas?' he asked, turning on what he considered his irresistible charm.

'I'm writing a piece for *Manhattan Style*,' she answered vaguely.

'Interviewing someone?'

'Antonio Lopez.'

'I'm betting on the other guy, but nothing like talking to the loser.'

'He won't be a loser, Joel,' she said. 'Spend a few hours with him and you'll understand.'

'You think he's gonna win?'

'*He* does. I don't know much about boxing, but Antonio is extremely confident.'

Joel moved in a little closer. 'You look *hot*.'

Her eyes darted around the crowded lobby searching for a way to escape.

'What's your plan tonight?' Joel inquired.

'Uh . . . meeting friends.' A quick glance at her watch. 'And, damnit, I'm running late.'

'Maybe we'll catch up with each other later?'

'Maybe,' she answered vaguely, thinking, *Not in this lifetime*.

Marika, observing this little exchange, obviously expected to be introduced. 'Hello,' she said.

'Uh . . . Madison, do you know Marika? My father's . . . uh . . . What do you call yourself, Marika? Girlfriend sounds kind of unimportant.'

'I'm Mr Blaine's partner in life,' Marika said, snap-dragon eyes flashing major danger signals. 'Mr *Leon* Blaine,' she added, in case Madison made the foolish

413

mistake of thinking she was with Joel. God forbid!

'Hi,' Madison said. 'Madison Castelli.'

'I read you,' Marika said. 'You have a distinctive style.'

'That's always good to hear,' Madison said politely.

'Yeah,' Joel said, joining in as if Madison were his best friend. 'This is one smart woman.'

'Thanks, Joel,' Madison said, dying to add, *I didn't know you could read.*

'I especially enjoyed your piece on Hollywood call-girls,' Marika said. 'Most informative. And rather sad.'

'Well,' Madison said, anxious to get away from both of them, 'nice meeting you. Now, if you'll excuse me, I've got to run.'

And she was on the move before Joel could say another word.

Chapter Forty-five

Age had not withered Kris Phoenix. At fifty-something, he was as raunchy as ever – a rock star for the ages. Peroxide blond hair, intense ice-blue eyes, a fake tan and rakish good looks. He was wearing well, this rock icon who was once a talented lad called Chris Pierce from Maida Vale, London. Kris still reigned supreme with hit records, sold-out concerts and a loyal fan base. Plus the women. Old, young and middle-aged, they loved him. They lusted after him. He was their fantasy.

Currently he was involved with Amber Rowe, a coltish young actress who had recently won an Oscar. Amber was tall and lanky with straight brown hair, amazingly long legs and absolutely no tits. In spite of the over thirty-year age gap, Kris felt he had finally found his match and was seriously considering asking her to move in.

Surrounded by an ass-kissing entourage, he held court in the outer room to his dressing-room suite before his one-night-only Vegas show, which was to

take place in the ballroom of the recently refurbished Magiriano Hotel.

Reluctantly, Madison trailed Natalie and her camera crew into the room. Natalie was all aglow in a short white Versace dress and python jacket. 'It's my rock star special,' she'd said, with a wild giggle, on their way in. 'Since I don't get to cover *real* news, I plan on grabbing as many good times as possible doing this crap.'

'Go for it,' Madison said, fading into a corner as Natalie began to do her stuff.

Amber Rowe faded into the corner right after her. 'I *loathe* this publicity circus,' Amber remarked, chewing her stubby fingernails. 'It's bad enough being *me*, but add Kris and we've got a major problem. We can't do *anything* without a trail of paparazzi. It's *such* a bummer.'

This was not the first time a total stranger had confided in Madison, it happened all the time. People seemed compelled to talk to her – often revealing much more than they should.

'You *could* stay home,' she suggested.

'Ha!' exclaimed Amber, blinking nervously. 'Try telling Kris *that*. He can't stand staying home. Always thinks he's missing out on something.'

'Then you must insist. Two or three nights a week wouldn't kill him.'

'Good idea!' Amber said, with a girlish grin. 'I'll try it.'

Across the room, Natalie flirted outrageously with Kris on camera. He played the game well, but when the interview was over they both knew what to do. Kris immediately began conferring with his publicist, while Natalie huddled with her cameraman and producer.

Madison and Amber made idle conversation until

Natalie came over. 'Okay, girl,' she said breezily. 'We're outta here. Entertainment Tonight TV is in the room, and that makes me want to *leave!*'

'Will I see you at the concert?' Amber asked Madison, a touch wistfully.

'Hey,' Natalie said, zeroing in as soon as she realized who the skinny girl was, 'can we talk on camera?'

'Sorry,' Amber answered quickly. 'I only do movie PR. And since I have nothing out now, it's a definite no.'

'Oh, *c'mon,*' Natalie said, flashing her best persuasive smile. 'How about a couple of comments about Kris?'

'Can't do it,' Amber said, shrinking away from Natalie, who sometimes came on too strong – especially when chasing an interview.

'An' what's goin' on 'ere?' Kris asked, strolling across the room, all tight pants and spiked hair. 'You after my girl?'

'Why not?' Natalie said boldly, with a brilliant smile. 'You two *are* together. Can't we talk about it?'

'No, luv,' Kris replied, shaking his head. 'Amber don't like to kiss an' tell, so leave her alone, okay?' Taking his young girlfriend's arm, he moved her firmly out of Natalie's way.

'You got it, Kris,' Natalie called out, to his retreating back. 'See you later, after the concert.' A beat. 'Asshole,' she muttered, under her breath.

'Can we get out of here?' Madison suggested.

'We sure can,' Natalie said, signalling to her producer that she was leaving.

When they got outside, Natalie was steaming. 'Let's go get a drink while I tell you how much I hate what I do,' she complained.

'You co-anchor your own very successful show,' Madison pointed out. 'What's so terrible about that?'

'Talking to ego-inflated assholes, that's my gig,' Natalie said gloomily. 'Gossip. Crap. Is Ricky Martin gay? Who's had a face-lift? Who's screwing who? I don't care! I wanna cover hard news – not so-called celebrities.'

'Join the club,' Madison said wryly, as they made their way through the crowded casino.

'At least you get to pick and choose *your* victims,' Natalie remarked.

'With a little help from Victor,' Madison said, as they entered one of the many cocktail lounges and sat down at a table.

'I need a drink before I have to sit through his show,' Natalie said, snapping her fingers for a cocktail waitress.

Madison wondered where Jake was and what he was up to. Damn! Why couldn't she get him off her mind?

She ordered a frozen margarita from a jaunty red-head in a fringed minidress and tried to forget about Jake altogether and concentrate on Natalie, who was still busy putting down her TV show and all it involved.

'The problem *is* the way I look,' Natalie said, pouting.

'So now pretty is bad?'

'I look too sexy.'

'You'd be pissed if you didn't.'

'No, I wouldn't.'

'Yes, you would. You get off on attention.'

'I do *not*,' Natalie said indignantly.

'And anyway,' Madison continued, 'if you wish to be taken more seriously, you'd have to change your image.'

'That's impossible. Where would I hide my boobs?'

'Hmm . . . let me see. Well, for starters you could

have breast-reduction surgery.'

'Get fucked.'

'I'm serious.'

'No, you're not.'

'Okay, then, what do *you* suggest?'

'It's easy for guys. Matt Lauer is sexy and *he*'s taken seriously. I want to be more like Matt Lauer.'

'So turn white, grow a dick and cut your hair.'

They both burst out laughing.

And as they were doing that, Jamie slid up behind them and shouted, 'Surprise!'

'Holy shit!' Natalie exclaimed, jumping up. 'Where did *you* come from?'

*   *   *

Carrie Hanlon had a dilemma, and she was confused. In the space of a few hours she'd been offered everything she'd ever dreamt of. Not that she didn't already *have* everything. She did. Fame. A successful career. Money. Adulation. What more could a girl ask for?

Only, deep down, Carrie possessed a nagging fear that one day it could all be taken away – just like that. Poof! Gone! And once again she'd be poor little Clarice O'Hanlon from the wrong side of town. And that thought petrified her.

Carrie had experienced her share of rich men willing to offer her anything, but none of them had been anywhere near as rich as Leon Blaine. And, quite frankly, none of them quite as fascinating. There was something special about Leon Blaine. Something powerful and exciting.

He obviously thought the same about her, because before they were half-way to Vegas, he began propositioning her. And it wasn't the usual *I'll buy you a Bentley, or Harry Winston's entire stock if you just glance in my direction.* No, this was different.

'I've been around a long time,' he'd said to her. 'I've travelled the world and seen many things. But, Carrie, I have *never* seen a woman as beautiful as you.'

She'd heard *that* before, but it was his next words that intrigued her. 'You are the woman who is capable of inheriting my fortune.'

'Excuse me?' she'd said, coolly. 'May I remind you that we only just met.'

'I'm a man of impulses,' Leon had said. 'That's how I *made* my money. And for the last ten years I've been looking for someone to leave everything to.'

'Really,' she murmured.

'You see, my dear,' he continued, 'Joel doesn't deserve it.'

'Why not?'

'My son is a pathetic joke. He has a trust fund from which he'll inherit a few million to gamble away. But we're talking about billions, and I need them to go to the right person.' A meaningful pause. 'You could be that person, Carrie.'

Billions! Carrie had millions, not very many of them, but Leon was speaking of billions! This was worth listening to.

Her eyes sparkled. 'And what would I have to *do* to inherit your fortune, Leon?' she'd asked, leaning closer.

'Have my baby. My true heir.'

'I thought you were married,' she'd said, gesturing across the plane at Marika, who was watching her from afar.

'Marika is more like my personal assistant,' he'd said. 'Yes, we've been living together for a time, but do you really imagine I want that woman to inherit everything? Do you think I want *her* to be the mother of my son?'

'You're a cold man,' Carrie had said.

'And you're probably a cold woman,' he'd answered. 'But your beauty and youth are what I desire. And a son. If you can give me a son, I will see that the two of you get everything. This is a business proposition, Carrie.'

'A business proposition?'

'Yes. There will be a contract drawn up by my lawyers, and in the contract it will stipulate a certain period of time for you to get pregnant.'

'And if I don't?'

'You will be enormously compensated.' He paused again. 'I understand you might find this a bizarre offer. However, when you walked on to my plane this morning, I knew at once that you were the one I've been searching for.'

His words had stayed with her. Now she was pacing around her suite at the Mirage in confusion.

Joel had called five minutes earlier to inform her he'd be picking her up in an hour. 'What for?' she'd asked blankly.

'We're all going to the Kris Phoenix concert over at the Magiriano,' he'd reminded her.

'Oh, yes,' she'd answered vaguely, remembering her fling with Kris Phoenix a year earlier. She'd soon discovered he wasn't her type. Rock stars expected to lie there and be ministered to. Well, she had news for him: so did models. The two of them had lain side by side on a giant waterbed in the Bahamas, both expecting the other to make the first move.

It had not been a magical experience.

Eduardo had been waiting in her suite when she'd

arrived. She was so shaken by the unexpected turn of events on Leon's plane that she'd sent him away. 'Come back later,' she'd said.

'What time?' he'd asked, disappointed that she didn't want to make love to him immediately.

'Around midnight,' she'd said, uninterested.

Leon had given her the weekend to make a decision. And the truth was, wild as it might seem, she was very tempted.

*   *   *

'You're bad,' Madison said.

'*I*'m bad,' Jamie said indignantly, her cheeks flushed. 'How about the prick I left behind?'

'What *is* that dress?' Natalie asked, surveying Jamie, who was clad in a sleek black dress with a neckline that plunged all the way to Cuba. 'Girl, your boobs are *out* there.'

'Some welcome,' Jamie said. 'I flew here to be with you guys, and *this* is the greeting I get?'

'Will somebody *please* tell me *what* is goin' on?' Natalie demanded.

So they did. Madison started the story and Jamie finished it.

'Man!' Natalie exclaimed, when they were done. 'This is unbelievable shit. Peter and another *guy*.' She shook her head in disbelief. 'Unfuckingreal.'

'I'm *never* going home,' Jamie remarked, matter-of-factly. 'I've made up my mind.'

'What are you planning to do?' Madison asked. 'Take up residence in Vegas?'

'No,' Jamie replied, very sure of herself. 'Tonight I'm going to fuck Kris Phoenix.' A languid pause. 'And then we'll see.'

Chapter Forty-six

While Rosarita was in the bathroom, Dexter sat on the side of the bed in their hotel room, trying to work out how he could contact Gem. She had mentioned the restaurant she worked at, and he was straining desperately to remember the name of the place. Finally it came to him. Quick as a flash he picked up the phone, dialled Information and got the number. He knew he had at least another ten minutes before Rosarita emerged from her nightly beauty routine. First she took a long, leisurely bath, after which she applied many expensive creams to her face to keep her skin soft and supple, and then it was the turn of the body creams and lotions.

Rosarita was proud of her skin. 'It's flawless,' she'd often told him. 'Absolutely flawless.'

And so it should be, considering she visited the best and most expensive dermatologist in New York twice a month.

He tried the number. 'Excuse me,' he said to the woman who answered. 'You have a waitress working there . . . um . . . I'm not quite sure of her surname, but her first name's Gem. Do you know who I'm talking about?'

'This line is for bookings only,' the woman replied. 'We don't accept personal calls for staff.'

'Is there a special staff line?'

'I suppose I can make an exception,' the woman said, relenting. 'Hang on, I think I see Gem.'

He did as she asked, nervously tapping the side of the phone. What if Rosarita emerged early and found him speaking to another woman? *That* would not go down well. He knew his wife: she did not take kindly to competition.

'Hello?' Lilting and lovely, it was her voice all right.

'Hi there,' he said, experiencing a rush of pure pleasure. 'This is Dexter Falcon.'

'Dexter?'

'That's me.'

'Where are you?'

'In California,' he replied, feeling ridiculously tongue-tied. 'Beverly Hills, actually. I'm, uh, staying at the Beverly Hills Hotel.'

'Oh,' she murmured, sounding impressed. 'That must be *awesome*.'

He laughed at her choice of word. 'Yeah, it's pretty awesome,' he said. 'One day you and –' He stopped abruptly: he couldn't start making plans, he had a pregnant wife in the bathroom.

Why was he calling this girl anyway? It was madness. 'I, uh, just wanted to say hello,' he managed, knowing he sounded awkward but unable to help himself.

'You did?'

At least she seemed pleased to hear from him. 'Yeah . . . What's your home number?' he asked. She hesitated before giving it to him. He scribbled it on a notepad by the phone, then shoved the piece of paper in his pants pocket. 'Maybe I'll call you later,' he said.

'That would be nice,' she said. 'How long are you staying in L.A.?'

'Tonight only. Then Vegas for two nights.'

'You're *so* cool,' she said, laughing softly. 'One of these days *I'd* like to be able to say something like that.'

One of these days you will, he thought. *You'll be with me, and we'll be here together and we'll be very happy indeed*. 'Okay, so maybe I'll call you later,' he said.

'Where are you staying in Vegas?' she asked. 'Somewhere glamorous and exciting?'

Without thinking, he told her, then regretted it. What if she called him?

No. She wouldn't do that.

He put down the phone, feeling unusually happy. A beat of ten, and Rosarita emerged from the bathroom. His timing was right on.

'Can you believe your mother trying to ask Tony Curtis for his autograph?' she said, busy rubbing scented hand cream up and down her arms.

'Why shouldn't she?' he said. 'Mom's always liked him. It's a thrill for her to be in a place like Spago seeing movie stars.'

A caustic 'Really?'

'You're jaded.'

'Ha!' Rosarita said. '*Me*? Jaded?'

'Yeah, you're too sophisticated.'

'*That's* better,' she said, liking the description. 'I *am* sophisticated. Perhaps it's one of the reasons you and I don't get along so well. What's the saying? You can take the boy out of the small town, but you can never take the small town out of the boy.'

'I don't get it.'

'Didn't imagine you would,' she said, climbing into bed.

'Think I'll take a shower,' he said.

Hopefully, if he stayed in the bathroom long enough, she'd be asleep by the time he emerged.

* * *

'Why do we have to go to bed so early?' Varoomba complained, hands on hips.

'Huh?' said Chas. He'd discovered her tweezers lying on the counter-top and was busy plucking his eyebrows, staring in the magnifying mirror mounted on the bathroom wall.

She stood behind him in her sexy yellow dress and very high heels, ready to hit the town. 'It's early,' she whined. 'Not even nine o'clock.'

'We got an early flight tomorra,' he mumbled.

'So what?' she countered. 'Can't we at least go down to the Polo Lounge for a drink?'

'You wanna do that?' he said, diligently plucking away.

'Yeah. I mean, the Polo Lounge is, like, where people go. We could sit there, have a peach brandy and talk.'

'What we gonna talk about?' Chas said, frowning.

'Stuff,' Varoomba said, with a petulant pout.

'Didn't I just tell ya we got an early-mornin' flight?'

'You know,' Varoomba said, snaking her arms around his waist from behind, 'when we get to Vegas, I'd like you to meet my grams.'

'Your *what?*'

'My grandma, the woman who raised me. She's a character.'

Chas made a disgusted face. Who needed to hear *this* shit? As far as he was concerned, Varoomba was there for one purpose only – and that purpose was to please him in the bedroom. Now she was coming up with a goddamn family, for Crissakes!

'You'll like Grams,' Varoomba said, as if meeting the old biddy was a done deal.

'Yeah?' Chas said, putting down the tweezers. 'She look like you?'

'You're so *funnee!*' Varoomba squealed. 'Course not.'

'Take off your dress, chickie,' he said, reaching for her tits. 'An', for God's sake, shut the fuck up.'

* * *

'Did you notice what Rosarita was eating?' Martha said, winding her hair on to pink foam rollers.

'No, I didn't,' Matt replied, inspecting the contents of the well stocked mini-bar, trying to decide what to select.

'She had a steak with sauce on.'

'So?' Matt said, pulling out a can of beer.

'That's not a very healthy meal for a pregnant woman,' Martha said, pursing her lips.

'Martha,' Matt warned, 'you'd better keep your mouth shut. Don't forget we're here on a free pass. It's not a good idea to muddy the waters.'

'But, Matt –'

'But nothing,' he said loudly. 'If you start messing with that girl, we're all in trouble.'

'I don't care,' Martha said stubbornly. 'This is our first grandchild. I'm talking to her about her diet.'

Matt glared at his plump wife. 'That's right, ruin it for all of us.'

'I won't ruin anything, Matt.'

'Yes, you will, you always do.'

* * *

Down the hall, Dexter lay next to Rosarita until he was sure she was asleep, then he slipped into the bathroom, dressed quickly and hurried downstairs to a pay-phone, where he tried the home number Gem had given him. It rang and rang, but there was no answer. Obviously she wasn't home yet.

Damn!

As he was about to return to the elevator he spotted Nicole Kidman and Tom Cruise crossing the lobby. Nicole was elegant and extremely tall, whereas Tom Cruise was shorter than his wife, with a huge grin on his face.

Why shouldn't he be smiling? Dexter thought. *He's got it all – a gorgeous, famous wife, stardom, kids, an Oscar.*

Or *did* he have an Oscar? Dexter wasn't quite sure about that, but he did know that Tom Cruise had been nominated. And more than once.

One day that's gonna be me, he thought. *I'll walk through the lobby of the Beverly Hills Hotel like a star with Gem beside me. And that day is not going to be too far off.*

Chapter Forty-seven

'*T*hat's the girlfriend?' Jamie questioned derisively.

'That's her,' Natalie replied. 'And she's damn talented. She won an Academy Award.'

'Who cares *what* she won?' Jamie said irritably. 'I came here to fuck Kris Phoenix, and *that*'s what I'm going to do.'

They were sitting at a front table in the huge ballroom where Kris was due to appear.

'Wow! You certainly are Miss Sure of Yourself,' Natalie said. 'But, then, you always *could* score any guy you wanted.'

'More or less,' Jamie replied confidently. She was drinking vodka martinis, a bad sign, and she was already half drunk.

'Tonight might be a problem,' Madison said, attempting to let her down easily. 'Kris seems very enamoured of Amber.'

'Oh, I see,' Jamie said, turning on her. 'You're on first-name terms with dear little Amber, are you?'

'We kind of met backstage,' Madison admitted. 'She's a sweet girl, very young.'

'What am I? An old hag?' Jamie said, narrowing her eyes.

'No, Jamie. Don't take it personally, it's simply that he's *with* someone. They're practically engaged.'

'They're not married,' Jamie said tartly, 'so as far as I'm concerned he's still fair game.'

'*This* I gotta see,' Natalie said, shaking. 'The beautiful Jamie in action. My money's on you, kiddo.'

'Well, mine isn't,' Madison said. 'I don't want anything to do with this.'

'Thanks,' Jamie said huffily. 'Support me in my time of need. It's good to have friends.'

'Oh, *c'mon*,' Madison said. 'He's in a relationship. Do you want to be the one to break it up?'

'Who cares?' Jamie said. 'He's a man, isn't he? He deserves everything he gets.'

'What does *that* mean?' Madison said.

'Figure it out,' Jamie replied. 'I'll fuck him, *then* I'll tell his girlfriend all about it.'

'Ooh, you've turned into a mean one,' Natalie purred.

'And so would you,' Jamie snapped back.

'Do not turn your heads,' Madison said, 'but approaching the table next to us is Mr Leon Blaine, billionaire supreme, with number one son, idiot supreme, *and* idiot son seems to be – believe it or not – with Carrie Hanlon.'

'You *gotta* be kidding,' Natalie said, turning her head immediately.

'Jeez,' Madison groaned. 'You're about as cool as a lobster in the pot.'

'There's nothing wrong with looking,' Natalie retorted. 'And, wow, *she*'s looking good.'

'Who?' Jamie asked.

'Carrie Hanlon, that's who.'

'By the way,' Madison said, 'how come you got such a great table?'

'It's Mr Mogul's,' Natalie said. 'He and baby bro were comin' to the concert. They couldn't make it so they gave me the table, otherwise we'd be stuck backstage with my crew. Pretty good, huh? Amazing what big bucks get you.'

'Yes,' Madison said. 'Especially when the big bucks belong to somebody else.'

* * *

The manager of the hotel, his wife and one other couple were sitting with the Blaines. To Marika's annoyance, Leon had organized the seating, placing himself next to Carrie and Marika across the table, where she put on a superior smile and downed her second Pernod on the rocks.

Joel had spotted Madison and was already trying to figure an excuse to make his way over to her table. He really had a thing about her. He considered her different. She wasn't like all the models he dated, and certainly she was nothing like Rosarita. She was the one woman who had it all going for her – beauty, class, intelligence. In fact, all the things he desired in a woman. Only problem was, she didn't seem interested.

'Have you considered my proposition?' Leon said to Carrie, in a low voice.

'How serious are you, Leon?' she replied, tossing back her mane of tawny hair while checking out the room.

'I never joke about important things,' he said.

'This is not the place to discuss it,' Carrie answered

restlessly. 'Your girlfriend is watching us the entire time. It makes me uncomfortable.'

'Take no notice of Marika. She does what I say.'

'That's a very chauvinistic attitude.'

'I'm a very chauvinistic man. But you can handle that, can't you?'

'Yes, Leon, I can. Being famous has taught me how to handle anything.'

'Do you enjoy your fame?' he asked.

'Sometimes,' she replied.

'Or do you think that perhaps one day it might all be taken away?'

She blinked rapidly several times. 'How did you know that?'

'I see it in your eyes.'

She sighed. 'This is a strange situation.'

'Is it?' he said, tapping his fingers on the table. 'Surely you believe in fate?'

'Yes,' she said tentatively.

'Then allow yourself to go with it.'

'Maybe I will,' she murmured.

'You're not interested in my son, so why *are* you here?' he asked.

'I wanted to come,' she answered evasively.

'Not because of Joel. You're too much woman for a man like Joel. And I use the word man loosely.'

'You're not very nice about him.'

'He's a moron.'

'That's cruel.'

'I didn't make my money by being Mr Nice Guy.'

'You're always talking about your money.'

'It's an intriguing subject to most people. You included.'

'I have my own money, you know,' she announced.

'And who looks after it?'

'My business manager.'

'Make sure he's not cheating you.'

Marika leaned across the table. 'What are you two talking about?' she asked, attempting to sound pleasant. Watching her, Joel could tell she was livid.

'Nothing that would interest you,' Leon said, dismissing her.

Marika's expression tensed. If this was headed towards war, she was ready to do battle.

* * *

The audience for Kris Phoenix's show was getting more famous by the minute. Gwyneth, George Clooney, a Baldwin or two, Al King, Gloria Estefan, the irrepressible Whoopi. A lot of celebrities were in town for the fight and they began piling in, filling up the best tables and creating an air of excitement.

'Showbiz reporter's dream,' Natalie said bitterly. 'And they'll all be my best friend as long as they've got something to plug. Other than that they won't even recognize me. They won't even remember *what* show I'm on. *Access, Showbiz Today, E.T.* Who gives a flying fart? *They* certainly don't. Celebrities. Ha! You can shove 'em *all* up your ass.'

'Hmm . . .' Madison said. 'And what's made *you* so pissed off with the world?'

Natalie shrugged. 'Dunno. Kris Phoenix an' his goddamn *attitude*. Stars do not treat us like equals. We're the worker squad, promoting their wares.'

'That's not our problem right now,' Madison said. 'Our problem is how to deal with Jamie and keep her *away* from Kris. Because the *last* thing she needs is rejection.'

Jamie had gone to the ladies' room, and Madison wanted to get a plan in place that would protect her. The trouble was that Natalie wasn't co-operating: she was more interested in putting down celebrities. Understandable in a way, because a lot of them *were* assholes.

However, in the overall scheme of things, whether they were assholes or not was simply unimportant.

* * *

On her way back from the ladies' room, Jamie was confronted by Antonio Lopez and his entourage.

'*Mamma mia*!' Antonio sighed, smacking his lips. 'You are one fine beauty, lady.'

She had no idea who he was. And even if she had known, it wouldn't have mattered because her mind was set on Kris Phoenix and *nobody* was going to change it. Especially not Madison and Natalie, who kept on muttering about some transient girlfriend he supposedly had.

'Hey, chickie baby,' Antonio said, clicking his tongue, 'wanna join the future champ's table?'

She threw him a haughty glare. 'I think not,' she said crisply. And, desperate for the boost of another martini, she returned to her table, whereupon Joel arrived and stood there with a stupid grin on his face. 'I swear I've never seen such a bunch of beautiful women,' he said. 'And, Madison, you're the crown jewel.'

She sighed. What was it with this guy? Why did he keep on chasing her? Couldn't he tell she didn't like him? 'Hi, Joel,' she said wearily.

'You should join *our* table,' Joel said, 'instead of sitting here all by yourselves.'

'Thanks, but no thanks,' Madison said. 'We're expecting friends.'

'I told you earlier,' Joel said, leaning in close, 'you, babe, are lookin' hot.'

'Joel, don't say that to me, okay?'

'Huh?'

'It's plain rude to speak to someone you hardly know in that way. How would you like *me* to say it to *you?*'

'Try me,' he said, leering.

'Okay, *honey*,' she said, eyeballing his crotch. 'You're looking hot.'

He took a step back. 'Hey, listen,' he said, pissed off at the way she treated him, 'did I say anything that would offend a normal person?'

Natalie laughed. 'Madison ain't normal, sweetie. You gotta know her to realize that.'

He turned his attention to Jamie. 'Where's your old man?' he said, staring down her cleavage. 'He shouldn't let a beauty like you out by herself.'

'Peter's in New York,' Jamie said. 'Where he belongs.'

'Trouble, huh?'

'No,' Madison interjected quickly. 'Go back to your table, Joel.'

'You're always so pissy with me,' he complained. 'Is it 'cause you like me an' refuse to admit it?'

'Yeah, sure,' Madison drawled sarcastically. 'It must be those sexy pants of yours. I'm so turned on I can barely think straight!'

* * *

Marika changed seats with the hotel manager's wife so

that she was sitting next to Leon. He was busy talking
to Carrie and didn't notice her until he felt her claw-
like hand on his arm. He turned to say something, but
before he could do so, she began whispering in his ear.
'Do you remember that whore in Saigon?' she hissed
fiercely. 'Do you remember what you *did* to her,
Leon?'

'What're you talking about?' he said, shocked.

'Cast your memory back. I'm *sure* you'll remember.'

'That was years ago,' he muttered angrily.

'Ah – but I have the photographs, such fond
memories,' Marika said triumphantly. 'I keep them
very safe.'

'Why are you telling me this now?' he said, furious.

'I'm merely reminding you,' she said, with a thin-
lipped smile, 'that *I* know you better than anyone.'

*　*　*

Antonio and his group were seated three tables along
from Natalie's prime spot. Madison glanced over, then
did a second take. Included in Antonio's entourage
were Jake and his teenage assistant.

She couldn't believe it. Jake playing hanger-on –
she'd given him more credit than that.

Oh, well, another loser. Too damn bad.

Chapter Forty-eight

And so Kris Phoenix hit the stage like a fireball, bouncing around, filled with energy – all sprayed-on leather pants, spiked hair and cocky grin. Time had not slowed him down, and the audience went crazy. This was good old-fashioned rock 'n' roll, and they loved it.

Madison remembered the first time she'd seen Kris Phoenix perform. Michael had taken her to an open-air concert in Central Park, and she'd fallen in love with the drummer from afar. She'd been fifteen and would've given anything to get backstage. But it was not to be. She and her dad had ended up eating hot dogs while walking along Fifth Avenue. It was a good memory.

Michael. Daddy. She'd tried to put him out of her mind – but there were moments when it wasn't possible. He was her father, the man she loved. And being estranged from him was incredibly painful.

The truth was she missed him.

How can you miss him? she asked herself scornfully.

Because I do.

That's bullshit. He's a murderer. HE KILLED
YOUR MOTHER.

Nobody knows that for sure.

Oh, yes, you do.

'I'll be right back,' she whispered to Natalie.

'Where you goin'?'

'Ladies' room.'

She got up from the table and made her way to the
back of the darkened room.

Kris was stomping across the stage belting out one
of his familiar hits. She didn't care. She didn't care
about anything. If it wasn't for Jamie she would've
made a fast getaway.

The ladies' room was empty except for an old
woman with an enormous beehive hairdo, who was
stationed next to an ashtray filled with five- and ten-
dollar bills. No cheap tipping at *this* hotel.

'Hello, luv,' the old crone said, in a thick Cockney
accent. 'Missing the show?'

'Looks like it.'

'Farrah Fawcett was in 'ere earlier,' the old woman
confided. 'Still got that lovely hair, she 'as.'

'Good for her,' Madison muttered, shutting herself
in a stall.

Damn Jamie for coming to Vegas. It was such a bad
idea, and now *she*, Madison, was supposed to be the
one to save her, because she couldn't depend on
Natalie. It simply wasn't fair. Didn't she have enough
to deal with?

She emerged from the stall.

'*I* used t' have lovely hair,' the old woman said with
a mournful sigh. '*I* was a showgirl 'ere in the early days.
Nearly went out with Bugsy Siegal I did.'

Madison fished out a twenty and left it in the ashtray.

Then she hurried from the room, and bumped straight into Jake. Literally.

'You know what I hate?' he said.

'Dating teenagers?' she said breathlessly.

'Ancient rock stars in too tight pants with socks stuffed in their crotch.'

'You know what *I* hate?' she said.

'Tell me.'

'Men who sleep in my bed for a week, run off to Paris and never call.'

'You know what I *like?*'

'Can't wait.'

'A quiet dinner for two in a romantic restaurant which, believe me, is not easy to find in Vegas.'

She sighed wistfully. 'Sounds good.'

He took her arm. 'Then let's go.'

'Can't.'

'Why?'

'It's too complicated.'

'What's complicated?'

'Everything.'

'C'mon, Madison, I don't have time to fight about this.'

'You've got to understand, Jake, I really would like to have dinner with you, but I've got this girlfriend, Jamie, and she's in trouble.'

'What kind of trouble?'

'The man kind, of course.'

'Wanna tell me about it? Maybe I can help solve it. I'm a guy, you know.'

'Really?' she said, shooting him an amused look. 'I was beginning to forget.'

He grinned. 'And she's quick with the quips.'

She loved his grin – it was boyish yet very masculine.

Why am I punishing myself? she thought. *What's wrong with enjoying myself with Jake and not taking it too seriously? After all, tomorrow I'm turning thirty. Better do* something *to celebrate.*

'Okay,' she said. 'Here's the sad story. Jamie discovered her husband was having an affair.'

'Happens all the time, doesn't it?'

'The affair *he's* having is with another man.'

'Oh – not so good.'

'Exactly.'

'So how are you helping?'

'Jamie's in Vegas. She came here to, uh, sleep with Kris Phoenix.'

'Does she know him?'

'Of course she does. He's been coming on to her for a while. Except now he has a permanent girlfriend by the name of Amber Rowe.'

'The actress?'

'That's the one.'

'So how is your friend planning to jump into bed with him?'

'That's the problem. I have to prevent her from making a fool of herself, because Amber is very much in evidence and Jamie is under the impression she can get any man she wants. Usually it's true.'

'So, you're telling me we can't have dinner 'cause you've got to protect this friend of yours?'

'That's what friendship's all about, isn't it?'

'How about we *both* go protect her?'

'And what would you do with your teenage assistant?'

'What am I *supposed* to do?'

'You're with her, aren't you?'

'No. Antonio asked us both if we wanted to come

along tonight. She's a big Kris Phoenix fan and said yes. I tagged along because I was looking for you. When I saw you go to the ladies' room I was right behind you.'

'You can't leave her alone with Antonio. He's a sexual predator and she's a baby.'

'Here's the deal,' Jake said. 'As soon as the concert's finished I'll send her home in a cab, you'll take your girlfriend back to her hotel, then you and I will have a late romantic dinner. How does that sound?'

'I . . . uh . . . don't know.'

'Well, *I* do,' he said. 'You think I'm an undependable schmuck, and I probably am. But I thought I explained to you when we had dinner in L.A. that after my wife died in a car wreck I couldn't get over the feeling that somehow or other it was my fault.' A long beat. 'Here's the thing, Madison. I don't want anything happening to you.' Another long beat. 'I know it sounds crazy, but *that*'s why I can't get involved.'

'We're not *talking* involved,' she said heatedly. 'I just got out of an *involved* relationship with someone who dumped me. So I'm not thrilled when people leave and don't bother to call. Anyway,' she added, 'didn't you tell me that you and your wife were separated when she was killed?'

'That's right. But the night she died we'd gotten together and ended up having a big fight, so maybe she wasn't concentrating. I dunno, Madison, but somehow I feel responsible.'

'Okay, Jake. After the concert I'll take Jamie back to her hotel, you put your teenager in a cab, then let's get together and talk.'

'Sounds good.' He looked at her quizzically. 'Y'know, that's what I like about you, Madison.'

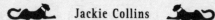

'What?' she asked softly.

Killer grin hitting her full force. 'You're the smartest woman I know.'

* * *

'I wanna go to the party,' Jamie said stubbornly.

'*Not* a good idea,' Madison said, wishing Jamie would sober up and calm down. Jamie was not used to drinking too much, and it showed.

'Why not?' Jamie replied, tilting her chin in an aggressive manner, ready for a fight.

'How many times do I have to explain this to you?' Madison said, exasperated.

'She ain't listening, girl,' Natalie joined in. 'Her head is somewhere else. But I'll tell you what, we'll go find my camera crew and walk around the party for a few minutes. That way Jamie gets to say hello to Kris, an' then we're outta there.'

'Doesn't anybody *get* it?' Jamie said crossly. 'Don't you *understand* my plan?'

'Yeah, yeah,' Madison said. 'We all *get* it. But you'd better put your plan into action tomorrow, 'cause tonight Kris is *definitely* taken.'

'Fine,' Jamie said. 'I'll make a connection with him tonight, and do the deed tomorrow. Does that please you?'

'No more drinking,' Madison warned.

'Christ!' Jamie grumbled. 'Why do I feel like I'm back in college?'

'Does Peter even know you're here?' Madison asked.

'Who gives a damn?' Jamie said, running her hand through her short blonde hair.

'At least you should let him know you're alive.

Otherwise he'll be sending out search parties.'

'Who cares *what* he thinks?' Jamie said defiantly. 'He's ruined my life.'

'No,' Madison said gently. 'Your whole life is ahead of you. Don't you ever forget that.'

'What's *wrong* with you?' Jamie said, her eyes filling with unexpected tears. 'Surely you *saw* those photos? Can't you *see* what he's done to me?'

'So I guess he's being punished.'

'Yes,' Jamie repeated, reaching for her third martini. 'I guess he's being punished.'

* * *

Kris had taken ten bows, waved to his adoring fans and vanished. Now it was time for all the invited to make their way to the main penthouse of the Magiriano Hotel, where the after-concert party was due to take place.

Madison stood up and looked around for Jake. She spotted him and waved. He waved back.

Hmm, she thought. *Am I making the right move seeing him later?*

What the hell? Why deny herself? She didn't want to *marry* him, all she wanted was some love and attention, and maybe some great sex. Was that so terrible?

The Blaine party had already left the room, escorted out before the final bow.

Madison grabbed Natalie's arm. 'Keep your eye on Jamie,' she said. 'I have to talk to Jake for a minute.'

'Oh, now we're talking to Jake, are we?' Natalie said, with a sly smile.

'Yes, Nat, do I have your approval?'

'Whatever gets you through the night, girl.'

'Thanks,' she said sarcastically.

'Although it's a shame he's not a *real* player,' Natalie mused. 'You know, super-rich, that kinda shit. How cool would *that* be? We'd be able to take free trips on his plane and stuff like that. Look at Carrie Hanlon – *she* was sitting with two of the richest guys in America.'

'Do you think she's sleeping with Joel Blaine?' Jamie ventured.

'Naw,' Natalie said. 'He's a creep.'

'*I* think he's sexy in a swarthy kind of way,' Jamie said.

'Oh, *please*,' Madison said. 'Right now, with all those martinis inside you, you'd think the *waiter* was sexy.'

'Well, he *is*.' Jamie giggled. 'Did you catch his cute little ass? If Kris is a no, maybe I'll settle for him!'

'Lordy, lordy!' Natalie sighed. 'Save this girl from her bad, *bad* self!'

Chapter Forty-nine

By the time Madison, Jamie and Natalie reached the party it was packed with press and guests all attempting to hustle their way towards the VIP section in the back.

'That's one place I *ain't* going,' Natalie said, rolling her eyes.

'Who wants to?' Madison agreed.

While Jamie said, 'Watch me, guys.' And before either one of them could stop her, she was on her way to the VIP area, only to be prevented from entering the inner sanctum by two burly bodyguards.

'I'm Mr Phoenix's interior designer,' she said haughtily. 'Would you please tell him I'm here? Jamie Nova, from New York.'

'Yes, ma'am, but you'll have to wait until we get clearance,' one of the guards said, placing a heavy hand on her arm.

She flicked it off. 'Kindly don't touch me,' she said imperiously.

'Sorry, ma'am. We gotta check you out.'

'Go ahead – I'll wait.'

445

By this time Madison had caught up with her. 'What are you *doing?*' she asked.

'Making arrangements for tomorrow,' Jamie said, slurring her words – but only slightly. 'Is that okay with you?'

'*Please* sober up,' Madison pleaded.

'Sure,' Jamie said, with an obliging smile. 'I'll be perfectly sober tomorrow when I fuck Kris Phoenix.'

* * *

Leon Blaine wanted to gamble; Joel Blaine wanted to go to the Kris Phoenix party; Carrie Hanlon wanted to get back to her suite and liaise with Eduardo; Marika wanted to leave Las Vegas and get away from Leon's latest infatuation.

Leon won. Naturally. So they were escorted to a roulette table, which was immediately closed to the public, and Leon began to play, piling stacks of chips on the table as if they were going out of style. To Joel's fury, Leon's number kept coming up. He was winning yet another fortune, the lucky old bastard.

After a while Leon handed a fistful of chips to Carrie. 'Cheval twenty-nine,' he commanded.

'What does cheval mean?' she asked.

'Place your chips around a number – surround it.'

As she did so, a crowd gathered. Several guards formed a barrier to keep them away from the table.

'This table is closed,' one of the guards told an eager fan, who was anxious to get a closer look at the very famous Carrie Hanlon.

'Can you do that?' asked a woman from Ontario, in bright orange Bermuda shorts.

'In this casino, ma'am, we can do what we like,' the guard replied.

Joel threw some chips down on the table, concentrating on thirty-five – his lucky number.

Leon placed a stack of chips worth a total of twenty thousand dollars on number twenty-nine.

The croupier spun the wheel.

'C'mon, thirty-five,' Joel muttered under his breath. 'C'mon, you motherfucker.'

He had to beat his father – at least at roulette.

'Twenty-nine,' the croupier announced.

'Shit!' Joel muttered. He couldn't catch a break. And Leon, one of the richest men in the world, had won over half a million dollars.

Carrie joyfully clapped her hands. This was *fun*! 'How much did I win?' she asked Leon.

He picked up his drink and sipped it. In his experience there was nothing like hard cash to make a woman happy. And even though Carrie Hanlon probably earned big bucks, it wasn't the same as the sexual charge of handling stacks of hundred-dollar bills.

'Enough,' he said, reaching for a Cuban cigar.

* * *

'Your New York apartment is really taking shape,' Jamie said, fingering the delicate diamond cross that hung on a thin gold chain around her swan-like neck.

'Thanks to you, luv,' Kris responded, mentally drooling as he checked out this blonde morsel.

Jamie tried the soft smile that melted most men's hearts. 'When will you be in New York, Kris?'

'Depends,' he said, admiring her small but perfect breasts.

'On what?'

'*You*, beautiful,' he said, giving her the full power of

the intense baby blues. 'I think you an' I could make –'
Before he was able to finish, Amber appeared. 'Where
you bin, luv?' he asked, grabbing her close, suffused
with sudden guilt.

'Talking to your manager,' Amber said. 'And
attempting to avoid the press. They're *everywhere*, Kris.'

'Oh, tryin' to come on to you, was 'e? 'E's a horny
old bastard.'

'Of course not,' Amber said, frowning at such a
thought. 'You know I like to stay in the background at
these things.' She stared at Jamie.

'Uh . . . 'ave you two met?' Kris said. 'This is Jamie,
uh –'

'Nova,' Jamie supplied, slightly put out that he
didn't remember her full name.

'Yeah, Jamie Nova,' he said confidently. 'She's my,
uh, interior designer in New York. Tarting up the
penthouse, she is.' He put an affectionate arm around
Jamie's shoulder. 'I'd like you to see it, luv.'

'Actually, I'll be in New York next week,' Amber
said. 'I can see it then.'

'Howzatt?'

'I have to do *The Letterman Show*, which I hate.'

'Why're you doin' it, then?'

'I promised. I never break promises.'

'So stay in the apartment. Is it ready, Jamie?'

'No, Kris, it won't be ready for several months.'
Damn! she thought. He was obviously interested in
this girl. Not that Amber was any great shakes to look
at: thin and waif-like, with angular features and long
lank hair. What could he possibly see in her?

But Jamie was not to be put off. Revenge was on her
mind. And what sweeter revenge than having a one-
night stand with Kris Phoenix?

'So, Kris,' she suggested, 'can we get together tomorrow? I have some concepts I wish to discuss with you. What's a good time?'

'Uh, dunno,' Kris mumbled. 'Maybe in the afternoon.' He turned to Amber. 'What've we got goin' on tomorrow?' he asked.

'Whatever,' she answered vaguely, shielding her face with one hand as a camera pointed in their direction.

'Amber's shy,' Kris explained.

'We should definitely get together,' Jamie said, giving him a long, innocent stare. 'Just the two of us. I want to be sure everything is exactly the way you want it, Kris. As you know, I've been dealing with your people, so it'll be good to speak to the real boss.'

'Got it, luv,' he said cheerfully. 'Whyn't you call me around one?' And he threw her a sneaky wink.

Jamie nodded, satisfied that tomorrow he would be hers.

* * *

It was past midnight by the time Madison and Jake finally got to consider having a romantic dinner for two.

'This is ridiculous,' she said, laughing as they stood in the crowded lobby of the hotel, slot machines ringing all around them. 'I can't eat this late.'

'Maybe we should dump on the restaurant idea and go for room service,' he suggested.

'Whose room did you have in mind?'

'Depends on who's got the best room.'

'Coming from you, that's funny.'

'Why?'

''Cause you couldn't care less about your surroundings. You're a maverick – a wanderer. You're not

449

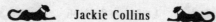

into material things, so why would you care who's got the best room?'

'Let's look at it this way,' he said. 'Who's got the best expense account?'

She stared at him, perplexed. 'What're you talking about now?'

'I'm in the mood for caviar and champagne.'

'*You* want caviar and champagne?' she said disbelievingly.

'We're in Vegas, that means we should indulge ourselves.'

'Hmm . . . I'm sure *I*'ve got the best expense account, so . . . my room it is.' A smile played across her lips. 'Actually, nothing would please me more than sticking Victor with a huge bill.'

'I know you think I'm unreliable,' Jake said, 'but I want you to know that I've really missed you.'

'Hey,' she said, 'missed you, too.'

'That's the best news I've heard all day.'

'Flatterer,' she said, determined not to take him too seriously.

'How about playing the slots before we go upstairs?'

'Slots are for chickens,' she said. 'May I suggest blackjack?'

'Never played. Is it complicated?'

'Oh, Jake,' she sighed, 'you're such an innocent.'

'*I*'m an innocent?' he objected. 'Hey, let's not forget that *I*'m the one who's covered wars in Bosnia and God knows where else, and you're calling me an *innocent?*'

'It's not an insult. It's simply that there's something unspoiled about you, which I personally find most admirable.'

'You do, huh?'

'I do. I was watching you today while you were photographing that stupid boxer. You get off on what you do. That's very appealing.'

'I'd like to photograph *you*.'

'*No* chance,' she said, making a face. 'I *hate* posing in front of a camera.'

'No posing, I promise. Let me take some photos of you tonight.'

'Are you *crazy?*'

'Sometimes.'

'So,' she said, quickly changing the subject, 'what have we decided? Room service? Blackjack? Or the slots?'

'Whatever you like, 'cause I'm happy just being with you.'

'In that case, I choose room service.'

They strolled through the busy casino, hand in hand. Suddenly Madison felt very much at ease. She'd delivered Jamie safely to her room, Natalie had gone off with her camera crew to cover yet another party, Jake had put his teenage assistant in a cab, so now they had no responsibilities.

They got into an elevator that was conveniently empty. Jake moved close to her, pinning her arms above her head against the side wall. Then he began kissing her.

He was a great kisser. Long soulful kisses that made her heart beat faster.

'How many girls did you sleep with in Paris?' she murmured, mad at herself for asking but unable to help it.

'What kind of a question is *that?*'

'Just curious.'

'Ha!'

'You're right,' she said quickly. 'It's none of my business.'

'How many guys did *you* have while I was busy working my butt off in Paris?'

'Not that many, actually,' she answered lightly. 'Although, of course, I wasn't counting.'

'You're a bad girl,' he said, shaking his index finger at her.

'You think?'

'Yeah – you're a beautiful, bad girl,' he said, kissing her again. 'The kind of girl I could easily fall for.'

'That's so sweetly old-fashioned, Jake.'

'What is?'

'Fall for. Who ever says things like that?'

'I do,' he said, flashing the killer grin.

The elevator reached her floor and they got out. Two fat men in matching Hawaiian shirts were arguing in the hallway, yelling at each other about a bet gone wrong.

'Evening,' Madison murmured, as they passed by.

She slipped her card into her door, and they entered her room.

'Okay,' Jake said, immediately searching for a room-service menu. 'What's it to be? A bottle of Dom Perignon? And some Beluga caviar?'

'Do you really *like* caviar?' she asked.

'I gotta confess,' he admitted, 'never had it.'

'It's an acquired taste, you know.'

'No, sweetheart, *you*'re an acquired taste. And one I can't wait to get my tongue around again.'

She felt a rush of excitement. 'Compliments will get you wherever you want to go,' she said breathlessly.

And they fell on the bed, locked in a fiery embrace of laughter and passion.

Chapter Fifty

'*G*oddamnit!*' Rosarita snarled. 'This flight is so bumpy I can't *take* it!'

'Not as bumpy as our flight yesterday,' Martha remarked smugly, leaning across the aisle. 'We're quite used to it now. Veteran travellers, aren't we, Matt?'

Matt grunted. He was busy studying the attractive flight attendant's legs and couldn't give a damn about the turbulence.

'Who cares *how* bumpy your flight was?' Rosarita said irritably. 'If this plane goes down, our entire family would be wiped out, and then Venice would inherit everything. God forbid!'

Martha shook her head. Sometimes words came out of her daughter-in-law's mouth that were downright shocking.

Rosarita tapped Chas on the shoulder. 'I hope you've arranged for a car to meet us at the airport,' she said waspishly. 'I'm not getting in a cab.'

'Yeah, I arranged a car,' Chas said, scratching his chin. 'An' whaddya mean, you're not gettin' in a cab? What're you? A freakin' princess?'

'I'm pregnant, Daddy. *Pregnant*. You keep on forgetting. I should be treated with care and consideration.'

'Yeah?'

'Yes,' she said, scowling.

Soon they would all have to treat her with extreme respect. As Mrs Joel Blaine, mother of the heir to the Blaine fortune, she *would* be a freakin' princess. And then they'd all be sorry they hadn't been nicer to her.

* * *

Madison awoke slowly, rolled across the bed, threw out her arm and hit another body. For a moment she was completely disoriented, then it all came back. Las Vegas. Jake. And today was her birthday.

Happy birthday to me, she thought wryly.

Oh, God! Thirty! Suddenly she felt incredibly old.

Jake was still sleeping. She propped herself up on one elbow and watched him, unable to resist running her fingers across his chest, discovering a small scar on his right shoulder. Funny, she hadn't noticed it before, but their week of passion in New York seemed such a long time ago.

She was secretly pleased that they'd got together again. Last night had been everything she'd hoped. He'd made her laugh and held her close, making her feel as if they had a truly special connection. And after great sex she'd gone to sleep in his arms, which was exactly the way it should be. So what if it wasn't a lasting thing? At least they were having fun.

He stirred slightly and opened his eyes. 'Hey,' he mumbled, stifling a yawn, 'gotta feeling I'm in a strange bed.'

'What's so strange about it?' she replied, straight-faced.

He smiled lazily. 'Have I ever told you how sorry I am that I screwed up?'

'I think it's time you stopped apologizing.'

'Does that mean I'm forgiven?'

'Surely you noticed?'

'Oh, yeah, I noticed all right.'

'Excellent.'

'And here's a promise.'

'What?'

'I won't screw up again.'

'You can do what you like, Jake, we're both free agents.'

'Now she's gonna give me the Miss Independent bit,' he said, sitting up. 'You used me for sex and now it's goodbye, sailor. Is that the way it goes?'

'Goodbye, *sailor?*' she said, giggling. 'Where did you come up with *that?*'

'I get around, you know.'

'I'm sure.'

'By the way,' he said, reaching over to touch her face, 'you look beautiful in the morning.'

'Thank you.'

'Think I'll go get my camera,' he said, jumping out of bed.

'I told you, Jake – no photographs.'

'Why?'

''Cause I look horrible in photos,' she said, wrinkling her nose.

'You couldn't look horrible if you tried.'

'Why are you being so nice to me?'

'It's your birthday,' he said, pulling on his pants.

'How do *you* know?'

'Happy birthday.'

'That's right,' she groaned. 'Remind me that I'm old and decrepit.'

'How old *are* you?' he asked, sitting on the edge of the bed.

'Can't tell you.'

'Be brave.'

'Thirty,' she confessed.

'Thirty! That's nothing.'

'To you it's nothing. To a woman it's a milestone.'

'You're talking like it's twenty years ago. Madonna is in her forties, so is Sharon Stone, and they both look damn good. So what're *you* worried about?'

'How do *you* know how old Madonna and Sharon Stone are?'

'Did a photo essay for *Newsweek* on women over forty.'

'I don't know, Jake,' she said, sitting up. 'What have I achieved? I mean, there's this book I'm writing, yet I never seem to find the time to finish it.'

'You will,' he said encouragingly.

'No, I won't,' she said. 'Not at the rate *I*'m going. I'm always too busy running here, there and everywhere, interviewing people I don't want to interview.' A beat. '*God*, now I sound like Natalie.'

'How come?'

'She's always bitching about interviewing celebrities.'

'So do something else, something you love.'

'Easy for you to say. And how am I supposed to support myself?'

'You'll get by. I do.'

'I'm sure you're not crazy about photographing Antonio "The Panther" Lopez, but you're doing it for

456

the money – right? So then you can go off and do whatever you want.'

'It's fuck-you money,' he said.

'Fuck you, too,' she countered.

'Hmm . . .' he said. 'Now that you've brought up the subject . . .'

'Yes?' she said, smiling.

He leaned over and grabbed her. 'C'mere, woman,' he said.

'You're insatiable.' She sighed.

'Only around you.'

* * *

Joel Blaine prowled around the casino like a predatory animal. He'd been up all night. What was the point in sleeping? First of all, Leon had won big, which pissed him off. Then the old man had handed a stack of bills to Carrie, who'd squealed like an excited schoolgirl – it was as if she didn't have money of her own. Later she'd gone off to spend the night with Eduardo, leaving him with nothing to do.

At that point he'd run into a couple of buddies from New York and they'd taken a cab to the best strip club in town. For two hours he'd sat there paying for lap-dances. One girl after another – all silicone tits and phoney smiles.

Whores. They were all whores. Otherwise why would they be doing this? Oh, yeah, sure, every one of them had their stories about a toddler at home, a dying mother, someone they had to support. Well, make your money working in a supermarket, bitch! Don't tell me your problems.

He tipped generously. Had to. He was Joel Blaine, after all. Didn't want people talking about him.

When he was finished with the strip club, he'd gone back to the casino and rolled craps for three hours, losing heavily. Then he'd gone up to his room, thought about calling a hooker, but decided against it, then returned to the casino, where he'd managed to lose another bundle.

Now he was tired and disgusted. He needed a shower and was pissed off that he'd lost big *and* stayed up all night.

He wandered over to the roulette table, threw his last few hundred on number thirty-five, waited for it not to come up, but to his amazement it did.

Shit, don't tell me my luck is changing, he thought, cashing in.

After collecting his winnings he went to a house phone and called Carrie.

It was apparent he'd awakened her. 'What's the matter?' she said, sounding sleepy.

'You up yet?'

A big yawn at the other end of the phone. 'Not really.'

'That's a shame, 'cause we could've had breakfast with Scorsese.'

'Why can't we?'

'He's got a meeting. We'll have to catch him later. How was last night?'

She yawned again. 'It was okay.'

'Anybody ever called you a dirty old woman?'

'No, Joel,' she said tartly. 'And I don't expect to hear it coming out of *your* mouth.'

'Marika's pissed at you.'

'Why?'

''Cause my old man's all over you. It's a good thing we're not fucking, otherwise I'd be pissed too.'

'Can I help it if he finds me irresistible? Most men do, you know.'

'Yeah, well, you'd better not cross the Asian prison guard, 'cause you'll be in trouble if you do.'

'I'm shaking in my Manolos,' she said sarcastically.

'Your *what*?'

'Forget it.'

'Get dressed and meet me for breakfast.'

'Why would I do that?'

'Christ! Is everything an argument with you?'

'Seems you bring out the worst in me, Joel.'

'We should discuss the Scorsese thing because your movie career is going nowhere. How long can you be a model? Movies are your future – I told you that before. Meet me in the coffee shop in half an hour.'

'God! You're bossy.'

'It's part of my charm.'

'*What* charm?'

* * *

Jamie opened her eyes and groaned. She had a major hangover – which she was not used to. Her head was pounding, her mouth felt like a rat had crawled in there and died, and every bone in her body ached.

Oh, God, she thought, what did I do last night? What crazy thing did I do?

Then she remembered. Nothing. Because Kris Phoenix had a girlfriend, thank God, which meant she hadn't done anything she would live to regret.

She got out of bed and went into the bathroom, whereupon the phone rang.

'Hello?' she said tentatively.

''Ello, luv.'

No mistaking *that* accent. 'Kris?'

'The very same.'

'Uh . . . hi.'

''Ere's the thing,' he said, getting right to it. 'Amber's gone off to ride a horse. So I was thinkin', whyn't you come by now?'

'*Right* now?'

'No. Tomorra mornin'.' A beat. '*Of course* right now.'

'For?'

'Breakfast. Nothin' like a bit of breakfast between friends.'

* * *

By the time their plane landed, Dexter's arm was black and blue, thanks to Rosarita clinging to him like a leech. He had to admit that it *was* a bumpy landing, but he had his thoughts to keep him calm. And his thoughts were concentrated on Gem, as he busily played the what-if game.

What if he said to Rosarita, 'Okay, I'll give you the divorce you've always wanted, but I must have custody of our child.'

No, she wouldn't go for that. Rosarita would use their baby as a pawn.

What if he scored a leading role in a major movie, made a lot of money and paid Rosarita off?

It still wouldn't work. She'd never give him the kid.

What if she gave birth and later that year was run down by a truck?

No. He wasn't that lucky.

So his dream of ending up with Gem was a no-go if he wanted to keep his kid. And he wanted to do that more than anything else because being a father was the most important thing that had ever happened to him.

'How's our baby doing?' he said to Rosarita, on their way out of the airport.

'What?' she said irritably.

'Our baby,' he repeated, wondering why she was always in such a bad mood. 'How's our baby feeling in your tummy?'

'Such crap!' Rosarita exclaimed. 'You sound utterly stupid.'

Pregnancy had certainly not softened her.

Chapter Fifty-one

Martha oohed and aahed all the way to the hotel, getting on Rosarita's nerves. Couldn't the woman *ever* shut up?

Chas led the way in, with Varoomba close behind. Rosarita hung back, embarrassed to be seen with Stripper Slut.

At the check-in desk, Martha spotted Leonardo DiCaprio and a group of his cronies. She nearly fainted on the spot. 'Oh, my God!' she wailed. 'Look – look who that is! I've seen Tony Curtis in Beverly Hills, now Leonardo DiCaprio in Las Vegas. My girlfriends in our book club will never believe me! I wish I had my camera!'

Rosarita rolled her eyes, although she had to admit that seeing Leonardo DiCaprio *was* impressive. He was shorter than she'd expected and much too young, but all the same, he *was* a major star.

She held on to Dexter's arm. At least he was a personality of sorts. Not a very famous one, but he did have a half-assed name, recognizable to anyone who watched daytime soaps.

She waited until Chas had finished talking to the desk clerk, then she sidled over. 'I'm Mrs Dexter Falcon,' she announced.

The desk clerk glanced up. 'What can I do for you, ma'am?' he asked politely.

'I thought I should make you aware that my husband is staying at the hotel. Dexter Falcon, the TV star. Perhaps you can inform your PR department. I know you have many celebrities here this weekend for the fight, and if there're any parties we should be invited to, I'd appreciate the invitation being sent to our room.' Satisfied, she turned away from the reception desk.

'What were you doing?' Dexter asked.

'Securing our position,' she answered, a smug expression on her face.

'*What* position?' he muttered.

*   *   *

Carrie made Joel wait. He sat in the coffee shop pushing scrambled eggs and bacon around his plate, wondering what time she was planning on putting in an appearance. Her promise of a half-hour soon stretched into an hour. He was severely pissed.

'Jesus, Carrie,' he said when she finally turned up, 'I thought you were a professional.'

'What?' she said, unconcerned.

'Why are you so late?'

'Am I?' she said, glancing at her watch.

'How was Baby Face last night?'

'Satisfactory,' she replied, casually inspecting the menu.

'We're supposed to meet the old man and the prison

guard for lunch,' he said. 'What were you an' Leon talking about yesterday? He didn't stop whispering to you all day. What the fuck was *that* about?'

'Confidential,' she replied.

'Are you kiddin'?'

'Leon wouldn't want me to repeat our conversation,' Carrie said, dismissing Joel's curiosity. 'Now, where is Mr Scorsese? I thought you said he'd be here.'

'I told you he had a meeting. I mentioned you to him. He's interested in getting together with you.'

'I don't do auditions.'

'Who's talking auditions? I made him aware you're into being a serious actress, not some tits-and-ass chase-movie queen.'

'He knows who I am?'

'Jesus Christ, you'd have to be an alien *not* to know you. Your goddamn face is on the cover of every magazine in America.'

This pleased her. She gave a satisfied smile. 'When do I meet him?'

'Later. At the party before the fight.'

'Good,' she said.

* * *

'What do you want to do today?' Jake asked.

'What do *you* want to do today?' Madison retorted.

'I've taken enough shots of Antonio, so no need to go back there. Did you get everything you need?'

'I'd say so. Enough dumb quotes to fill a book. The guy is a walking disaster – his own worst enemy.'

'So what *would* you like to do?'

'I'm easy.'

'I found *that* out last night.'

'Hey!' she said, throwing a pillow at him. 'No sexist-guy remarks around here.'

'I have an idea,' he said, grinning. 'How about we rent a boat and go out on Lake Mead?'

'Mmm . . .' she said, stretching languorously. 'That sounds great. Just let me check in with Natalie and Jamie.'

'Why? Do they have to come too?'

'Of course not. Natalie's working, and Jamie – well, I'm hoping she'll get on a plane back to New York and confront her husband.'

'Is she in the mood to do that?'

'I think so.'

'She's a truly beautiful woman.'

'Are you trying to make me jealous?' Madison asked mildly.

'You're not the jealous type. You're too secure.'

'I am?'

'That's the impression you give, although . . .'

'Yes?'

'I *have* noticed a vulnerable side.'

'You don't say?'

'Oh, yeah.'

She smiled and reached for the phone. There was no answer from Jamie's room. 'Did Ms Nova check out?' she asked the operator.

'No, ma'am,' the operator replied.

She then called Natalie. 'What's going on?' she asked.

'Met a guy,' Natalie said. 'An actor. Well . . . not *really* an actor, more like a model. Black and gorgeous! Exactly my type. We ended up in the pool at one a.m.'

'What were you doing in the pool?'

'Everything!' A slow beat. 'What time is it now?'

'Past ten.'

'Jeez, I gotta roll out of bed, meet with my producer and decide what assholes we're talkin' to today. What are *your* plans?'

'I'm with Jake.'

Natalie chuckled softly. 'That's good news.'

'We're renting a boat and going out on Lake Mead.'

'*Veree* romantic.'

'I'm sure it will be.'

'So I'll catch you later. Don't forget there's a party before the fight tonight.'

'What party?'

'The VIP party. One of those big-deal events. I'll get you invited.'

'No, thanks.'

'Hey, girl, you're in Vegas, what else you gonna do?'

'I can think of *plenty* of other things to do.'

'So check in later.'

'I will.'

'Are we on for Lake Mead?' Jake asked, as soon as she put down the phone.

'Let's do it,' she decided, leaping out of bed. 'I feel like taking the day off.'

'This time I *will* go get my camera,' he said, moving towards the door.

'Why do you need your camera?'

''Cause I never go anywhere without it. And today, Miz Castelli, whether you like it or not, *you* are having your photo taken.'

* * *

Rosarita was not happy with their accommodation. 'I hate this room,' she complained, stamping around in circles. 'It's too small.'

'We're only here for two nights,' Dexter pointed out, opening his suitcase.

'Who cares if it's two nights or a thousand?' she said. 'I want to see what kind of room Chas has. I bet he's got himself a luxury suite, and he's stuck us with this poky little deal. I'm not standing for it.'

'Nothing you can do about it,' he said, hanging up his suit.

'Ha! You'll see,' she said, picking up the phone and calling the reservations desk. 'This is Mrs Dexter Falcon,' she announced grandly. 'Mr Falcon, the star of *Dark Days*, was supposed to be getting a suite for the same rate as a room. There's obviously been a mistake. Can you please send someone up to move us?'

'You'll never get away with it,' Dexter said, when she hung up.

'I just did. What have we got to lose? They'll either move us or they won't.'

'You're using my name.'

'What have you *got* a name for if we can't use it?'

'It's embarrassing. They probably don't even know who I am.'

'I agree with you, Dex – that *would* be embarrassing. But, then, you've been an embarrassment to me for our entire marriage.'

He stared at her, hurt and angry. If she wasn't pregnant, he would be granting her the divorce of her dreams.

*　*　*

Sober, Jamie wasn't sure *what* she wanted. But she dressed anyway, then took a cab over to Kris's hotel. In the elevator on the way up to his suite, she started

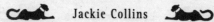

wondering *what* she was doing. Did she really want to go to bed with a rock star merely to get revenge on her cheating husband?

Yes. Why not? She had to do *something*. She couldn't sit around like the poor hard-done-by wife. And after she'd completed the deed, she *would* tell Peter. 'Oh, by the way, Peter, while *you* were out with your *boyfriend*, *I* was screwing Kris Phoenix.'

One thing she knew about her husband – he was insanely jealous.

She wished she had a drink to fortify herself. Doing this while drunk was one thing, but sober, she wasn't sure if she could carry it off. Besides, her hangover was kicking in with a vengeance.

Kris greeted her at the door of his suite wearing a white terrycloth robe and not much else. His hair was wild and sticking up, and he looked older in the sunlight, but still cocky and cute. And very English.

'I thought you didn't get up until lunch-time,' she remarked.

'Like the sweater,' he said, pulling her through the door. '*Veree* sexy.'

She'd worn a baby blue angora one: the colour brought out her eyes, the fabric made men weak.

A room-service table was set up in the centre of the living room, with two large jugs of freshly squeezed orange juice and a pot of coffee.

'Can't stomach food in the mornin',' Kris said, making a face.

'Where's Amber?' she asked.

'We had kind of a fight last night. So, like I told you, she's run off in a huff to ride a horse or somethin' stupid.'

'What was the fight about?'

'She doesn't want to be seen with me. She doesn't get that you gotta use publicity like it uses you. Amber's young – she doesn't realize you gotta put out. Know what I mean?'

'How *old* is she?' Jamie asked, pouring herself a cup of strong black coffee.

'Twenty-two.'

'I'm twenty-nine, does that mean I'm too old for you?'

He gave a cocky grin. '*You*, my little darlin', are not too old for anybody. C'mere an' gimme a hug.'

'Can I ask you something?' she said, taking a step back.

'Ask away.'

'What exactly do you have on under that bathrobe?'

'A hard-on an' a smile!' he said, with a cheery wink. 'Anythin' wrong with that?'

Chapter Fifty-two

Not only did Rosarita get their room changed for a suite, she also received a printed invitation to a VIP party in the Magiriano Leopard Suite at six o'clock that evening. She fingered the white and gold card triumphantly. Having balls was good, it paid off every time.

'Look,' she said, waving the invitation under Dexter's nose, 'we're invited and we're going.'

'What about the others?' Dexter said.

'They're *not* invited, so they're *not* going.'

'That isn't fair,' Dexter said. 'You know how my mom would love it.'

'God, Dex, you're *such* a mommy's boy,' she jeered. 'Grow up. They can go do something else while we party. We'll meet them later.'

'You're *sure* you can't get them invited too?' he asked, certain she could if she put her mind to it.

'No, Dex,' Rosarita said, pursing her lips. 'This is a VIP party.'

'You're positive?'

'Oh, for God's sake!' she snapped. 'I'm going shopping.'

'You went shopping yesterday in Beverly Hills.'

'Are *you* paying the bills?' she asked testily. 'Is *that* the problem here?'

'No, but I thought we might all hang out together today.'

'Not me. I'll meet everyone later for lunch.'

'Chas mentioned Spago. My mom's all excited.'

'Christ! A tube of *toothpaste* would excite her!'

'Don't be bitchy, Rosarita. You were never like that when we first met.'

'That was a long time ago, Dex.'

'It hasn't even been two years.'

'It seems like twenty-two.'

It was pointless to argue with Rosarita. She always made sure she had the last word.

'I'm going jogging,' he said. 'I'll meet you at Spago in Caesar's Palace at one o'clock. Don't be late.'

'Can't wait,' she muttered.

As soon as he left the room, she hurried into the bathroom and extracted the bottle of lethal poison from its hiding place at the bottom of her makeup case. Now that the time was drawing near she was beginning to get nervous. What if the poison didn't work? What if Dex *didn't* die and she was stuck with him for ever?

She couldn't stand it. It *had* to work. Why wouldn't it?

The next question was, how to do it? Her original plan had been to slip it into his drink before they went downstairs. But if she did that, she'd be the only one around, therefore she might be accused at a later time.

No, the place to do the deadly deed was at the VIP cocktail party. That way she could slip it into his drink

471

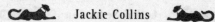

while they were surrounded by people, and she would never be a suspect.

But how to achieve that without anybody noticing?

It shouldn't be *that* difficult. Rosarita was excellent at solving problems.

* * *

The moment Chas opened his eyes after taking a short nap, he was ready to gamble. 'Let's go,' he instructed Varoomba, thrusting a couple of hundred dollars at her. 'Get yourself some chips and cruise the casino. We're gonna make us some money.'

'Did you book the table for lunch?' she asked.

'Yeah, yeah, I did it.'

'Remember you promised to meet my grams?'

'I didn't promise nothin',' he growled.

'Yes, you did.'

'So?'

'Well, um . . . can she come to lunch?'

'*Lunch?*'

'That way she can meet everyone. I don't ask you for much, Chas. *Please* let me invite her.'

'Ah, Jeez!' he mumbled, under his breath, he hated it when women pleaded.

'Is that a yes?' she asked eagerly.

'It's a maybe.'

'Thank you, hon,' she said, throwing her arms around his neck. 'You're such a big sexy teddy bear. I love you *so* much.'

Love? The L-word had never entered Varoomba's vocabulary before. Hearing it made Chas extremely nervous. He reminded himself to call the house to make sure that they'd packed up her things.

Never leave anything to chance – that was his motto.

* * *

Now that it was daylight and she was sober, Jamie decided that maybe this wasn't such a good idea after all. But how to stop something *she*'d started?

Kris had fast-moving and nimble hands, and it was glaringly obvious he hadn't lied when he said he had nothing on under his white terrycloth robe. She tried not to look, but his erection was poking through the material like a signal.

First he kissed her, bending her back, his tongue darting in and out of her mouth, his hands in her hair. Then he started feeling under her sweater like a schoolboy on a sure-thing date.

'Take it easy, Kris,' she gasped, backing off. 'You're moving *way* too fast.'

'Cor blimey,' he muttered. 'We don't 'ave much time, luv. Let's get to it. It's what you've bin after, isn't it?'

'I thought it was *you* who was after me,' she said. 'You were always calling me in New York.'

'Your old man didn't like that, did he?' Kris said, chuckling. 'What's the deal with you an' 'im, anyway?'

'I caught him cheating,' she said flatly.

'So *that*'s why you're 'ere.'

'Maybe. But I also find you attractive.'

'I bin told *that* one before, 'aven't I?' he said. 'Is it *me* you find attractive or the whole rock star bit?'

'*You*, Kris. I couldn't care less about your fame. It's completely irrelevant.'

'You sure?'

'Of course I am.'

Before she realized what he was doing, he'd deftly unhooked her bra. She felt a shiver of excitement, but at the same time she still wasn't sure that she wanted to rush into anything. It was one thing to boast that she was going to fuck Kris Phoenix. It was something else to go through with it.

His hands dived under her sweater, reaching bare tit.

Once more she backed off.

Once more he came after her.

'Got somethin' t' show you,' he said, leering.

'What?' she said.

'This.'

And then he flashed her, opening his bathrobe to reveal an extremely impressive erection.

'Oh . . . my . . . God . . .' she managed.

And as she uttered the words, the door of the suite opened and in walked Amber.

Chapter Fifty-three

'This is great,' Madison said, lying on the sundeck of the boat they'd rented, her head thrown back to the sun, enjoying doing nothing, thinking about nothing, merely relaxing and having a nice time with a man she liked.

'I'm kind of liking it myself,' Jake agreed. He'd been snapping away with his camera, but she'd hardly noticed.

'I feel so relaxed,' she said, well aware that when this assignment was over she had to get her life together and discover exactly what her father was all about. But right now she didn't have to do a thing. Right now she could live in the moment and simply enjoy being with Jake.

'Do you have a ringside seat tonight?' he asked.

'I guess so. Can't *wait* to have their blood splattered all over me.'

'That's a gruesome thought.'

'Boxing is *such* an archaic sport. Two guys beating the crap out of each other. For *what*? Entertainment? Isn't that going back to Roman times and the gladiators?'

'Things never change,' he said. 'They just go round in circles.'

'And he's philosophical too,' she murmured.

'Last night was special, Madison,' he said, leaning over to kiss her. 'You make me feel incredibly comfortable.'

'That's exactly how you make me feel,' she said.

'I think this means we're going to be seeing more of each other,' he said.

'That depends on you, doesn't it?' she said, adding a flippant, 'got any trips to Paris coming up?'

'Very funny,' he said, kissing her again.

'I'm serious, Jake. Where *is* your next assignment?'

'No idea. You hit on it last night when you called me a wanderer. It's true – I am like that. I have no home, I prefer staying in hotels.'

'Where's your stuff?'

'Who has stuff?' he said quizzically.

'Normal people.'

'Maybe I'm not normal.'

'Well,' she said, stretching, 'I'm considering going to L.A. for a few weeks after I leave here. I need to get my head straight about my father. I miss him and yet I *don't*. I love him and yet I hate him. Does that make sense?'

'Maybe.'

'I *have* to find out the truth.'

'You will. In your own time.'

'Jake,' she said seriously, 'you don't have to follow me around. We can keep in touch and get together when it suits both of us. I'm not a clingy person, you know.'

'You're not clingy at all. And, believe me, *I* can tell you about clingy women.'

'Can you now?' she said, amused.

'There *have* been other women.'

'No!'

'Bitch!'

'What happened to that blonde you were seeing? The call-girl?'

'You *have* to remind me.'

'She *was* very beautiful.'

'I told you before, *you*'re beautiful – *she* was pretty.'

'And he has a way with words.'

'And *you* have the most kissable lips I've ever had the pleasure of getting close to.'

* * *

Martha decided that cruising the Magriano Hotel in Las Vegas was the most amazing thing she'd ever experienced. She had already spotted a Latin singing star, three movie stars and Al King, one of her all-time favourites. Her level of excitement was in overdrive as they left the Magriano and walked along the strip towards Caesar's Palace for lunch at Spago.

'The women in my book club will *never* believe me,' she babbled, repeating herself. 'It was exciting enough when Dickie landed on a daytime soap. Now this!' She hung on to Chas' arm. 'I'm so *grateful* to you, Chas. You are such a wonderful man, and *very* generous, if I may say so.'

'It's the least I can do,' Chas said, enjoying his role as the purveyor of good times.

Varoomba followed a few steps behind them. She had chosen to wear a tight red tank top with no bra, and everything was on show – including, to Matt's delight, her very prominent nipples. He'd spent the morning imagining what it would be like to chew on

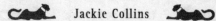

them, and wondering if there was any chance of visiting a strip club. He knew Vegas was famous for its lap-dancing, but he also knew there was not much hope of him sneaking off to visit a club by himself. Dexter wasn't the kind of son who'd arrange it, and why would Chas be interested, considering he had a piece like Varoomba at his disposal?

Martha oohed and aahed all the way to Caesar's Palace. 'The hotels here are out of this world,' she exclaimed. 'I've never seen anything like this place. *Everything* is magnificent!'

Varoomba was hoping that Renee would be on time. Grams had a habit of always being late, and even though Varoomba had called her as soon as they'd arrived, Renee was never a sure thing. 'Meet us for lunch at Spago,' Varoomba had said. 'And don't be late.'

'Christ!' Renee had complained. 'Do I *have* to?'

'Yes,' Varoomba had insisted. 'I told you, this one's likely to propose. Wouldn't you like to see your little granddaughter happily married to a rich man?'

'Did you bring money?'

'I brought a coupla hundred.'

'Is that all?' Renee said scornfully. 'You, who make a fortune shakin' your boobies? Shame on you.'

'A few hundred is better than nothing, isn't it?' Varoomba said. 'If I can get this guy to marry me, you'll get more.'

'Okay, I'll see you there.'

Now, as they headed towards Spago, Varoomba wondered if it was such a good idea. She hadn't seen Renee in a couple of years and her grams was hardly the grandmotherly type. If Renee wore one of her outfits and managed to knock back a few drinks . . .

Oh, no . . . It didn't bear thinking about.

* * *

Jamie was mortified. Not that she'd been caught with her pants down, but Kris certainly had. Although she had to admit, Amber was quite cool and collected.

'Hello,' the young actress said, walking into the suite as if she hadn't noticed Kris standing there with his dick hanging out.

'Uh . . . 'ello, luv,' Kris said, hurriedly closing his bathrobe and knotting the belt. 'What's up?'

'My horse was temperamental, so I decided to come back,' Amber said, helping herself to a glass of orange juice.

'I can see that,' he said.

She glanced over at Jamie. 'Hope I'm not interrupting anything.'

'Not at all,' Jamie said, flustered. 'If you'll excuse me, I need to visit the powder room.'

She raced into the sanctuary of the guest bathroom, and quickly did up her bra. This whole incident was so stupid. She'd come all the way to Vegas to sleep with Kris Phoenix, and now she'd gotten caught – by his girlfriend, of all people, before anything had happened. This was like a bad joke.

She peered in the mirror, brushed her hair, applied some lipstick and hurried back into the room, anxious to make a fast getaway.

'Well, uh, Kris, I guess we've covered everything,' she said, calm as it was possible to be under the circumstances.

'Yeah, luv, we did.'

'So I'll hear from you in New York.'

'Look forward to it,' he said awkwardly.

'Amber, nice to see you again.'

'You, too . . . um, Jamie, isn't it?'

'That's right.'

'I won't forget your name again,' Amber said, with a vague smile.

'I'm sure you won't,' Jamie said. 'Don't worry – I'll let myself out.'

She travelled down in the elevator feeling totally humiliated. This was all Peter's fault. Why hadn't he come to her and confessed? Why hadn't he said, 'You know what? We'd better get a divorce because I've discovered I like men.' That would've been the civilized thing to do.

But, oh, no, Peter couldn't do that, he'd had to let her find out the hard way. Bastard!

She got out her cell phone and tried to call Madison at the hotel. No answer. Then she attempted to reach Natalie. The same there.

She needed to talk to Natalie about Madison's birthday dinner. Hopefully, Natalie had already taken care of ordering a cake.

She sighed and got into a cab. The driver was talkative. She gave him monosyllabic answers, hoping he'd get the hint. He didn't.

She was paying off the cab outside her hotel when she noticed Joel Blaine walking out.

'Hey,' he said, seeing her at the same time. 'And still no husband?'

'I told you, he's in New York.'

'What kind of a man lets *you* run around Vegas by yourself?'

'A dumb one.'

'Whoa . . . Somebody's angry.'

'Where's your girlfriend, Joel? Aren't you with Carrie Hanlon?'

'She's kind of boring. You know what those models are like, nothin' much to say. Where's your friend, Madison?'

'I haven't seen her today.'

'She's different. I like her.'

'You do?'

'Yeah, she's a smart cookie.'

'You should ask her out.'

'You think she'd go out with me?'

'No. But you may as well ask.'

'Why *wouldn't* she go out with me?'

'She thinks you're a player.'

'Is that a bad thing?'

'Madison's not into serial daters.'

'Maybe I'd change for a woman like her.'

'Meanwhile you're here with Carrie Hanlon.'

'Wanna go play blackjack?'

'Why not?' Jamie said, with a weary little sigh. 'I have nothing else to do.'

*   *   *

'Charlie?' Renee shrieked.

'Ren?' Chas bellowed.

The two of them fell upon each other with loud whoops and hugs.

Varoomba's mouth fell open. Her grandmother and Chas *knew* each other! How could this be?

'How many years has it been?' Renee said, taking a step back.

'Too goddamn many,' Chas said, beaming. 'Ya look senfuckinsational!'

And she did. Renee was a tall, statuesque ex-showgirl with a strong resemblance to Raquel Welch. At fifty-two she had lost none of her in-your-face good looks, and she knew it.

'Jesus Christ!' Chas exclaimed. 'What're you *doin'* here?'

'Looks like I'm meeting you, doesn't it?' Renee said, smoothing down her black, fake leather microskirt.

'It sure does. Ya gonna join us for lunch?'

'I think that's the whole idea.'

'Huh?'

She laughed loudly. 'Don't you *get* it, Chas? *I'm* Varoomba's grandma.'

Chapter Fifty-four

People stared at Leon Blaine. They stared even harder when they realized that Carrie Hanlon was in his party. It was the kind of group that made people step back. Of course, they were surrounded by several not-so-discreet bodyguards as they headed for a limo to take them from the Mirage to Caesar's Palace for lunch. Carrie was dressed for attention in a man's-style pale blue pin-stripe suit with a low-cut waistcoat. She looked stunning.

'Marty promised to drop by,' Joel informed her.

'As in Scorsese?' she replied.

'You got it, babe.'

Although Joel didn't fancy Carrie Hanlon, it was definitely a kick to be seen with her. The way people gaped! It was like she was a movie star or something.

Joel had only dated one movie star, and that had been a miserable experience. He'd always thought models were the ego queens, but he had been wrong, movie stars were way ahead in that field. All the girl had talked about was her next movie, her co-star, her director, and every producer in town. Also, he soon

483

found out that if someone more important entered the room, she was away and running.

No, movie stars were not for him.

He'd noticed Amber Rowe lurking around the casino. Skinny piece of ass. Not his style at all. Although he had to admit that actress-wise she was the real deal.

After breakfast with Carrie, he'd spent the morning flitting from one casino to another. The Magiriano was on his case. He owed money. Big.

So what? His credit line was good anywhere.

Eventually he'd run into Jamie Nova and played a couple of games of blackjack with her. When it came to gambling she didn't know shit. But she was his entrée to Madison, so he kept on her good side.

Leon had an entourage of friends join them for lunch. A Bolivian tin billionaire with his decades-younger wife. A jockey and his stately black girlfriend. Two financiers, and an Internet mogul.

They were settled at a prime table, whereupon dishes of food were laid out for them to sample.

Joel nibbled on a piece of duck pizza and considered returning to the strip club to while away the afternoon before the big fight.

Why not? Maybe he'd discover a stripper he fancied fucking.

* * *

From across the room, Rosarita spotted Joel walking in with Carrie Hanlon, and was rendered speechless. How could this be happening? Joel, in Vegas, with the most famous supermodel of all? This was a bad joke.

She slid down in her seat, unwilling for him to see her with this group.

Chas and Varoomba's grandma were apparently old friends and, boy, were they making up for lost time. Varoomba was livid. She sat at the table, silicone tits sticking out, mouth slightly open as she listened to Chas and Renee reminisce.

'Hey, Charlie, remember that time in Atlanta when you couldn't find your pants?' Renee said loudly, trying to break his balls.

'The racetrack thing?' he said, chuckling at the memory.

'Yeah, remember that? An' I thought you were such a winner. Little did I know you were busy cheating.'

'Watch it!' Chas said, roaring with raucous laughter. 'I don't cheat, get that into your pea-sized brain.'

'Pea-sized brain, huh?' Renee shrieked. 'Better than havin' a pea-sized dick like *someone* I know.'

'Stop it,' Chas said, still laughing. 'I got a daughter sittin' here.'

'I'm sure she's heard the word dick before,' Renee said. 'Haven't you, dear?'

Rosarita jumped. She wasn't really listening, she was too busy watching Joel. 'Excuse me?' she said.

'Nothing, honey, forget it.' Renee turned her attention back to Chas. 'What a blast!' she exclaimed. 'Who would've thought?'

'Ya got that right,' Chas agreed.

Varoomba was confused. It seemed, from what she was gleaning from their conversation, that Chas and her grams had once had a serious affair. And now it appeared that they were all set to light the fire again, because Varoomba hadn't seen Chas this turned on in the entire time she'd known him. Renee had always had a way with men. She might be fifty-two, but she was a looker. Unfortunately, she was also a drinker, and Varoomba noticed she was knocking back the wine with a complete disregard for the fact that it was only one o'clock in the afternoon.

Just my luck, Varoomba thought. *I get a guy who I think might marry me, and what happens? It turns out he's got a hot nut for my grandma. Too damn much!*

She turned to Matt, who'd been ogling her tits all through lunch. 'Life's a bitch, isn't it?' she said, with a sour expression.

'Sure is,' Matt replied.

'Sometimes I don't understand anything,' she said mournfully.

'I know what you mean,' Matt agreed, happy she was paying him some attention.

Martha gave him a swift kick under the table. 'Stop encouraging her,' she whispered.

'What are you talking about?' he whispered back.

'You don't want to upset Chas. Can't you see what's going on? His old flame turns out to be his girlfriend's *grandma*. Now *you*'re talking to the girl, and *she*'s trying to make him jealous. So stop it. Right now!'

'For Crissakes,' Matt muttered, scowling.

Dexter, meanwhile, was oblivious to everything. He'd jogged in the morning, then he'd taken a swim in the hotel pool. After that he'd called Gem.

Bad news! A man had answered the phone. Dexter was so thrown that he hadn't uttered a word.

'Hello?' the male voice had said. 'Hello? Who's there?'

Dexter had quickly replaced the receiver in a state of panic. Was Gem living with someone? Did she have a boyfriend? A husband? Jesus! He hadn't bothered to ask, and now that he came to think of it – why would a girl like Gem be on her own?

He had to find out. He decided to get away from the table on the pretext of going to the men's room. Then he could try phoning her again. It was imperative that he find out the truth.

* * *

'I'm glad I caught you,' Jamie said, as she sat with Natalie on the patio at Spago.

'Me too,' Natalie said. 'If I don't eat lunch I am one *bad* interviewer. Food is on my mind most of the time.'

'Not when you're talking to someone like Brad Pitt,' Jamie said.

'Whoever. I gotta have that meal before I deal with them.'

Jamie laughed and waved at Joel across the room.

'He's a jerk,' Natalie remarked.

'No, he's not, he's sweet,' Jamie responded. 'He taught me how to play blackjack.'

'So,' Natalie said, 'what else did you do this morning? Anything I *shouldn't* know about?'

'Not what I threatened to do,' Jamie said glumly.

'You mean you didn't run over to see Kris?'

'Well . . . *he* called me, and I *did* run over. Only the moment we were about to get into it, in walked Amber.'

'No way!' Natalie said, and burst out laughing. 'You mean you and Kris were busy gettin' it on, and the *girlfriend* walks in on you?'

Jamie nodded. 'How embarrassing is *that*?'

'Hmm . . . I guess it means you are *not* destined to fuck Kris Phoenix.'

'I have to do *something* before I see Peter and tell him it's over,' Jamie said, frowning. 'I can't sit there and say, "Oh Peter, I found out you're screwing another guy, and that's fine – let's get a divorce." I have to make him feel like shit. Can you understand that?'

'Sure, honey,' Natalie said soothingly. 'I'm into revenge big time.'

'It's not revenge. It's more like getting even.'

'Revenge,' Natalie said, rolling the word across her tongue. 'Call it like it is.'

* * *

Varoomba left the table to visit the upstairs ladies' room. As she undulated through the restaurant every male eye was upon her, including Joel's.

Holy shit! he thought. *There goes my favourite stripper – the one who never came to my office. What the hell is she doing in Vegas?*

'Excuse me,' he said, getting up from the table, determined to get an explanation.

As he began following her, he recognized Dexter Falcon, also on his way upstairs. They'd never actually met, but Joel knew who he was: Rosarita's husband – the dumb schmuck soap actor.

Wasn't *this* something? Maybe Dexter was with the stripper. Now he'd have something to tell Rosarita when he returned to New York.

He glanced back in the direction Dexter had come from and, to his shock, sitting there at a large table filled with people, was Rosarita.

He looked away quickly, wondering if she'd spotted him.

So what if she had? Rosarita made him happier than any of these other bitches. As a matter of fact, he wouldn't mind a session with her right now. She was sexier than all his models put together.

He continued following Dexter up the stairs, noticing that the soap star was a tall motherfucker, and handsome in a bland way.

Once upstairs, Dexter didn't go into the men's room, he headed straight for the pay-phone. Joel hovered. Interesting, he thought.

Dexter dialled a number and waited. Joel lit up a cigarette and continued to hover.

'Hey,' Dexter said, into the receiver. 'Gem? It's me. Where were you last night? I phoned, there was no answer.'

A pause as whoever was at the other end of the line gave him some kind of explanation. Then Dexter said, 'I called this morning and a guy answered. Who was he?' Another pause, then a relieved 'Oh, your *brother*.'

Joel knew he was on to something.

'You know what?' Dexter continued. 'As soon as I get back I want us to get together. There're things I have to tell you.'

Joel smiled to himself. So old Dexter had a girl-friend. Wouldn't Rosarita find *that* an interesting piece of news.

Chapter Fifty-five

'I think we'll skip the party,' Madison said, on the drive back to their hotel.

'What party is that?' Jake asked.

'Some kind of VIP party Natalie wants us to go to. I'd sooner catch the action in Antonio's dressing room. And I'm sure you wouldn't mind getting more photos before the fight, huh?'

'Good idea,' Jake said. 'I'm not into parties.'

'Nor am I.'

'Although your friend *did* mention that we're all having dinner after the fight.'

'What friend, and who's *we?*'

'Natalie. She called while you were in the shower and invited us to dinner after the fight.'

'Why didn't you tell me before?'

'I forgot.'

'Thanks, Jake. You take great messages.'

'So *that*'s what you want me for – to be a message-taker?'

'No,' she said teasingly. 'I want you for your great big sexy . . .'

'Yeah?'

'*Body*.'

'I wondered what you were about to say.'

'I *bet* you did.'

'Anyway, sweetheart, is dinner okay with you?'

'I'd sooner have room service,' she said wistfully. 'Last night was memorable. The things you can do with caviar that I'd never even thought about!'

'Not to mention champagne.'

'I heard no complaints.'

'So, dinner is on, then?'

'Okay, but let me warn you, Natalie *loves* celebrations, and *I* happen to hate them. So *no* birthday cake. I repeat, no cake. Make sure, okay?'

'I hardly know Natalie, so how am I supposed to persuade her not to do something?'

'Tell her *I don't want it*. You can do that, can't you?'

'It's your birthday, sweetheart, I can do anything you want.'

* * *

Rosarita dressed for the party in the best Escada had to offer. She'd thought long and hard about what to wear for the big fight, and the very expensive Escada black and white dress purchased on Rodeo Drive was the perfect choice.

She'd thought about Joel all afternoon, reasoning that he was probably in Vegas for the fight. But why hadn't he told her? If she'd known in advance they could've set up a meeting. And she was horny, because ever since Dexter had learned she was pregnant he had not approached her sexually. Rosarita did not like going without sex. It didn't suit her.

Anyway, what did she care? Dexter Falcon was a stiff, and tonight he'd be a stiff in more ways than one.

* * *

To Carrie's annoyance, after Leon's original come-on he had not mentioned contracts, heirs, marriage, billions, *nothing*. She was most put out. Did he think he could *play* with her? Did he think she could be tempted and then discarded? Not Carrie Hanlon. Oh, no. Men did not mess with Carrie Hanlon.

Marika kept giving her the evil eye. Carrie knew the evil eye when she saw it – she'd experienced it enough times from fellow models.

Every attempt she made to get close to Leon was thwarted by Marika.

Damn the woman. She was a witch.

Carrie hadn't mentioned to Joel that nothing had happened between her and Eduardo the previous night. It was none of his business. The problem was that after her conversation with Leon, she wasn't in the mood for a toy boy. No. She was more in the mood for Leon to fulfil his promise.

Eduardo did not make her feel as sexy as billions of dollars.

She was determined that tonight she would corner Leon and ask him exactly why he was treating her in such a disrespectful way. Screw him if he thought he could make an offer then rescind it all in one day.

She dressed in a skimpy green Versace dress that left little to the imagination. Carrie Hanlon did not need much adornment – she could carry off sackcloth, if need be.

* * *

'How can you do this to me?' Varoomba wailed.

'Whaddya carryin' on about now?' Chas said irritably.

'Inviting my grams to go with us to the fight. How did you get another ticket anyway?'

'I have my ways,' Chas said mysteriously.

'It's not fair,' Varoomba whined, her eyes filling with tears.

'What's not fair?'

'You and my grams.'

'Stop calling her your grams, for Crissakes. She's Renee, an old friend of mine.'

'Did you screw her?' Varoomba said suspiciously. 'Did you an' my grams have *sex?*'

'Mind your freakin' business,' Chas snorted.

'It's *plenty* my business,' Varoomba insisted. 'She's my grams.'

'I don't give a fuck if she's your freakin' *sister*. What the two of us did twenty years ago has nothin' t' do with you.'

'I'm sure it doesn't,' Varoomba said huffily. 'But what the two of you do today has *lots* to do with me.'

'Yeah?'

'Yeah.'

'Ya think you got some kinda claim on me?'

'We live together, remember?'

'I've bin meanin' t' talk to ya 'bout that.'

'And say what?'

'I got ya set up in an apartment.'

'Me?'

'Yeah, ya got your own place. I'm havin' your stuff moved there while we're away. It don't suit me livin' with somebody. You gotta understand, my kids ain't happy 'bout it.'

'Your *kids?*' she said scornfully. 'They're grown women.'

'Anyway, that's the way it is. I'll give ya some cash an' you'll do what ya wanna do.'

'This is shit!' Varoomba exclaimed, her silicone boobs shaking with indignation.

'Take it or leave it.'

'It's all *her* fault.'

'Who's her?'

'Grams.'

'It ain't nothin' t' do wit' Renee. I told ya before, we're old friends.'

'You're a bastard, Chas – a genuine two-bit bastard.'

'Thanks, kid. I bin called worse.'

'You won't get away with treating me this way,' Varoomba warned. 'You might think I'm just a dumb stripper, but I'll get my own back on you. And don't you forget it.'

Chapter Fifty-six

I nvitations to the very exclusive party at the Magiriano had to be presented at the door before entry was gained.

Rosarita thrust her invitation at the girl with the list. 'Mr and Mrs Dexter Falcon,' she said grandly.

'Oh, hi, Mr Falcon,' the girl said, smiling straight at Dexter and ignoring Rosarita. '*Love* your show.'

It seemed people in Vegas knew him a lot better than people in New York. Well, they'd certainly hear about him today when he dropped dead somewhere in the hotel. Rosarita patted her purse. The bottle of poison was in place. All she had to do was pour it in his drink and make sure he drained his glass. Then it was goodbye, Dex – and hello Joel.

Although now she had a new problem. How was she supposed to get Joel to dump Carrie Hanlon?

Of course, she could slip *her* some poison, too.

Ha ha! Very funny! A serial killer she was not.

Anyway, Rosarita felt secure that once she told Joel about the baby, Carrie Hanlon would be history. The cocktail party was already crowded. Rosarita recognized a few famous faces and felt pleased to be mixing with the stars. She and Joel would do this in the future – come to the fights in Vegas and mingle with celebrities.

She recognized Bruce Willis, incredibly sure of himself, with a smirky smile. And George Clooney – quite sexy. Martha would be in heaven!

'Why did we have to come to this?' Dexter asked, not comfortable at all.

'Because,' Rosarita explained patiently, 'it's good for your career to be seen and have your photograph taken in such illustrious company. Look who's over there. It's Nick Angel. And there's Al King talking to Will Smith – oh, God, I used to love Al King when I was younger. It's quite a stellar group, Dex, we should mix.'

'If you say so,' Dexter said, wishing he was in New York with Gem.

'And you have the temerity to call *me* jaded,' she mocked. 'I think the shoe is on the other foot, my dear.'

'Excuse me?' he said, frowning.

'Nothing. What are you drinking?'

'I'm not in the mood for a drink.'

'Oh, c'mon, Dex – we're in Vegas for God's sake, you have to have *something*.'

'I don't understand why my mom couldn't have come to this party,' he grumbled. 'I could've given her *my* invitation.'

'Stop being ridiculous,' she said sharply. '*Your* invitation is what got us in here.'

'She would've loved it.'

'So what?'

'You're a mean woman, Rosarita. You could've arranged for another invite.'

'I could *not*. This party is very exclusive. We're lucky to be here ourselves. Can't imagine *how* I pulled it off.'

'*You* pulled it off by using *my* name.'

'Why are you always bickering with me?'

'Because . . .'

'Because *what?*'

'Oh, forget it.'

* * *

Walking into a crowded party with Carrie was definitely a kick. The few photographers who'd been allowed inside immediately went ballistic.

Joel got off on the attention. Oh, sure, he was used to being photographed at premières and Broadway openings with some gorgeous model on his arm, but Carrie was the model of the year – the decade, actually. Carrie Hanlon was a supermodel, the real deal.

He looked around to see if he could spot Madison. He'd decided that, with Jamie's help, he might be able to score there. How many other guys would be thinking about another woman while out with Carrie Hanlon? Not many. It showed he had class and taste.

Across the room, Marika was giving his father an earful. God knows what she was saying, but he could see Leon's lower lip quivering with annoyance.

Why did his father put up with her shit? Why didn't he trade her in and get himself a *real* girlfriend? It's not like Marika was a looker. She was a dragon lady. Quite scary, actually.

Oh, well, it wasn't *his* problem.

* * *

'And this is Mr Mogul,' Natalie said.

'Nice to meet you,' Jamie said, distracted, because

before leaving for the cocktail party, Peter had tracked her down and actually called her.

'What the *hell* do you think you're doing?' he'd demanded, over the phone. 'Are you *insane?*'

'How did you find me?'

'What does *that* matter? I found you, didn't I? So get your ass back here. And do it fast.'

'No, Peter,' she'd said, standing up to him for once.

'What do you mean – *no, Peter?*'

'It's over,' she'd said, and hung up the phone, ignoring the persistent ringing that continued until she'd left her room to meet Natalie.

'*You*'re a beauty,' Mr Mogul said, checking her out.

'Don't worry, he's gay,' Natalie's brother, Cole, interrupted, hanging on to his arm. 'Take no notice of his compliments.'

Mr Mogul laughed.

'Cole,' Jamie exclaimed, grabbing a glass of champagne from a passing waiter, 'I haven't seen you since college. Madison's right – you look sensational.'

'Is that what she said?' Cole asked, pleased.

'I remember a tough little teenager running around trying to bum money off his sister. *Now* look at you.'

As a much-in-demand Hollywood fitness trainer, Cole kept himself in perfect shape. He was an extremely tall, muscular and handsome man.

'How did you two meet?' Jamie asked, draining her glass and reaching for another one.

'I went to break his balls, and he ended up breaking mine,' Cole said, with a wicked grin.

Mr Mogul gave him an affectionate pat on the arm. 'Try not to discuss balls in public,' he said. 'It's *so* not done.'

'I thought that's what you liked about me,' Cole

said, grinning. 'That I do all the things I'm not supposed to. Where is Madison anyway?'

'She won't make this party,' Natalie said. 'She had to go interview one of the boxers.'

'Lucky her!' Cole said.

'There's a birthday dinner for her later, which you guys will come to, right?'

'Wouldn't miss it,' Cole said. 'Anyway, I want her to meet Mr M.'

'Am I going to be called Mr M. for ever?' Mr M said good-naturedly. He was an older man, but attractive, with a bald head and a wide smile.

'I think you're stuck with it,' Natalie said. 'I started it because I hated you. Now I like you. In fact, you can be my brother-in-law.'

'May I remind you that marriage is not legal between two men?'

'Damn! Just give him some kind of document, so that if you drop dead he gets everything.'

'You're a feisty one, Natalie.'

'Yeah,' she said grinning. 'Nobody ever said I wasn't.'

* * *

Waiters in black tie were serving Cristal champagne in fluted glasses with the place and date etched on the side in gold.

Rosarita took two glasses from a silver tray and handed one to Dex. 'We'll take these glasses home,' she said, 'as a souvenir. So drink up, Dex, while I go visit the little girls' room.'

She had come up with a new plan. She'd pour the poison in *her* drink, then when she got back she'd switch glasses with Dex. It was perfect.

Once in the powder room, she shut herself in a cubicle, took out the bottle of poison and carefully tipped it into her champagne glass. Her heart was beating so fast that she didn't know what to do. She hoped that handling it wouldn't harm the baby. Joel's baby – which she would tell him about soon.

Holding her glass like precious cargo, she made her way back to the party.

On her way across the crowded floor, she bumped into Joel. Neither of them was surprised.

'You didn't tell me you were coming to Vegas,' he said, stepping in front of her.

'Nor did you,' she countered.

'I flew in for the fight on my father's plane.'

'Coincidence. I'm with *my* father too.'

'It's family night in Vegas,' he said drily.

'And who did Carrie Hanlon fly in with?' she couldn't help asking.

'Carrie's kind of hanging with my dad. She's under the impression he's going to be signing her to a big fat contract.'

'What kind of contract would that be?'

'A makeup deal,' Joel lied. 'He owns three cosmetics companies. You know these models – they're always desperate for a bigger and better deal.'

'I wouldn't think Carrie Hanlon was desperate for anything.'

He moved closer. 'What've you been up to while you're here?'

'Not a lot,' she said, licking her lips. 'And you?'

'I haven't been having sex, if that's what you mean.'

'Nor have I,' she said, with a secret smile.

'How about we meet up before the fight?' he suggested. 'I know you're with your husband, but I'm sure you'll be able to sneak away . . .'

She took a deep breath. 'Where did you have in mind?' she asked.

'The swimming pool with the fountains.'

'That's a little *too* public, isn't it?'

He laughed. 'It'll be deserted,' he said, sipping his drink. 'Of course, if that's too risky for you . . .'

'Not at all,' she answered boldly, almost sipping *her* drink, until she remembered what a disaster *that* would be.

'Fifteen minutes,' he said.

'Twenty,' she countered. She didn't want him thinking she was *too* easy.

A sudden commotion across the room attracted their attention. 'What's going on?' she said.

'Aw, Jesus, it's my dad,' Joel said, putting his glass down on a side table.

'What happened to him?' she asked.

'He's on the floor. Christ! I hope he's not having a heart-attack.'

Without thinking, Rosarita placed her glass beside his and followed him over to the scene of the commotion.

'Let me through,' Joel said, billions dancing before his eyes as he shoved his way over to Leon, who did not look dead, merely embarrassed.

'Your father tripped,' Marika explained. 'It's nothing. He's fine.'

Joel put his arm out to help Leon up. His father glared at him. 'Goddamn chair.' He glowered. 'I'll sue this fucking hotel.'

'You should, Dad, you need the money,' Joel said, kind of getting off on Leon's anger and embarrassment.

Rosarita backed away. Oh, God, where had she put her drink? Then she remembered. It was on a side table next to Joel's. She retrieved it and looked around for Dexter. Had to get this done, and then she'd be free to meet Joel.

She was starting to sweat, which she never did. This was nerve-racking, and yet – in the end – it would all be worth it.

* * *

While an irate Leon Blaine was being dusted down by a bodyguard, Marika took the opportunity to corner Carrie. 'I feel I should tell you something, dear,' Marika said, her voice an icy blast. 'Nothing is ever as it seems.'

'Excuse me?' Carrie said, flashing her whiter than white teeth at a hovering photographer.

'*Nothing* is ever as it seems,' Marika repeated slowly. 'And you, as a fairly smart woman, should realize that.'

'I have no idea what you're talking about,' Carrie said, tossing back her magnificent mane of thick hair.

'I'm talking about Leon,' Marika said. 'Leave him alone, my dear, because you will get *nothing* except promises from him.'

'I don't want anything from Leon,' Carrie said. 'I have plenty of my own.'

'I'm aware of that. But one can never have enough, can one?'

'What?' Carrie said rudely.

'Of course,' Marika continued, quite enjoying herself, 'when Leon found out you had a sixteen-year-old boy waiting for you in your suite last night, he wasn't impressed. It's so *pathetic* when one has to *pay* for sex.'

'I have no idea what you're talking about,' Carrie said, paling slightly.

'Don't you, dear? Well, all you need to do is remember what I said – stay away from Leon.'

'And if I don't?' Carrie said boldly.

'Ah . . .' Marika said. 'Let me see . . . if you don't, you and your sixteen-year-old toy boy are destined to appear on the front pages of *all* the tabloids. I can see the headline now – "Desperate Carrie Hanlon Can't Get a Man – Has to Settle for a *Child*".'

'You bitch!' Carrie said.

Marika honoured her with an inscrutable smile. 'Takes one to know one.'

* * *

'Hi, honey,' Rosarita said, wondering if Dex could hear her heart beating. It was now pounding so loud that it was making a racket in her ears.

'Can we leave?' Dexter said. 'I promised my mom we wouldn't stay long.'

'Such a mommy's boy,' she mocked. 'Drink up and we'll be out of here. I'm taking the glasses as a souvenir.'

'I don't know what I did with mine,' he said.

'Have this,' she said, thrusting her glass at him.

'All right,' he said, taking her glass of champagne and draining it in three large gulps.

Things were working out better than she'd imagined. She removed the empty glass from his hand. 'I'll go rinse it out,' she said. 'Then we'll leave.'

'Isn't it kind of dumb, taking a champagne glass to a boxing match?'

'What's dumb to you, Dex, is not dumb to me,' she said, hurrying back to the ladies' room.

Fortunately it was deserted. Setting down the glass, she crushed it under her high-heeled shoe. Then she picked up the pieces with a Kleenex and dropped them into the trash.

Her breathing was out of control, yet she was suffused with a feeling of immense triumph.

She'd done it! She'd actually done it!

How long would it take before the poison worked? Oh, God, how long? One hour? Two? Better not be alone with him. Had to make sure they were always in crowds. And what better place to be in a crowd than at a boxing match?

'Can we go now?' he said, as soon as she returned.

'Yes, Dex. We'll meet the others and go straight to the fight.'

'About time.'

'Are you feeling all right?' she ventured. 'You look a little pale.'

'I'm perfectly okay,' he said.

'Good,' she said.

And once again she wondered how long the poison would take to do its deadly deed.

Chapter Fifty-seven

The heady excitement of a championship fight about to take place was in the air. The lobby and casino of the Magiriano Hotel were alive with people – some going to the fight, others trying to score last-minute tickets, and a slew of wide-eyed tourists star-gazing as a continual parade of celebrities made their way down the red carpet into the arena where the preliminary bouts had already started.

As Martha and Matt trailed behind Chas, Renee and Varoomba, Martha wished that she was standing with the fans. Watching everything out here would be much more entertaining than having to go directly to her seat.

She couldn't wait to get home and tell her friends *everything*. All these celebrities – beautiful women and handsome men, TV cameras everywhere, it was almost too much to take.

'I thought Dexter and Rosarita were meeting us,' she said, tapping Chas timidly on the shoulder as they entered the huge arena.

'Yeah, yeah, they're gonna see us inside,' Chas said. 'They got their tickets.'

'But it would have been so nice to have walked in with Dexter.' Martha sighed. 'Perhaps I would've been photographed with him. I often see celebrities photographed with their moms.'

'Mebbe on the way out,' Chas said offhandedly. 'Hang on to him, they'll catch a shot or two.'

'Do you think so?' she said, eyes gleaming.

'Yeah, yeah,' Chas said, more interested in talking to Renee, who was strutting beside him in thigh-high boots, a snakeskin miniskirt, and wide-shouldered jacket. The woman might be over fifty, but she was pure dynamite. She left Varoomba trailing *way* behind, in her stupid pink dress, with her big silicone tits forging the way like a pair of headlights.

Everything about Renee was the real McCoy. Chas could vouch for that.

* * *

There were so many people crowded into Antonio's dressing room that Madison had no chance of getting near him – not that she had any desire to do so: she already had all the dumb quotes she could use.

Jake was manoeuvring himself into corners to catch various shots of movie stars and sports personalities who kept dropping by to shake Antonio's hand and wish him luck.

After twenty minutes of this, Madison was all set to move on. 'Are you ready to get out of here?' she asked Jake, who'd managed to catch most of the action.

'I certainly am,' he replied.

'Damn! It's crazy in there – just crazy,' she said, as they made a quick exit. 'How can he prepare? Isn't he supposed to be by himself?'

'I heard the champ won't allow anybody in,' Jake

said. 'Only his manager, a couple of trainers and his sidekick. He's *very* focused.'

'Shall we make a bet?' she suggested, suddenly getting into the spirit of Vegas.

'*Do* you bet?' he replied, giving her a sceptical look.

'No. Do you?'

'No, but since it's your birthday we could put five hundred bucks on Antonio to win.'

'What are the odds?'

'She doesn't bet,' he said, smiling, 'yet she wants to know the odds.'

'Do what you like. I don't care.'

And she didn't, she was happy just being with Jake.

'We could grab a bite to eat before the main fight. Or have sex,' he said, with a smile. 'Whatever turns you on.'

'Later,' she said, smiling back.

'Later.' He nodded. 'Then how about a hamburger now? I'm starving.'

'I thought you didn't eat meat,' she said accusingly.

'You thought that, did you?'

'Yes, Jake,' she teased. 'I had you pegged as one of those, like, um, *tofu* guys.'

'*Me?*' he said, eyebrows shooting up.

'You.'

'Jesus! You certainly know how to insult a person.'

'I learned at an early age.'

'I can eat a hamburger with the best of 'em, okay?' he said, grabbing her hand. 'So let's go order, then on to the fight, and then – oh, shit,' he said, stopping abruptly.

'What?' she said quickly.

'I was forgetting – we've got dinner with your friends.'

'Is that an absolute must?' she said, wishing nothing more than to spend the night alone with Jake.

''Fraid so.'

'Whatever.' A beat. 'As long as there's no cake.'

* * *

'I forgot my wrap,' Rosarita said.

'What?' Dexter said.

'My wrap,' she repeated, peering at him to see if he was exhibiting signs of any ill-effects. 'I must've left it at the party.'

'And I suppose you want *me* to run back and get it?' he said brusquely.

'No, Dex, that's all right. You go on – *I*'ll get it. I have to visit the little girls' room again anyway.'

It was unlike Rosarita to be so obliging.

'If you're sure,' he said.

'I'm sure. Give me my ticket. I'll meet you inside.'

He handed over her ticket, and she took off. As soon as she was certain Dexter was out of sight, she switched direction, slipped outside and made her way to the swimming-pool with the built-in fountain.

It wasn't too hard to find, and Joel had been right, at this time of night it was deserted. Not *that* deserted, there were a few people strolling around.

She smiled in anticipation. Trust Joel to come up with a good idea.

* * *

Meanwhile, Dexter made a stop at a pay-phone on his way in to the fight. Over the last twenty-four hours he had become obsessed with Gem, she was all he could think about, and there was absolutely nothing he could do about it.

She answered her own phone. No brother this time. 'How are you?' he said, clearing his throat.

'It's you again?' she said, laughing.

'Yeah, it's me again.'

'Didn't we speak at lunch-time?'

'I know. I'm on my way to the fight.' A long pause. 'Uh . . . Gem, there's something I've got to tell you.'

'Go ahead,' she said.

'Maybe it can wait,' he said nervously. 'We're flying back tomorrow morning.'

'Who's *we*?'

Another long pause before he spoke. 'Well, uh . . . *that*'s what I've got to tell you.'

'What is it, Dexter?'

He loved the way she said his name: it sounded so smooth coming out of her mouth. 'I, uh, I have a wife,' he mumbled. 'And, uh, we're shortly going to be separated.'

'Oh,' she said, very quietly.

'Look, I mean, not that you and I are anything to each other,' he said, his words tumbling over each other, 'but I've got a strong hunch we have a future together, and I can't start anything until I separate and begin my new life with you. I know this sounds crazy and we've only just met, but I've never found anybody like you. You're everything I ever dreamt of. Beautiful inside and out.'

'No one's ever talked to me like that before,' she whispered.

'And nobody ever will again,' he said, gaining confidence. 'Because you're mine. Immediately after the fight tonight, I'm telling my wife.'

'Are you *sure*?' she said, not the least bit argumentative.

'Yes. And if I can get a late flight out I will. So if I'm very lucky I'll see you later.'

'Yes, Dexter,' she said softly. 'Later.'

He walked in to the fight with a broad smile spread across his handsome face.

* * *

On his way to meet Rosarita, Joel was accosted by a couple of goons. They sidled up beside him, each took an arm, and frogmarched him through the casino.

'What the fuck –' he began.

Then he was jabbed in his left side by something that felt suspiciously like a gun, so he abruptly shut up.

They headed for a side door behind a bank of slots. As they got outside, the hot night air hit him like a blast of steam.

'Where are you taking me?' he asked, angry and scared – so scared that he was fast developing a bellyache.

'Never ya fuckin' mind,' said goon number one, a classic broken-nosed hood in a creased brown suit.

'You know who I am?' Joel questioned, sure that this must be a case of mistaken identity.

'Fuckin' right we do,' said goon number two, younger and tougher than the first, although it was the first one who had the gun jammed into Joel's side.

'So what's the problem?' Joel muttered.

'Fuckin' problem's one million fuckin' bucks,' said the man in the creased brown suit. 'Five hundred thou the last time you was here. Now you're into us for another five.'

'If you know who I am, then you know I'm good for it.'

'Sure we do,' the man sneered. 'That's why our boss wants payment tonight.'

'Are you *crazy?*' he said angrily. 'Who carries that kind of money with them?'

'Get it,' the younger, tougher one said. 'Pay your markers by midnight, or you're a fuckin' dead man.'

And with that he hauled off and smashed Joel in the face, followed by a right to the stomach that took him straight to the cement. And in case he wasn't getting the message, the man in the brown suit kicked him in the groin. Twice for good measure. Then they were gone.

Groaning, Joel staggered to his feet, blood pouring from his nose, which felt like it was broken. 'Shit!' he mumbled – a mumble that turned into a furious yell: 'Shit! Shit! SHIT!'

* * *

'Where's Rosarita?' Chas inquired, happily ensconced between Varoomba and Renee.

'On her way,' Dexter replied. 'She left her wrap at the party.'

'Was the party nice, dear?' Martha asked plaintively. 'I suppose you saw all kinds of stars.'

'Didn't notice.'

'Dick!' Martha admonished.

'Dexter,' he corrected, glaring at his forgetful mom.

'Excuse me,' Madison said, making her way along the row of seats past Dexter, who seemed vaguely familiar.

'Hi,' he said, recognizing her too.

'You're my friendly neighbourhood jogger, right?' she said, with a pleasant smile.

'That's right. How's that magnificent dog of yours?'

'Pining, I'm sure,' she said, moving on to her seat. Not quite ringside, but near enough. She searched for Jake, spotted him in the photographers' area.

He saw her and waved. She blew him a kiss. He mouthed, 'Happy birthday.'

'Nice going,' said Natalie, already in her seat. 'That's two days in a row, isn't it?'

'Will you *stop*?' Madison said, leaning across her to kiss Cole, who immediately introduced her to Mr Mogul.

And then the fanfares began, announcing the entrance of the two boxers.

Antonio appeared first, waving his arms in the air as if he'd already snagged the title, resplendent in a gold and blue cape, with matching satin trunks, black boots and white and silver striped socks. He jumped into the ring like a tiger, threw off his cape, made a victory sign with his hands, and the crowd went wild. Antonio was a big favourite.

Next came the champ, a more serious man, clad entirely in white. Bull Ali Jackson was bigger than Antonio and quite ferocious-looking. His skin was ebony, his head bald. His eyes said he was ready to kick the shit out of anyone who dared to get in his way.

The crowd was impressed, they began chanting his name – 'Bull Ali! Bull Ali! You're the champ! Bull Ali!'

His wife, a serene black beauty, took her seat ringside, clutching a string of diamond and pearl prayer beads.

And so the fight commenced.

Chapter Fifty-eight

Trying to staunch the flow of blood pouring from his nose, Joel staggered back into the hotel. He was beyond furious. That he, Joel Blaine, had been subjected to the indignity of being beaten up by a couple of hired thugs was unfuckingbelievable.

His father could buy and sell Las Vegas. And *they* were worried about a measly million bucks. It was unreal. It didn't make sense. Fuck 'em all. He'd leave town and never come back. They could whistle 'The Star-spangled Banner' for their lousy money.

He made it to a men's room, stuffed Kleenex up his nose and splashed cold water on his face. Then he set off for the front of the hotel.

* * *

Jamie elected not to go to the fight, even though Mr M assured her he could get her a ticket.

'Not interested,' she'd said. 'I'll meet you all at Madison's dinner.'

'Stay away from Kris Phoenix,' Natalie said, wagging a warning finger.

'Of course.'

'What'll you do?' Natalie asked.

'Play blackjack,' she'd said. 'Joel Blaine taught me everything I need to know.'

'Stay away from *him*, too. We'll see you at the restaurant.'

'Call me when the fight's over so I'm not sitting there by myself.'

'You got it.'

She hadn't told anyone about Peter's upsetting and belligerent phone call. How dare he track her down and demand that she come home? Did he honestly believe she was too stupid to have found out what was going on? She ran a very successful interior-design business, she was no dummy.

Peter simply didn't get it. And he sure as hell didn't get her.

She sat at one of the blackjack tables, accepting pointers from a fat, red-faced man, in a too-tight, striped seersucker suit, who squeezed in next to her. The man made sure the champagne flowed, and her hangover from the night before soon vanished.

Gambling was definitely the perfect way to pass the time.

* * *

Rosarita paced back and forth by the pool, getting angrier by the minute. Was Joel Blaine actually standing her up? What kind of a shitty move was *that*?

'Hi, honey,' slurred a drunken man, with a bad rug perched crookedly on the top of his head. 'Lookin' for company?'

'Get lost,' she snapped.

'I won me two hundred bucks, now I gotta find a place t' park it,' he said, with a lascivious twitch of his right eye. 'Get my drift, cutie?'

Outraged at being mistaken for a hooker, Rosarita stalked off.

* * *

Round one. Antonio on the attack. Cocky. Bouncing on the balls of his feet. Diving right in on the offensive, using his fists as lethal assault weapons.

Bull Ali taking it all in his stride. Standing tall. Unfazed. He is, after all, the champ.

The crowd picked up on the rumble and began a steady yell of encouragement.

The vibes were in the air. This championship match was destined to be a good one.

* * *

'You *see?*' Madison said, hunching up in her seat. 'I told you he's full of confidence.'

'Sexy with it, too,' Natalie remarked, crunching a handful of popcorn.

'He's got me sold!' Cole said. '*Nice* abs.'

'Be quiet,' scolded Mr Mogul. 'It's not polite to admire other men's bodies when you're in my presence.'

* * *

'Joel?' Jamie said, reaching out to grab his arm as he passed by the blackjack table she was sitting at. 'We've got to quit meeting like this.'

515

'Huh?' So intent was he on getting out of there that he almost didn't stop.

'Guess what?' Jamie said, gathering her chips and getting up from the table.

'What?' he said shortly, as the fat man in the seersucker suit gave him an if-looks-could-kill glare.

'I won a thousand dollars! You taught me well.'

'Yeah?' he said, not remotely interested.

'What *happened* to you?' she asked, taking in his dishevelled appearance. 'You're a terrible mess.'

'I, uh, had a nose bleed.'

'You're very pale. And, anyway, why aren't you at the fight?'

What was she – dense? ''Cause I had a nose-bleed,' he said, repeating himself.

'You don't look good at all. Come upstairs to my room and I'll try to clean you up.'

'That's sweet, Jamie, but . . . aw . . . Jeez,' he said, almost doubling over from a sudden shooting pain. 'Maybe I'll take you up on that.'

'You should,' she said, holding on to his arm. 'It's the least I can do after you helped me win all that money.'

'Yeah,' he mumbled. 'An' I didn't think you could play for shit.'

'Thanks,' she said, with a wry laugh, leading him over to the elevator.

He stifled a groan. His balls felt like they'd been through a shredding machine.

'How come *you*'re not at the fight?' he managed.

'Too violent,' she said, screwing up her nose. 'I can't stand the sight of blood.'

* * *

As the elevator doors closed on Jamie and Joel, Rosarita stalked past, missing them by seconds. She was fuming. Next time she got hold of Joel Blaine, he would *pay* for keeping her waiting and making her miss the beginning of the fight.

How rude! No fucking manners.

Busily muttering under her breath, she strode through the casino until she reached the red carpet that led into the arena. The area was deserted as everyone was now inside.

'Damn!' she exclaimed, still furious with Joel. 'Damn, damn, damn!'

She sought out an attendant at the back of the arena and thrust her ticket at him.

'You can't go in now, ma'am,' he explained. 'They're in the middle of a round.'

'I can see that,' she said shortly.

'You'll have to wait.'

'I'm not waiting for anybody,' she said, steaming. 'My seat's ringside. Take me there right now.'

'People don't like being disturbed in the middle of the fight,' the attendant said, foolishly arguing.

'Fuck 'em,' she said forcefully, sounding suspiciously like Chas. 'Lead the way, or I'll make damn sure you're fired.'

* * *

'Tell me the truth about what happened,' Jamie said, as they entered her room.

'What truth?' Joel said, collapsing in a chair.

'Well, frankly, Joel, you look like you've been beaten up. Your jacket's ripped, and you're white as a ghost. I repeat – what happened?'

'Aw, shit, *I* dunno,' he mumbled. 'Coupla guys had a beef with me about money they think I owe.'

'How can *you* owe money?' she said incredulously. 'Your father's one of the richest men in America.'

'Yeah, yeah, yeah – tell me about it. Stupid, huh? A bad fuckin' joke.'

'I'm sorry,' she said quietly.

'Yeah, so am I.'

'I've got an idea,' she said. 'Why don't we order a bottle of champagne and celebrate?'

'Celebrate *what?*' he said sourly. 'I've got nothing to celebrate.'

'My thousand dollars,' she said, smiling brightly. 'Pretty good for a novice, isn't it?'

'I guess so,' he conceded.

'Some man was trying to give me pointers. He wasn't as helpful as you, though.'

'No?' he said, perking up, because if he wasn't mistaken, Jamie was coming on to him.

'Oh God, I've had *so* much champagne.' She sighed, throwing herself down on the bed. 'I feel a little bit crazy.'

'You do?' he said, taking another look at her. How come he'd never thought about Jamie Nova in a sexual way? Was it because she was married and he didn't care to deal with her husband? No, that couldn't be the case. What did *he* care about husbands? His affair with Rosarita had proved that wasn't an issue.

The truth was that he didn't find Jamie that sexy. She was too pure-looking, too Grace Kelly in those old TV movies. There was something about her that wasn't his style. She looked like she'd have *clean* sex, not *dirty* sex – the way *he* liked it.

But, still . . . she *was* a beauty. And those legs! Jeez! They went on for ever.

He wondered if she realized that her skirt was riding up so high, revealing acres of succulent thigh. Then he wondered if she was doing it on purpose.

'Order the champagne, Joel,' she murmured, yawning. 'I'm feeling mighty thirsty.'

Who was he to turn down an opportunity when it was staring him in the face?

'Yeah, sure,' he said, trying to forget about his aching balls. 'I'll order the champagne. You put on the music.'

'Music?' she said, amused. 'Oooh, are you trying to get me in the mood, Joel?'

'Why would I wanna do that?'

She rolled over on to her stomach. 'I've always found you *very* attractive,' she murmured seductively.

'You have?'

'Yes.' A soft laugh. 'I kind of . . . you know, had little fantasies about you.'

'No kiddin'?' This might work out better than he'd imagined. 'Wanna tell me about 'em?'

'Well,' she said, pausing provocatively, 'you're different. You've got energy. Peter is too uptight, he *never* has energy. Peter is actually a walking, talking Ralph Lauren ad.'

'No shit?' Joel said, grinning.

And suddenly the ache in his balls was not as bad as he'd thought.

*   *   *

Round two belonged to the Bull, and he took it with a great deal of pride.

Antonio was surprised. Round one had definitely been his, but now the Bull was all over him like a Mack truck and he didn't appreciate it.

He tried giving back his best, but the Bull was having none of it. *I'm getting rid of this cocky little bastard up front*, the Bull was saying to himself.

And it showed.

* * *

Rosarita squeezed past Bruce Willis, allowing her ass to graze his knees. *Hmm . . .* she thought with a self-satisfied smirk, *that'll give the famous movie star something to think about.*

Finally she made it to her seat next to Dexter, out of breath and still furious with Joel.

'Where have you been?' Dexter asked.

'I told you, I had to get my wrap,' she replied, peering at him, wondering when the poison was going to take effect. 'Then I got stuck in the bathroom.'

'What do you mean, stuck in the bathroom?'

'Oh, forget about it,' she said irritably, turning her attention to the ring.

Two half-naked, sweaty men and the promise of blood.

What more could a girl ask for?

Chapter Fifty-nine

T he room service waiter was Cuban and, although unfortunately short, he was quite attractive. He delivered the champagne in an ice bucket with two glasses. 'Would you like me to open it?' he asked, slyly checking Jamie out.

'Yeah,' Joel said, reaching in his pocket for a tip.

'Oh, yes,' Jamie agreed, giggling. The waiter was so cute that if she didn't score with Joel, he'd definitely be a contender.

* * *

Round three, and Antonio was making another stab at dominating the champ.

No go. Bull Ali was a wall of muscle. A solid brick wall of a man with a devastating right-handed punch, which he now started to use to good effect, pounding away at Antonio's face. *Not* a popular move with the Panther, who was very protective of his handsome features.

By the end of the round, Bull Ali had opened a cut

above Antonio's left eye, and blood was dribbling down his face.

The crowd loved it.

* * *

'Your message light is blinking,' Joel pointed out.

'*You* pour the champagne while *I* listen to my messages,' Jamie said, feeling deliciously light-headed. 'Then we should do something about cleaning you up. Maybe you should buzz the valet and get them to fix your jacket.'

'I'll take care of it at my hotel.'

'Don't wanna take your clothes off, huh?' she teased, pointing her tongue at him in a provocative fashion.

Talk about a come-on. This babe was *panting* to climb Mount Everest, no doubt about *that*.

Only drawback, he still felt like shit. The ache in his balls was not abating, and his stomach was continuing to cramp – which was all he needed. 'Gotta use your bathroom,' he mumbled.

'Go ahead,' she said, picking up the phone and pressing the message button. 'Jamie!' Peter's angry voice screaming in her ear. 'What are you *thinking*? Goddamnit! I know you wanted to be with Madison on her birthday, but to sneak off to Vegas without telling me is stupid and childish. I'd come get you, but you know I can't stand that city. You and I need to sit down and have a serious talk because I refuse to put up with this spoiled, selfish behaviour. Grow up, Jamie. It's about time you realized you're a married woman.'

She put down the phone incensed, his words ringing in her ears. *Stupid. Childish. Spoiled. Selfish.*

How dare he?

Peter's harsh words were too much, considering what *he* was busy doing.

'Joel,' she yelled, jumping off the bed and stepping out of her dress, 'get in here. I'm ready to fuck your brains out!'

* * *

Round four belonged to Bull Ali, and Antonio was in trouble. The cut above his eye had deepened and split and now the blood was gushing like a geyser. Bull Ali dogged him around the ring, and Antonio was taking a lot of punishment.

Mrs Bull Ali raised her expensive prayer-beads to her lips and kissed them with a fervent murmur of thanks.

As far as she was concerned, it was all over.

* * *

'If one spot of blood splashes on my dress, I'm out of here,' Rosarita complained shrilly.

'Go,' Dexter responded.

She spun round to favour him with a malevolent glare. '*What* did you say?'

'Go. Get out. Do what you want.'

Well, obviously the poison was doing its stuff, because she'd never witnessed Dex act like this before. 'Ex*cuse* me,' she said, still glaring.

The crowd roared as Bull Ali landed another punch above Antonio's damaged eye.

'I said get out, because that's what *I*'m doing.'

'Ha!' Rosarita jeered. 'A touch late in the day for *you* to be making threats.'

Chas leaned across from his seat. 'Will you two shut the fuck up?' he said gruffly. 'I'm tryin' t' watch a slaughter here, an' who can concentrate wit' the two of you yammerin' away?'

* * *

'I can't watch this,' Madison said, covering her eyes. 'It's totally barbaric.'

'No,' Mr Mogul said. 'It's two big hunks of masculine flesh hammering out their aggressions.'

'Get real,' Natalie said succinctly. 'It's two greedy jerks beatin' the crap outta each other for big bucks.'

'Whatever it is,' Madison said, 'I loathe it. The way this guy's pounding Antonio, he'll *have* no face left by the time they put a stop to it. And aren't they supposed to do that when it gets bad?'

'The promoters cater to the crowd, not the boxers' welfare,' Mr Mogul said.

'Oh, really? Well, it's about time the rules were changed.'

'Try gettin' them to ban cigarettes first,' Natalie said. 'It's all big business. Ouch!' she exclaimed. 'Did you see that?'

And as Antonio fell to the canvas, Madison suddenly felt desperately sorry for him.

* * *

Never one to turn down an out-and-out invitation, Joel emerged from the bathroom.

Miss Clean Sex herself had removed her dress and thrown herself down in the middle of the bed, clad only in a pristine white lace bra and bikini-cut panties.

524

Not even a thong to get him in the mood.

Some guys would go ape-shit over Jamie Nova – the classic blonde beauty. But he simply couldn't get *that* excited.

He threw off his ripped jacket, pulled his black silk turtle-neck over his head and dropped his pants. Surveying him from her position on the bed, Jamie noticed that he was extremely well endowed – or, as Natalie would say, 'The dude is hung like an award-winning stallion on a good day!' Natalieisms were quite memorable.

Jamie reached for the champagne and took a few gulps from the bottle to bolster her courage. This was a revenge fuck. Nothing more. Nothing less. But she might as well enjoy it.

Unfortunately, the only way she could do that was if she was ever so slightly drunk.

* * *

Round five. And Antonio was still taking a lot of punishment. Not only was Bull Ali pounding him with a series of vicious right jabs, but the blood from the cut above his eye was beginning to blur his vision.

Antonio tried counter-punching, hitting the taller boxer with a flurry of blows to the body.

Bull Ali wasn't having it. He'd knocked Antonio to the canvas once, and in this round he planned for him to stay there.

* * *

To his horror, Joel could not get a hard-on. This had never happened to him in his life. Oh, sure, he'd heard about it happening to other guys – but to *him*? Never.

He was on top of what most guys would consider a very delectable piece and, goddamnit, he couldn't get it up.

Quickly he tried to summon a mental picture of Rosarita in one of her leopard-print thongs and a nippleless bra. She *always* got him horny.

Christ! He suddenly remembered his rendezvous with her, which he'd failed to keep. Rosarita would be madder than a crazy wildcat.

Of course, when she heard his story, perhaps she'd understand. Especially if he embellished, and he was good at that.

And if she didn't understand – screw her. There were plenty of Rosaritas in New York. Maybe it was time he found himself a *new* married woman.

Thinking about Rosarita did not solve his problem with Jamie. Jesus! The *reason* he couldn't get it up was because his balls were giving him hell, his stomach was a mass of shooting pains and he was sick. Those creepo paid bastards had made him fucking *sick!*

'You okay?' Jamie asked, acutely aware that nothing was happening and naturally blaming herself.

'Huh?' he muttered, sprawled on top of her like a dead weight. 'I . . . I don't feel so good.'

'Oh?' she said, wriggling out from under him. 'Is it . . . something about me?'

'No, honey,' he assured her. 'You're a babe. It's me, I feel like shit. I didn't tell you before, but those motherfuckers kicked me in the stomach, an' I think they've . . . Jesus Christ, I think they've done something bad to me.'

She knelt up on all fours, still clad in her underwear.

'I'm sorry,' she said sympathetically, before bursting into floods of tears.

Christ! This was all he needed – almost doubled over with pain, and a sobbing, half-naked woman on his case.

'What's your problem?' he managed to say. 'I don't go for all this crying stuff.'

'I'm upset about Peter and what happened.' She sobbed mournfully. 'All I wanted was to get my own back on him. I was planning on doing it with Kris Phoenix, but then his girlfriend walked in on us. Now you can't even get an erection. Is it something about *me*? Is that why Peter had to go off with a man?'

Joel's eyebrows shot up. 'Peter is into guys?'

'Yes. Why do you think I'm *doing* this? Oh, God,' she wailed, 'I shouldn't be here,' and she jumped off the bed.

'You'd better call a doctor,' Joel groaned, clutching his stomach. 'An' do it fast.'

'You feel *that* bad?' she asked, staring at him, upset because she was certain it was her fault that he was incapable of having sex.

'I promise – it's not you, babe,' he gasped. 'It's those fuckin' guys . . . They kicked the shit outta me, an' . . . Aw, *Jesus!*' He rolled over and closed his eyes.

'Joel?' Jamie said, shaking his shoulder. 'Wake up. What's going on?'

He groaned, and brought his legs up to his chest. Then he let out a long, strangled cry, choked a little bit, and after that there was silence.

Chapter Sixty

Round Six. Bull Ali was the champion, and everyone knew it. Everyone, that is, except Antonio. Between rounds he'd huddled in his corner with his handlers while they'd lectured him on his next moves.

'Stop tellin' me what to do,' he'd said, spitting blood into a bucket. 'I listened to you guys an' it got me nowhere. I'm goin' back in there and doin' it *my* way.'

'Be cool, Tonio,' his manager warned. 'That's all you can do. An' if he drops you again, stay there before he does more damage.'

'Fuck you!' Antonio had mumbled. 'I'm gonna be champ. Y' can bet your fuckin' *cojones* on it.'

Now he could barely see out of his left eye, but he knew if he could avoid any more punishment to the area he had a chance. And the champ did have one big weakness. His arrogance.

Antonio got in a couple of quick body jabs. And then he went with his prize move – a solid left hook to the jaw that took Bull Ali by surprise, and almost knocked him off his feet.

The crowd roared. The underdog was fighting back.

Bull Ali slammed into motion, but now Antonio was fired with adrenaline and knew he had to seize the opportunity to win the battle.

Stay focused, he told himself. *Ignore the pain. You, Antonio 'The Panther' Lopez, are destined to be champion.*

And from out of nowhere he turned into a ferocious dynamo, swift on his feet, skilfully avoiding Bull Ali's attempts to do further damage to the cut above his eye. He was finally living up to his reputation as The Panther. Sleek and fast, he was back in action.

As he circled his opponent, he knew for sure that there was no way he could win this fight on points. Too late for that. His only chance was to knock the champ out. Otherwise he would definitely lose.

Summoning every ounce of strength he had left, he slammed two more solid left hooks straight at Bull Ali's jaw – one sledgehammer blow after the other.

To the crowd's surprise and shock, Bull Ali fell to the canvas like a lead weight and failed to get up.

The referee started the count. 'One . . . two . . . three . . .'

'Get up,' the crowd began chanting. 'Get up!!'

'Four . . . five . . . six . . .'

'Get up, you piece of shit!' screamed Bull Ali's beautiful, serene wife.

'Seven . . . eight . . . nine . . . *ten!*'

Pandemonium reigned.

Antonio 'The Panther' Lopez was the new champion – exactly as he'd predicted.

* * *

The crowd poured out of the arena, buzzing with the

heady excitement of the surprise ending to a truly great fight.

'I never thought he'd pull it off,' Madison said, as they made their way towards the entrance.

'I did,' said Cole, close behind her. 'He's got killer eyes.'

'Enough about the eyes,' said Mr Mogul, stopping to air-kiss Pamela Anderson, a blonde vision in a red rubber tube dress.

'Mr Mogul knows everyone,' Cole confided.

'Ah, but *you* know all their dirty little secrets,' Natalie said wickedly. 'Like who's had breast implants, lipo, penile enhancements . . .'

'Do you, Cole?' Madison asked, quite amused. 'That could be a fascinating story. The plasticization of Hollywood. Lipo in La La Land. Victor would love it!'

'We did a segment on lips,' Natalie said. 'I wanted to call it "Who's Been Kissing Whose Ass?" but the midget brains who run the network didn't get it.'

Jake caught up with them as they continued to jostle their way out of the arena. He grabbed Madison and hugged her. 'We won!' he said happily. 'Now I can buy you a present.'

'We did?' she replied, ridiculously pleased to see him.

'Yes, and we got our cover too. I know the shot I want Victor to use.'

'I'd better call him,' Madison said. 'He'll be screaming for the piece I'm writing like yesterday.'

'Where are we meeting Jamie?' Cole asked.

'Oops, I'd better call her room,' Natalie said, pulling out her cell phone. 'And then – I don't know about anybody else, but *I*'m in the mood for food!'

* * *

'We lost, damnit,' Chas growled, not at all pleased. 'Five thousand big ones.'

'*You* lost,' Renee pointed out with a triumphant smile. 'But *I*,' she boasted, 'being such a smart cookie – bet on the winner.'

'Ya did?'

'Should've followed my lead, darlin'. You *know* I always pick winners.'

'Ya sure do,' Chas said, chuckling.

'Remember that time at the racetrack –'

'When ya begged me to bet on –'

'The horse that was twenty to one –'

'An' I told ya it was crazy.'

'An' I said *you* were the crazy one.'

'An' then –'

'Oh, for God's sake!' Varoomba yelled hysterically. 'Can you two *stop* with the reminiscing? It's making me *sick!*'

* * *

'What was that all about before?' Rosarita said, as they were swept along by the crowd toward the exit.

'It was about us,' Dexter said grimly.

'Us?' she questioned, wondering why he was still standing. Damn Holland and its phoney mail-order poisons.

'I'm leaving you, Rosarita.'

'You're doing *what?*' she said incredulously.

'I've met someone else. Someone sweet and decent. Someone who will make me happy.'

Oh, this was rich. *He* was leaving *her*. Before or *after* he dropped dead?

'You're pathetic,' she sneered. 'A sad excuse for a man.'

531

'I understand you have no respect for me,' he said evenly, keeping his temper, because above all else he was a gentleman, 'so this'll be best for all concerned. But I'm warning you, if I give you the divorce you've wanted for so long, and ask for nothing in return, then you must swear to me that I will receive free access to our baby.'

'*Our* baby, huh?' Rosarita said, in a state of simmering fury. '*Our* baby? Sorry, Dex, but what makes you foolishly think that *you*'re the father?'

And just as she said those words, they reached the press line – and Martha leaped forward, hanging on to her son as if he were the last lifeboat in a stormy sea.

'Dickie!' Martha shouted joyfully, sensing her moment in the sun was at hand. 'Tell the photographers to take a picture of you with your mommy! It's all the rage!'

* * *

'She wants to see us,' Natalie said.

'*Who* wants to see us?' Madison said.

'Jamie.'

'She will, any minute. Didn't you tell her we're on our way to the restaurant?'

'I did, but she's adamant that we go to her room. Just you and me.'

'Just you and me, huh?' Madison said disbelievingly. 'Come on, Natalie, what kind of an idiot do you imagine I am?'

'What?' Natalie said.

'Oh, yeah, she opens her door, ushers us in, and there's a bunch of people yelling "Happy birthday", and a surprise cake and a studly cop who conveniently turns into a male stripper. I know your games.'

'I promise you, Mads,' Natalie said, 'nothing like that is going to happen. Jamie insisted that we go to her room immediately. You and I, not the others.'

'I swear to you,' Madison said, frowning, 'if you're having me on, I'll kill you.'

'I'm not,' Natalie said.

'Jake,' Madison said, turning to him, 'do you know anything about this?'

He held up his hands. 'I'm totally innocent.'

'I *bet* you are. And I'm the Pope in drag.' A beat. 'You know, guys, you're not fooling me, not one little bit.'

'Call Jamie,' Natalie said.

'Oh, yeah, like *she*'ll tell me the truth.'

'No, *I*'m telling you the truth. She sounds too upset to say much of anything.'

'If she's so upset, why does she want to see us?'

'Probably to tell us what she's upset *about*,' Natalie said patiently. 'You know Jamie, she can't deal with confrontation. Peter's probably called her, and she's sitting there having an uptight *fit*.'

'Okay,' Jake said. 'Here's the deal, you girls go get Jamie, and we'll meet you at the restaurant.'

'Do me a favour,' Madison said coldly. '*Don't* call me a girl.'

'What *should* I call you?'

'A woman. We *women* will go get Jamie.'

'Fine. You *women* go get Jamie, and make it quick.'

Madison grumbled all the way to the elevator. 'I know this is a scam,' she said, 'and I hate it. I hate birthday cakes and singing and all the shit that goes with it. And *especially* now that I'm thirty. Do you *realize* how old thirty is, Nat?'

'Yes, I do, because *my* birthday was a month ago,

remember? I'm already an old bag, and I'm hosting a show I don't give a shit about.'

'You get off on every minute of your new-found fame. I noticed Jack Nicholson waving to you at the fight like you were old friends.'

'Jack flirts with everyone.'

'He does?'

'Constantly. It's part of his dubious charm.'

Three Chinese couples joined them in the elevator as they travelled up to Jamie's floor.

'I'm telling you,' Madison warned, as they walked down the corridor. 'One male stripper, one cake, one anything, and I'm out of here.'

'I promise you,' Natalie said, knocking on Jamie's door, 'I have no idea what this is about.'

'Who is it?' Jamie called out.

'Us,' Natalie said. 'Your loyal friends – remember?'

Jamie inched the door open, keeping the security chain firmly in place.

'Hi,' Natalie said. 'Can we come in? Or would you sooner we camped out in the corridor?'

'*What* is going on?' Madison demanded. 'And why are you wearing a bathrobe?'

'Maybe *she*'s the surprise stripper,' Natalie suggested with a giggle.

'It's just the two of you, isn't it?' Jamie said, nervously trying to peek past them. 'You didn't bring anybody with you?'

'Yeah, we've got Kris Phoenix and his girlfriend right behind us,' Madison said drily. 'He mumbled something about coming over to fuck you.'

'That's not funny,' Jamie said, quite distraught. 'Something terrible has happened.'

'What?' Madison said.

'I'm opening the door,' Jamie said. 'When I do, come in quickly and close it right behind you.'

'Jamie, stop acting like you're in the witness-protection programme,' Madison said impatiently. 'Is Peter here?'

'No,' Jamie replied, tentatively opening the door.

They entered the room, and the first thing they saw was a naked Joel Blaine sprawled face down across the bed.

'I knew it!' Madison said. '*I knew it!* This is some kind of weirdo birthday *joke*.'

Jamie stared at them, her eyes wide and fearful. 'This is no joke, guys,' she whispered. 'Joel is dead.'

Chapter Sixty-one

Antonio 'The Panther' Lopez was born to be champ. Carried aloft to his party like a king, he was surrounded by stars. He was the champion. He was the fucking champion! And he was one happy guy.

The cut above his eye had been treated and dressed, and although – much to his chagrin – his face was swollen, he still looked good as he hit his party like a tornado, accepting all the congratulations and adulation that came his way.

His manager was a sweating, happy wreck, as he fended off well-wishers, hangers-on, predatory females, and members of the press.

'Mr Leon Blaine wants to meet you,' his manager whispered, shaking and sweating at the same time. 'You know who he is, Tonio?'

'No, who is he?' Antonio said, grinning widely. 'Some big important mother-fucker?'

'Mr Blaine is one of the richest men in the world,' his manager said reverently. 'And he's with Carrie Hanlon.'

'*Aha!*' Antonio exclaimed. '*Now* you're talkin'. Is she gonna be my prize cunt for the night?'

'Watch your mouth,' his manager warned, wondering how he was ever going to control Tonio now that he was the new champion.

* * *

'I still don't understand where Joel is,' Carrie said irritably, unwilling to be stuck with Leon and the Asian prison guard, as Joel had so aptly labelled Marika.

'Who knows with that boy?' Leon said. 'He's always been a fuck-up, excuse my language.'

'Aren't you concerned that he missed the fight?' Carrie said casually.

'I'm never worried about anything Joel does,' Leon replied. 'As long as it doesn't cost me money.'

Carrie checked out the crowded party to see if she knew anyone there who owned their own plane. *Anything* was better than hanging out with Leon and Marika.

She wondered what had happened to Eduardo. Now that she was in the mood, he could be just the diversion she was craving. Sex with a hot *young* bod. Always a kick!

Across the room she spotted Jack Nicholson talking to Oliver Stone, both acquaintances of hers. Without a word of goodbye, she made her way over to them and joined in their conversation.

'That girl is common,' Marika said, to her retreating back.

Leon nodded. Marika was a smart woman. He was fortunate to have her: she always came through and saved him from doing anything too indiscreet.

* * *

Dexter's mind was on fire. Rosarita was even worse than he'd imagined. 'What makes you think you're the father?' What kind of woman *said* a thing like that to her husband?

He was right to leave her. She'd practically told him to his face that it wasn't his baby.

But, then, she *could* be lying. Rosarita was a proficient liar, he knew that only too well.

He'd grant her the divorce she'd always wanted, but as soon as the baby was born, he'd insist on a blood test to ascertain who the real father was. If she thought she could get away with keeping their baby from him, she was very much mistaken.

He sought out his father, who was hovering by a roulette table. 'Listen, Dad,' he said, 'I have to leave.'

'How can you leave?' Matt said, frowning.

'I'm flying back to New York. Tell Chas I'm sorry.'

'Is Rosarita going with you?'

'No, she's not.'

'But we're *all* leaving tomorrow. Why can't you stay until then?'

'Because I have something else to do, and I want to start doing it now.'

* * *

'I'm getting Jake,' Madison said.

'You can't do that,' Jamie said, panicked.

'Well, my *God*, we've got to do something.'

'What happened here anyway?' Natalie asked, circling the bed.

'It was – it was an accident,' Jamie said. 'We were

about to make love . . . and then . . . he was on top of me . . . and he . . . he couldn't get an erection. And then he just . . . began to feel bad.'

'Pretty *damn* bad,' Natalie interjected.

'Oh, my God!' Jamie gasped. 'Have I killed him? Is this my punishment for leaving Peter?'

'Don't be so Catholic,' Natalie said, holding out her arms. 'Come here, baby. You haven't killed anyone. The guy probably had a heart-attack.'

'No, I killed him,' Jamie fretted. 'I know I did.'

'You *didn't*,' Madison insisted.

'Yes, I did!'

'We'd better call the paramedics,' Madison said.

'No,' Natalie said sharply. 'Do you realize what this'll look like? We have to figure out how to deal with this before we call *anyone*.'

'That's why I need to get Jake here,' Madison said. 'Let *him* get his mind around it.'

'Nobody else must know,' Jamie said, panicking again. 'Only you two.'

'Then how *should* we handle this?' Madison said, thinking aloud.

'*I* don't know,' Jamie said, bursting into sobs, which didn't help matters.

'Oh, Jesus,' Natalie said, staring down at Joel's hairy back. 'Are you *sure* he's gone?'

Madison ventured over and felt his pulse. 'He's gone,' she confirmed.

'What the hell were you doing with Joel Blaine anyway?' Natalie said, turning on Jamie. 'I *warned* you about him.'

'He was here, Kris Phoenix wasn't,' Jamie said tearfully. 'I had to do *something* to get back at Peter.'

'*Fuck* Peter,' Natalie said adamantly. 'That bastard.

Look at the mess he's got you in.'

'I have an idea,' Madison said. 'When I was a kid, I remember my father flying to Vegas all the time. He always stayed at this hotel. He said he had investors whom he had to see personally. I don't know if he can help us, but since he obviously knows Vegas well, I think we should give it a try.'

'Give *what* a try?' Natalie said.

'Attempt some sort of cover-up,' Madison said. 'Let's be realistic. You're right. If Joel is discovered dead in Jamie's room, *she*'ll be a suspect. It could turn into a big scandal. So . . . maybe Michael can come up with a solution.'

'You'd really call your dad for me?' Jamie said.

'Yes. And I'd better do it before I change my mind.'

'Okay,' Jamie said meekly.

'Use my cell phone,' Natalie suggested. 'That way there's no records.'

Madison took a deep breath and checked her watch. It was ten thirty in Vegas, which meant it would be after midnight in New York. She hadn't spoken to Michael in a while now. She'd been planning not to speak to him at all until she felt ready to deal with his lies. But this was an emergency, so she had no choice.

Her throat was dry as she punched out his number.

'Yeah?' He answered the phone sounding terse.

'Michael?' she said.

'Maddy – is that you?'

'It's me.'

'Jesus, what time is it?'

'It's late. Were you asleep?'

'I was watching television, must've drifted off.' A loud yawn. 'What's up?'

'I'm in Vegas.'

'What're you doing there?'

'I'm here on a story, but . . . something bad has happened.'

'What?' he said, sounding more alert.

'It's – it's my friend, Jamie. She, uh, she's in her room at the Magiriano, and . . . she was in bed with this guy – who happens to be Joel Blaine, the son of Leon Blaine.'

'And?'

'We think he might have had a heart-attack 'cause he's dead in her bed, and we don't know what to do.'

'Who's we?'

'Jamie and Natalie. My friends from college.'

'So you're telling me that you're standing in a hotel room with your girlfriends, and there's a rich guy's son dead on the bed?'

'Yes, and I'm calling you because you're the only person I can think of who might be able to help us.'

'Oh, I'm good for helping with a dead body, huh?' he said drily.

'Michael, I'm begging for your help. We're kind of desperate.'

'What's your room number?'

'503.'

'Stay tight. Don't move. Within fifteen minutes I'll have somebody at your door.'

'You will?'

'His name is Vincent Castle. You got that? Vincent Castle. He'll take care of everything. Is that good enough for you?'

'Yes, Michael,' she said, and clicked off the phone. 'It's taken care of,' she said turning to Natalie and Jamie.

'What're you *talking* about?' Natalie said. '*Nothing*'s

taken care of. The three of us are still in here with a dead body.'

'I trust my father.'

'Oh, so now you trust him? Last week you didn't want anything to do with him.'

'Things change.'

'Man, you can say that again.'

'Anyway,' Madison said, 'I think it's best if you go to the restaurant, and tell everyone Jamie's gotten the flu or something and won't be joining us. That way they won't get suspicious.'

'This is a fucking nightmare,' Natalie wailed.

'I know. But we're going to work it out.'

* * *

'Congratulations,' Varoomba said, zeroing in on Antonio, batting her over-extended false eyelashes. 'I was *sooo* impressed with your moves tonight.'

'*Mamma mia*!' Antonio crooned, checking her out. 'You gotta have some pretty cool moves of your own.'

'I've been told that,' she said coyly, thrusting her boobs towards him.

'What is it that you do, gorgeous?'

'I'm a specialty dancer.'

'No shit?' Antonio said. A knowing wink. 'Mebbe you'll show me your specialty *privately*? How about later tonight, chickie?'

Varoomba glanced across the room at her grandmother and Chas, laughing and joking and putting their arms around each other.

'Yes, champ,' she said, flirting outrageously. 'It'll be *my* pleasure.'

* * *

'I want to depart tonight,' Leon said abruptly. 'Alert the pilots, tell them to get the plane ready.'

'What about Joel?' Marika asked.

'He can get a commercial flight back tomorrow. Leave him a message.'

'And his girlfriend, Carrie?'

'She can look after herself,' he said curtly.

Marika gave a small, triumphant smile. 'I'll arrange everything, Leon. The limo will pick us up in half an hour.'

Chapter Sixty-two

By the time there was a knock on the door, Madison had managed to get Jamie dressed, packed and ready to leave.

'Who is it?' she said tensely.

'Vincent Castle.'

She looked through the peephole and observed a tall man standing there. Releasing the chain, she let him in.

Jesus Christ! Vincent Castle was a younger, even more handsome version of Michael. Mid-thirties, he had black curly hair, olive skin and dense green eyes.

She stared at him. He stared back at her with the same startled expression. 'So you're Madison?' he said, entering the room.

'That's me,' she said, trying to regain her composure.

'And this is Jamie?'

Jamie nodded nervously.

'So, Jamie,' Vincent said, 'I have somebody waiting outside to take you to the airport. We've already booked a seat for you. Now all you have to do is go back to New York and forget this ever happened. Not one word to anyone. Do you understand?'

She nodded again.

'And when I say anyone,' Vincent added, a touch menacingly, 'I mean *anyone*.'

'She gets it,' Madison said, giving Jamie a hug. 'Everything will be okay. Go straight to my apartment. I'll call you tomorrow.'

As soon as Jamie left, Madison indicated the body on the bed. 'Don't ask me how,' she sighed, 'but I can assure you, he's definitely dead.'

'Were they having sex?' Vincent asked, checking out the room.

'They were about to, but apparently he couldn't uh . . . get it up. According to Jamie, he'd taken a beating in the parking lot by a couple of heavies – something about him owing money.'

'So this is Leon Blaine's son?'

'Jamie didn't kill him,' Madison said, still reeling from Vincent's uncanny resemblance to Michael. 'He must've had a heart attack.'

'You understand that this is not good PR for the hotel,' Vincent said, picking up the almost empty champagne bottle. 'Which is why I'm going to deal with it.'

'Are you connected to the hotel?' she asked.

'Let's just say I'm an investor,' he said, discarding the bottle in the trash.

'I know this'll sound crazy,' she said, 'but you look so much like my father.'

'I know,' he said, picking up the two champagne glasses and throwing them in the trash too.

'You do?'

'Hey – you also look like him. The female version.'

'How do you know that?'

A shadow of a smile. 'Happy birthday, Madison.'

'And how do you know it's my birthday?'

'C'mon, Madison, you're a smart girl, surely you've figured it out by now?'

'Figured what out?'

'We're family.'

'Family?' she said blankly.

'You'd better sit down, I'm about to rock your world.'

'What are you talking about?'

'Don't you *get* it? I'm your brother.'

'I – I don't have a brother,' she stammered.

'You do now.' A long, steady beat. 'I'm your half-brother, the one Michael never bothered to tell you about.'

'Oh . . . my . . . God!' she gasped. Was this another of Michael's surprises? Did she know *nothing* about her father?

'We'll have to talk another time,' Vincent said, all business. 'Right now I have to deal with this, uh, incident.'

'It's not an *incident*,' she said furiously. 'It's an accidental death. And I'm not so sure we shouldn't call the police. Maybe his death has something to do with him getting beaten up.'

'Whatever,' Vincent said coolly. 'But nobody wants publicity, so here's what I want you to do. Go back downstairs, enjoy your party, get on a plane tomorrow and leave Vegas. Don't even think about this again. Can we trust Jamie to do the same?'

'You can't casually inform me you're my half-brother and expect me to leave it at that,' she said, outraged.

'Why?' he answered calmly.

Goddamnit, he even *acted* like Michael.

'Because you can't, that's why,' she said churlishly.

'Okay,' he said. 'Here's the Cliff Note version. My mother was in Michael's life before Beth. He never wanted Beth to know about her and me, so he moved us to Vegas, where he visited every month. We had a great relationship, only we weren't allowed to mention his other family. When we heard about Beth's murder, it made things bad. And then came Stella. I don't know why he had to keep us a secret then, because there was no Beth to get upset. But he got off on leading two separate lives. It was his secret. It was the way he wanted it. Satisfied?'

'No.'

'Too bad.'

'And tonight, when he called –'

'He didn't instruct me *not* to tell you.'

'Michael is more of a stranger to me every day,' she said stiffly. 'I have no clue who he really is.'

'Yeah, Michael. He's something else, right?'

She wasn't about to get into a discussion about her father with a total stranger – brother or no brother. 'Uh . . . what will you do with – with Joel?'

'That's not for you to worry about. It'll be taken care of.'

'And how do *I* take care of finding out I have a brother I never knew about?'

'One day we'll get together and talk. But not now, 'cause I have business to attend to. You go downstairs and enjoy your birthday.'

She nodded wearily. 'Yes, Vincent. But you must understand that now I know you exist we are very much unfinished business, and I intend to find out everything.'

'Got it,' he said, totally unfazed.

She hurried downstairs in a daze, and as she entered

the restaurant, Natalie and the group stood up and began singing 'Happy Birthday' while an obliging waiter wheeled out a huge cake with thirty candles she didn't want.

Her eyes met Jake's. He was the only honest man in her life, and she wanted to be with him more than anything. She rushed into his arms.

He held her close and whispered, 'Happy birthday, sweetheart.'

'I told you, no cake,' she scolded.

'Not my fault,' he said. 'I'm just an idle bystander. And I didn't buy you a present, but I do have something nice to tell you.'

'What?' she murmured.

He held her very close. 'I think I love you.'

'You *think* you love me?' she said, gazing up at him. 'You *think* you love me. What kind of crap is *that*?'

'Okay, let's just say that I definitely do.'

'Really?'

'Yeah.'

'Okay, that's not so bad.'

'It's not, huh?'

'I can live with it.'

'You can?'

'I can,' she said, thinking, *What a night! It couldn't get any weirder*.

'And you?' he said.

'What *about* me?'

'Got any feelings *you*'d like to share?'

'Uh . . .'

'Come here, woman.'

And he soul-kissed her, long and hard until she could barely breathe.

Finally she felt safe.

EPILOGUE

J oel Blaine vanished into the night. For weeks and
months, Leon Blaine waited for a phone call from
his son's kidnappers demanding an enormous
ransom, but none came.

He was as puzzled and mystified as everyone else,
but not that sad.

Six weeks later he married Marika in a civil ceremony
conducted on a yacht cruising off the coast of Sardinia.

She did not sign a pre-nuptial.

* * *

Carrie Hanlon returned to New York and had quite a
hectic time playing the abandoned, bewildered
girlfriend of the missing heir to the Blaine fortune.

It was better than being simply the most famous
supermodel in the world.

She received two movie offers, a lucrative cosmetics
contract and six hundred proposals of marriage.

She never did meet Martin Scorsese.

* * *

Varoomba moved in on the champ big-time. He had a thing for lap-dances, and she gave the best.

After several steamy weeks of togetherness, she relocated from New York to Antonio's brand new Hancock Park mansion in L.A.

The press went crazy about them. They became the new hot couple in town, and they both luxuriated in the publicity.

* * *

Chas rediscovered Renee with a vengeance. She might be an older broad, but she stood up to him every inch of the way, and he delighted in the challenge. She sold her phone sex company in Vegas and started a new one in New York.

Chas backed her all the way.

* * *

Dexter obtained the quickest divorce he could get, promptly married Gem and signed a contract to star in a low-budget action-adventure film set in Sicily. Annie, his agent, advised him to do it because she was anxious to get him off her daily phone list. Little did she know that the cheapo movie would become a cult hit, and Dexter Falcon the biggest action-adventure star in the world.

* * *

Rosarita almost lost her mind trying to puzzle out what had happened. Did Joel die instead of Dexter? Had the poisoned drink somehow been switched?

But if that *had* happened, where was Joel's body?

She lived in fear that he'd turn up one day and accuse her of attempting to murder him.

In the meantime, she suffered a miscarriage fighting for a cab in the rain outside Bergdorf's with a skinny socialite in a black mink coat.

It simply wasn't her year.

* * *

Jamie, petrified of what the outside world held, reconciled with Peter for exactly six weeks. Then she caught him flirting shamelessly with a shirt salesman at Barney's, and she knew the time had come to be brave and move on.

She tried to put Vegas and all that had happened there behind her. And she never drank again.

* * *

Natalie resigned from her highly popular TV entertainment show and got a very lucrative gig on talk radio as a shock jockette, catering to women in a humorous, honest and cutting edge way.

Her show was a huge success.

* * *

Madison took time off and accompanied Jake on a trip to India and the Far East. They experienced a magical time together, forgetting about the frenetic worlds of Vegas, New York and L.A.

She brought her manuscript with her and almost managed to finish her book.

When they returned to New York, Jake took off on an assignment to Russia for *Newsweek*, and Madison returned to her job at *Manhattan Style*.

Was she happy? She didn't know.

But she did know that soon, very soon, she would be ready to research her father's past and find out everything.

In the meantime, she had a brother in Vegas, an aunt in Miami, and she was determined to get to know both of them, whether they liked it or not.

Madison was a survivor, and life went on. She didn't know what her future held, she only knew that, whatever it was, she could deal with it.

**SIMON &
SCHUSTER**

This book and other **Jackie Collins** titles are available
from your local bookshop or can be ordered direct
from the publisher.

978 1 84983 423 0	Married Lovers	£7.99
978 1 84739 436 1	Hollywood Wives	£7.99
978 1 84739 437 8	Deadly Embrace	£7.99
978 1 84739 438 5	Hollywood Divorces	£7.99
978 1 84983 421 6	Lethal Seduction	£7.99
978 1 84983 422 3	Lovers & Players	£7.99

Please send cheque or postal order for the value of the book,
free postage and packing within the UK, to
SIMON & SCHUSTER CASH SALES
PO Box 29, Douglas Isle of Man, IM99 1BQ
Tel: 01624 677237, Fax: 01624 670923
Email: bookshop@enterprise.net
www.bookpost.co.uk

Please allow 14 days for delivery. Prices and availability
subject to change without notice